DARK SIDE OF THE MOON

Dark Side

OF THE
Moon

Sherrilyn Kenyon

St. Martin's Press
New York

www.stmartins.com

Design by Mary A. Wirth

ISBN 0-312-35743-5
EAN 978-0-312-35743-6

First Edition: June 2006

10 9 8 7 6 5 4 3 2 1

For the most important person in any writer's life . . . you, the reader.
Thank you for taking this trip into the
Dark-Hunter realm with me.

Acknowledgments

For the entire team at SMP for all the hard work you guys do on my books. I have no idea what I'd do without you, and I don't want to find out.

For Monique, who definitely needs an award for going above and beyond the call of duty. Thank you. And for Merrilee, who had no idea what she was getting herself into.

Most of all, I want to thank all the readers and fans who visit the Dark-Hunter.com bbs and loops. You guys are always a joy to see. To my RBL women, who never fail to entertain and inspire. And to my personal friends, who give me encouragement and strength when I need it most: Janet, Brynna, Lo, Carl, Loretta, and Christine.

And last, but most definitely not least, my family, and that includes my brother Steve, who wanted to be named. I love all of you. Thank you so much for making my life what it is and for taking this journey with me.

He [the ravyn] is the warrior's bird of battle, exults in slaughter and carnage . . .

—BEOWULF

DARK SIDE OF THE MOON

PROLOGUE

Wales, 1673

The air whispered with psychic electricity. It was a sensation that could only be felt by a particular nonhuman sect or by humans with highly developed senses.

Ravyn Kontis was most definitely *not* human. He'd been born into the world of nocturnal predators who commanded the hidden magicks of the earth—who ruled its darker arts—and he had died as one of their toughest warriors. . . .

By the hand of his own brother.

Now Ravyn walked the earth as something else. Something soulless. Something ferocious and even deadlier than what he'd been before. There was no heart left inside him. No pity or compassion. Nothing but a pain so deep, so profound, that it lacerated what little humanity he had until there was nothing left but a beast so feral that he knew it would never be tamed again.

Leaning his head back, he roared the cry of the angry beast

that snarled inside him. The stench of death encircled him just as the blood of his enemies coated every inch of his human flesh. It dripped from his hair and his fingertips in slick rivulets that dappled the battle-trampled earth at his feet.

Still it wasn't enough to appease the rage that lived inside him.

Vengeance was a dish best served cold. . . .

He'd foolishly expected it to ease some of the crippling grief that haunted him. It hadn't. It only left him even colder than the betrayal that had caused his death.

Ravyn winced as he saw Isabeau's beautiful face in his mind. Even though she'd been fully human, they had been chosen as mates. Thinking that she loved him, he'd trusted her with the secret of his world.

And how had she repaid him? She'd told the humans of his small clan of brethren and they had attacked the women and children while he and the men had been out on patrol.

No one had been left alive.

No one.

The males of his clan had returned to find the smoldering remains of their village . . . the scattered bodies of their children and women.

They had turned on him then, not that he blamed them. It was the only time in his life he hadn't fought back. At least not until his last breath had come.

As it had rattled in his chest, his fetid rage had taken root and grown into a monster, feeding the darkest part of his nonhuman being. His human soul had screamed out for vengeance against those who had destroyed his people. The anguished cry of both man and beast had echoed in the sacred temple of Artemis far away on Mount Olympus—so loud and demanding, it had summoned the goddess herself to him. And there in the faint light of the waning moon, he'd taken her bargain and sold his soul to her for the one chance to return the favor to Isabeau and her people.

They were dead now, by his hand . . . all of them. Just as he was. Just as his family had been.

It was over. . . .

Ravyn laughed bitterly at that thought as he clenched his bloodied fists. No, it wasn't over. It was only beginning.

CHAPTER ONE

Seattle, 2006

BOY EATEN BY KILLER MOTHS.

Susan Michaels groaned as she read the headline for her latest story. She knew better than to read the rest of the article, but something inside her just wanted to feel kicked this afternoon. God forbid that she ever took pride in her work again. . . .

> Bred in a lab in South America, these top secret moths are the next generation of military assassins. They are genetically engineered to think their way into an enemy's lair where they bite the neck of the target and infect them with a concentrated poison that is completely undetectable and that will render the victim dead within an hour.
>
> Now they have escaped the lab and were last seen heading north, straight for the central U.S. Be on guard. They could be in your neighborhood within the month. . . .

Dear Lord, it was worse than she'd imagined.

Her hands shaking in anger, she got up from her desk and headed straight into Leo Kirby's office. As usual, he was online, reading some poor slob's blog and making copious notes.

Leo was a short, lean man with long black hair that he always wore in a ponytail. He also had a goatee, cold gray eyes that never laughed, and a strange spiderweb tattoo on his left hand. He was dressed in a baggy black T-shirt and jeans, with a giant Starbucks travel mug at his elbow while he worked. In his mid-thirties, he'd be cute if he wasn't so damned annoying.

"Killer moths?" she asked.

He looked up from his notepad and shrugged. "You said we were going to have a moth invasion. I just had Joanie rewrite the story to make it more marketable."

She gaped in total astonishment. "Joanie? You had *Joanie* rewrite the story? The woman who wears tinfoil in her bra so that the people with x-ray vision can't see her breasts? *That* Joanie?"

He didn't flinch or miss a beat. "Yeah, she's my best writer."

Talk about insult to injury. . . . "I thought *I* was your best writer, Leo."

Sighing heavily, he swiveled his chair to face her. "You would be *if* you had any imagination whatsoever." He held his hands up dramatically as if to illustrate his point. "C'mon, Sue, embrace your inner child. Embrace the absurd that lives amongst us. Think Ibsen." He put his hands down and gave another weary sigh. "But no, you never do, do you? I send you out to investigate the bat boy who lives in the old church belfry and you come back with a story about moths infesting the rafters. What the hell is that?"

She gave him a droll stare as she crossed her arms over her chest. "It's called reality, Leo. Reality. You should stop shrooming long enough to try it."

He snorted at that before he flipped to a blank sheet of paper on his notepad. He set it beside his coffee. "Screw reality. It don't feed my dog. It don't make my Porsche payments. It don't get me laid. Bullshit does that . . . and I like it that way."

She rolled her eyes at his beaming face. "You are such a toad."

He paused as if an idea had struck him. He reached for his pad, where he quickly scribbled something. " 'Employee Kisses Toady Boss to Discover an Ancient Immortal Prince' . . . better yet, a god. Yeah, an ancient god"—he gestured at her with his pen—"a Greek god who's been cursed to live as a sex slave to women . . . I like it. Can you imagine? Women all over the country will be kissing their bosses to test the theory." Then he looked back at her with a wicked grin. "Shall we try the experiment and see if it works?"

She screwed her face up at him in disgust. "Hell, no. And that wasn't a come-on, Leo. Trust me, even with a thousand kisses you'd still be a toad."

He was totally undaunted, mostly because the two of them had been teasing each other this way since they attended college together. "I still think we should give it a try." He wagged his eyebrows at her.

Susan let out a long, exasperated breath. "You know, I would bring you up on sexual harassment charges, but that would imply that you have actually had sex in your lifetime, and I intend to maintain that you are a prime example of what happens to people when they're too sexually frustrated."

That brought another glassy look to his eyes before he scribbled again. " 'Sexually Frustrated Boss Turns into Screaming Lunatic. Disembowels Woman Who Excites Him.' "

Susan groaned deep in her throat. If she didn't know better, she'd think he was threatening her, but that would involve actual action on his part, and Leo was nothing if not a complete delegator. His maxim had always been why do it yourself when you can hire or bully someone else to do it for you.

"Leo! Stop turning everything into a cheesy headline." And before he could respond, she quickly added, "I know, I know. Cheesy headlines pay for your Porsche."

"Exactly!"

Disgusted, she rubbed at the sudden pain she felt behind her right eye.

"Look, Sue," he said as if he felt an uncharacteristic wave of sympathy for her. "I know how hard these last couple of years have been for you, okay? But you're not an investigative reporter anymore."

Her chest tightened at his words. Words she didn't really need to hear, since they haunted her every minute of every day. Two and a half years ago, she'd been one of the foremost investigative reporters in the country. Her former boss had nicknamed her Hound Dog Sue because she could sniff a story from a mile away and then run it to ground and bring it home.

And in one moment of gross stupidity, her whole world had come crumbling down around her. She'd been so hungry that she'd run headlong into a setup that had completely destroyed her reputation.

It'd almost cost her her life.

She rubbed at the scar on her wrist as she forced herself not to remember that awful night in November—the only time in her life when she'd actually been weak. She'd come to her senses, and then vowed to never let anyone make her feel that powerless again. No matter what, this was her life and she was going to live it on her own terms.

But for Leo, whom she'd met in college when they'd worked on the staff of the campus paper together, she'd have never worked in journalism again. Not that working for the *Daily Inquisitor* could ever be construed as true journalism, but at least it allowed her to pay off some of her gargantuan debt and court costs. And though she hated her job, it kept her fed and off the street. For that she owed the little toad.

Leo tore off a sheet of paper and slid it toward her.

"What's this?" she asked as she took it from his desk.

"It's a Web address. There's some college kid who goes by the name Dark Angel who claims she's working for the undead."

She stared at him. Oh, yeah . . . her life was definitely a lemon and she wanted her money back—with interest. "A vampire?"

"Not exactly. She says he's an immortal shapeshifting warrior who annoys the hell out of her. She's local, so I want you to check it out and see what else she has to say. Then report everything back to me."

Oh, this couldn't be happening to her, and yet that old internal voice in her head was already laughing at her. "Shapeshifter, huh? Is this before or after she drops acid?"

Leo made an irritated noise. "Why don't you at least try to get into the spirit of the job? You know, it's really not bad at all. In fact, it's actually highly entertaining. Live a little, Sue. Let go of the venom. Enjoy it."

Enjoy it . . . enjoy being a laughingstock after she'd been working for the *Washington Post* . . . yeah. It was hard to Carpe Crap when what she really wanted to do was get her reputation back.

But those days were over. She'd never be a real reporter again.

This was it. Her life. Joy, oh joy—the bad-luck fairy had really screwed her over.

No, she thought as her chest tightened again, that wasn't true. She'd screwed herself over and she knew it. Heartsick, she turned around and headed back to her desk as she looked at the blog address in her hand.

It's stupid. Don't do it. Don't even go to the site. . . .

But before long, she did, and there it was . . . a black page with some hand-drawn Gothic artwork on a Web site called deadjournal.com. But her absolute favorite part had to be the header that read: "Musings from the Dark and Twisted Mind of a Damned College Student."

The girl, Dark Angel, was certainly that. Her entries showed the typical angst of an average student . . . who was seriously delusional and in need of years of therapy from between the walls of a padded room.

JUNE 3, 2006, 06:45 A.M.
Someone please shoot me. Please. I really can't stress the "please" part enough. So here I was trying to study for my test tomorrow. Note the word "trying." So here I am engrossed in the complexities of Babylonian Math, which isn't really engrossing, to say the least, when all of a sudden my cell phone rings and scares the total shit out of me because the house is even more silent than a tomb—and trust me, I've been in enough tombs and crypts to know this for a fact.

At first I stupidly thought it was my father harassing me, until I looked closer at the number and no. Not him. Those who've been reading my journal know that it's my boss, 'cause who else

*would call me at this ungodly hour and think that I have no life
whatsoever except to serve his every whim and need? Really,
take my advice and never work for an immortal. They have no
respect whatsoever for those of us with finite lives.*

*5:30 in the morning, there he is. Calling to tell me that he's
just killed off a bunch of undead people (okay, vampires, but I
really hate to use that word 'cause it draws out all sorts of lunatic weirdos who want to know how they, too, can become
vampires and where to find the ones I know, which wouldn't do
anything but get you killed, but back to my original thought)
and that I need to pick him up since it's about to be dawn and he
can't make it home before the sun turns him into grilled toast.
You know this isn't the way to motivate me, since a grilled toast
boss = one happy Dark Angel.*

*Now here's where I tirade against the fact that if he were just
a regular shapeshifter, I wouldn't have to go get him. He'd be
able to get home without help. He could just teleport himself
into the house, but back when he made the bargain to become
immortal, that ability was taken from him, along with the one
that allows him to travel through time and the ability to walk as
a man in daylight. And why was this taken from him? One reason. To make my life a living hell of servitude, that's why.*

*Oh, and I have to bring him clothes since he'll most likely be
in cat form at Pike's Market, which is the only way he can be in
daylight and not be a crispy critter (really). So when he switches
back into human form he'll be naked and will need clothing—
yes, for those with gutter-bent minds, he's a buff god in theory,
but since I've known him all my life it's like seeing your brother
naked—can we say "ew"?!*

*All right, it pisses me off, but I go since he pays me and if I
don't he'll tell on me again and get me into all kinds of trouble,
none of which I want to hear right now. So after I hoof my butt
over there to get his sorry ass, what do I find?*

*Yes, you guessed it. Nothing but a couple of homeless people
who think I've lost my mind as I search for my "cat" while holding male clothing which I slowly remember won't do any good
since he can't shift back into a human until after I get him home.
That rank bastard and his pranks. A curse of poxes on his head.
Better yet, I hope he gets fleas (I would wish ticks, but then I'd
probably get Lyme disease from him). So fleas. Lots and lots of
fleas!*

I'm sure Catman Moron found some bimbo to shack up with and shag for the day, but damn it all. Couldn't he have called and told me that? No. So here I am, chugging extra-caffeinated espresso and hoping I stay awake for my test this afternoon. Thanks, boss. Appreciate it. You are the best. Where's Animal Control when you really need them? Better yet, get me an ax so I can cut off his head, and I don't mean the one on his shoulders.

Mood: Pissed

Song: "Everything About You": Ugly Kid Joe

Susan let out a tired breath as she rubbed her brow. Oh, yeah. The girl needed some serious professional help. But what the hell? It wasn't like she had anything else to do other than go and investigate the Immortal Catman of Pike's Market.

Susan cringed at the thought. "Now I'm doing it, too . . . Cheesy headlines are us." Groaning, she rubbed her eyes. "You know, if my life was a horse, I'd shoot it."

No *matter the* location or day, every animal shelter in the United States seemed to always hold the same pungent odor of cleaning antiseptic mixed with wet fur. And even though the shelters were warmed, there was always an odd chill to the air. One that penetrated straight to the bones.

Today was no different. The cat cages were lined along two walls where some of the felines slept while others played, ate, or groomed.

All except one.

That one crouched as if ready to kill and it watched everything around it with the sharp intellect of a vicious predator that belied its smaller size. It wasn't like the others. Only a fool would make that assumption.

At first glance, it appeared to be a regular Bengal house cat, but if one looked closer, it was obvious that it didn't hold quite the same facial characteristics that marked the Bengal breed. In fact, it looked just like an Arabian leopard—only it weighed a scant fifteen pounds instead of sixty.

More than that, its eyes were an eerie shade of black . . . an unnatural color for such a beast. And if one was really paying attention, they would definitely notice that while the other cats wore plain white collars, this one wore one of silver. It was a very special collar that caught the light and flashed with a preternatural gleam.

And what made it so special? Certainly not the thinness of its strap or the fact that it had no buckle on it. No. It was the unseen circuitry that ran along the underside of the silver fabric. Circuitry that had been designed to send out inhibitors that couldn't be felt by man or beast—unless the creature was both man *and* beast.

A devilish invention by those who wanted some control over the magick of others, this collar kept this particular cat in its current feline form.

And that seriously pissed the cat off.

Ravyn hissed as a man ventured near his cage. If he could get out of this, he'd tear the bastard's arms off and beat him with them. But unfortunately, he couldn't—that would require him to actually have arms of his own, which in his current form he didn't possess.

And it was all his fault. Damn him and his libido anyway. If he'd simply trotted past the sex goddess in the extremely short skirt at dawn, he'd be happily home by now—well, maybe not happily, since he'd have to listen to Erika bitch, but certainly he'd be home in his own bed and not locked in this damned cage.

What could one little stroking possibly hurt?

He looked at the bars on the cage and hissed at the apparent answer. Yeah. Ash would have a field day with him on this one.

Provided he got out of it. As it stood, he wasn't so sure he was going to make it this time. So long as he wore the collar, his powers as both a Dark-Hunter and a Were-Hunter were seriously restricted. As an Arcadian Were-Hunter, his natural form was human. To be trapped as a cat during the light of day was both painful and extremely disconcerting. Even with the metriazo collar on that inhibited him from using his paranormal powers, there was only so long he could hold this form before his own magick turned on him and killed him.

It was one frightfully sobering thought.

"How's he doing?"

Ravyn narrowed his eyes on the tall, blond male veterinarian who was an Apollite. As a rule, most Apollites stayed out of the war that raged between the Daimons and the Dark-Hunters. It wasn't until Apollites started stealing human souls to elongate their short lives and thereby becoming Daimons that Dark-Hunters bothered with them. After all, that was the whole reason Dark-Hunters had been created. They were the ones who killed the Daimons so that the stolen human souls could be released before the Daimon possession destroyed them.

Obviously this Apollite wanted a head start on being hunted.

The human assistant, who was a short man around the age of thirty with black hair and a shaggy beard, answered. "He's pissed and glaring. What else?" He cocked his head as he studied Ravyn from a safe distance. "You think he's Arcadian or Katagari?"

The vet shrugged before he bent down to look into the cage. "I don't know, but I'm hoping for Arcadian."

"Why?"

Ravyn bared his teeth at the prick who smiled in response. "'Cause if he is, the magick that's holding him in cat form will eventually cause his head to explode. It'll be painful as hell before he dies."

The assistant laughed. "And no nine lives to bring him back. Damn shame. But I like it." He turned to look at the doctor. "What say you neuter him while he's like this, too?"

"You know, you have a great idea. . . ."

Ravyn snarled as the vet reached for the clipboard that hung outside his cage and made a note. Ravyn hissed at him before he sent out a mental note to the Apollite vet. *"You neuter me, you bastard, and I'll dance in your entrails."*

That bit of spite came back on him tenfold as it caused the collar to constrict and shock him enough to seriously hurt, but not so much that it caused him to change forms.

The vet smirked before he hung the clipboard back on the peg. "I don't really see how you're going to do that in your current position. Do you, furball?"

The human assistant high-fived the vet. "I can't wait for Stryker and Paul to get here and finish him off." Then laughing, the two of them left Ravyn alone with the rest of the animals.

Ravyn charged the bars of his cage, but all he succeeded in doing was hurting himself. Damn them all. How had they managed to get him trapped like this? How had they known where to find him?

One minute he'd been hiding in the shadows of Pike's Market, waiting for his Squire, Erika, to come get him, and the next thing he'd known that *puta* in the red skirt had grabbed him and snapped the collar around his neck before he could fight or sense her intentions. Once the collar was in place, he'd been powerless without his magick.

Keeping a tight grip on him, the woman had wrapped him in her shawl, picked him up, and handed him off to a group of waiting humans who'd paid her fifty dollars for her services. Afterward, the humans had tossed him into the local animal shelter.

And here he would stay until either his head exploded from the inhibitors in the collar or he figured out some way to escape this cage without having either his magick or opposable thumbs.

Yeah. Great odds there . . . not. His only hope was that Erika would get concerned when he didn't show up after nightfall—

Wait, he was talking about Erika Thomas here. Erika. The girl who liked to pretend she didn't have to work for him. The girl who went out of her way to avoid *him* and her duties. She wouldn't notice for days that he wasn't home.

No, the little mutant would throw a party the instant she found out that while she'd ignored his absence, some mad Apollite had gelded his ass and left him impotent. Then, she'd call all her friends and laugh about it.

I am so screwed. . . .

Susan sighed as she toyed with the small gold medallion that she kept in her purse. Only a hair larger than a silver dollar, it didn't look like much, but on the night she'd won it, it'd held even more value than a hundred-million-dollar lottery ticket.

She paused to look at it as old memories assailed her. She'd won the Sterling Award for Investigative Reporting for Politics in 2000. She'd been on top of the world that night. . . .

Clenching the award in her hand, she cursed under her breath. "Just sell the damned thing on eBay."

But she couldn't and she hated herself for that. It was hard to let go of a glorious past even when all it did was bring her pain. Maybe she shouldn't have been so cocky back then. Maybe this was her comeuppance.

Bullshit. She didn't believe in that kind of divine retribution. She was where she was because she'd allowed herself to be deceived and she had been after more glory. There was no one to blame but herself. She'd been stupid and trusting, and she would pay for that one moment of fallacy for the rest of her life.

Her phone rang.

Grateful for the interruption to her morbid ruminations, she picked it up and answered. "Susan Michaels."

"Hey, Sue, it's Angie. How you doing?" Her buddy sounded a little less than upbeat, but it was still good to hear a friendly voice.

"Fine," Susan said as she tucked her award away into her purse. If anyone could make her feel better, it was Angie. A smart-mouthed vegan veterinarian, Angie had a way of cutting through the thick of any matter and pointing out the ludicrous—it was truly a gift Sue appreciated. "What are you up to?"

"Five by five as always."

Susan rolled her eyes. The statement wasn't just a reference to the *Buffy the Vampire Slayer* show Angie loved, it was also the way Angie described herself, since she was round and cuddly.

"I'll only give you five by three . . . maybe."

"Yeah, right. Trust me, I am as wide as I am tall, but that's not the point of this. You got a minute away from your lunatic boss?"

"Yeah. Why?"

" 'Cause I've got some news that I think you're going to want to hear."

In spite of Angie's dire tone, Susan smiled. "Hugh Jackman has divorced his wife and happened upon my picture in some old article and decided that I'm the woman for him?"

Angie laughed. "Damn, you have been working for that paper for a long time. You're now starting to believe the rubbish you publish."

"Har, har. Is there a real point to this conversation?"

"Yes, there is. You know those strange missing-person reports

Jimmy's been talking about that've been going on for a while? The ones Jimmy said might be related?"

"Yeah?"

"They are."

Susan froze as her old reporter self leaped to the forefront. "How do you mean?"

"I can't say anything more on the phone, okay? In fact, I'm on a pay phone, and you don't want to know how hard one of these things is to find nowadays. But I can't take any chances. Can you come by work in about an hour to look for a cat?"

Screwing her face up, Susan let out a disgusted breath. "Ew! I'm deathly allergic to those things."

"Trust me, it'll be worth your wheezing and then some. Just be there." The phone went dead.

Susan hung up as a thousand scenarios went through her head. She'd heard real panic in Angie's voice. *Real* panic, and that wasn't like her friend. This was a serious situation and Angie was scared.

Susan tapped the phone with her fingernail as her thoughts scattered into a million different directions. But they all came back to one single thing—this odd call just might be her own road back toward salvation and respectability.

CHAPTER TWO

In many parts of the world and in many religions, the concept of hell has long been one where the dead were punished for the evils they participated in or perpetrated while living.

In the Atlantean hell realm of Kalosis, there were wicked souls aplenty, but none of them were being punished for what *they'd* done while alive. Indeed, most of them had led calm, peaceful lives. As Urian—a Spathi Daimon who'd once called Kalosis home—so often said, "We're not the damned, folks, we're the categorically fucked."

And it was true. Those here were all being punished not for their transgressions, but rather for something a long-forgotten queen in Atlantis had done centuries ago to strike back at her former lover. In one fit of anger against the Greek god Apollo, she'd sent her soldiers out to murder his child and mistress. By doing so, she'd damned all of her Apollite people not only to a life spent in darkness but to a life span of only twenty-seven years. A life that would end on their birthday as their body slowly, *painfully* deteriorated over a twenty-four-hour period until there was nothing left but a faint dust.

It was a cold, callous fate that each man and woman here in Kalosis would have met had their leader Stryker not found the mythical portal that allowed him to descend from the world of man into this realm where he'd met another god. A god whose indignant fury had made a mockery of Apollo's.

Trapped within the hell realm by her own family who had feared her powers, Apollymi wasn't one to let Apollo get away with his cruelty. She had embraced Apollo's cursed son, Stryker, adopting him as her own before she taught him how to harvest and use human souls to elongate his life. It was a lesson Stryker had gladly shared with others of his race as he brought them here to serve not only his own code of vengeance but Apollymi's as well. Currently he commanded legions of Daimons who used the pathetic humans as cattle.

And even though he owed her so much, Stryker truly hated the goddess who had saved his life and adopted him.

Now, he sat in the banquet hall of her home and watched as his Spathi warriors celebrated their latest victory.

"Death to the humans!" one of his warriors shouted above the din.

"Fuck that," another replied. "We need them. Death to all Dark-Hunters!"

An echoing cheer rang out through the barren hall. Stryker leaned back in his cushioned throne as he watched the Apollites and Daimons congratulate each other on their most recent success—the capture of Ravyn Kontis. The darkened hall was lit only by candles as they poured Apollite blood—the only thing that could sustain their cursed bodies—from pitchers and spilled it all over themselves.

Like the other Spathis gathered here, Stryker envisioned a better world. A world where his people weren't condemned to die at the tender age of twenty-seven. A world where they could all walk in the daylight that he'd taken for granted as a child.

And all because his father had knocked up a whore and then

gotten pissed when the Apollites had killed her off. Apollo had cursed them all . . . even Stryker, who had been the ancient god's most beloved son.

But that was eleven thousand years ago. Ancient, ancient history.

Stryker was the present and the Daimons before him were the future. If everything went as planned, they would one day soon reclaim the human realm that had been taken from them. Personally, he'd have rather started with another city, but when the human official had come to him with a plan for the humans to help rid Seattle of Dark-Hunters it had been a perfect opportunity to start aligning the race of man with the Apollites and Daimons. Little did the humans know that once the Dark-Hunters were cleared, there would be no one to save their souls. It would be open season on all mankind.

"How many Dark-Hunters are left in Seattle?" he asked his second in command.

Like the other Daimons who were present, Trates was tall and lean, with golden blond hair and dark brown eyes—the epitome of youthful beauty. He drew his brows together as he thought for a second. "Once Kontis is dead, we're down to seven."

Stryker curled his lips. "Then we're celebrating too soon."

Silence rang out at his words.

"How so?"

Stryker turned his head to see his younger half-sister approach his carved throne with a bold, determined stride. Unlike the Spathi Daimons who made this place home, she bore no fear of him. Dressed in a black leather catsuit that laced down the front and hugged her lithe, muscular body, she stepped up on the dais to lean against the arm of his chair. Her dark eyes were completely devoid of emotions as she arrogantly cocked a questioning brow.

"He's not dead yet." He spoke each word slowly, with careful enunciation. "I've learned when dealing with these bastards to take nothing for granted."

She gave a sarcastic half laugh before she pulled his cell phone off his belt and dialed it.

In theory, the phone shouldn't work in this nether realm. But never ones to let the humans get the better of them, his Spathis had found a preternatural wave that could carry the signal out of Kalosis and up into the human world. It was a dubious trick that served them well.

Satara gave Stryker a bored look as he heard the good Apollite vet in Seattle answer the phone. "Is he dead yet?" she asked, mocking Stryker's earlier tone.

He could only hear the faint muttering of the Apollite on the other end.

Satara gave an evil laugh. "Ooo," she said, wrinkling her nose in a seductive manner. "You're so nasty, gelding him before he dies. I like that."

Stryker reached up and grabbed the phone from her. "You've done what?"

Even over the static of the line, he heard the Apollite sweating. "I . . . um . . . I'm planning to neuter him, my lord."

Stryker saw red at that. "Don't you dare."

"Why not?" Satara asked in an offended tone.

Stryker glared at her as he answered for both her benefit and that of the vet on the other end. "For one thing, I don't want Kontis out of that cage until after he's dead—he's too dangerous for that—and for another, I won't stand by and see a worthy opponent emasculated. He's earned the right to die with some dignity."

Satara scoffed. "Some dignity. His head's going to explode. Where's the dignity in having your brains splattered all over a cat box because you wanted to look up some human whore's dress? If he'd truly been worthy, we'd have never caught him so easily."

Stryker tightened his grip on the phone. "Trickery isn't worthy of our species."

"Oh, get out of the Stone Age, Strykerius. There's no such thing as noble duels anymore. This is a world where the better sneak wins."

Perhaps, but he remembered a time and place where things didn't work quite that way and after eleven thousand years he was too old to change his ways. "Even so, he is a cousin to us and—"

She sneered at him. "The Were-Hunters turned their backs on the Apollites and Daimons a long time ago. They don't consider you family anymore."

"Some do."

"Kontis doesn't," she shot back. "If he did, he'd have never been able to sell his soul to the Dark-Hunters and join their ranks. For hundreds of years he's hunted and killed your kind. I say geld the bastard and wear his shriveled balls as a trophy."

Trates cringed at her words, as did several other males in the room, some of whom instinctively cupped themselves.

And Satara wonders why no man will date her. . . .

"Leave him intact," Stryker ordered the Apollite over the phone while he glared at his sister. "I'll be there after sundown to check on him myself and he better be as he was when you captured him."

Before the Apollite could respond, Stryker hung up the phone and returned it to his belt.

Satara rolled her eyes. "I can't believe *you* would show mercy to an enemy. You who cut the throat of your own son to appease Apollymi."

Acting on pure instinct, Stryker reached up and grabbed her by the neck to silence her. "Enough," he growled as her eyes bulged. "Unless you want to see the exact nature of my mercy, you'll take a more respectful tone when you address me. I don't care who you serve. Let Artemis find another handmaiden. One more word and I'll silence you eternally." Shoving her away from him, he stood up.

Utter silence filled the hall as he scanned the gathered Spathis. Physically no older than twenty-seven, each member of their clan was as beautiful as an angel . . . of death.

And they were his to command.

Ignoring his sister, he addressed them. "We have been given a rare opportunity to work with the humans to bring about the end of the Dark-Hunters in Seattle and give us the foothold we need in their world. But don't think for one minute that this war is over. And as soon as Acheron realizes how many of his Dark-Hunters are missing, he will come here himself to see what's going on."

Stryker pinned a fierce look on Satara. "Are you ready to battle the Dark-Hunter leader?"

Her eyes flashed with bloodlust as she rubbed her throat. "With every breath I have."

Stryker scoffed. "Suicidal bravery will get us nowhere. Apollymi protects that bastard of hers. It will never be by a Daimon hand that he dies. . . ."

"It'll be by a human one," Trates said from his right.

Stryker nodded. "And it will take a great deal of planning and careful execution if we're to do this. Kill Acheron and the other Dark-Hunters will be easy to manipulate or eliminate." He looked around the room as his army nodded in agreement.

"So who do we kill next?" Trates asked.

Stryker considered the seven Dark-Hunters who were left. Each one of them had been a fierce warrior in their human lifetime. There wasn't an easy target in the bunch.

But with the humans helping them for once they had a distinct advantage. Like the Apollites and Daimons, the Dark-Hunters couldn't survive in daylight but their human helpers could. What's more, the Dark-Hunters couldn't sense a human the same way they could an Apollite or Daimon. Humans could easily sneak up on them and deliver an unexpected death blow. Not to mention the small oath that all Dark-Hunters took to preserve human life even at the expense of their own. . . .

It was an oath that would be their undoing.

"We'll let the humans choose. This is their war. We'll support them for now, but in the end, should they fail it'll be their funerals and not ours."

S*usan knew better* than to get her hopes up as she parked in front of the animal shelter. This could very easily be nothing more than a major waste of time.

Or it could be your ticket back—

"Oh, shut up, Pollyanna," she snapped at herself as she grabbed her purse. She hated that little bit of an optimist who still lived inside her. Why wouldn't it die?

But no, she always had to have hope even when it was pointless. What was wrong with her anyway? Other people got to be jaded . . . why not her?

I'm just cursed, I guess.

Sighing in disgust, she got out of her car and headed for the entrance. She pushed open the door to walk into a brightly lit reception area.

There was a perky blond teenager standing behind a counter

where the girl was tucking papers into file folders. "Hi," she said, glancing up at Susan. "Can I help you?"

"Cats. I'm here looking for cats."

The girl gave her an odd look. Not that Susan blamed her. There couldn't have been less enthusiasm in her voice if she'd tried. For that matter, she might even have been curling her lip as she said it. She wasn't quite sure. It was hard to hide as much distaste as she had for the creepy four-legged creatures who'd made her miserable as a child.

The girl pointed to the left. "They're over there."

"Thanks." Susan headed toward the light blue door that was marked ironically enough with the word *Cats*.

She pushed it open and had to fight the urge to run back to her car as her sinuses immediately clogged. And this after she'd taken Benadryl half an hour ago in expectation of such misery.

"Good grief," she said, pulling a Kleenex from her purse while she pretended to peruse the evil allergy beasties. Her eyes were even starting to swell, she could feel it.

She sneezed loudly, then dabbed at her nose. "Where are you, Angie?" she asked in a low whisper from between her clenched teeth.

She was just about to abandon the thought of sticking this out when she caught sight of the strangest cat she'd ever seen. Long and lean, it looked as if someone had shrunk a leopard into the size of a house cat. But more than the beauty of its small body was the blackness of its eyes. She'd never seen a cat with black eyes before.

And it looked really angry.

She cocked her head to study it. There was something about the cat that seemed highly intelligent. "Hey, Puss in Boots, you unhappy here?" She sneezed again. Cursing and wiping her nose, she sniffed as her eyes started tearing. "I can't blame you. I'd rather be hit in the head with a tack hammer than stay here."

"Hi there. Can I interest you in a cat?"

She jerked around at Angie's voice. Short with black hair and brown eyes, Angie looked about nervously and by that she could tell Angie didn't want anyone to know they were friends. Catching the cue, Susan looked back at the cat and could have sworn it had one eyebrow raised as it waited for her response. Yeah, the Benadryl was working on something besides her sinuses. "Sure."

"Let me show you to a room where you can play with him for a few minutes." It was obvious Angie had been practicing that speech for a while.

Good thing Angie was a vet and not an undercover agent—she'd be shot in a heartbeat. But Susan didn't say anything more as Angie gently took the miniature leopard out of the cage and put it in a cat cage before she led her toward another blue door that opened into a small petting room.

Pausing outside the door, Angie handed her the cage and gave her an artificial smile. "Take your time. You really want to make sure you know the cat before you take him home."

"Will do," Susan said in the same stilted tone. She took the box, holding it as far away from her body as she could, and entered the windowless room, which she thought was empty until the door closed and she saw Angie's husband standing behind it. A detective, he'd been a friend of hers for years, too.

"Hi, Jimmy."

He put his finger to his lips. "Keep your voice down. Someone could be outside. Listening. Why do you think I had Angie tell you to meet me here? I can't afford anyone to see me meeting with a reporter after what happened last night."

Ooo, he'd gone seriously paranoid.

"Someone like who?" she whispered. "What happened last night?"

He didn't respond. Instead, he took the cage from her outstretched hand and set it right beside the door before he pulled her to the farthest corner, where a small bench rested. "You don't know what I've seen, Sue," he whispered. "What they're capable of. My life, your life . . . all of us. It means nothing to them. Nothing."

Her heart picked up its pace at his fearful muttering and the panic she saw in his light blue eyes. "Who are *they*?"

"There's a major cover-up going on and I have no idea just how high up the food chain it goes, but it does go up."

Susan leaned forward eagerly. Exposing high-level cover-ups had once been her specialty. "Major cover-up for what?"

"Remember those missing kids I told you about? The college

students and runaways that we've been getting reports on? I've found a couple of them. Dead. Now I've been pulled from the cases and told that they're being handled by a special task force that doesn't exist. That I shouldn't worry about them."

A chill went down her spine at those words. "Are you sure?"

"Of course I am," he said angrily. "I found evidence . . . and when I went to report it, I was told that it would be in my best interest not to do any more investigating. So I did a little more of it with my partner Greg and now he's missing, too, and . . ." He swallowed hard. "They're after *me* now."

"Who?"

"You wouldn't believe me if I told you. I don't even believe it and I know the truth." His eyes were round in fear. "I'm taking Angie tonight and we're leaving town."

"Where are you going?"

"Anywhere but here. Anywhere there's no people in league with the devil."

Susan went cold at his words as a wave of suspicion went through her. "And who's the devil?"

"I told you, you wouldn't believe it. I don't and I saw it. Do you understand? They're out there and they're coming for all of us."

"Jimmy—"

"Sh. Don't lecture me on this. Get out of this town, Sue, while you can. There are things here that aren't human. Things here that shouldn't be alive, and we're the food for them."

She pulled back with a grimace at his bizarre turnabout. "What the hell is this? A bad joke?"

"No," he snarled, his nostrils flaring. "You can be stupid if you want, but this isn't a game. I thought it would be safe to talk to you here in this shelter of all places. And then I find out that one of them is working with Angie. Working *here*. Right here in this clinic. He could be listening in on us right now and reporting back to the others that I'm on to them. None of us are safe."

"Who's here?"

He swallowed hard. "The other vet. Dr. Tselios. He's one of *them*."

"Them who?"

"The *vampires*."

Susan ground her teeth as she fought the urge to roll her eyes. It was a battle she was amazed she won. Surely, Angie and Jimmy wouldn't be so cruel as to play this game with her. Not when they knew how much she loathed her job at the *Inquisitor*. "Jim—"

"Don't you think I know how crazy I sound?" he hissed, cutting her off. "I was just like you, Sue. I thought it was all bullshit, too. There's no such thing as vampires, right? We're the top of the food chain. But that isn't true. They're out there and they're hungry. If you know what's good for you, you'll get the hell out of here. Please write it up to let other people know before they kill them, too."

Now that was just what her bloody reputation needed. More wounds. *Thanks, Jim.*

Jimmy's eyes narrowed on her as if he knew what she was thinking. "It's your ass now, Sue. I did my best to save it. You can do what you want, but I'm out of here."

Before she could say anything more, he left her standing alone in the room . . . and returned the cat cage to the floor by her feet.

Susan sneezed.

As she dabbed at her nose, the door opened to show her Angie, who stared at her with a frown. She entered the room and shut the door behind her. "What did you say to Jimmy?"

"Nothing really. Why?"

"He wants me to leave with him right now."

Susan sighed at the fear in her friend's voice. "Did he tell you what was going on?"

She shook her head. "Not exactly. He said too many people were missing and dying and that he's terrified that the ones responsible will come after him next. He wants us to head out for his parents' house in Oregon."

"Did he also tell you about the vampires?"

"The what?" By Angie's face, Susan could tell that Jimmy hadn't shared that bit of information with his wife.

"Yeah. According to him, the vampires are out to kill all of us off. No offense, Ang. I think Jimmy needs some help. Has he been doing a lot of overtime?"

Anger flared deep in Angie's eyes. "Jimmy's not crazy, Sue. Not by a long shot."

Maybe, but she didn't want to argue with her friend. "Yeah, well, thanks for the hot news tip."

As she started for the door, Angie stopped her. "Here. Take the cat with you."

She gaped. "Excuse me?"

"Please. For whatever reason, Jimmy is terrified. Take the cat to keep up appearances and I'll come by and pick him up after work."

Sue cringed at the thought, but she would do anything for her best friend. "All right, but you owe me. *Big*-time."

"I know."

Growling low in her throat, Susan picked up the box and followed Angie to the counter out front.

Angie handed her some papers while she wrote out a check for the adoption fees. "Now don't forget to spend time with him until he gets used to you." She was back to being stilted and odd again.

"No problem."

"Hope you enjoy your new pet," the receptionist called.

Yeah, when pigs fly. "Thanks," Susan said with a smile so fake, it would make a politician proud.

Sneezing again, she headed for her car and set the cage in the backseat. "Thanks a lot, Puss in Boots," she said as she eyed him with malice. "I hope you seriously appreciate the misery I'm enduring for you."

A*ngie watched as* Susan pulled out of the parking lot and headed south toward her house. Releasing a relieved breath, she turned to see Jimmy motioning for her on the other side of the door that led to the employees only area of the shelter.

One minute, she mouthed to him.

She was just about to grab her coat from behind the counter when she saw Theo heading straight for her. His handsome face was paler than normal as he slammed the door shut from the cat room. Two seconds later, his assistant, Darrin, came out of the cat room just behind him.

Theo's dark brown eyes were flaming angry. "Where is he?" Theo demanded as he stopped in front of her.

Angie was baffled by his anger and accusing tone. "Who?"

"The cat." He spat those words at her as if they were evil. "The one that was brought in early this morning. Where the hell is he?"

"Is that the one that was just adopted?"

Angie cringed as the receptionist spoke. "Is there a problem with him?"

Theo and Darrin exchanged a hostile glare. "Yes. He's feral."

"Oh." Angie started to say she'd go get the cat back when she saw Jimmy making odd gestures at her through the door. It looked like he was telling her to run toward him. She frowned at her husband.

Theo turned to see what she was looking at. Jimmy dropped his hands and tried to look nonchalant.

Something dark descended over Theo's face as it turned to stone. "Darrin?"

"Sir?"

"Lock the door and shut the blinds."

CHAPTER THREE

Ravyn wasn't sure if he should be happy or not by his rescue. One thing was certain, he'd be a whole hell of a lot more grateful had his rescuer not put him in direct sunlight on her backseat. The painful rays forced him to cower in a corner, and cowering wasn't something he relished.

He sniffed the air. Damn. Was that his fur getting singed? Of course it was . . . what would make him think for one minute that it wasn't him getting burned?

Nothing was worse than to have burning hair and a heightened sense of smell. Well, maybe there was something worse—burning flesh and turning into a pile of flaming ash, which was exactly what he'd be doing if he were in human form.

Okay, on second thought, this was better, but even though he could tolerate the sun as a cat, it still hurt like a mother. He might not burst into flames like this, but if they didn't get him out of here soon, he would be blistered pretty badly.

"What's that smell?"

He ground his teeth at Susan's question. *It's me, genius.* He would project that thought out to her if it weren't for the fact that it would shock him and he'd been shocked enough for one day. Ravyn hissed as sunlight cut across his footpad and blistered it. He jerked his paw and tucked it up under him.

His head was throbbing and honestly, he didn't know how much longer he could maintain his form or hold back his magick. Time was running out for him.

"Is that you, Puss in Boots?"

Ravyn glared at her as she stopped for a red light. Irritation at her aside, she was rather cute in a very girl-next-door kind of way. Not a knockout by any means, but wholesomely pretty. With dark blond hair and bright blue eyes, she looked like she should be on a farm somewhere, tending a dozen or so kids. There was something about her that reminded him of a no-nonsense Mennonite woman. She wasn't wearing any makeup and her hair was pulled back into a ponytail. If it were down, it'd probably fall just below her shoulders—the same length as his.

She rolled down the car windows. "Gah, what did you eat, Puss in Boots? I'm thinking I shouldn't have taken that Benadryl. A stopped-up nose would definitely improve this aromatic nightmare. Someone shoot me."

Oh, to have the ability to speak as a human right about now. . . . Get me out of the sunlight, lady, and we'll both be a hell of a lot happier.

Ravyn tried to swallow only to learn that he couldn't because the collar was suddenly constricting his throat. His body was starting to grow again even with the ionic inhibitors of the collar that were keeping him in small-cat form. Since it wasn't his natural form and it was daylight, his body wanted to return to being human, and before much longer he would switch back whether he wanted to or not.

If he were still wearing the collar when the change came, it would kill him.

Drive faster.

Susan jerked as she heard what seemed to be a man's voice in her head. It was followed by the cat hissing in the backseat.

"Great," she mumbled under her breath. "I'm losing my mind now. Next thing you know, I'll actually see one of Jimmy's vampires or, better yet, I'll buy into Leo's psychosis." She shook her head. "Get a grip, Sue. Your sanity's all you have left and as worthless as it is, you can't afford to let it go."

And still she had this prickly feeling on the back of her neck as if her skin were crawling. It was so disturbing. It was as if someone were staring at her, but as she looked around at the traffic, she couldn't find anyone. Completely unsettled, she closed the windows and wished that she hadn't left her gun at home this morning.

By the time she pulled into her own driveway, she half-expected something freaky to happen. She wasn't sure what that freakiness would involve—maybe her Toyota coming alive like Christine or Herbie (which begged the question, if the car could talk would it have a Japanese accent?), or her newly adopted cat talking like Morris, or even one of Jimmy's vampires waiting in her house.

"I should write fiction," she mumbled as she pulled the cage with the cat out of the backseat and slammed the car door. "Who knew I had this kind of imagination?"

Yeah, right. She really wasn't creative at all. Her feet had always been planted firmly on the ground, with her only trips into the fantastic being the occasional *Star Wars* movie.

As she fumbled with her keys in the front-door lock, the cat started jumping around in the box as if he were in pain. "Stop it, Puss, or I'm going to drop you."

The cat calmed instantly as if it understood her. Sneezing and miserable, Susan pushed open the door and set the carrier down just to her right before she shut and locked the door. She headed for the Kleenex, intending to keep Puss in Boots in the cage until Angie came to retrieve it, but as she blew her nose, she looked to see the cat crawling out of it.

How had the door come open?

"Hey!" she snapped. "Get back in the box!"

But the cat didn't listen.

She took a step toward it only to realize that it was acting strangely. The cat could barely walk and appeared to be choking. It fell down and rolled to its side.

Her heart stopped beating. "Oh, don't you dare die on me. Angie'll kill me. She'll never believe I didn't do something to kill you."

Wiping her nose, she crossed the room in short strides to reach for the lump of fur. Its breathing was labored and pain filled.

What on earth could be wrong with him?

It was then she realized that the cat's collar was extremely tight on its neck. Poor Puss appeared to be asphyxiating. "Okay," she said calmly. "Let's get this thing off you." She reached for the latch only to realize that it didn't have a buckle.

Susan frowned. *What on earth?*

"Pull at it. Hard."

It was that same deep, masculine voice in her head and it coincided with the cat hissing and squirming as if in even more pain.

"Just relax," she said soothingly as she grabbed the collar and pulled. What the hell? Maybe the weird voice knew something she didn't.

At first the collar seemed to tighten even more, causing the cat to wheeze and choke. Susan pulled at the collar with all her strength. Just when she was sure it was useless, the collar snapped in half with a foreign surge of electricity so powerful, it actually knocked her back three feet.

Cursing, she righted herself, then froze as she caught sight of the cat, which was growing on the carpet, right before her eyes. In a matter of heartbeats, it went from small house cat to full leopard size.

And still it writhed on the floor as if it were in agony.

"Run!"

She flinched at the man's voice in her head. Far from a coward, she moved forward . . . at least until all hell broke loose. Lightning shot from the ceiling and rebounded all over her room, shattering frames and breaking lightbulbs. The hair on her body stood up on ends as the air was rife with static electricity that snapped in her ears.

The leopard let out a feral snarl as it clawed at her carpet.

Unsure of what to do and unable to get to her gun since the cat was between her and the staircase, Susan took cover behind her couch as more lightning flashed and the windows rattled so badly that she wasn't even sure why they hadn't shattered. She shrieked as a bolt came dangerously close to her, making her hair stand on end in what she was sure was a truly attractive sight.

Just as she thought her house would ignite into flames from the powerful bursts, the lightning stopped abruptly. It was eerily quiet as she sat cringing with her hands over her ears. So quiet that all she could hear was the pounding of her own heart. The heaviness of her own breathing.

She half-expected the lightning to return.

But after a minute of waiting with nothing else running amok, she dared a glance over the back of the couch to discover the most incredible thing of all had happened. . . .

Her leopard was gone and in its place was a naked man.

I have got to be dreaming. . . .

But if she were, wouldn't she have given herself a better house than this?

Ignoring that thought, she narrowed her eyes. The man lay unmoving on her dark green carpet. From her angle, all she could see was a well-muscled backside with a strange double bow and arrow tattoo on his left shoulder blade. Long black wavy hair was plastered against his damp body and he had the nicest naked butt she'd ever seen in real life.

Granted he looked mighty fine lying there, but then Ted Bundy hadn't been hard on the eyes, either.

Susan grabbed the closest thing she had to a weapon—her table lamp that had fallen over during the chaos—and crouched low, waiting for him to move.

He didn't.

He just lay there so still and quiet she wasn't even sure he was alive.

With her heart lodged firmly in her throat, she unscrewed the lamp shade and crept closer to him. "Hey?" she said sharply. "You alive?"

He didn't respond.

Preparing to run just in case he was faking, she poked him with the tip of the lamp. *Okay, I've seen this movie before*, she thought. *Hapless moron sticks head over unconscious body to check vital signs and the bad guy opens his eyes and grabs her.*

She wasn't about to fall for that. So she decided to creep around to the front of him.

Still, he didn't move. "Hey," she tried again, poking him with the lamp.

Nothing.

Nothing but a body so prime that it made her want to take a bite out of it to see if he tasted as good as he looked. *Stop it, Sue!* She had much more important things to think about than how good he looked naked.

Susan narrowed her eyes as she sat back on her heels. It was hard to get those thoughts out of her head. He had a long, lean body that was dusted with short black hairs and lean, hard muscles that let her know he would be extremely formidable while awake. He was well over six feet tall and there was something about him, even while out cold, that said he wasn't meek or mild.

A body like his wasn't something a woman came up against often. In more ways than one. He was all tanned flesh from tip to toe. But what captured her attention was the beauty of his hands. He had elegant, strong fingers and the palm of his right hand appeared to be blistered.

How absolutely odd. But that wasn't what concerned her. The fact that he was on her floor did.

Ready to whack him hard if he moved, she used the lamp to roll him over onto his back. Something that wasn't exactly easy to do, since he appeared to weigh a small ton, but eventually she had him there. His long hair completely obscured his face even though the rest of him was laid out bare to her gaze.

Feeling a teensy bit better that he hadn't made any moves to grab her, she crept closer. So close that she could finally touch that delectable skin. Susan frowned as she saw a line of awful bruising around his neck—like the cat might have had from the collar. . . .

She wasn't sure if that comforted her or scared her. Lowering the lamp, she reached to touch the bruised area so that she could feel for his pulse. God, he had a sexy neck. The kind a woman dreamed about teasing between her teeth.

Focus, Susan, focus. This isn't about sex, this is about a naked stranger in your house.

One she wanted out of here, ASAP. And luckily his pulse was beating strongly against her fingertips.

Still, he didn't try to grab her.

Maybe he wasn't faking after all.

"Okay," she breathed. He was alive and unconscious on her floor. Where did that leave her?

Up stinky creek sans a paddle.

Sighing, she continued to stare at the bruise on his neck. He couldn't really be the cat, could he?

"Oh, don't be stupid. This so can't be happening. Not now. Not to me."

And yet it was. She couldn't deny the fact that there was a gorgeous naked man on her floor and the cat appeared to have completely vanished.

No, it had to be some kind of trick. Something like a Criss Angel stunt—he was the king of pulling off incredible illusions while millions of people watched. Never had she believed in magic of any kind and she wasn't about to buy into that crap now. She only believed in what she could see and feel.

And you could feel him right now. No one would ever *know. . . .*

"Oh, get thee behind me, Id." But then it had been way too long since she'd had a naked guy around, and she'd never had one around who was quite this fine. Of course there was a really good reason for that. Most guys who looked like this weren't exactly date material. They were more the players who came and went so fast that they often left skid marks on a woman's heart and in her bedroom.

That was the last thing she needed in her life.

Returning her thoughts to her dilemma, Susan glanced to her couch, where she'd taken cover when the lightning had started—an easy trick to pull off probably. They could have rigged something to her outlets to cause the lightning and friction. Maybe that's what had thrown her back when she'd pulled the collar off—it could have been some kind of remote. Then, while she'd been distracted by the light show, this guy must have traded places with the cat.

Yeah, that was it. That made sense.

Now he was pretending to be unconscious. He had to be.

She looked up at the ceiling. "If you're filming this, I'm not amused. It'll take more than this to make me believe the cat turned into Mr. Gorgeous."

There was no response. Fine. Let them laugh. At least she got some good eye candy out of it.

Licking her dry lips, she studied him carefully. He lay as if in some kind of coma, but if he was an actor, that would be easy to fake, too. Against her better judgment, she reached out and brushed the hair from his face until she could see him.

Her breath caught. His features were chiseled and perfect. His eyebrows finely arched, his cheekbones high and covered by at least two days' worth of black whiskers. He had an almost sullen, bad-boy look to him. It was smoldering and animalistic. Magnetic. That moody, dark sexuality that made every woman pant whenever a guy like this came on the scene.

And those sensuous lips of his, completely kissable. Yeah, it was hard to be this close to him and not take advantage of it. Honestly, he was the best-looking guy she'd ever seen in the flesh.

All of a sudden, she started laughing. Deep and loud. She couldn't help herself. Good Lord, how weird was this?

Over and over, she could hear Leo's voice in her head:

"CAT TURNS INTO STUNNING NAKED MAN IN
SINGLE WOMAN'S HOME . . . WOMEN STAMPEDING
LOCAL ANIMAL SHELTERS EVERYWHERE.
KEEP YOUR CAT UNDER LOCK AND KEY."

It made her wonder who she should call . . . a doctor or a vet.

She froze as that thought triggered another. "Angie."

That was it. Angie had to have been in on this. No wonder Angie had insisted that she take the cat home in spite of her allergies. Now it all made sense. Jimmy's insanity, Leo insisting that she check into the Catman story. Angie's fake acting—nobody was *that* bad an actor.

Not to mention the fact that she was no longer sneezing. . . .

Yeah, they were all playing some kind of prank on her. She

was positive. And damn them for it. Like she didn't have anything better to do with her life. *Well, you don't.* Narrowing her
eyes, she chose to ignore that irritating little voice in the back of
her mind.

There for a second, they'd almost had her going.

Well, fine, two could play this game and she could play it a
whole lot better than all of them combined.

Disgusted at herself for even buying into it for a second, Susan
grabbed the cell phone from her pocket and called Angie's number.

There was no answer.

"Come on, babe. Pick up the phone." She called again, only to
have it roll over to the voice mail. Deciding to continue her friend's
game, she added a tremor of panic into her voice. "Hey, Ang. It's
me. Give me a call, okay? I *really* need to ask you about this cat you
gave me. Something really weird has happened. Give me a call as
soon as you get this. Talk to you later."

Susan tucked the phone back into her pocket and glanced at the
unconscious hottie as another thought went through her head. . . .

*I'm sure Catman Moron found some bimbo to shack up with
and shag for the day, but dammit all. Couldn't he have called and
told me that?*

That would be Round Two. The girl, Dark Angel, and her
blog. Leo probably had her in on this, too. Then again, Leo could
very well be Dark Angel for all she knew. Anyone with an Internet
connection could set up a blog page.

After all, there couldn't be more than one Catman in Seattle. *I
mean, really, what were the odds of there being one, never mind a
whole tribe of them. Right?*

So it was time to tackle that leg of the hoax. Grabbing the pink
throw from her couch and tossing it over her unwelcome guest, she
took her laptop off the coffee table and opened it up. It didn't take
her long to boot it up and find the blog again. She quickly located
the e-mail link for Dark Angel. Susan clicked on it, then sat there
staring at the blank e-mail screen.

How should she even begin?

Might as well be blunt. She honestly didn't know any other
way to live her life or write.

Dear Dark Angel,

I've found your missing Catman in a local animal shelter. He's currently passed out on my floor. Please respond soon and let me know what you want me to do with him as I am highly allergic and I don't have time to housebreak him.

Thanks,
Susan

Okay, so it read like she was on some serious medication. But what the hell? If this was real, she'd probably start needing some.

She reread the post about Dark Angel losing her boss last night. Glancing over to the man on her floor, Susan gave a wicked smile. "Well, if I lost something like you, I'd certainly want him back."

Okeydokie, she thought as she sent the e-mail off. Now it was time for her to see about securing the Catman of Seattle until she heard from either Dark Angel or Angie. Hmmm . . . here's where being a rock climber would have come in handy, or even a serial killer. Any kind of hobby that would've allowed her to have had some kind of rope on hand. But she didn't.

As she searched the room for something to use, her gaze fell to the collar that she'd pulled off the cat. Frowning, she went over to it and picked it up. It was the strangest thing she'd ever seen. The material felt like both metal and cloth. Truly, it was odd. And unfortunately, it was too small to use on the guy.

You do have some bungee cords in the closet. . . .

Would they work?

All she could do was see.

As she headed for the closet, she heard the ping from her computer, telling her that mail had arrived. Her cords forgotten, she went over to it and paused as she saw an e-mail from Dark Angel.

Clicking on it, she couldn't wait to see what the girl had to say.

Dear Psycho Susan,

You need help. Really. This isn't a game here, but let's say for argument's sake that by some long stretch of the imagination you're not lying and that you did find him. If I were you, I'd be on my knees, praying. 'Cause when he wakes up, he'll rip your heart out and laugh about it, then drink your blood and dump your body in the nearest ditch. Shapeshifters don't have a sense

of humor and they can't stand to be trapped anywhere. There-
fore, I'm not worried about getting him back from you. He'll
come home when he's ready to.

DA

Susan stared at the words as a feeling of anger filled her. What
kind of crap was that?

They were screwing with her. They had to be.

And to think there for a minute she'd almost bought into it.

What about the lightning?

Special effects. Really, what were the odds? Out of all of Seattle, *she* would be the one to find the missing cat that Leo had told
her to investigate. . . .

Yeah, right. Leo and Angie were always saying that she needed
to loosen up. What better way than to pay some cute guy to come
play a prank on her?

"That's it, Puss," she said, aggravated at all of them. "It's time
to get you out of here."

Shutting the lid for her laptop, she headed for the unconscious
man. She was no more than a foot from him when one long, muscular arm shot out and swept her feet out from under her.

Two heartbeats later, she was pinned to the floor and staring
up into the blackest eyes she'd ever seen.

CHAPTER FOUR

Ravyn paused as he stared into pale blue eyes that seared him. Not to mention the fact that his body was being cushioned by the softest curves he'd ever felt, curves that would only feel better if she were naked underneath him.

The scent of woman mixed with sweet perfume filled his head and it was enough to silence the beast inside him as he wondered how she'd gotten into his house while he slept.

It took a full ten seconds before he remembered that he wasn't in his own home. Another five before he remembered everything that'd happened since last night. The woman, Susan, had taken him out of the animal shelter and brought him to her house. As soon as she'd taken the collar off, his suppressed magick had run riot.

Now he was—

About to be creamed by the lamp she was lifting up to beat him with. Rolling away from her, he came to a crouch at the same time Susan lunged at him with her lamp.

"Hey, hey, hey!" he snapped, deflecting it with his arm. "What are you doing?"

She forced him back with the tip of the lamp. "Keep your hands to yourself, buddy."

Ravyn struggled to disentangle his feet from a pink Power Puff Girl blanket while he dodged her pokes. "Put the damn lamp down."

She refused.

Too aggravated to argue, Ravyn tried to disintegrate it with his mind. Unfortunately, all that happened was a sharp pain to his head. Cursing, he put the heel of his hand against his forehead to combat the ache. He realized that he'd worn the collar so long, it had all but drained him of his powers. He was completely lacking all magick until he had time to recharge. Damn.

So instead, he jerked the lamp from her hands and made as if to hit her with it—not that he ever would, but dammit he was pissed, and the stupid blanket that seemed to be melded to his legs wasn't helping any. Irritated, he set the lamp down behind him as he finally succeeded in stepping out of the mess at his feet.

The woman seemed every bit as aggravated with him as she tried to reclaim her property. "You know, that wasn't cheap. I want my lamp back."

He kept her from reaching around him to grab the lamp. Finally, he forced her back, toward the brown leather sofa. "Yeah, and people in hell want ice water. Doesn't mean they're going to get it, especially when someone can't keep herself from poking me with it."

He glanced around the spartan living room, grateful that all the shades were drawn shut to keep the daylight out. The whole house was done in simple, contemporary lines with earth tones and only a bare minimum of furniture. It was obvious that she wasn't into anything too fussy, frilly, or complicated. "It's still daylight, isn't it?"

"You think?"

A tic started in his jaw. His luck just kept improving every step of the way. "Whatever you do, don't open those blinds."

"Why? You gonna burst into flames or something?"

He looked at her drolly but didn't answer. How he wished he had enough juice to summon clothes for himself. But that, too, would have to wait, so instead he retrieved the evil pink blanket from the floor and wrapped it around him. He grimaced as he realized the word *Puff* covered his cock—yeah, he was feeling really manly at the moment. "You got a phone I can use?"

Susan folded her arms over her chest. All things considered, she had to give Leo and Angie credit, the guy was scrumptious—even with the childish blanket wrapped low around his lean hips. His shoulder-length black hair was tousled but looked really good with his sullen features. As he raked a hand through his hair to settle it into place, the muscles of his arm and side flexed in a most captivating way.

He had the deepest voice she'd ever heard—the kind that just rippled down her spine like a hot caress. And he had the most intriguing way of speaking without opening his mouth more than a tiny bit. Truly the man was sex on a stick.

She didn't know where they'd found him, but given his build and beauty, she'd guess he was probably a local stripper. It would explain why he was so comfortable with being naked in front of a complete stranger.

But since they'd gone to such trouble, she might as well play along to see how far Mr. Buff carried the charade. "A phone? For what? Can't you mind meld to your cat people or something?"

He sneered at her as if that offended him. "Just how much TV do you watch?"

"Very little."

He looked less than amused. "So can I have a phone or not?"

"Who are you going to call?"

"Someone to get me out of here."

"Well, why didn't you say so." She tossed him her cell phone.

Ravyn wasn't sure if her quick capitulation amused him or pissed him off. Deciding on the former, he flipped the cover up and dialed for Erika.

"This is Erika. I can't answer the phone right now, but please leave your name and number and I'll get around to chatting later."

He glanced over to the clock on the wall. It was just after four in the afternoon.

"Dammit, Erika, where are you? You're not in class and you should be home studying with your phone turned on. It's me and I need you to bring me some clothes and come pick me up pronto.

Call me back for directions." Disgusted with his wayward Squire, he hit the CANCEL button.

He dialed Acheron's number.

Yet another voice mail. Great, just great. He really hated these things. Hanging up, he growled deep in his throat.

He considered calling the other Seattle Dark-Hunters and warning them about the Apollite uprising but decided it would wait a bit. Either they were safe at home or they were dead. If the latter, then there wasn't anything he could do for them.

He glanced at the woman who was still watching him with a strange look of perturbance. "I don't suppose you have some clothes I could borrow, do you?"

"Sorry. Extra-large male isn't my specialty. Besides, can't you just poof some clothes on?"

"Not at the moment."

She gave him an arch look. "Let me guess, you need to recharge your batteries or something, right?"

She was eerily astute. "Yes."

The disbelief on her face was almost comical. "I do have some pink sweats that might not be too bad."

"I'd rather go naked."

"Suit yourself. Not like it bothers me."

"Then we're even." Like patience, modesty had never been his virtue. But one thing he did hate was being around people he didn't know. Then again, he didn't like being around people he did know, either. He much preferred solitude—it couldn't betray him.

She cocked her head. "So how long have you known Leo, anyway?"

"Leo who?"

"Kirby."

He frowned at her. He'd known Leo vicariously for years. Like his Squire substitute, Erika, Leo was one of the humans who served the Dark-Hunters. Paid employees, they helped to keep the paranormal world hidden from the rest of mankind, who would most likely panic if they ever learned what inhuman beasts prowled the night, waiting to prey on them. "Are you a Squire?"

"No, I'm a Michaels."

He rolled his eyes. She had to be the biggest smart-ass on the planet; well, maybe second only to Erika. "That's not what I mean and you know it. Do you work with Leo?"

"Of course I do. Why else would you be here?"

Ravyn nodded. It explained her snotty attitude. For some reason, the latest generation of Squires seemed to have a problem with their duties. "Why didn't you tell me you worked for him?"

"I assumed you knew it."

"Yeah, right. The way you guys come and go, it's impossible to remember more than one or two of you at a time."

She nodded in agreement. "Leo does have a way of burning people out. So how did he talk you into this?"

"Into what?"

"Showing up here, naked to yank my chain."

Yeah . . . like Leo could have *ever* done that. "He didn't. I assumed he sent you to me to get me out of the shelter."

"I guess in a roundabout way he did. So tell me something, how did you do that earlier trick?"

Ravyn grimaced. "What trick?"

"The cat thing. How did you switch?"

Why did humans always want that question answered? Even if he explained it, it wasn't like they could do it. "It's magick," he said sarcastically. "I mumble hocus-pocus and the next thing you know, I'm a cat."

She narrowed her eyes at him. "I suppose it's a step up. The last guy I had in my house could only turn into a beer-drinking pig."

In spite of himself, he gave a short laugh at her dry tone. He had to give her credit, she had a quick sense of humor, and he was quirky enough to appreciate that in other people.

Suddenly, he was exhausted. He hadn't been able to sleep since the Apollites had captured him—to have done so would have caused him to revert instantly to human form, which would have resulted in head explosion. Now he felt the deep need to rest. "So can I take the bed until tonight?"

Her eyes widened. "Excuse me?"

"I need sleep. You know? Whole point of you getting me from the shelter? You said Leo sent you, right?"

She put her hands on her hips and gave him a sharp glare that said she wasn't keen on that idea. "Yeah, but not to let you sleep in my bed. This isn't a flophouse, you know?"

That raised his ire. "What is happening to the Squire's code? I remember a time when that actually meant something."

"What Squire's code?"

"Up the ginkgo, babe. Don't you remember the one you had to take when you went to work for Leo?"

Her eyes snapped blue fire at him. "Leo didn't make me promise anything other than to leave my sanity at home."

His disgust tripled. "That figures. You must be first-generation."

"What has that got to do with anything?"

"It explains why you don't know your job any better than you do."

She crossed the floor to stand right in front of him as she glared her anger at him. "Excuse me? I don't know *my* job? At least, I'm not the one standing naked in a stranger's house, clutching a throw to cover *my* vital parts." She raked him with a less than complimentary glare. "Who the heck are *you* to lecture *me* on what *I* should be doing?"

"I'm a Dark-Hunter."

Susan stiffened. He said that as if it explained everything. "And that's supposed to mean something to me?"

He curled his lip. "Of course it should. What the hell has gotten into all of you that you no longer care about us? Or your duties? Have the Daimons sucked you in to work for them, too?"

What was he talking about? "Who are the Daimons? Last time I checked, the paper was owned by the Kirbys."

He curled his lip at her. "Like you don't know who they are. Look, Susan, I don't have time for you to jerk me around. I need some sleep before tonight. We've got a lot of stuff we have to do and I'll need for you to e-mail the rest of your group and let them know what's going on."

Boy, he had some nerve. She'd never seen anyone so commanding and sure of himself. Especially given the fact that he was standing here bare-butt naked. "Excuse me? Do I look like your personal secretary or slave? Uh . . . no. You don't own me. I don't even know you and I don't care how cute you look naked in my living room, I don't take orders from anyone. So there's the door—"

"You know I can't go out there. There's daylight outside."

She gave him a droll stare. "Well, that's what happens when the big yellow ball comes up over the mountains. Amazing, isn't it?"

Ravyn wanted to choke her. And he'd stupidly thought Erika was a pain. *That's what you get for thinking there couldn't be a worse Squire in existence . . . here's Erika in another fifteen years or so.*

And Acheron thought that saving mankind from the Daimons was nothing. Gods spare him from women such as these two.

Just as he opened his mouth to speak, there was a knock on the front door.

Ravyn exchanged a puzzled frown with Susan. A small preternatural frisson went up his spine. Since it was daylight, he knew there couldn't be a Daimon or Apollite out there—daylight would fry them on the spot.

Yet that's what it felt like. There was no denying or excusing away the unique sensation.

Which meant it had to be a halfblood. Only a half-Apollite would be able to set off his senses and still walk in daylight without dying.

"Ms. Michaels?" a deep, masculine voice called through the door.

Susan started toward it only to have Ravyn pull her to a stop. "No."

"No?" she asked, her voice frigid. "Boy, I'm not your bitch or your ho. You don't order me about. Ever." Susan twisted away from his grip.

Ravyn cursed at her stubbornness. Something wasn't right. He could feel it with every heightened sense he possessed.

Susan ignored him as she opened her door to find two uniformed police officers on her front porch. One of them was incredibly tall, probably around six six or so, with short blond hair and dark brown eyes. The other officer was a brunette who only stood about four inches taller than her.

"Can I help you?"

The brunette looked up at the blond as if he were the one in charge. "Are you Susan Michaels?" the blond officer asked.

She nodded.

"Were you at the Seattle Animal Shelter a short time ago?"

"Is there a problem?"

The blond gave her a smile so fake that someone should post it in a toothpaste ad. "No problem. You just left the facilities with a cat that wasn't meant to be adopted. We're here to collect him."

Every nerve in her body rang out with suspicion. Why would two cops—

Oh wait. Jimmy. He'd probably put them up to this just to get her goat. Susan stared blankly at them. "Don't you guys have something better to do, like actually investigate real crimes or something?"

"This *is* a matter of public safety, ma'am," he said seriously. She had to give him credit. He was much better at acting than Angie had been. "That cat is extremely feral and might be rabid."

Sure it was. "Well, I'm afraid you're too late. The cat has already turned into Mr. Supermodel and has now taken up residency in my home. I don't know what Jimmy paid you guys for this, but whatever it was, I'm sure it wasn't enough. Have a nice day, gentlemen." She closed the door.

But before she could step away, she heard a faint voice through the door. "It's her and he's here in human form. She won't hand him over, so what do you want us to do?"

Susan scowled as she heard a voice answer him, but she couldn't make out any of the words.

"Yes, sir." There was a brief pause until she heard footsteps on her porch. At first, she thought it was the police leaving. But the sound was getting closer, not farther away.

"He said to kill the Dark-Hunter and take the woman back to the shelter for questioning. If she gives us any problems, kill her, too."

Her heart shrank at those words. They had to be joking . . . right? This wasn't real. It couldn't be.

"I told you not to answer it, didn't I?" Ravyn snarled as he pulled her away from the door.

Two seconds later the front door flew open. The two uniformed officers angled guns at them. "Don't move."

She raised her hands up as fear gripped her hard. They were going way out of line on this one. "What's the meaning of this?"

They didn't answer as she saw two more men in street clothes coming in behind them. Large and tough, they each looked like they had a rap sheet to make Scarface proud.

Ravyn silently debated on how to handle this. The tall blond was half-Apollite without a doubt, but the other three were humans. By Dark-Hunter code, he wasn't allowed to harm humans. Then again he'd never lived by anyone's code but his own.

For now, he had to move quickly to keep Susan safe and himself alive. "Susan . . ."

She looked at him as he reacted instinctively.

He dove for her at the same time the cops opened fire on him. Ravyn cursed as the bullets sliced into his flesh. They wouldn't kill him, but it didn't mean they didn't hurt.

Susan was momentarily stunned by what was happening. This wasn't a practical joke. They were trying to kill him and take her. The horror of it all held her immobile as she stared at the blood pouring out of Ravyn's body while he shielded her from the gunfire.

"He's still moving," one of the thugs said to the blond officer.

"The bullets won't kill him. Tear down the blinds."

She heard Ravyn's curse before he breathed in her ear, "Run for the back door while I distract them."

He rolled from her as the men started ripping her blinds from their tracks, causing the afternoon sun to spill through her living room.

That's my house, you assholes, she wanted to shout at them, but thought better of it. They didn't seem to be in the most reasonable of moods as they riddled her home with more bullets while tearing it apart. She was amazed that they hadn't shot her in the chaos.

Ravyn hissed as a ray of sunlight cut across his skin. But what stunned her most was that his skin blistered and began smoking.

That wasn't normal and that wasn't fake, especially not the stench of it . . . what was going on?

"Kill him!"

Ravyn dropped the blanket and shoved her toward the back of her house. "Go!"

"What about you?"

He recoiled as they opened fire on him again. "Go, Susan. Run!"

She did, but she didn't go far. She ran to her closet and pulled out her baseball bat that she kept there just in case of intruders. And this definitely qualified as that. Too bad she hadn't had time to get to her gun before all this started.

Susan ran back to the fray. Ravyn went down hard on the floor as she swung at the thug closest to her.

She caught him against the arm with enough force that it caused him to drop his gun. Then she swung another blow at him with all her strength, catching him against the head. He hit the ground hard. The brunette officer turned toward her and took aim. She ducked as he unloaded his clip into her wall.

Ravyn was dazed as his body burned. Daylight was now all around him so much so that he could barely move for it.

He saw Susan swinging at the other thug as the halfblood officer grabbed him by the ankle and tried to pull him toward the light on the floor. Every fiber of his body ached as he watched the brunette officer grab Susan from behind. The thug took the bat from her hand and shoved it into her stomach. She cried out before doubling over in pain.

Screw this. He was through playing with them. As a Dark-Hunter he wasn't supposed to ever attack a human being, but then humans had never been all that high in his estimation and he wasn't about to die and let these bastards live to do whatever they wanted with Susan. Pain though she was, she was a Squire and that brought with it a certain degree of protection.

Not to mention, it wasn't in his genetic makeup to go quietly into that good night and since one of these assholes was part Apollite . . . well, he knew of one way to rejuvenate his weakened powers. Apollites and Daimons liked to feed on Were-Hunters so that they could not only steal the Were-Hunters' souls but claim their psychic powers as well.

That channel worked both ways. . . .

His rage swelling, Ravyn kicked out at the officer holding him. He felt the beast inside him snarl as it rose to the forefront. His eyesight changed from human to that of a vicious predator.

Lowering his head, he ignored the bullets that riddled him as he rushed toward the half-Apollite and caught him about the waist. "You stupid fool," he snarled as he turned the man so that his back was against Ravyn's front. "You should have brought a Taser."

"Shoot me!" the blond officer screamed at the other two who were still standing. "Quick!"

Susan froze in her struggling as she caught sight of Ravyn. He held the blond cop in front of him, but that wasn't what stunned her. It was the fact that his eyes were no longer black. They were a deep, insidious red. He tilted his head back, opening his mouth so that she could see long, sharp incisors. The other men in the room froze as if they were every bit as terrified as she was.

And before she could release her pent-up breath, Ravyn sank his teeth into the officer's neck.

I don't believe in vampires. I don't believe in vampires. . . . The litany repeated itself over and over again in her mind as she watched the blood pour down the officer's shirt while he struggled to get away from Ravyn, who effortlessly held him with one arm.

Suddenly, the two thugs opened fire on both Ravyn and the cop he held. The cop's entire body shook in response to the bullets pummeling him as his eyes turned glassy and dull. Ravyn laughed evilly as he released the lifeless body to sink slowly to the floor at his feet.

He threw his hands out and some kind of invisible wave went through the room, knocking the two men off their feet. His eyes matched the red blood that still dripped from his chin as black clothing appeared on his body.

"You don't knock on the devil's door, boys, unless you want him to answer," he said, his voice deep and evil. He wiped the blood from his chin.

"Th-they said you wouldn't attack us," one of the thugs said in a frightened tone.

"*They* lied."

Some unseen force ripped her out of the arms of the officer who held her. Ravyn rushed the thug closest to him and hit him so hard that he was knocked off his feet, and three feet up, into her wall, which shattered as the thug hit it. The brunette officer rushed at Ravyn, who spun about and caught him a powerful blow to his jaw. The sound of bones breaking echoed in the room as the officer fired more bullets.

Ravyn's eyes turned an even brighter red before he waved his hand in the air. The bullets stopped dead in the air, hanging there for two heartbeats before they reversed direction and struck the cop.

Susan couldn't breathe as her gaze scanned the carnage of the four men who'd entered her home. Now the only one standing was . . .

The male stripper.

"Please, please tell me that I'm having an acid flashback."

His eyes faded back to black. "You drop acid?"

All she could do was shake her head no as some foreign coldness invaded every part of her body. This couldn't be real. She couldn't have seen what she'd just seen.

I'm having a psychotic episode.

Maybe they weren't dead. Maybe all of this was still part of the hoax Leo had perpetrated. She took a step toward the blond officer to feel for a pulse . . . only there was no way to press her fingertips against his carotid since it was no longer intact. It had been ripped out.

And that wasn't makeup. It was real. Disgusting and real. At one time, she'd been on the police beat and seen more than her fair share of dead bodies. This was no hoax. Her male stripper had just killed four men in her house, which would make her an accomplice if she didn't report this.

"We have to go to the police," she said in a strangely serene tone. "Tell them what happened."

He shook his head. "We can't go to the police. They're in on this."

"No, they'll—"

"Susan," he snapped, shaking her lightly. "Look at me."

Even though she wanted to run, she stood her ground and met those spooky black eyes.

"This isn't a game. Didn't you hear what your friend was trying to tell you earlier? There's some serious shit going down here. Now that I know what's going on, I can take care of myself, but you're another matter. We have to get you to a sanctuary before more of them come to find *you*. Do you understand?"

"But I didn't do anything wrong. I didn't kill them. *You* did."

"Bobby? Alan? What's going on? You got the woman yet?"

Her breath caught as she heard the officer's radio going off. Were there more of them outside waiting to come in?

"Bobby? Respond. Over?"

Ravyn cursed as he heard heavy footsteps outside. "There's two more men coming up the walkway."

"How do you know?"

Before he could answer, her door was kicked wide open. Ravyn shoved her toward the kitchen before he slung his hands and knocked the two human males down. He took a step forward only to realize that these two were smarter than the others . . . they had the one weapon that would incapacitate him. A Taser. One shot and the electricity would bounce around his cells, turning him from cat to man and back again without his control. His magick would be haywire and he would be defenseless against them.

As much as he hated it, it was time to retreat. Changing to cat form, he ran after Susan, who was making her way toward the back door.

"We have to get to your car."

Susan froze as she heard the male voice in her head and saw the small leopard back in her house. "Please tell me I'm having some kind of stress-induced hallucination." It was better than the thought that she had actually lost her mind completely.

But insane or not, she needed to get out of here until she figured out what was going on. Since there was no way to get to her front door without confronting the two newcomers, she grabbed the spare set of car keys from the small hanger inside her back door. She rushed out of her door as bullets sprayed the wall beside her, narrowly missing her.

Too afraid to look back, she ran to the driveway only to realize that they'd blocked her in. Damn. Another shot rang out before the passenger window of her Toyota shattered. Susan crouched down as she made her way around the car, to the driver's side. She didn't dare glance back until she had the door open.

She couldn't see anything until the small leopard came bounding out of the door, headed for her. Before she could move, it leaped into her car and jumped into the backseat.

Deciding not to argue, she got in, slammed the door, then started the engine.

"Duck!"

Normally, she didn't obey anyone's orders, never mind a disembodied voice in her head, but given the oddness of this day, she decided not to argue or hesitate. No sooner was she down than more bullets sprayed her Toyota.

"This is ridiculous!" Infuriated over the damage done to her car, she put it in drive and gunned the engine as more shots were fired. The car lurched as it went tearing through her neighbor's yard, over their small white garden fence. "Jenna is going to kill me." But she'd deal with her neighbor later, provided she survived this and had a later.

Her heart pounding, she sat up so that she could actually see where she was going. Off in the distance, she heard the sound of sirens. The saner part of herself wanted to head toward them, but she thought better of it. Those had been cops at her door. . . .

Jimmy had been terrified of his compadres in uniform. For argument's sake, what if that part of his psychosis had been real? She knew more about police corruption than any human had a right to, and though she'd always thought of the Seattle cops as much more honest than others, there could very well be more than one dirty apple in the barrel.

"I need to speak to Jimmy," she said under her breath. He was the one cop she could trust.

"*Head toward Pioneer Square.*" There it was again . . . that deep masculine voice in her head that she now recognized as Ravyn's.

"Why?" Oh good grief, she was now buying into the talking-cat thing. Great.

"*Just trust me. Three-seventeen First Avenue South.*"

Sure, why not? "And who's there, the Addams family?"

"*Yes.*"

Of course. Who else would live there? "This is one hell of a delusion I'm having. All I can say is that I hope whatever put me into this coma doesn't leave any lasting damage."

"*Since I'm the one with all the bullet wounds, I don't want to hear it from you.*"

"Lay off me, Puss in Boots. I'm having a really bad day."

"*Ditto.*"

Deciding to listen to the voice that sounded like her own, she headed back toward the clinic.

"*This isn't the way to Pioneer Square.*"

"Yes, voice in my head, I know. But I'm doing things my way, so sod off."

At least that was the plan until she got to the animal shelter and saw it marked off with yellow warning tape. Her heart rose in her throat to choke her as she saw the coroner, newspeople, officers, and a gathered crowd.

What had happened?

Part of her wanted to check it out, but given the fact that her car was currently riddled with bullet holes, that might not be the prudent thing to do until she found out what was happening and why the police seemed to be after her. No, she needed to get the hell out of here. But where could she go?

Leo.

He was . . . "Oh, don't say it," she whispered. She couldn't believe that he, of all people, was her lifeline. Yet she couldn't think of anyone else who might know why the police were at the shelter. Pulling her phone off her belt, she pressed 3 and waited while it rang.

"Yo?"

Never in her life had she been more thrilled to hear that goofy little-boy voice of his. "Leo?"

"Susan? Is that you?"

"Yes, and I—"

"Listen," he said sharply, cutting her off. "Don't talk." His curt tone irritated her, but for once she didn't argue. "There's been some odd things happening this afternoon. Did you by any chance go see your friend Angie today?"

"Yes. Why?"

He was silent for a full second. "Where are you now?"

"I'm in the car."

"You still got the cat?"

If there were any doubts Leo was in on the prank, that eliminated them. How else would he know that she'd taken a cat home from the shelter? "Yes. Puss in Boots is safe."

"Oh thank God." There was an unwarranted amount of relief in his voice. "Whatever you do, don't let that cat out of your sight."

"Why?"

"Just trust me." She heard a muffled sound like Leo was covering up the phone with his hand. "Tell them just a second." Then he returned to her. "I have to go. You need to head to Three-seventeen First Avenue South. Hold up there and I'll be over as soon as I can." He hung up the phone.

Three-seventeen First Avenue South. There was that address again. What was it with that place? Deciding that it must be important to her delusional mind, she finally succumbed and headed for it.

Susan really wished she knew what to think as she worked her way through the relatively light Seattle traffic. She could hear the cat moving around in her backseat from time to time, but for the most part, he was quiet.

Until she finally reached Pioneer Square.

"Pull around to the loading dock in back."

Convinced she was utterly insane, she did as the disembodied voice said, then parked the car. Her nerves were pretty much shot by the time she opened the door and got out. She half-expected the cat to leap out, but instead it was lying on the backseat . . . completely covered in blood. Her heart clenched at the sight.

Was it dead?

Terrified, she opened the back door. She touched the cat's shoulder only to have it hiss at her. "Easy," she said, pulling back.

The cat rose up slowly so that it could limp out of the car, toward the dock.

"Hey!" a cute young man with short black hair snapped at her. "You can't park . . ." His voice trailed off as he caught sight of the cat.

His face went instantly pale before he shouted inside the door. "Mom, we got Ravyn out here! Code Red." He grabbed a coarse blanket from a stack of them that was piled on the edge of the dock, then jumped down to wrap it around the cat.

Carefully, he picked the cat up, cradled it in his arms, then took it back to the loading dock.

Unsure of what she should be doing, Susan locked her car (and immediately wondered why she bothered since one window had been completely shot out and the rest of the car looked like it'd survived a war zone—but then old habits die hard) and followed them into the dock, which led to a small storeroom. As soon as the kid shut the door and set the cat down, Ravyn returned to being human. He braced one bloodied and blistered hand against the right wall and kept his head bent down as if he was exhausted.

Sure, why not? He really *was* the cat. Made about as much sense as the rest of her day. And hey, if she had to be delusional, at least he had the best naked backside she'd ever seen, except for the fact that there were numerous bullet holes riddling almost every inch of his exposed flesh.

But then he was only naked for a few brief seconds before a pair of jeans and a T-shirt appeared on him. It didn't take long before the shirt was saturated in blood.

Susan cringed at the sight of it. How could he still be alive, never mind standing upright? *Just play along with the delusion, Sue. What the hell?* "He needs an ambulance," she said to the kid.

Ravyn lifted his head to look at her over his shoulder. There was a small bit of blood on his lips, and for the first time she saw his fangs when he spoke. "I'll be all right. I just need some sleep."

"I have got to start taking drugs," she mumbled. "At least then I'd have an explanation for all this."

A door on the opposite side of the small storeroom was flung open to show two more people running in. A young woman who was around the age of the boy and a tall, dark-haired woman in her mid-fifties. The older woman paused as soon as she saw Susan. "Who are you?"

Ravyn rubbed his bleeding arm. "She's with me, Patricia."

Patricia gave her a suspicious look but didn't argue. "What happened?" she asked Ravyn, moving to examine the bullet wound he had in his right biceps.

"The Daimons have declared war on us and they have some of the police department on their side. I don't know how they managed it or how many they have, but it's enough to warrant our undivided attention. They claimed they killed at least one Dark-Hunter, didn't say who, and they almost got me. We need to warn the others, ASAP."

The color faded from the older woman's face. "How is that possible?"

Ravyn shook his head. "I don't know. But they're coming after us one by one."

Patricia turned to the girl behind her, who was a younger version of her—obviously her daughter. "Alicia, start the calls." Then she looked to the guy who'd met them on the dock. "Jack, I need you to make sure someone goes to Cael's to warn him. Since he lives with Apollites, he's probably in the greatest danger, and I've never known the man to answer his cell phone until the sun goes down."

"Okay, Mom." Jack took off immediately to obey her.

Susan was completely baffled by what the woman was talking about. Apollite? What was that? Some sort of diet soda? And what the devil was a Daimon? The only time she'd ever heard that term was when her e-mail bounced back with *mailer-daimon* attached to it.

Alicia handed her mother more bandages before she left to do her mother's bidding.

As soon as they were alone, Patricia moved to grab a small doctor's bag. "We'll need to get those bullets out of you so you can heal."

Sure, and why not just give the man a piece of leather to bite on for the pain, too, while they were at it? How backwards were these people?

"He needs a doctor," Susan insisted.

Patricia ignored her as she started setting out her supplies on a nearby table while Ravyn sat down on a stool. "Are you sure she's a Squire?"

Ravyn shrugged. "She said she worked with Leo."

Patricia paused. "With . . . or for?"

"For," Susan said.

That got Ravyn's full attention as he turned those deeply annoyed black eyes on her. "You're not a Squire?"

Before she could answer, the door opened again. "Mom," Jack said. "We have a serious problem."

"What?"

Jack held up a Sony portable TV monitor that had a breaking news story.

Susan's heart froze as she saw the news cameras that were trained on her little Cape Cod house.

"According to police, three unidentified men and two local officers were just reported as slain while trying to apprehend two people suspected of murdering a local veterinarian, her husband, and a clerk earlier this afternoon in a local animal shelter." Disbelief filled her.

The scene flashed to one of the men who'd chased Susan from her home. He was covered in blood and had a bandage wrapped around his head.

"I knew I should have ripped his throat out, too," Ravyn snarled.

"It was insane," the man said into the microphone. "We were just trying to sell magazine subscriptions and as soon as we knocked on the door, they pulled us in and killed my friend. I thought I was dead. I really did. If I hadn't been pretending I was dead, they would have killed me, too. They're crazy, man, crazy."

The scene went back to the anchorwoman. "As you can see, this is quite an unsettling event. Authorities are posting a reward for any information that leads them to the whereabouts of Ravyn Kontis and Susan Michaels, the two suspects for the murders. If you see either of them, please do not attempt to apprehend them, as they are considered extremely dangerous. Call the special line at 555-1924 and let the police know where they are."

Susan's jaw went slack as they flashed an old photograph of her and a police sketch of Ravyn. It was followed by a shot of her leaving the animal shelter with the cat cage. Jimmy had been right. There was a police conspiracy.

Her sight dimmed as her heart started racing. This couldn't be happening to her. It couldn't be.

But as shocking as that was, it was nothing compared to the next picture they showed.

It was the animal shelter again with all the yellow warning tape that kept it sectioned off from a small crowd of people.

"We finally have the names of the couple who was killed . . . Angela and James Warren. James, or Jimmy as he was known, had been married to Angela for the last five years and was known to often visit his wife at her clinic. . . ."

Susan staggered backwards until the wall stopped her. Angie was dead? Jimmy?

And *she* was wanted for their murders. . . .

From the deepest part of her soul, deep, wrenching sobs overwhelmed her.

Ravyn cringed as he heard the sound of her tears—he'd never been able to stand the tears of a woman. They tore through him and reminded him of a past he'd just as soon forget. "We've seen enough, Jack."

Jack cast a sympathetic look to Susan before he turned the monitor off and left.

Patricia moved toward Ravyn, but he brushed her off. "Give us a moment, okay?"

She nodded before she left them alone.

Ravyn's heart ached for the pain he heard in those soul-deep sobs. Better than anyone, he understood that kind of agony. The kind of loss that reached so far down into your being that it was all you could do to stand still and not launch into a hysterical tantrum of rage.

He'd been bred to that kind of misery. A Were-Hunter's life at best was one of burying family.

His had been even worse than that.

He wanted to tell her it would be all right, but he wasn't heartless enough to hand her that lie. In life, there were never any guarantees other than the one that said when you were down and out, someone would definitely come along to kick you.

So instead, he did something he hadn't done in countless centuries, he pulled her into his arms and held her. She wrapped her arms around him as she continued to sob. Ravyn ground his teeth as ragged emotions tore through him. Like her, he'd lost everything when he'd been mortal. . . .

Even his life.

She would need to cry this out. To let out all the rage and agony until she was spent from it. All he could do was offer her some physical comfort. As paltry as it was, it was better than nothing.

And it was more than anyone had ever offered him.

He leaned his head against hers and closed his eyes while she clung to him.

Susan wanted to scream as countless memories of Angie and Jimmy haunted her. They were her friends. Her *best* friends. Both of them. She'd known Angie ever since they were children, playing house and dress-up together. As for Jimmy, Susan had been the one to introduce them. They'd even made her the best man at their wedding as a goof.

How could they be gone now? Like this? Who could have hurt them?

"Why?" she sobbed, wanting some kind of solace. Some kind of answer.

But there wasn't any. It was senseless and stupid, and it hurt so deep inside that she wanted to claw the pain out.

Why hadn't she believed Jimmy? Why? She should never have left that shelter without both of them being with her.

Now they were dead.

And it was *her* fault for being so stupid!

From the deepest part of her soul, anger swelled as she remembered Jimmy's earlier fear. That anger allowed her to gather her strength, and as it overrode her grief she became aware of the fact that she was clutching a complete stranger.

Pulling back, she stared into those obsidian eyes. "What the hell is going on here and don't lie to me. I want the truth about what happened today."

He took a deep breath before he answered. "You're not a Squire, are you?"

Her frustration mounted. "You keep asking me that. What *is* a Squire?"

He looked ill at her question.

Her gaze fell to the bullet wounds in his chest, which were no longer bleeding. They were all over his arms, his neck, and the bloodstains on the black shirt betrayed all the places where he'd been shot on his chest and back. Yet he was acting as if they were nothing but a nuisance.

Susan touched the bullet wound on his arm that had torn straight through the muscle and tissue. It wasn't makeup or some special effect, it was real and it was gory. "What are you?"

A tic worked in his jaw before he gave a clipped answer. "In short . . . the only hope you got."

CHAPTER FIVE

Wiping her eyes, Susan pulled back from him and gaped. "Best hope for what, Catman? Death? Bankruptcy? You know, my life was going along . . ." She paused as she considered what she was about to say. "Well, rather crappily, to be honest, but at least no one was trying to kill me and no one was dying around me. Since I met you, my life has taken the high road to Shitsville with no off-ramp in sight. My best friends are dead. I've seen you kill a total of five people in—"

"Four," he said, interrupting her. "You took the one out with the bat crack upside his head."

Did he have to remind her of that? "And why was I playing Hank Aaron, huh? Because I stupidly took a stray cat home. Now I'm out the eighty-two dollars it cost to spring you from the shelter, my house is destroyed, my car has become Swiss cheese, and I owe my neighbor God only knows what for the little fence she keeps around her petunia bed. Thanks, Puss in Boots. Really. Thank you."

He looked aghast at her. "I can't believe you're thinking about money at a time like this."

"What am I supposed to think about?" she asked, her voice cracking, "The fact that the two people who mean the most to me in this world are gone and I can't even go to their funeral because everyone thinks *I* killed them?"

She ground her teeth as grief and frustration overwhelmed her. "If I'd just listened to Jimmy and got them out of there, they'd be alive now. I should have *never* left them alone. They're dead and it's *all* my fault. . . . Yeah. That's really what I want to dwell on." She fought the tears that stung her eyes and her heart. She couldn't afford to think about Angie and Jimmy right now. Not if she wanted to stay functional. That pain was too deep, too severe for her to cope.

She could see compassion in his eyes as he cupped her cheek in his warm, callused palm. "Look, I'm really sorry for what happened to them. But you're not responsible for it. You hear me? They're dead because Jimmy found out about the Daimons and was dumb enough to think he could run from them. Trust me, he wouldn't have gone far before they found him and killed him anyway. With the information he was carrying, he was dead before you ever got there."

She scowled at him. "If you're trying to make me feel better, it's not working."

"I know." And by the look on his face, she could tell he meant that as he stroked her cheek with his thumb. "You've had one hell of a shock today." She saw respect in his eyes and something in there she couldn't identify. "You're entitled to a momentary meltdown, but believe me when I say that a momentary one is all you can afford. You are in way over your head and you've got a long road ahead of you."

"And how is that?"

"You're used to dealing with humans who don't have psychic abilities. Well, baby, the world you know just got ugly. Everything Jimmy told you at the shelter is true. You just stumbled into a war that your kind isn't even supposed to know is happening. Forget everything you thought you knew about physics and science, and now imagine a world where mankind is nothing but food to a whole race of people who want to subjugate you."

She shook her head in denial. "I don't believe in vampires."

He opened his mouth to show her his vicious set of fangs. "If you want to live past tonight, you better learn to start."

Susan wanted to reach out and touch his teeth just to make sure they were real, but she knew the truth. She'd actually seen them in action. "What are you? Really? You said a Dark-Hunter. What is that?"

Ravyn hesitated. Having spent three hundred years as a Dark-Hunter and taken an oath to never let those outside of their circle know anything about their world were deeply ingrained in him. But this wasn't the usual set of circumstances. The Daimons had dragged her into this and if he didn't give her the truth, she was defenseless against them. Whether she wanted to be in this or not, she was.

"No. Dark-Hunters are immortals who have sworn to protect mankind by hunting down the Daimons who prey on them."

"And Daimons are?"

He took a deep breath as he thought about the easiest way to explain it to her. "Long ago, in ancient Atlantis—"

"Atlantis is real, too?" she asked, screwing her face up.

"Yes."

She shook her head. "What next? Unicorns?"

Her spunk amused him. "No, but dragons are."

She narrowed those blue eyes on him. "I really hate you," she said in a voice that was laden with venom.

He offered her a kind smile while he let the softness of her cheek soothe the heat of his blistered fingers. He should be tending his own wounds and yet he wanted to soothe her first. That didn't make sense to him. It was contrary to everything that came naturally to him, and yet here he was, explaining to her a world that she would no doubt consider preposterous.

"I don't blame you. I'd probably hate me too if I were in your shoes. But back to Atlantis. There was a race of beings there who were called Apollites."

"God, I was really hoping they were some kind of diet apple drink."

He laughed, then cringed as a shard of pain went through him. "No, they're definitely not that. Their name comes from the fact that they were created by the god Apollo. It was his plan to have them dominate the humans, but as with all best-laid plans, it blew up in his face. The Apollites turned on him by killing his mistress and son and he cursed them all to die at age twenty-seven. Slowly. Painfully."

"I bet they loved that."

"Yeah. Needless to say, it wasn't to their taste, so a group of them somehow learned that they could kill humans, suck their souls into their bodies, and elongate their lives. Since that day, whenever Apollites near their twenty-seventh birthday, they have a choice—die or start preying on humans and become Daimons. The only problem with that is that the souls they feed on aren't meant for them. As a result, the soul starts to die as soon as they pull it into their body. If it dies and they haven't taken in another one, they die, too."

She stepped back from him and ran her hands over her face as the horror of that sank in. "So they're on a constant quest to keep killing in order to stay alive."

He nodded. "And now it appears they've been able to get some of your people to help them."

"Why?"

"I don't know. You have Hollywood to thank for that. Most humans who help them have the misguided belief that the Daimons can make them immortal by biting their necks and converting them. They can't. You're either born an Apollite or you're not. There's no way for them to pass along their powers or false means of elongating their lives to a human."

She shook her head as if she couldn't believe what he was telling her. "Have you any idea how hard this is to believe?"

"Yeah, well, you might not believe in Santa Claus either, but that doesn't mean someone isn't leaving presents for the kids on Christmas Eve."

She frowned at him. "What's that supposed to mean?"

"It means that behind every myth, there's usually some degree of truth."

Startled by the new voice, Susan turned to find Leo standing in the doorway behind her. She couldn't believe it, but she was actually happy to see him.

"Hi, Ravyn," Leo said in greeting.

Ravyn inclined his head to him.

Leo met Susan's gaze. "Patricia needs to get the lead out of Ravyn before he heals over it. Why don't you come out here with me while she works on him?"

His blasé tone amazed her. Oh sure. Why not? After all, the man or Dark-Hunter or whatever the hell he was had more lead in him than her plumbing.

It was just such a normal comment. . . .

Forcing herself not to roll her eyes, Susan followed Leo out of the room and passed the older woman in the hallway, who didn't speak to either one of them. It was obvious that Patricia wasn't any happier about all this than Susan was.

While Patricia entered the storeroom they'd just vacated, Leo led Susan up a back metal stairway to a large conference room. He turned on the lights and held the door open for her. The white walls and black ceiling gave the room a cold, contemporary feel that wasn't helped by the glass conference table and black leather chairs. It had all the appeal of an emergency root canal, and something about the room made her feel like a grade school student getting called into the principal's office.

"Have a seat," Leo said before he shut the door.

It wasn't in Susan's nature to follow anyone's orders, but she was too tired and upset at the moment to argue. She just wanted five minutes of peace so that she could lick her wounds and pull herself together.

"Are you okay?"

"Oh, I don't know," she said as she sat down. The leather creaked under her weight, which really just made her feel so much better about herself and her situation. "I woke up this morning, had my cornflakes and coffee as usual. Went to work for my sleazeball paper and saw my prized story had been butchered and turned to crap. Had my boss crawl all over my butt because I can't leave reality behind me. So to help me with that, he gives me this assignment to track down some kid writing about a catman who prowls the market. Then while I'm contemplating the total absurdity that is my life, my best friend calls and tells me she has a lead for a real story that could get my reputation back. Only that story turns out to be one about the cops helping vampires eat us. I adopt a cat that I'm allergic to because my girlfriend is paranoid. I take him home to have him become the very thing I'd been told to find by my eccentric boss. And the next thing I know, my house is blown to shit. The Catman eats a guy in front of me, and my two best friends on the planet are now dead."

She paused to pin an angry stare on that stone look of his. "Gee, I'm not sure how I should feel right now, Leo. If you have a clue could you please let me know? This isn't exactly within my scope of past experience. I'm tired, I'm stunned, and I just want to go to bed and have all of this be some really awful nightmare. But I have a bad feeling that when I do wake up tomorrow, it's just going to get worse."

Leo gave her a sympathetic smile as he neared her chair. He put a gentle hand on her shoulder. "I'm really sorry, Susan. But I wanted you—"

The door opened to show her a group of two men and one woman joining them. The first to enter was a tall, dark-haired man who had a lethal look about him. He was incredibly good-looking and dressed in an expensive gray sweater and black pleated pants. The man behind him looked every bit as dangerous, but his hair was a medium brown, while the woman was tall, athletic, and blond. Oddly enough, the woman looked a lot like Patricia and Alicia.

Leo straightened up and an air of authority literally settled onto his shoulders. No longer the quirky little boss she knew so well, he now struck her as a no-nonsense predator.

"Susan," he said, indicating each of the three in turn. "Meet Otto Carvalletti, Kyl Poitiers, and Jessica Addams."

She sighed. "Hi."

They didn't respond in kind. Instead, they took up stations around her in a mafia-like manner. As Susan lowered her gaze, she noticed something that they had in common with Leo . . . all of them had the same spiderweb tattoo on their hands.

A bad feeling went through her. But she wasn't about to let them intimidate her. She'd been through enough today without that. Rising to her feet, she gave them each her own take-no-shit glare. "What's going on, Leo?"

He ignored her to address the other three. "Knock off the Big

Bad Scary, guys, and have a seat. We have a lot to go over and only a few more hours before the sun sets."

To Susan's complete shock, they actually obeyed him. It was extremely surreal and reminded her of a Chihuahua calling down a pack of Dobermans.

"What about her?" Otto jerked his chin in Susan's direction. "Is she secured?"

Leo sighed as he sat down beside her. "I'm really sorry that you got dragged into this, Susan. I never meant for you to find out about any of it. That's what I was trying to tell you when they walked in. I just wanted you to trace Dark Angel. You were supposed to keep living in your blissful ignorance, never learning that vampires exists."

Ah, God, it just kept getting better and better. "So all the crap we write about in the paper is real?"

"No," Leo said, to her surprise. "It's all, as you say, crap. I only run the paper to make sure that none of the true stuff gets out. I mean, let's face it, the 'I adopted a cat and he turned into a man in my living room' story isn't exactly something you call the *New York Times* about. You call papers like ours. For the last sixty years, my family has run the *Inquisitor* so that they would get first dibs on any story that could expose us to the public."

In a weird way that made sense, and the fact that it did truly scared her. "And the other reporters at the *Inquisitor,* are they like you, hiding the truth?"

"No," he said, his face earnest, "they're all pretty much insane. I usually hire crackpots because even if they stumbled onto the truth and tried to expose it, no one would believe them."

Well, that explained so much about her coworkers and her own position. So much so that it cut her deeply. "You hired me because I'd lost all my credibility in journalism."

His eyes burned into hers. "No. I hired you because you were one of the few friends I had in college. Without your help, I'd have never graduated, so when you got into trouble, I offered you a hand-up . . . the fact that no one would ever again take you seriously was just an added bonus."

She glared at him. "Thanks a lot, Leo."

He brushed her anger aside with a wave of his tattooed hand.

"I'm not going to lie to you, Susan. I respect you too much for that."

"Yet you've been lying to me all this time."

He looked offended by that. "When? Have I ever denied that vampires were real?"

"You said it was bullshit."

"No, I said bullshit pays for my Porsche . . . and it does. I'm the one, as I recall, who kept telling you to embrace the ridiculous. To believe in the unbelievable."

He did have a point now that she thought about it. That had been his rant at her since the day she joined his staff. Sighing, she retook her seat. "So why did you send me after Ravyn if you didn't want me to find out the truth?"

"Because I was hoping it wasn't Ravyn that the student was talking about. I mean, let's face it—there are a *lot* of Were-Hunters in Seattle, and since they live for centuries, to the uninformed it might seem like they're immortal. I was hoping you'd go, get me a name and address, and then I could clean it up if it were real."

"Why not just go yourself?"

He scoffed at her. "I'm not an investigative reporter. I have all the subtlety of a brick, which is why I'm more of an enforcer. Besides, I knew that even if you found out the truth and saw it with your own eyes, you'd never believe it. Somehow you'd find a logical, legitimate way to explain it all away that I could then use with other people. See?" He looked past her, to the other three, who'd been eerily silent all this time. "Now we have a bit of a problem."

She snorted at Leo. "*You* have a problem? Try being in my shoes."

Leo rubbed the back of his neck nervously. "Yeah, well, you *are* the problem, Sue."

Her heart stopped beating. "How do you mean?"

"Civilians aren't allowed to know about us," Otto growled from his seat across from her. "Ever."

"Uh-huh," she said slowly. "You know with that sinister tone you should look into working for the IRS. I'm sure they're desperate for people who can cow others with a single growl."

Leo sat forward. "Sue, don't taunt the cobra. He tends to bite."

And by the look on Otto's face she could see that Leo wasn't kidding. She looked back at Leo as Kyl handed him a shiny black folder. He opened it briefly, then set it on the table.

Leo drummed his fingers on it while he addressed her. "Normally, we recruit members who have skills we can use. But sometimes we have unexpected things come up, such as the last twenty-four hours, where innocent bystanders accidentally get caught up by mistake. Those mistakes have to be corrected." His tone was deadly and threatening.

Refusing to be intimidated, she crossed her arms over her chest and gave him an equally withering stare. "And how do you propose to correct me?"

"You have a choice," Kyl spoke at last. "Either you become one of us or . . ."

She waited. When he didn't finish, she gave him an arch stare. "Or what? You kill me?"

It was the woman who answered. "Yes."

"No," Leo said sternly. He looked back at Susan. "But we can't take the chance that you'll expose us. Do you understand?"

Was he serious? But then all she had to do was look at the doom squad to know that answer.

"And what are *you* in all this, Leo?" she asked, needing to fully understand what she'd inadvertently been sucked into. "Why do these guys," she indicated the other three at the table with her, "listen to you?"

"Because I'm the Squire Regis for Seattle, since my dad retired. I run the Theti branch which, by default, makes me the head of all the Squire branches in this area."

"Theti?"

"Blood Rites," Otto said in a low, guttural tone. "We do other Squire jobs as well, but we're the ones who are licensed to enforce the Council's mandates."

"And we use any means necessary to keep our world a secret." Kyl narrowed his eyes meaningfully on her.

This had to be the weirdest day of her entire life, and given the fact that she spent time with her grandmother, who swore that her female dog was Susan's reincarnated grandfather and wore her clothes wrong side out to keep the lightbulbs from fading the dye, and with her coworker Joanie, who had a penchant for putting

Post-it notes over her desk drawer to keep the little men from leaving it, that said something.

They really meant to kill her.

"So what's your decision?" Otto asked. He looked just a little overeager for her to say no.

"What?" she asked, unable to resist teasing the cobra—it just seemed like a moral imperative. "Had a dry spell of killing people lately?"

His face completely stoic, he responded dryly, "As a matter of fact, yes. If it doesn't end soon, I might get out of practice."

"God. Forbid," she said in a mock tone of awe.

Leo cleared his throat, drawing her attention back to him. "Sue, I need an answer."

"Do I really have a choice?"

"No," they said in unison.

Leo's face softened ever so slightly. "You know too much about us."

Susan sat there in silence as the events of the day replayed through her mind. It was all too much to take. God, how she wished that she could just go crazy like her grandmother to get away from it all. But life wasn't being that kind to her at present. Her sanity was intact, because heaven forbid she have any escape from her sucky situation. "And this new life you're offering me. What does it entail?"

Leo glanced to the others before he answered. "Not much. Really. You swear an oath to us to keep your silence and you go on our payroll and into our system so that we can monitor you."

Those words, combined with his tone, sent a chill down her spine. "Monitor me how?"

"It's not as ominous as it sounds," Leo assured her. "We just keep a tab on you from time to time to make sure you haven't been talking to any civilians about us. So long as you maintain your silence, you get a lot of perks."

"Such as?"

Leo pushed the folder toward her. "Private planes. Exclusive vacations. A 401(k) and stock options to beat the band. Funds to start your own business if you want." He paused to give her a stern stare. "And the one thing you've never had. A family that'll be there whenever you need it."

That last bit stung and Leo knew it. Her father had abandoned her and her mother when Susan was only three years old. She had no memory of him whatsoever, and her mother had never taken her to meet his side of the family. An only child like Susan, her mother had been close to her parents, but they, too, had died while Susan was a small child and then her mother had died in a car wreck three days before Susan turned seventeen.

She'd been alone ever since.

Family had been the one thing in her life that she'd always craved with a burning passion, and much like her respectability, it was as elusive as a unicorn's horn. It was the one carrot Leo knew to dangle in front of her.

Sighing, she flipped through the folder to see a contract and a list of phone numbers for different kinds of services. She closed it and pinned Leo with a frigid glare. "You make it all sound so rosy, but one thing I've learned: If it sounds too good to be true, it probably is. So what's the catch?"

"There isn't a catch, promise." Leo made a cross over his heart. "You can go about your life any way you please. You'll just be privy to a lot of things that the average person is clueless about."

"The drawback is you'll have a lot more days like today," Jessica said in an emotionless voice. "As a Squire, the Daimons will be drawn to you and they will come after you from time to time."

"But we'll train you," Leo added. "You won't be left alone to fight them."

Oh, joy! Who in their right mind would ever turn *this* down? It was all she could do not to laugh at their offer. "Is that it?"

Otto gave her a dry grimace. "Isn't it enough?"

"Oh, yeah," she said with a humorless laugh, "it's enough and then some." Susan grew quiet as she considered everything Leo had just dumped into her lap. But in the end, she knew what they did . . .

She had no choice.

Her heart heavy, she looked over at Otto. "Looks like I'm going to ruin your day, Big Boy. I choose to live my crappy life a little longer."

"Damn." Otto let out a long-suffering sigh.

Leo appeared relieved. "Welcome aboard."

Funny, she didn't feel welcomed. She felt ill. A condition that wasn't improved when Leo paused and said, "Oh, and one more thing."

This she couldn't wait for.

"As Squires, we're all answerable to the Dark-Hunters. To the men and women like Ravyn and in particular to their leader, Acheron. In essence, we're their servants who help them and who guard them from the public."

She widened her eyes in feigned happiness. "Oh gee, golly, goodie, Mr. Leo! Can I have my eyes gouged out, too?"

Otto actually laughed. "You know, I think I'm really going to like you."

Well, at least the pit viper thought she was amusing. Leo, on the other hand, looked less than amused as he shook his head at Kyl and Jessica.

Sobering, Susan picked up her folder and addressed her biggest concern now that certain death at Otto's hands had been avoided. "So what happens to me now? How are you going to hide me while I'm wanted by the cops?"

"We'll worry about that," Jessica said. "The police are the least of our problems. It's who's pulling their chains that concerns us."

"The commissioner?" Susan suggested.

Kyl rolled his eyes. "Think outside human parameters."

She gave him a droll stare. "Yeah, but if there's a cover-up, someone in the police department is helping out, right?"

"Yes," Leo said in a strained tone, "but right now that's not a big deal. What we need to know is who's targeting us. If they're able to take out a Dark-Hunter, then we're nothing but fodder to them."

"Speak for yourself," Jessica said smugly. "I assure you, I'm not at the bottom of this food chain."

Otto snorted at her bravado. "Knock it off, Jess. When Kyl and I were in New Orleans a year ago, there was a major Daimon uprising led by a Spathi named Stryker."

Susan frowned at the unfamiliar term. "Spathi?"

"A special warrior class of Daimons who are old," Kyl said. "Really, *really* old. They're a lot stronger than the typical Daimon who roams around looking for an easy target to suck dry."

"Yeah," Otto agreed. "These usually have a serious ax to grind against the good guys and humans. Last year, we lost a lot of Dark-

Hunters in Northern Mississippi and New Orleans to them. The last thing I want to do is lose any more."

Kyl turned toward Otto. "You think we should call Kyros or Rafael and see if they can help us. They got a lot closer to the Spathis than anyone else . . . and unlike Danger, Euphemia, Marco, and the others, they actually survived the encounter. Maybe they can remember something that could help expose a weakness we could exploit."

Otto nodded. "Good idea."

"I'll ring them," Jessica volunteered.

"And I'll call Kyrian," Kyl said. "Any of you know where he is at present?"

Otto answered, "He never left New Orleans. None of the Dark-Hunters, current or former, evacuated for Katrina. They got their families out, but they stayed behind to help. Last I heard, even Amanda and the kids were back."

"Cool. I'll buzz him then and see if he knows anything more concrete about Stryker or the others."

"What about Ash?" Leo asked.

Jessica shook her head. "He's been MIA for the last few days now. Last I heard, he was in Australia anyway."

You know, Susan thought wryly, *it would really help if I had a clue as to who and what they were talking about.* But they were so absorbed and earnest, she didn't want to interrupt them. Besides, what they were discussing seemed to be far more important than her ignorance and no doubt, if she lived, she'd begin to understand all of it soon enough.

Leo let out a frustrated breath as if he was way too tired. He turned toward Susan. "By the way, were you able to find anything out about Dark Angel before all this went down?"

"Yes. She's a snotty little booger."

Leo looked ill at her description. "Oh gawd, it is Erika."

Otto frowned. "What are you talking about now?"

Leo let out another weary sigh. "Someone local has been blogging that she works for an immortal shapeshifting warrior who hunts vampires. I had Sue check her out."

Otto looked even more perplexed. "Erika's not a Squire."

"Not technically," Leo said, "but while her father's off on his honeymoon, she's subbing for him and running errands for Ravyn."

"Well, if you really think it's Erika then why didn't you have Tad run a trace on the blog?"

Leo cocked his head in an offended manner. "Because that would involve me actually talking to Tad now, wouldn't it?"

"Yeah, and?"

Clearing his throat, Leo became sullen. In a low, almost embarrassed tone, he said, "I owe him money."

Otto gave him a droll stare. "What has that got to do with anything?"

Leo narrowed his eyes. "I owe him a *lot* of money."

"Good God, Leo," Kyl said angrily, "given how much you have, how much could you be into him for?"

"Everything, and I mean *everything*. Hell, I even owe him my Porsche."

Otto's jaw went slack. "You jeopardized us because of debt? You've got to be kidding me."

"Do I look like I'm joking?" No, he looked completely pissed. "Besides, it's not my fault. He cheats at cards."

Kyl made a disgusted noise. "You've been playing poker with him? Are you insane? That man's brain functions like a computer."

"*Now* you tell me."

Otto disregarded his outburst. "And because of that you put a civilian on a case that should have been turned over to one of us? Jeez, man, what were you thinking?"

Leo rose to his feet. "Get off my back, Otto. I'm the one in charge here in Seattle."

Otto sat back with his arms folded over his chest in a demeanor that said he answered to no one else. "Not if I kill you for incompetence."

Jessica gave an evil smile. "Need us to turn a blind eye?"

Leo narrowed his eyes on her. "Ha, ha. But that doesn't change the fact that we still need to find out definitively if Dark Angel is Erika. And if not Erika, then we need to know if Dark Angel is another one of us, or just a local lunatic."

Otto shook his head in disgust. "I'll check into it."

Leo looked less than convinced Otto could handle it. "And what are you going to do, Otto?"

"What you should have done. I'll simply ask her."

Leo laughed. "You haven't met her, have you?"

"No, why?"

He laughed even harder.

"Wear a Teflon jockstrap," Jessica said under her breath.

Otto rolled his eyes. "Oh, please."

"Please nothing," Leo said, "she's a vicious piranha. She looks all cute and cuddly, then she opens that mouth and lets loose so much venom she could double as a nest of scorpions."

Still Otto looked less than intimidated. "I think I can handle her."

Leo glanced over at Kyl. "Add a call in to the florist to send flowers to either his hospital room or funeral parlor."

Otto shook his head before he stood up. "It looks like we all have our marching orders. Should we reconvene later tonight?"

Leo nodded. "Eight thirty. Be here."

Susan got up to leave with the others only to have Leo pull her to a stop.

"I'll get a handbook from Patricia for you. You'll also be stuck here for a while."

"Okay." Her gaze dropped down to his hand where the tattoo was. "Do I have to get one of those, too?"

He snorted. "No." He flexed his hand. "These are used solely for Blood Rites."

"Is that like special ed?"

"Hardly."

She still couldn't believe it. Oddly enough, it was easier to buy into the vampires than it was to believe Leo could hurt anyone. "Uh-huh, you who calls me into your office to kill spiders because you're squeamish?"

"That's different," he said defensively. "Those are disgusting."

"And yet you expect me to believe you'd kill a human?"

His eyes turned dark and forbidding. "I took an oath a long time ago, Susan, and I will abide by it. Whatever it takes. What we deal with is bigger than spiders. It's bigger than you and me."

For the first time, she saw the man behind the teasing friend she'd known all these years. And in truth, she missed the old anal-retentive, smarmy boy she'd befriended in college.

"You know what I want, Leo?"

"Your life back."

She nodded. "I really need a do-over on this day. Then again, I could really use one for the last five years."

"I know." He gave her a gentle hug. "But it'll be okay, Sue. I promise. We take care of our own and you're here with us now. Don't worry. You're safe."

Stryker *came to* his feet as a rage so raw, so potent, went through him that he wasn't sure how he managed to maintain himself.

"Kontis did what?" he asked in a low, calm tone that belied his turbulent mood.

"He escaped us, my lord," the Apollite vet, Theo, explained as he stood cringing before Stryker's throne in Kalosis. Wearing a blue, blood-spattered lab coat, the half-Apollite should amuse him, but there was nothing amusing about the man's news.

Stryker met Satara's disgusted stare before he narrowed his eyes back on the worm who dared to deliver such news to him. "I told you, Theo, that you only had one thing to do. Keep him in a cage until I arrived."

Swallowing hard, Theo wrung his hands. "I know and I did just as you said. I swear it. I didn't take him out of the cage. Not once. We just wanted to have a little fun with him until your Spathis killed him." He glanced up with imploring eyes. "It was the human I work with who took him out while I was speaking to you on the phone earlier. By the time I found out about it, he was already gone."

Did the fool honestly think that by indicting a human as an accomplice he would get leniency? These stupid tools were getting dumber and dumber every year.

Stryker curled his lip. "Where is Kontis now?"

"He was taken home by another human. The other vet we killed said her name was Susan Michaels. We have a team of humans out, looking for the two of them now."

Styker ground his teeth as all of his dreams of easily grabbing

Seattle as a home base came sliding down around him. By now Kontis had no doubt notified all the other Dark-Hunters in Seattle. Every one of them would now be on high alert. So much for the element of surprise. Their job would now be a thousand times harder.

He wanted blood for this. "Do you have any idea what this means, Theo?"

"I do, but we still have enough daylight left that we should be able to get to him before he reaches the others."

Stryker scoffed. He knew better than that. Ravyn was like him—a survivor. If they wanted to take the city, they'd have to move quickly.

He turned toward his sister. "Gather Trates and the Illuminati."

"You're planning to hunt?" Theo asked, his eyes sparking a degree of relief and hope.

"Yes," Stryker said slowly.

"Good. I'll get my team ready."

"Don't bother, Theo."

His nervousness returned tenfold. "My lord?"

Stryker approached him slowly, methodically. He reached out and cupped the man's cheek in his palm. It was smooth and supple, as were all of theirs. Perfect. That was the beauty of never growing old.

Theo might be stupid, but he was as beautiful as the angels that many of the humans believed in. "How long have you served me now, Theo?"

"Almost eight years."

Stryker smiled at him. "Eight years and in all that time, tell me what you've learned about me."

He could feel the man shaking as he answered. The scent of fear and perspiration hung heavy in the air—gods, how he loved that smell. It was like an aphrodisiac to him.

"You're the Daimon King. Our only hope."

"Yes." He stroked Theo's cheek. "Anything else?"

Theo glanced nervously toward Satara before he returned to frown at Stryker. "I don't know what you mean."

He sank his hand into Theo's blond hair and balled his fist tightly in the strands so that the half-Apollite couldn't escape him. "The one thing you should have learned, Theo, is that I don't accept failure in any shape, form, or fashion. Your first mistake was letting the Dark-Hunter escape. Your second one was being stupid enough to come tell me about it."

Theo tried to pull away, but Stryker held him in place. "P-please, my lord, have mercy. I can find him! I can!"

Stryker smirked at his pathetic cries for clemency. "So can I. In fact, I intend to find more than just Ravyn. Before I'm through tonight, I intend to hunt and feed to my heart's content. But it won't be human." He licked his lips as he stared at the throbbing vein on Theo's neck. "Tonight I feast on Apollite blood and carnage . . . On you and your entire family."

Before the man could speak again, Stryker sank his teeth into Theo's neck, ripping out the carotid as he drank his fill.

Theo only fought for a second, before death finally claimed him. Stryker let Theo's limp body fall to his feet before he wiped the blood from his lips with the back of his hand.

"You didn't take his soul?" Satara asked incredulously.

Stryker scoffed. "Why bother? He was too weak to even whet my appetite."

"So what is our plan then?"

Stryker walked down the steps of his dais to stand beside his half-sister. "To run the bastards to ground. Ravyn has a Squire, right?"

She nodded.

"Then let's put the fear of us into the Squire and he or she is bound to lead us straight to Ravyn."

"How do we do that?"

"Simple, sweet Satara. You're not a Daimon. You can enter Ravyn's house and then invite us in. Trates and the others will go for the Squire, and she will run to Ravyn for protection."

Satara considered that for a moment. "What if you're wrong? The Squire might run to others of his kind."

Stryker shrugged nonchalantly. "Then we eat our fill of Squires. At best, it'll put fear into the other humans who serve the Dark-Hunters and it'll be an emotional blow to them. At worst, we just have a stomachache from the blood."

CHAPTER SIX

Susan was a bit confused by the vastness of the Addams layout. It wouldn't take much to get lost in the ten-thousand-plus-square-foot building that had some secured areas and some that were open to the public.

One of the first things Leo did was take her to an electronic scanner for a hand and retinal imprint that would allow her access to their locked facilities. It would also allow them to find her if she ran, or, her favorite part of all, identify her remains should the Daimons get their hands on her for torture and mayhem. She would also need to get a copy of her dental records for their files . . . just in case.

Yes, she was really enjoying the prospect of being part of this world. Maybe they could even manage a few ritual slayings just for fun and practice!

But one of the more interesting parts of the building was the very front, which was a small coffee and pastry/deli shop that let out onto Pioneer Square. It was dark in tone, with pine paneling and a black ceiling. Even so, it still managed to have a homey, old-fashioned feel to it. And spookily enough, it was one she'd eaten at several times in the past with Angie and Jimmy whenever they came down here for the antique store on the corner that Angie had dearly loved.

While they showed her around the shopfront, from behind the scenes innocent people came and went without realizing that just past the business area was the Twilight Zone. Only a few hours ago, she would have been one of them, too.

In fact, with the exception of the small eating area, the counter, the bakery area, and one small storeroom, the rest of the monstrous building was essentially command central for the Seattle-based Squires. There were high-tech computers that kept tabs on virtually everything to do with them. Where they lived, shopped, and patrolled. There were databases of local businesses they owned. Lists of who worked for the city, state, and federal government, and those who were assigned to particular Dark-Hunters in the area.

Apparently, there were nine main Dark-Hunters in various parts of the city while another six were assigned to outlying areas such as Bainbridge Island, Bremerton, and Redmond.

There was also a hospital set up to tend any Dark-Hunter or Squire who was injured in a way that didn't lend itself to visiting a traditional medical facility without freaking out the "ords." *Ords* being a slang term for "ordinaries," who were people who had no clue about their world. Personally, Susan wanted to return to being an ord, but she knew better than to even ask.

But what fascinated her most was the one lone man who sat in an office where he monitored all the local emergency bands. He'd been the one to tell her that the call hadn't gone out on dispatch to those cops who had come to her house, when she and Ravyn had been attacked. If it had, he'd have known it. They had been sent from behind the scenes, which begged the question who had sent them.

"Here, Sue."

She turned to find Leo behind her with what appeared to be a leather-bound phone book in his hand. "What is that?"

"The Squire's handbook I told you about."

He handed it to her and she almost dropped it. The huge thing had to weigh at least fifteen pounds and it smelled like her grandmother's old mothball-infested cedar closet. "You've got to be kidding me."

He gave her a grim stare. "And you'll be tested on it, too."

She gaped.

"Just kidding." He smiled. "But it will explain exactly who and what we are. There's also a lot more information in there about Daimons, Apollites, and emergency numbers for every major city."

"And the Dark-Hunters? Is there anything about them?"

"Oh, yeah. Lots of stuff about them. Their history and origins. If you go to our Web site, Dark-Hunter.com, there's an online database that tells you the names of all the Dark-Hunters, as well as a profile page about their general age and background."

"Really?"

He nodded.

Now that could be useful. "Is it safe? I would think having all that online would just be inviting hacker trouble."

Screwing up his face, he shook his head. "Not really, but we have our own hackers who keep the rest at bay. And if someone does, perchance, find their way around our security precautions, they get a rude visit—"

"Let me guess, from Otto?"

"No . . . people who make Otto look fluffy."

Now that was something she would love to see, but not knocking on *her* door.

Susan tried to balance the book in one hand to flip through it, but it was too big for that. So she resorted to asking more questions. "What about Squires? Does the Web site tell about them, too?"

"Only a handful. We keep a lower profile as a rule. And there are a lot more of us than there are Dark-Hunters. They number in the thousands while we are tens of thousands worldwide." He tapped the cover of the tome and winked at her. "Happy reading."

Susan grunted at him. "Up yours, Leo."

He gave her a devilish grin. "Yeah, I know."

Sighing, Susan decided to find herself a quiet room to read in. She opened the first door she came to and pulled up short as she found herself in the same room as Ravyn, who was asleep on a red futon.

It was all she could do to catch her breath as she saw him lying facedown, entwined in the stark white sheets that seemed to just highlight how tan his skin was. And the man was tan *all* over. That dark, tawny shade appeared to be his natural skin tone.

It was enough to set her heart pounding. He was all sinewy muscle. All man—in a shapeshifting . . . leopard . . . undead kind of way. And even stranger than that, most of the bullet wounds on his back were nothing more than puckered scars. Leo had told her that the Dark-Hunters healed fast, but dang. They really didn't waste any time with mending those wounds.

He opened one black eye to stare at her. "You need something?" His voice had a rumbling quality to it that was deepened by his sleep.

"I thought this room was empty. Sorry."

He stretched before he rolled over, and the sheet slipped to give her a nice view of one bare hip and the trail of black hair that ran from his navel to a thicker patch of hair. A wicked part of herself was hoping the sheet would pull down another few millimeters so that she could glimpse the rest of him.

Okay, so she already knew what he looked like naked, but earlier she'd been a bit occupied to notice the finer details of his body. Now she was feeling a little greedy and if the man wanted to run around naked . . .

Well, far be it from her to complain.

"No problem." He yawned as he scratched the arm that up until a short time ago had also had a bullet in it. Now it appeared all healed like the rest of him. "You doing any better?"

His question and the concern she heard in his deep voice surprised her. Why would he even care, and yet a part of her was grateful that even if he didn't, he at least pretended to. Having spent her entire adulthood alone, she really ached to have someone just for her. Someone whose love she didn't have to share. It was selfish, but she really did want to find that one person who could love her unconditionally. "I honestly don't know. What about you?"

He looked down and ran his hand over his tight, perfect chest. "Pretty much healed."

It was so strange to try to reconcile this man with the one she'd seen viciously kill the half-Apollite earlier. A chill went down her spine at the memory. Ravyn might be acting friendly toward her at the moment, but he was a ruthless killer. He hadn't even blinked or hesitated at taking the lives of those men in her house. Whether justified or not, it was a sobering thought that life meant so little to him.

Suddenly uneasy, she stepped back into the hallway. "Well, I won't keep you. You probably need more sleep."

He pulled the sheet up higher and tucked his exposed leg under it. "Yeah."

Nodding, she pulled the door closed and backtracked to the room she'd been in earlier that held the computers Leo had told her were for regular Squire use.

Kyl was in there alone, typing furiously at one station.

"Can I borrow one?" she asked hesitantly. Kyl, like Otto, still acted as if he'd like to kill her.

He looked up but didn't break in his typing at all. "The one on your left."

She sat down, placed the book beside her, then wiggled the mouse. As soon as the screen came up, she tried the site Leo had mentioned, only to pull up a porn site. "Holy cripes. I don't think this is right."

Kyl frowned at her. "What?"

"Leo said there was a Dark-Hunter Web site, but I don't think I have the right URL."

He laughed at her. "You didn't put the dash in between *Dark* and *Hunter,* did you?"

She looked at the field and realized he was right. "No."

"Put it there and try again."

Susan did and breathed a little easier as the right page came up. It was all black-and-white. "How very monochromatic."

Kyl snorted. "It's easier on the Dark-Hunters' eyes. They're a lot more sensitive than human eyes. The dark background is the easiest one for them to read."

Hmmm, that was interesting. "Why's their sight different?"

"If you'll read your manual, which should be used for information and *not* a doorstop, you'll see that since they hunt during the night, they have special night vision. Their eyes are always dilated, so bright light is painful to them. It's why many of them wear dark sunglasses even indoors."

Tucking that away into her brain in case she ever needed to blind one of them, Susan clicked for the Dark-Hunter profiles and paused as she saw Ravyn Kontis's name. Oh, it was too much to resist. Clicking on it, she quickly read what they had listed for him.

It was actually highly fascinating. He was born in ancient Greece—304 B.C. to be precise. Dang, he was an old coot. She hoped she looked that good at two thousand plus years.

She somehow doubted it though.

But as she was reading, she realized that the Were-Hunters, the shapeshifting branch in all this, didn't live normal life spans. Rather, they lived for hundreds of years and, unlike humans, they didn't have to live chronologically. They could move through time.

Impressive, but it also begged one major question. "Is Ravyn's family still alive?"

Kyl paused in his typing. "Technically yes, but no, not really."

"What do you mean?"

"Ravyn's a Were-Hunter. They're *cousins* to the Apollites and to the Daimons who are hunted by the Dark-Hunters. Since they share the same bloodline, many of the Were-Hunters run sanctuaries that protect the Daimons from the Dark-Hunters. Because of that, Ravyn was denounced when he became a Dark-Hunter. He's not allowed near any of his kinsmen in any incarnation."

Susan's heart clenched. Having had her own father turn his back on her, she fully understood the pain of rejection. But at least she'd never known her father. How much worse would it be to have someone she loved turn her out?

"Here in Seattle. His father owns one of the sanctuaries just a few blocks over."

Her jaw dropped at that. "And none of them ever talk to him?"

He gave an odd half laugh. "Nooo." He stretched the word out with meaning. "They're not even allowed to say his name. He's completely dead to them."

"If they felt so strongly about that, why did he become a Dark-Hunter?"

Kyl shrugged. "You'll have to ask him."

"Hey, Kyl?"

They both turned to look at the doorway where Jack stood in the small opening. "Have you heard anything from Brian?"

"No, why?"

"We sent him over to check on Cael, but he hasn't come back yet and he's not answering his phone."

Kyl scowled. "That's weird."

Jack agreed with him. "We thought so, too, and it's dusk already. Should we send someone after him?"

Kyl hesitated. "Has the sun set?"

"Ten minutes ago."

He cursed.

Susan was perplexed by his hostility. "Is that bad?"

Both men gave her a "duh" stare. But it was Kyl who answered. "Just a little bit. At sunset, the Daimons are free to prowl." He let out a tired breath. "Man, times like this I really miss home."

"Home?" she asked.

"New Orleans. Down there, the Daimons are much more laid-back and tend to take their time before they hunt. Up here, they're way too caffeinated. As soon as the sun sets, they call for parties." He looked at Jack. "How many Blood Rites are around here right now?"

"You and Leo. Otto should be back in a few and Jessica later tonight."

Kyl stroked his chin as he considered that. "Let me know the instant Otto gets back and we'll go check on Brian."

There was something in his demeanor that struck her. He was scared and trying hard not to show it. After Jack left, she got up and approached him. "What are you *not* saying?"

His face turned stoic and cold. "Nothing."

Yeah. Right. Susan cocked her head and narrowed her eyes on him. "Look at me, Kyl. No bullshit. I used to be one of the best reporters in this country and if there's one thing I know, it's body language. And yours tells me that you're lying about 'nothing.' "

He dropped his gaze and took a deep breath. Deep sadness darkened his eyes as he rubbed his right biceps. "I probably shouldn't tell you this since it'll only scare you, but what the hell? If I'm right, you need to know." He paused a few seconds as if he were gathering his thoughts before he spoke again. "We had a bad situation about eighteen months ago in New Orleans. A *real* bad situation. We lost a lot of good people in one night, including one of my best friends and his mother."

It was obvious that he was still haunted by that night and her heart went out to him. There was nothing worse than trying to deal with tragedy.

"And you think this is going to be the same?"

His gaze burned her. "It's just a feeling I have. I know it sounds hokey. But I'm a Creole with a long line of people who know the mojo. As my grandmother would say, 'I can feel the evil on the wind.' It's the same feeling you get whenever someone steps on your grave."

Okay, now he was really beginning to freak her out.

All of a sudden, there was a loud crash outside that sounded like someone trying to break down a wall.

Susan jumped as her heart lodged itself in her throat. Good grief, what was happening now?

Kyl dashed from his seat, out of the room. Susan followed hot on his heels as he led her back toward the loading dock where there was a red Saleen S7 that someone had crashed into a Dumpster.

The door of the expensive sports car lifted open to show a young woman around the age of twenty, dressed as a Goth. Wearing all black except for her bloodred stockings and biker boots that had flames on them, she was cute enough as she leaped out of the car with bright blue eyes that were round in terror.

"Dammit, Erika!" Ravyn shouted from behind Susan as he joined them. "What have you done to my car?"

Susan put her finger in her ear and cringed as Ravyn bellowed as if he were in pain. She turned to see that he was dressed in a pair of black jeans, with a loose button-down black shirt that was opened at the neck. The look on his face promised Armageddon to the girl who'd damaged what appeared to be a prized possession.

Erika was completely undaunted by his rage as she ran up the dock and tossed her fuzzy black scarf over her shoulder before she confronted him. "Screw your car, Rave, straight up the sphincter. You can buy another one. *I,* on the other hand, am completely irreplaceable."

His eyes actually turned red as a fierce muscle worked in his jaw. "Not to me you're not. I'm not your daddy, little girl."

"Oh, shut up," Erika said in a way reminiscent of some vintage 1980s Valley girl. "Why don't you ask me why I'm driving the seven-hundred-and-fifty-horsepower car and not my adorable little Beetle, huh?"

Ravyn ignored her as he went to his car, which had the entire left bumper caved in. He raked his hands through his hair as if he were trying not to wrap them around her skinny little neck and choke her. "Why the hell were you in my car?"

Still on the dock not far away from Susan, Erika put her hands on her hips as she glared at Ravyn, who was now inspecting the inside of his car. " 'Cause Daimons tried to eat me, okay? Someone came to the house and rang the bell only a few minutes after the sun set. I thought it was you, so I opened the door, and there they were, so I slammed it shut, turned around, and there were three of them. In. The. House." She punctuated each word with a smack of her hands together.

Closing the car door, Ravyn stared at her.

"Did you hear me, Rave?" Erika asked when he didn't respond. "They were in your house. *Your. House.* And just how the hell did they get there, huh? I thought they had to be invited in."

She looked at Susan, then Jack, before she returned to Ravyn. "You invite one in and forget to tell me about it? I know I didn't. I'm not *that* stupid. But they got in and I want to know how."

Ravyn was aghast as he headed back up the metal stairs. "How did you escape?"

"I grabbed that round weapon thing you have on the wall and threw it at the one closest to me, then I ran screaming like a demon for the garage. You're lucky you still have me!"

Susan felt the grisly pain that Ravyn had on his face as he gave Erika a look that said he didn't think himself particularly lucky that she hadn't been eaten.

"Question," Susan asked Ravyn. "Is this the same Erika who's Dark Angel?"

Erika gave her a look that confirmed it.

Rage, dark and forbidding, came over Susan instantly. If not for this little Goth hoyden, her life wouldn't have taken the off-ramp to hell this afternoon. "Oh, forget it, Ravyn. I'm going to kill her for you!"

Kyl grabbed her as she started for the girl.

Squeaking, Erika took three steps back. "Who are you?"

She fought against Kyl's hold, but the little bugger was stronger than he appeared. "Psycho Susan and I have an ax to grind against your little selfish head."

"Take a number," Kyl growled in her ear.

Erika screwed her face up as if she smelled something really rotten. "Psycho Susan? The lunatic who e-mailed me earlier? Was that *you*?"

Suddenly a whistle rent the air. "Ladies," Leo snarled from where he stood beside Jack and Patricia. "Focus a minute. Ravyn, screw the car. We have a bigger problem here. How did Erika, Ms. I Can't Drive a Car If My Life Depended on It, elude a group of Daimons?"

Kyl finally released Susan. "She couldn't."

They all cursed as they realized it was a setup.

"Get inside," Leo said quickly.

"It's community property," Kyl snarled. "We have no protection here. They can get inside."

Leo glared at him. "You got a better idea?"

"No."

Erika and Jack were already running for the door that Patricia held open for them.

As Kyl and Leo made to join them, Susan, who noticed the look on Ravyn's face, paused there on the dock.

Patricia closed the door.

"What?" Susan asked as Ravyn turned his head as if he was listening for something.

When he spoke, his voice held a distant tone. "There's something strange here."

Now that had to be the understatement of the year. "You think? FYI, I haven't seen normal since I left my house this morning."

He gave her an irritated smirk. "No. I mean there's something really wrong with this—"

Before she could ask him what he meant, a bright ball of light flashed near his car. Two seconds later, a dozen men and women stepped out of it like some bad alien movie.

They were all tall, all blond, and all breathtakingly beautiful. Dressed all in black, they looked like angels except for the fact that they immediately attacked Ravyn.

"I'm assuming those are Daimons."

Ravyn grunted as he flipped the first one to reach him onto the ground. He pulled a knife from his boot, then stabbed the Daimon in the center of his chest. Screaming, the Daimon burst into an odd, gold powder that dusted the tops of Ravyn's boots.

He gave her a dry stare as another Daimon was headed for his back. "No, they're Avon ladies." He elbowed that one in the throat, then turned to confront him.

Susan started to run inside to get help, only to find her way blocked by another Daimon. He opened his mouth and hissed at her.

"Oh, get some Listerine," she growled before she drop-kicked him as hard as she could where it would do the most damage.

Cupping himself, he staggered back.

Relieved that maneuver worked on the undead as well as the living, she started for the door only to realize that Ravyn was in trouble. They had him pinned against the wall of the alley. His mouth and nose were bleeding profusely.

"Hold him still," one of the women said gleefully as she pulled out a hilt. She pressed a button and it extended to a sword.

Reacting on pure instinct, because if she'd thought about it for one instant she would have run the other way, Susan rushed the Daimon female. She knocked her away from Ravyn.

Cursing, the woman swung the sword at her. Susan jumped back, into the arms of another one.

She heard a fierce growl before she was released. Ravyn shredded the Daimon who'd been holding her, then he went for the woman with the sword. The female Daimon swung and missed. As she tried to recover the move to swing at him again, Ravyn caught her forearm and backhanded her.

The sword flew from her grip and rattled onto the pavement not far from Susan's feet. She quickly picked it up and turned toward the man who was rushing toward her. She twirled the sword, and planted it straight into his heart. He burst into a golden powder.

Her heart hammering, she turned to confront the next one.

"Retreat!" a second female shouted. She waved her hand to form another ball of light.

The remaining Daimons rushed into it.

Susan started to run in after them but caught herself as she realized that Ravyn wasn't so concerned about following. "Shouldn't we go after them?"

Shaking his head, he wiped at the blood on his lips as he faced Susan. "No. Trust me. You don't ever want to follow a Daimon into a bolt-hole. That takes you right into a banquet hall at Daimon central, where the poor fool who follows is quickly served up as an appetizer."

"Oh, *that* would be bad."

"Yes. Yes, it would." Ravyn smiled in spite of the fact that his entire body ached. He had to give her credit, she'd handled herself really well and even managed to maintain her humor. "Where did you learn how to sword fight?"

She twirled the sword around her like an expert, and since he'd once lived in the Middle and Dark Ages, he had plenty of firsthand knowledge of sword afficionados. "Society for Creative Anachronism. I lived in the Kingdom of Meridies for six years."

He scratched his jaw as he recognized that area of the southern U.S. There were a lot of Squires and even a few Dark-Hunters who were members of the SCA. "Yeah, but An Tir kicked their asses at Pensic."

"Not while I was fighting for them, they didn't." No sooner had she spoken those words than she slipped with the sword and almost sliced a chunk out of her leg. She straightened up immediately and held the sword still in an indignant way that said, *I meant to do that.*

He laughed in spite of himself. She certainly had a lot of salt and vinegar in her personality, and it captivated him. There was nothing he appreciated more in life than someone who could maintain their spirit when all odds were against them. "C'mon, Xena Warrior Princess, we need to get you inside."

She blew him a raspberry before she rested the sword on her

shoulder and moved to join him. He opened the door and let her enter first.

No sooner had they entered the building than they heard the screams and sounds of people fighting inside.

Ravyn rushed past her, toward the command room. There were Daimons everywhere. He grabbed the one closest to him, who was fighting Jack, spun him around, and slammed him back against the wall. Ravyn manifested a knife in his hand so that he could stab the Daimon.

Then he went for the one with Patricia. Before he could reach her, the Daimon sank his teeth into her neck and ripped it open. Cursing, Ravyn shot a psychic blast from his hand to knock the Daimon back. Patricia fell to the floor as Ravyn launched himself and caught the Daimon about his waist.

The two of them went tumbling.

As they wrestled, the Daimon sank his teeth into Ravyn's shoulder. Hissing, he stabbed him, then kicked him back. The Daimon began spitting out the poisonous Dark-Hunter blood, but it was too late. The Daimon was dead three seconds later.

Ravyn turned right as another Daimon exploded behind him. His gaze met Susan's. "Thanks."

She inclined her head to him.

Ravyn's eyes flared as he saw another Daimon heading for Susan. Reacting on instinct, he tossed his knife, straight into the Daimon's heart.

Susan turned around with a gasp just in time to see the Daimon explode. "Thanks to you, too," she said in a breathless tone.

"Anytime."

All of a sudden, Erika launched herself at Ravyn, who caught her against his body as the Daimon who'd been chasing her skidded to a halt. Setting her aside, Ravyn lunged for him, only to have him vanish into another bolt-hole. All of the remaining Daimons followed suit.

"How do they do that?" Susan asked.

Ravyn tucked his knife back into his boot. "Magick. Certain members can summon or request a bolt-hole from Kalosis and if the keeper likes them or believes them worthy, they get in."

"I'm picturing this decrepit old man who's in charge, laughing at them."

Ravyn snorted. "No. Imagine a beautiful ice goddess who decides whether or not she wants them in her realm."

Somehow Susan liked the idea of the old man a lot better.

Ravyn frowned as he caught sight of Patricia, lying on the ground while her son, Jack, was trying to staunch the blood flow at her neck. He made his way over to them.

"We've got to get all of you to safety."

Jack looked at him doubtfully. "Where's safe? They came in here like we were nothing."

Ravyn's face turned to stone. "The Serengeti. As a sanctuary, it's the only place that they can't breach." He picked Patricia up in his arms. "I'll meet all of you there and if I were you, I'd hurry."

"You need any help?" Susan offered.

Ravyn hesitated. "It'll be a tight squeeze, but yeah, someone needs to keep pressure on her wound."

"I'm not claustrophobic."

By his face she could tell he was grateful. "Then retract that sword and let's go."

Susan did as he said, then followed him out to his trashed car. She got in first. Ravyn carefully set Patricia in her lap. "Don't press too hard."

Her heart lurched at the sight of the unconscious woman's neck. Honestly, she didn't know how the woman could still be alive. "Is she going to make it?"

"I hope so for her family's sake. The Addamses are one of the most prominent of Squire families, and she's their grand matriarch."

Ravyn dashed to the other side, got in, and started the car. He certainly knew how to handle a crisis well. And he could rival any race car driver's skill as he whipped his car in and out of traffic.

Thankfully, they didn't have to go more than about ten blocks before they reached the famed Seattle Serengeti Club. The windows were tinted so dark that she couldn't tell if anyone was inside or not. There didn't appear to be any cars in the area that could belong to the club or its workers.

"Is it open?"

Ravyn put his car into park and got out. He didn't answer her until he'd opened up her car door. "It opens at dusk and the owners live here."

Before she could ask about the odd note in his voice, he took Patricia from her lap and carried her through the back door of the club.

Wondering why the door wasn't locked, Susan followed him down a short corridor, toward an office area.

"Excuse me!" an attractive redhead snapped as she saw them. "Who are you and what are you doing here?"

Ravyn didn't hesitate or stop as he carried Patricia toward a door off to his right. "Get Dorian. Now."

The woman sneered at him. "And who are you?"

"Don't worry about it. Just go get Dori."

Arms akimbo, the woman looked like she wanted to lash out at him. She cast a dire go-to-hell look at Susan before she left.

Ravyn paused at a door. Susan stepped around him to open it, then stepped back for him to enter what appeared to be a clinic. He laid Patricia down very carefully on the hospital bed that was closest to the door.

"Is there a doctor here?" Susan asked.

"Yeah."

Just as she started to blink, a man appeared directly in front of her. Out of nowhere. He just poofed into the room like some weird TV show effect. With shoulder-length black hair, he bore a striking resemblance to Ravyn. "What are you doing here?" he demanded between clenched teeth.

Ravyn's face was completely stoic. "The Addamses have been attacked by Daimons. Patricia needs medical attention immediately or she's dead. The others will be here as soon as they can make it."

The man, whom she assumed must be Dorian, slid an irritated gaze to Susan. "I don't know her."

"She's a new Squire."

There was a loud commotion outside before the door flew open. Jack came in along with a short African-American woman who rushed to the bed. By the way the woman started examining Patricia, Susan figured she was the doctor.

"Who else was hurt?" the doctor asked Jack.

"Most of us. But Mom was the only one who got seriously damaged. Will she be okay?"

The doctor didn't answer. "You need to wait outside with the others, Jack."

He went white.

The man, who still hadn't identified himself, took Jack by the arm and led him toward the door. "I think we all need to leave Alberta to her work."

Susan felt for the boy as tears gathered in his eyes. "It'll be okay, Jack," she said, praying she was right. Having lost her own mother at Jack's age, she couldn't stand the thought of him losing his.

Ravyn gave her a knowing look. "Yeah, Jack. Alberta won't let anything happen to your mom. She'll be back on her feet, yelling at you, real soon."

Jack nodded bravely as he walked out of the room.

Susan followed Ravyn into the hallway where he drew up short. Looking around him, she sucked her breath in sharply to see a group of extremely handsome but angry men.

An older man who appeared around the age of sixty curled his lip at the sight of Ravyn before he spat on the floor at Ravyn's feet. "You know better than to come here. Ever."

An air of exhaustion settled over Ravyn, as if he didn't want to deal with this right now. "It was an emergency."

That didn't seem to appease the man at all, and it was then she realized this was the sanctuary his family owned. "You should have let the humans bring her."

"Dad—"

He hissed at the man who'd joined them in the clinic. "Don't defend him, Dorian. If not for the laws of sanctuary, I'd already be tasting his blood."

Ravyn's features hardened as he approached his father. Anger mixed with hurt deep inside him. They hadn't seen each other in more than a century, and still his father couldn't look at him without curling his lip. Ravyn remembered a time when he had respected this man. When he would have done anything for him.

Part of him hated his father for the fact that he'd just stood by and watched while Phoenix killed him all those centuries ago. But another part was the little boy who'd once thought the world of this man. The little boy who used to ride on his wide shoulders and play chase with him. That part had wanted some kind of comfort over the death of his family.

Instead, they'd killed him, too. His father had even kicked him as he lay dying on the floor and spat on him. He looked at the spittle beside his boot. His father still spat at him.

And that awoke a potent rage inside him. It was what he focused on now. "What galls you most, old man? The fact that I betrayed you, or the fact that I had the balls to set it right when you didn't?"

He lunged at Ravyn only to have Dorian catch him. "Don't, Dad. He's not worth it."

Ravyn smiled sinisterly. Dorian had no idea just how right he was. "Yeah, *Dad,* I'm so not worth it."

"Get out," his father snarled, his voice thick with hatred, "and don't come back here ever."

"Don't worry."

Ravyn started for the door until he realized that Susan was still following after him. What the hell was she thinking? "You need to stay here with the others."

"I don't think so."

"Susan . . ."

"Look," she said sternly, "you're the one who dragged me into all of this. No offense, Otto, Kyl, and Jessica look at me as if they want to kill me. I want to kill Erika and you're the only one of them who seems to be bulletproof. So between my choices, you look like the safest bet for my continued survival."

Even though his features were angry, there was a glint of humor in his black eyes. "Trust me, I'm not. I'm headed out there into the lion's den. If you stay here, the bad guys can't get you. But if you go with me, they can."

Maybe he was right, but something in her gut told her that she needed to stay with him, and if there was one thing in her life she'd learned to trust, it was her gut. "Ravyn—"

"Listen to him, human," a brittle voice said from behind her. "Getting innocent people killed is what he's best at."

Grief so profound that it took her breath flashed into Ravyn's eyes before he hid it. "Go to hell, Phoenix."

Susan turned to see a man behind her who was an exact duplicate of Dorian. The only reason she knew it wasn't him was that this guy had on a pair of jeans and a denim button-down shirt instead of the pleated pants and black shirt Dorian had been wearing.

Phoenix narrowed his eyes before Ravyn opened the door and stepped through it. Susan headed out behind him just as Otto and Leo were coming in from the back alley.

"Where you going, Ravyn?" Otto asked.

"To check on Cael."

Leo frowned. "We were going there t—"

"No," Ravyn said in a tone that brooked no argument. "We've already got one Squire MIA and I'm sure he's dead. No need to get another one of you killed. I'll handle it."

Otto scoffed. "Are you insane? You can't fight beside Cael. You'll just weaken each other."

That didn't seem to faze Ravyn at all. "I'll have a good fifteen minutes before being in his presence weakens me. So will Cael. Believe me, the two of us can do a lot of damage to anyone who might attack us in that amount of time. I'm pretty sure we'll be all right."

Otto shook his head. "Then I'm going with you."

"So am I," Leo said.

Ravyn growled at their unreasonable insistence on joining him. He couldn't stand the thought of anyone dying so needlessly. If he had more time, he'd waste it arguing with them. But he already had a bad feeling about one of the very few friends he'd had all these centuries. The last thing he wanted was to see Cael dead, and he was too tired to argue anymore. He needed to get over there and find out if Cael was still alive. And if Cael was dead, then he wanted to hunt for the ones responsible. "Fine."

Without another word, he got into his car, only to find Susan getting in on the passenger side.

"What are you doing?"

She gave him a blasé stare. "I told you. I'm going with you."

Like he really wanted that. In truth, all he wanted right now was to be alone to deal with the turmoil of this day. "I thought you'd ride with Otto since, in direct contradiction to common sense, they're going, too."

She let out a very undignified snort. "And I told you that the man acts like he's looking for a reason to kill me. Not to mention he, unlike you, isn't Kevlar."

Ravyn sighed as he started the car and dropped it into gear. He might be bulletproof, but he wasn't completely invincible. They could chop off his head and kill him easily enough. But he decided not to worry her with such trivial details.

"Where are we going?" Susan asked.

"Ravenna." Cael lived over by the university, in the basement of a less than refined club that was owned by a family of Apollites. Ravyn had been telling Cael for years that he was playing with nitro by having the enemy so close.

Sod off, he'd always say. *I like danger. Besides, all I have to do is throw on some clothes, walk upstairs, kill a few Daimons, and come home. You can't beat that.*

Ravyn only hoped his friend wasn't paying for that arrogance now.

"You okay?"

He glanced over to Susan. "Fine."

"You know when people say fine, it generally means 'leave me the hell alone because I don't want to talk about what's really bothering me.'"

"And sometimes it just means they're fine and there's nothing else to say."

She made a face as she considered that. He could tell she wasn't buying it. "Maybe, but can I ask a question?"

Ravyn shrugged. "Free country, which means I don't have to answer it."

By her pinched features he knew that she didn't care for his answer. But after a few minutes, she turned toward him. "Knowing how they were going to treat you, why did you take Patricia to your family when you could have taken her to a hospital?"

Aggravated at the reminder of how much his family hated him, Ravyn tightened his grip on the leather steering wheel. He'd forgotten about the fact that Susan was a journalist, which made her observant and nosy—two things that were lethal to a man who didn't like to talk about his past or his present. Damn, he'd have to be more on guard around her.

He also knew that when dealing with such beasts, it was pointless to hedge. She would just pursue him until she had an answer . . . or he killed her.

Nah, they had enough problems without him doing that. Besides, she was oddly appealing to him. Especially the gentle curve of her lips and the way they turned up ever so slightly whenever she was waiting for him to answer her.

It was almost enough to make him drag this out . . .

But in the end, he answered her with the truth. "One, she wouldn't have been safe at a hospital. The Daimons can come and go there since it's public domain, and I have a feeling that they would have been back to finish her off since she's so significant in the Squire world. The only protection a human has against them is to be in the privacy of their own home. No Daimon can enter a private residence unless they've been invited in. Two, and most importantly, can you imagine trying to explain away the bite wound on her neck? I think the average doctor might get a little concerned to see what appears to be human teeth and yet not human teeth shredding a woman's neck. This was the easiest way to get her help without attracting unwanted attention from someone like, oh say, a journalist."

"You might just have a point with all that," she admitted in a grudging tone.

Susan fell silent as she watched the streetlights cut across Ravyn's face. He really was a good-looking man. But it wasn't just that that she found appealing. There was something more to him. Something that was in pain and at the same time feral. It made her want to soothe him, especially since she understood what it was like to be alone in the world.

Don't think about it. Her mind was right. She had much more important things to focus on at present than how good he looked and how attracted she was to him.

Her thoughts went to Erika. "So how do you think they got into your house?"

"Hell if I know. Someone would have had to have been inside the house to invite them in. She swears she didn't do it, and it damn sure wasn't me."

That wasn't comforting.

"Have you any idea what's going on with the Daimons to-night? Is this normal for them?"

"No," he said sincerely. "It's highly unusual for them to attack like this. Normally they pick off a few humans and we kill them before they get much age on them. Since their goal is to keep living, they usually run from us, not toward us. And I've never seen them attack a Squires' facility before."

She digested that and wondered why it was different now. What was the catalyst? Could it be the Stryker person that Kyl had mentioned earlier or was it something else?

"What about this Cael? I take it he's a friend of yours."

"Yes."

"How long have you known him?"

"Almost three hundred years."

"Wow. I'm impressed. I guess long-term relationships don't scare you, huh?"

He frowned at her teasing. "What's that supposed to mean?"

"Nothing." He still looked perturbed and she strangely found that amusing, too. She didn't normally tease people she didn't know. Yet there was an air about him that just begged her to nettle him. It must be that same suicidal tendency humans had to jump whenever they stood on the edge of a cliff.

Or maybe it was the fact that she liked the way his face softened whenever she amused him. It was extremely beguiling and made her wonder if he'd always been as stern and serious as he was now.

Ravyn slowed as he drew near the Happy Hunting Ground. Yeah, he'd always loved that tongue-in-cheek name for a well-established Apollite/Daimon bar that catered to college students. The college crowd thought it was a play on the singles scene. What they didn't know was that the black dragon shadow flying against a yellow sun on the club's sign was a welcome mat for an Apollite to his Daimon brethren, to let them know they were safe here. Originally Cael had been sent in to shut them down, but the Apollites had quickly offered to make a bargain with him. They would be respectable so long as he protected them. They had even invited Cael to live on the premises. For reasons unknown, Cael had accepted. Now the Daimons tended to stay away. And it was open season on those Daimons who hadn't gotten the word there was a Dark-Hunter in the basement, and who were unlucky enough to wander into the Happy Hunting Grounds to snack on some young college student.

Ravyn just hoped Cael still lived in the basement and hadn't become a casualty of his own trusting stupidity.

"I know this place," Susan said as he parked around back. "I love the recycled trash sculptures out front. I tried to find out who the artist was, but no one would tell me. In fact, the people who work here are really rude."

Ravyn dropped his car into park as Otto pulled his Jaguar to a stop beside them. "The artist would be Cael. The rude people would be the Apollites who own this place."

"Are you serious?"

"Yes."

"Isn't that kind of like playing with your food or something?"

"Something. Definitely something. But Cael likes it here and the Apollites seem to tolerate him. Who am I to question it?"

Ravyn got out of the car and took a minute to get his bearings while Otto joined them. The music from the club was loud and thumping. Susan tilted her head, it was Black Eyed Peas with "Don't Phunk with My Heart."

"Back door again?" Susan asked.

Ravyn shook his head. "You still got that sword?"

"Yeah."

"Keep it close. We're walking into the dragon's den here and I don't know what we're going to find." He exchanged a warning look with Otto. "Any trouble breaks out, I want the two of you to run for the door, and make sure Susan is with you."

Otto gave him a vicious glare that would make a serial killer proud. "No offense, I don't run."

"Neither do I," Susan said firmly.

Leo held his hand up. "For the record, I do."

When Otto scowled at him, Leo rolled his eyes. "It was a joke, Carvalleti. Get a sense of humor."

"I'd really rather not, and don't pull a Gilligan on me. I tend to shoot Gilligans."

Leo flipped him off. "Don't worry. I'm in for the long haul."

Ravyn made a sound of disgust. "Fine. Your deaths are your own business. Just remember I told you how *not* to be a Gilligan." He tucked his knife into his pants at the small of his back.

They walked around to the front. The brick building was just over a hundred years old. Painted baby blue with black windows that had been decorated with vintage hippie symbols, it looked like a million other college clubs. This early, it wasn't particularly busy as people milled around the front, chatting and panhandling.

There was a café and bookstore, Ravenna Third Place Books and Honey Bear Bakery, next door that had a much larger crowd of people. Unlike the club, it was bright and inviting. There was an air of sex and seediness that clung to the Happy Hunting Ground, but then maybe that was what appealed to the regulars.

Trying not to think about how many people had lost their lives because they'd foolishly ventured here for a drink with their friends or a one-night stand, Ravyn opened the door of the club and came face-to-face with a huge Apollite who was waiting in a small foyer area to check IDs. He stood at least six foot seven and had to weigh a minimum of three hundred pounds. It wasn't often he had to look up at anyone.

Damn. As a rule, Apollites were taller than most humans, but due to their liquid diet, they were usually lean. The Apollites here could easily rent this guy out as a major bruiser . . .

Or a Macy's Thanksgiving Day float—except the sunlight would kill him. Then again, float and fireworks. You couldn't beat that.

The Apollite tensed as soon as he saw them. "What do you want here, Dark-Hunter?"

"Just came to see a friend."

The Apollite moved to block his access to the club. "You ain't got no friends here."

Ravyn gave him a withering stare. "I better have at least one."

Still the Apollite wouldn't let him pass. "Then you can call him on the phone. Your kind isn't welcome here."

"Does that go for Cael, too?"

The Apollite's face turned to stone. "He's none of your business. Now leave."

Ravyn started past him only to have the Apollite take a swing. He ducked the blow, then added one of his own. The Apollite staggered back.

Out of nowhere three more Apollites appeared. They formed a line between him and the second door that led to the club. "You're not wanted here, Dark-Hunter. Go home."

"Not until I see Cael."

Otto swung open a butterfly knife. "You know, you guys have a pathetically short life. It'd be a shame to lose even one day of it."

"Put that away!" an extremely attractive blond woman said as she came around the bouncers. She was dressed in a lime green go-go outfit, complete with white vinyl ankle boots and white lipstick. Unlike the men, she didn't bother to hide her fangs while she spoke. "No weapons are tolerated in this club, ever."

She gave Otto, Leo, Susan, and Ravyn a scathing glare. "Why are you here?"

Ravyn took a deep breath for patience. "I'm really getting tired of saying this. I want to see Cael and if I have to say that one more time, I'm going to start Daimon-killing practice on the whole lot of you."

The Apollite woman crossed her arms over her chest. "I'm sure he doesn't want to see you."

Otto narrowed his gaze on the woman. "I think he's already dead, Ravyn."

"He's not dead," the woman said, her tone offended. "But you've got no business here with him. He didn't put you on the guest list and the last time we checked, he wasn't exactly social with the lot of you. How do we know you're friends of his?"

Ravyn gave her a toxic look of his own. "Enemies don't come in the front door, baby."

The bruiser said something to her in Apollite. She looked a little nervous as she glanced at Ravyn. "Smart enemies might. For all I know, you're not as dumb as you appear. Maybe you're here to kill Cael."

Ravyn was through playing this shit with her. "There you would be wrong. And unless you want this club to go up in flames tonight, I suggest you let us pass."

She stiffened at his threat. "You can't harm us, it's against the code. No Dark-Hunter is ever allowed to harm an Apollite until we turn Daimon."

"Fuck the code," he said between clenched teeth. "If my friend is dead, I honor nothing but that which gave birth to me . . . vengeance."

The man spoke to her again.

She hesitated before she answered him. Her eyes worried, she looked back at Ravyn. "You have fifteen minutes with him before you drain his powers. After that, I want you gone."

To his complete shock, the Apollites actually broke apart to let them pass.

Expecting a trap, Ravyn made sure that Susan was between him and Otto while Leo pulled up the rear as they followed the woman through the club, which actually had a fairly large crowd, dancing to the hip-hop music. Strobe lights flashed off three different mirrored balls that spun high above them. To the sides were tables that were covered with black tablecloths that held Apollite and hippie symbols painted in neon colors. Black lights helped the colors to leap out in the darkness. They also served a dual purpose of making Ravyn's eyes ache.

The motion and lights would weaken a Dark-Hunter while leaving Daimons and Apollites unaffected. Smart thinking on their part.

The woman took them past the bar area, through an industrial kitchen, to a narrow door that opened onto a stairway for the basement.

She held it open with one arm and stood back for them to enter without her. "His room is the last one on the left."

Ravyn went down first.

"You think this is a trap?" Susan asked after the woman shut the door behind them. The light in the basement was very faint, but it actually felt good to his eyes after the hostile lighting above. Here, he could see perfectly.

"At this point," Ravyn said in all seriousness, "nothing would surprise me."

Ravyn paused as he approached the door that the woman had

said led to Cael's room. He could hear someone grunting as if in severe pain, then suddenly, Cael let out an anguished cry.

His heart hammering, Ravyn kicked open the door and then completely reevaluated his prior comment about surprise.

This . . . *this* shocked the total hell out of him.

CHAPTER SEVEN

His jaw dropping, Ravyn stood in the doorway in total stupefaction as he saw Cael entwined on his bed with an Apollite woman. Completely flagrante delicto. "I so did not need to see *that* hairy full moon tonight," Ravyn said as he turned around to give them his back. "Gawd, I think I've gone blind."

Susan gasped as Otto and Leo laughed, then stepped back into the hallway, out of sight range for the naked couple.

Cael snarled a fetid curse. "What the hell is this shit?" he demanded angrily in a thick brogue that was an odd Scot-Irish mix. Ravyn could hear the two of them shuffling about on the bed, no doubt trying to cover themselves. "And for the record, I'm not the one with the hairy arse. That would be you. Don't you people knock?"

"Usually yes," Ravyn said snidely. "But not when I think you're being attacked."

"I *was* being attacked . . . in a most desirable way. You should try it once in a while, Rave, and maybe you wouldn't be such a bastard."

Ravyn rolled his eyes. "I don't know. You're the one who seems obsessed with my hairy ass. What's that say about you, bud?"

A shoe struck the wall not far from Ravyn's head. "Your aim's off, Cael."

"That wasn't Cael," a soft, venomous voice said in an agitated tone. "And next time I won't miss."

Before Ravyn could comment, Cael cleared his throat. "Why are you here anyway, Catboy?"

"That's Cat*man* to you, and I need a word with you."

Cael let out an aggravated sigh. "Wait outside while Amaranda and I get dressed."

Ravyn cast a glance over his shoulder to see Cael and Amaranda wrapped in a sheet before he joined the others in the hallway and shut the door.

"I think I'll go wait upstairs," Leo said, heading down the hallway. "Call me if you need any more help busting up horny couples."

"Shut up, Leo," Ravyn snarled. "You're not so necessary to my world that you can lip off and not get hurt."

"Yeah, yeah," he said dismissively as he headed back up the stairs and disappeared from sight.

"Well, that was certainly embarrassing," Susan said in a tone that should be entered in the Sarcastic Hall of Fame. Looking up at him with those clear blue eyes, she folded her arms over her chest. "Now that I've seen the mating rituals of the Dark-Hunters up close and personal, got any more fun places to take me tonight? You know, I haven't been this embarrassed since the elastic broke in my gym shorts in high school and I learned the hard way that I had a hole in the back of my panties."

And for some reason that made no sense whatsoever to him, the thought of her butt peeking out from a tear in her panties actually turned him on . . . yeah, he was losing it.

Before he could comment on her causticity, the door opened to show Cael wearing nothing but a red and black plaid kilt wrapped low around his lean hips. Raking his hands through his wavy black hair to settle it into place, he glared at them before he wrapped his arms around his bare chest, which bore a number of red scratches. "To what do I owe this extreme displeasure and interruption? The answer better be 'Armageddon' if you want to live."

Susan tried not to gawk, but it was hard. Like Ravyn, the man had the build of a taut gymnast . . . with a full eight-pack of abs. He, too, had a bow and arrow tattoo, only his was low on his left hip while another tattoo of a heart pierced by a dagger went down one arm. Vines rose up from it to twine over one shoulder and down to his right pecs. His thick black hair fell to his shoulders in waves of masculine perfection. At least one day of beard covered his handsome face, and he had dark eyes ringed by eyelashes so long, they should be illegal.

Ravyn had a tic in his jaw as he faced his friend. "Close. I came to tell you that the Apollites are going to try and kill you."

Cael gave an evil smirk at that. "You're too late. Amaranda's been trying all day, but I won't go down." He wagged his eyebrows.

Susan cringed at his bad double entendre.

Ravyn's nostrils flared as he directed a heated glare toward the closed door. "This isn't a joke, Cael. This is serious. I can't believe you're shacked up, shagging the enemy. What the hell are you thinking?"

All the humor fled Cael's face as he tightened his grip on his arms. "Caution, *braither*. You'll put respect in your tone when you speak of her, you ken?"

The bedroom door opened to show Amaranda. Tall and ethereally beautiful, she was the kind of woman Susan had spent her entire life envying. There wasn't an ounce of fat on her, and it was obvious, since she wore a pair of skintight jeans that barely came up over her pubic area and a slinky red halter top that left most of her upper body bare. Her slender upper left arm was encircled by a gold snake slave bracelet that matched a pair of gold earrings, and a ruby red moon hung from the loop she had pierced in her belly button. As she turned toward Susan, she noted that Amaranda also had a small red stud in her right nostril.

Susan started to mention the fact that it was a bit nippy outside for the outfit but held her tongue. Maybe the woman would get a cold and gain some weight. . . . At the very least, she'd cover up that perfect body so that Susan wouldn't feel quite so inadequate.

Note to self: Start a new diet tomorrow.

Tossing her waist-length, perfectly white-blond hair over her shoulder, Amaranda glanced quickly at them before she looked up at Cael. There was no mistaking the deep, adoring love in that gaze. It was only matched by the one Cael gave her back before he smiled at her. He said something in a language Susan didn't recognize.

Amaranda responded in kind. Like Cael, she also flashed a bit of fang as she spoke.

Ravyn curled his lip as Amaranda withdrew from them. "You even speak their language?"

Tilting his head down, Cael rubbed at his eyebrow with his middle finger.

"Fine," Ravyn snarled. "But let me tell you what's been going on while you were making nice with your little girlfriend."

Cael gave him a peeved glare.

"At dawn, I was picked up by the Apollites and taken to an animal shelter where they came dangerously close to killing me. After I got out of that by the skin of my teeth, they sent a group of humans and a half-Apollite out to kill me during the daylight hours. They've already killed one as yet unidentified Dark-Hunter and then tonight they attacked the Addamses at their base. Patricia might not even survive the night."

With every word Ravyn spoke, Cael's face turned more deadly serious. "What?"

"It's true," Susan said in Ravyn's defense. "The police and Apollites are working with the Daimons and they're out to hunt all of you down." Even as those words left her lips, they sounded ludicrous. How she wished they really were.

"Yeah," Otto added. "We sent a Squire over here three hours ago, before the attack on the Addamses, to warn you."

Cael scowled at that. "No Squire came over here. Kerri would have told me."

"Kerri?" Ravyn asked.

Cael hesitated as he cast his dark gaze toward the stairway that led to the club upstairs. By his face she could tell he was debating something extremely important. He looked highly uncomfortable before he finally answered. "My sister-in-law."

Ravyn couldn't breathe as those words went through him like a hot knife. *What the hell was he thinking?* "Your *what?*"

His features tightened. "Amaranda's my wife."

Rage and disbelief made for a hostile mixture inside Ravyn. "Have you lost your friggin' mind?"

Cael started to shove him, then thought better of it. After all, whatever one Dark-Hunter did to another, the antagonist felt ten times worse. A simple shove to Ravyn would rebound to Cael as a staggering blow. "I know *exactly* what I'm doing."

Yeah, right. Tangling like this with an Apollite was like milking snake venom for a living. Sooner or later, one of them was bound to turn around and bite him—it was just the nature of the beast. "You fucking idiot! Have you any idea—"

"Of course I do, Rave," he said between clenched teeth. "Don't you dare think for one minute that this has *ever* been easy for either one of us. It hasn't. We're well aware of the downside and drawbacks of this relationship." The pain in his eyes was raw and powerful.

Part of Ravyn felt sorry for him. The other part just wanted to beat the shit out of him until he saw reason. This wasn't a game they were playing. It was a war they were fighting. And how could a man fight while his loyalties at home were with the very enemy they were sworn to kill?

"How old is she?" Susan asked quietly.

The pain flared even brighter in Cael's eyes. "She turns twenty-six in a couple of weeks."

"Damn, Cael," Ravyn said under his breath. He wanted to argue with him, but to what purpose? They were already married. Even though this had to be the dumbest move Ravyn had ever heard of, Cael wasn't a child. He knew the score and he was the one who would have to live with the consequences of it. Having screwed up his own life over a woman, Ravyn wasn't about to lecture anyone else about their love life. But it never ceased to amaze him how stupid a man could be over a woman. "Well, at least now

I understand why the Apollites tolerate you living here. How long have you been married?"

"Four years."

Ravyn let out a disgusted breath as he exchanged a look of disbelief with Otto. It amazed him that Cael had managed to keep it quiet for so long. But then Dark-Hunters didn't usually visit one another's homes and Cael had never asked for a Squire. Even before he'd moved into the Apollite-owned building ten years ago, Cael had been alone, so it would have been relatively easy to keep his marriage hidden from them.

Since Dark-Hunters were forbidden to date or have any kind of long-lasting romantic entanglement it wasn't something that would have come up or been asked.

But then that begged one particular question. "Does Ash know?"

Cael shrugged. "If he does, he hasn't said anything."

Ravyn had to give Cael credit—he was good at hedging around a question. "Did you *tell* him?"

"No," Cael admitted, "but I haven't hid it, either. I am not ashamed of my wife or my marriage. But I figured as long as no one asked, I wouldn't talk about it."

"What about her family?" Otto asked. "Since Apollites tend to breed a lot of kids, I'm sure she has more than a sister. What do you do when they turn Daimon?"

Cael's entire posture turned defensive. "Who says they turn Daimon?"

Both Otto and Ravyn gave him a doubting stare.

"You saying they've all died?" Otto asked.

Cael refolded his arms over his chest as his expression turned a bit sheepish. "Not exactly. Some of them have vanished."

"Vanished . . ." Ravyn mocked. "You mean went Daimon."

Cael's face was stone. "I mean *vanished*."

The look of disgust on Otto's face was tangible. There was so much tension in the air that it made the hair on Susan's arms stand up. She kept expecting one of them to lunge at the other, but to their credit no one was getting phsycial.

"Don't ask, don't tell, right?" Otto asked.

"They're my family, Otto," Cael said from between clenched

teeth. "I don't go looking for them when they go walkabout. There's enough other Dark-Hunters here to take care of them if they go to the dark side."

Otto released a long, tired breath. "Family? Are you sure they feel the same way about you? Tell me what you're going to do when you wake up with your head detached from your body because your so-called family got nervous. . . . Don't delude yourself, Cael. You're enemies. Always. Sooner or later, one of them is going to sell. You. Out."

"I think he has a bigger problem than that," Ravyn said, drawing their heated attention toward him. "What are you going to do when Amaranda turns twenty-seven?"

The agony in those dark eyes wrung Susan's heart as he looked away. "We don't talk about that."

"Why?" Otto asked. "You planning to hold her hand while she feeds on humans?"

That succeeded in breaking the hands-off truce. Cael grabbed Otto and shoved him back against the wall with so much force, Susan was amazed it didn't crack the plaster. His fangs bared, she half-expected Cael to rip out Otto's throat. "It's not your problem, human."

Ravyn separated them and put his body between Cael and Otto. "It's all our problems, Cael. All of ours."

Cael curled his lip into a feral snarl.

"You know this might not be so bad," Susan said, drawing their attention to her. "Cael can ask them what's going on, can't he?"

Cael shook his head as Ravyn gave him a curious stare. "No," he said firmly. "I don't call in those kind of favors. They don't ask me about the Dark-Hunters and what we're up to, and I don't ask them about other Apollites or Daimons."

"Unbelievable."

Cael sneered at Ravyn. "Don't cop a superior attitude with me, dickhead. It's not like you're not hunting family, too. At least I don't have any Apollite blood in me. How can you hunt your own kind?"

Susan caught Ravyn as he moved toward Cael. "Enough, boys."

"She's right," Otto said, backing her up. "Besides, you two should be weakening each other by now."

"We are," they said in unison.

The door at the end of the hall opened to show Amaranda coming back toward them, carrying a small sack of what smelled like food. As she walked past them, Susan noticed a small Dark-Hunter bow and arrow entwined with a rose tattoo on the small of the woman's back.

Amaranda looked pointedly at Ravyn, who somehow managed to keep his face completely stoic. "Cael needs his strength. You need to go."

Ravyn's gaze fell to the teardrops that were tattooed on the hand Amaranda placed on Cael's arm. "She's Spathi?"

Cael's features hardened again. "She's not a Daimon."

"But she's trained to fight us."

Amaranda lifted her chin to stand firm against Ravyn and his criticism. "I'm trained to protect myself and those I love."

"From what?" Otto asked in a dry tone.

She gave him a withering stare. "Whatever I have to."

Again the air was rife with unspent anger and hostility. The frisson of it went down Susan's spine like a phantom touch that set her on edge.

It was only broken when Cael looked at his wife and his anger seemed to fade immediately into a much softer emotion. "Baby, was there a Squire here earlier asking to talk to me?"

"No." Her features were completely sincere and open.

"You sure?" Otto asked.

She nodded. "Kerri would have told me if there were. She wouldn't have kept something like that secret."

Otto looked ill. "He didn't come back and he didn't make it here. They must have intercepted him. Damn. I wonder when we'll find the body."

Ravyn released a heavy breath. His exhaustion and sadness reached out to Susan. She wanted to place a comforting hand on him but decided that wouldn't be prudent. Unlike Cael and Amaranda, they weren't a couple. And she didn't know him well enough to gauge if Ravyn would welcome her comfort or resent it.

"At least we know Cael's safe, so we can relax there." Ravyn narrowed his eyes on the other Dark-Hunter. "Stay in touch and remember what I said. Sooner or later, this battle will come to your door."

Worry darkened Amaranda's brow as she looked up at her husband. "What battle?"

He took her hand into his. "Nothing, baby. They're just paranoid."

Otto scoffed at his words. "And cockiness kills."

"C'mon," Ravyn said, pushing Otto toward the stairs. "We have other places to go and other people to annoy."

Otto shrugged his grip off as he headed down the hallway, away from Cael and Amaranda. Ravyn followed after him.

Susan pulled up the rear, but as she reached the stairs, she turned back to see Amaranda drop the sack of food on the floor as Cael pulled her into his arms and cupped her face in his large hands, before he gave her a passionate kiss.

Gone was all of his toughness and in its place was the gentleness of a man who was obviously head over heels in love with his wife.

"You need to eat something," Amaranda said as she pulled back from his lips.

He gave her a teasing smile. "Trust me, I'm going to eat now . . . the food can wait till later."

Amaranda laughed as he picked her up and headed back into their bedroom.

A bittersweet pain sliced through Susan at the sight of them. God, what would it feel like to be that in love? She couldn't even imagine it. The closest she'd ever been to it had been Alex back when she'd been a reporter. He'd worked for a competing paper and they had dated for almost three years—they'd even talked about getting married.

Until she'd been disgraced. Then he'd left her life so fast, she still had a skid mark on her heart.

I can't stay with you, Sue. Can you imagine the gossip? No one would ever trust me. You ruined your career. I won't let you ruin mine, too.

The truly sad thing was, she understood it and, honestly, she'd rather have him gone if he didn't love her enough to stand by her.

But understanding didn't stop it from hurting, even after all this time. How she envied Cael and Amaranda for being able to love even when everyone else condemned them for it.

But that was tempered by what would happen to Cael next year when his wife was destined to die . . .

Her heart heavy for them, Susan dashed up the stairs after Ravyn and Otto, who'd already policed up Leo. The club was still thumping as college students and Apollites mixed and danced. She walked past a group of tall blonds whose black eyes watched them with tangible malice. Susan felt like a guppy in a shark tank. There was something extremely disconcerting about the way the blonds watched them, and the reporter in her went on full alert.

"Ravyn?" She pulled him to a stop. "I've got a bad feeling."

"About what?"

"I don't know. Something's not right. I can't explain it. . . ."

A teasing light came into his eyes. "Don't worry, my spidey-sense is going off, too. I think it best we get out of here as quickly as we can."

She nodded as they followed Leo and Otto out of the club, back to the street.

Ravyn couldn't shake the bad feeling Susan had mentioned. He hadn't been kidding. There was a scent on the air that he couldn't place. It wasn't Daimon or Apollite. Nor was it human. It was something else . . . something sinister and powerful, and that concerned him. He needed to get the humans back to safety before whatever it was made its presence known to them.

"What now?" Leo asked as soon as they were outside the club.

"Were all the other Dark-Hunters notified about what's going on?" Ravyn asked.

Leo nodded.

"Then—" Ravyn's voice broke off as he felt a sharp stab in his shoulder. The sting of it made his arm start to tingle and burn immediately. "What was that?"

He met Otto's scowl.

"What?" Leo asked.

Ravyn couldn't speak. It felt as if his tongue was swollen so large that it wouldn't move. His head started throbbing. His vision blurred and dimmed.

"He's hit!" Otto shouted. He handed Susan the keys for his Jaguar before he grabbed Ravyn around the waist and pulled him toward the car. "Get us out of here. Now. Leo, take Ravyn's car and run."

Susan fished the keys from Ravyn's pocket and tossed them to Leo.

Leo dashed off to comply.

Susan barely had time to recover before she saw the brigade of five Daimons coming out of the alley to their left. Four men and one woman, they walked with determined strides in a killers' formation with the sharp Seattle wind billowing out their long coats. Each one wore a pair of dark wraparound sunglasses and held a sharp, stern face that said they were out for blood.

Their blood.

Her heart hammering, she got into the car and turned the key in the ignition at the same time Otto shoved Ravyn into the backseat. Something hard struck the hood.

Startled, she looked up to see a male Daimon standing on the hood, baring fangs at her as he drew a gun out of the folds of his coat to shoot through the windshield.

"Screw you, asshole," she snarled, putting the car in reverse and cutting the wheel even though Otto still had the car door open. The Daimon went flying as the car slung sideways. She laid her weight on the brakes, causing the car door to slam shut as Otto let out a foul curse from the backseat.

"Buckle up and hang on," she warned him, dropping the gearshift into drive. She stomped the gas and headed for the others, who quickly dove out of her path. "Damn, I missed them."

"Where did you learn to drive like that?" Otto asked.

"I was a reporter, Otto. You ever notice that reporters rank up there with lawyers and politicians in terms of public opinion? There's a lot of people in the world who'd like to hurt us. As soon as I got my first job out of college, Jimmy made me take self-defense classes in both martial arts and driving. Believe me, I can J- and K-turn with the best of them." She glanced into the rearview mirror to see Ravyn trying to stay awake. "What happened back there? Is he okay?"

Otto pulled a small dart out of Ravyn's shoulder, then sniffed the tip of it. "Apparently, they tranked him."

"Can they do that?"

He met her gaze in the rearview mirror. "The answer should be no. Dark-Hunters as a rule are impervious to drugs of any kind, but since he's part animal, it appears he's a little different, and whatever the drug, it worked on him."

Susan glanced all around the car to make sure they weren't being followed by the Daimons, then slowed down so as not to draw any attention from the police. The traffic appeared normal, but then what did she know about normal? All her preconceived notions about that had been splintered the instant Ravyn walked into her life.

"Where am I headed?" she asked Otto.

He sighed. "Good question. I only wish I had an answer. I'm sure between the police and the Daimons, they have both Ravyn's house and your place staked out."

Not to mention, her house was a crime scene. She couldn't go to the Addams house. Leo's house was too far . . . "Where's your house, Otto?"

"New Orleans."

That was the last place she expected him to answer with. "That's really not useful."

"I know."

"Where are you living here?"

"I was living with the Addamses."

That was even less helpful. Fine. She only knew of one place that was safe for them.

She glanced at the men in the backseat. Otto watched the traffic even more carefully than she was doing while he fidgeted with his armpit under his jacket. "You got some kind of rash there, Otto?"

He frowned. "What?"

"You keep scratching at your arm like that and people are going to think you've gone mad or something."

He snorted. "I want to keep my hand close to my gun . . . just in case."

That should scare the crap out of her, but instead it made her feel a little less tense. She glanced at Ravyn, who was slumped over against the other window. His long black hair obscured his face but she could still see the bruises on his neck from where the collar had almost killed him. If anyone had had a worse day than her, it would be Ravyn. And he had yet to voice a single complaint. That amazed her. He had more strength and courage than anyone she'd ever met before, and it made her wonder how his family could have turned their backs on him.

Maybe it was because she had no family of her own that she understood its value, but one thing was certain; if she ever had someone like him in her life, she'd fight to keep him, no matter what.

"How's Puss in Boots doing?" she asked Otto.

"Out cold."

Susan let out a tired breath. The day was really starting to get to her and she just wanted a minute to sit down and have five seconds of peace. A moment to catch her breath before something else was thrown at her. Since lunch, her life had been careening madly out of control.

Was this what she had to look forward to as a Squire? If it was, then Leo could shove it. Granted, as a reporter, she loved the thrill of the chase, but this was entirely different. Give her a regular human killer any day over one who could attack without warning and vanish into thin air.

If this was normal, then it went a long way in explaining why Leo was such a rank toad most days at work.

"So is this how you guys live your lives? One major disaster after another?"

Otto gave a short laugh. "No. Not really. It's usually rather quiet. There's something here in Seattle specifically that's behind this uproar."

That made her feel a little better . . . well not really. She still felt like crap. "Any idea who's behind it?"

"Apollites," he said dryly. "Big ones, with a few Daimons thrown in for fun."

"Har, har, Otto. I'm serious." Susan gripped the wheel tighter as she remembered the look on Jimmy's face in the shelter. "My friend Jimmy said to me earlier today that some of the police were working with the vampires. I thought he was nuts, but now I'm not so sure."

"That doesn't make sense, though. I can understand the Hollywood generation who fall for it, but cops? They have more sense than that."

"Unless someone higher up the food chain is sending them out. Think about it. I saw the list earlier. You guys have people all over the government. Why couldn't they?"

"For one thing, there's not as many of them who can walk in daylight."

"Yes, but there are a lot of cops on night shifts. How do you know they're not Apollites covering up the murders their people are committing?"

"Now that isn't unheard of. A lot of them do that. But this is more organized than that. They're not just Apollites and Daimons attacking. They have humans working with them."

"Which plays right into what Jimmy was saying. He told me that this ran high up. There has to be a human leading them."

Otto stroked his chin in thought. "What exactly did Jimmy know?"

Susan took a deep breath as she tried to remember everything. "It started a couple of years ago. He'd have these isolated incidents of college students or runaways who turned up missing. Every now and again, they'd even find a body. The cases would be solved, but he'd never see the reports. At first he didn't think anything about it. But a few months ago, they started getting more frequent, and that's when he became suspicious."

"Did you ever investigate it?"

Pain sliced through her. "No. I can't show my face at City Hall. I'd be laughed outside before I could even begin my research."

She met Otto's sympathetic glance in the mirror, but he made no comment. "Were the disappearances all in a certain area?"

"Ravenna. In and around the area where the Happy Hunting Ground is."

"That would make sense, wouldn't it?"

She nodded. "I think Jimmy was right. Someone fairly high up is interfering and helping the Daimons. Someone like the mayor, maybe."

Otto made a noise of disagreement. "He's too high up. He couldn't push that many members of the police department around without someone getting suspicious."

"Yeah, not to mention that it started before he took office." Susan chewed her lip as she considered more suspects. "What about the commissioner?"

"That's more a possibility. Or maybe a detective?"

"No, Jimmy said it went higher than that."

Otto nodded. "He'd be the one to know."

Her heart clenched remembering the fact that Jimmy couldn't tell her anything now.

Damn, if only she had a clue of some kind. . . .

"There has to be a reason for this. Are you sure they've never attempted something like this before?"

"Positive. And in my mind, I can't imagine what would prompt a cop to help a vampire prey on other humans, especially a high ranking one."

"But it is happening."

Otto nodded. "Whatever's going on though, I'm thinking Cael needs to be replaced since he's obviously distracted and not paying attention to what the humans and Daimons are doing."

She could understand that. "Is it normal for a Dark-Hunter to date an Apollite?"

"No. Hell, no. I've never heard of a Dark-Hunter hooking up with an Apollite before. The only time anything close to this has happened was with Wolf, and he wasn't technically a Dark-Hunter. He was just a human who got caught up in this by a Norse god. Dark-Hunters aren't supposed to date anyone at all. And marriage is strictly forbidden."

That had to stink. She couldn't even begin to wrap her mind around that concept. "So they live for eternity, but they're never allowed to have a significant other of any kind?"

"That's the deal."

"That sucks."

"Yeah," Otto agreed. "It does, but as Ash would say, when you sign with the devil, you're bound to get burned."

"Ash?"

"The Dark-Hunter leader, Acheron."

She remembered reading about him earlier. Although there wasn't much on him other than he was rather eccentric and hard for a Squire to get ahold of. "How old is he?"

"Eleven thousand plus years."

Her jaw dropped as she imagined a shriveled up old man who looked like Merlin from a King Arthur movie. "That's a long time to putter about."

"Yeah," Otto said with a light laugh, "it is."

They fell silent as Susan ran all of the information through her mind, but honestly at this point, she was beginning to have information overload.

She slowed as they neared the Serengeti.

Otto cursed as he realized her destination. "You can't take him in there again, Susan."

She parked on the curb, near the back door. "You got a better idea?"

She expected him to argue. Instead, he held a hand up to tell her to wait, while he pulled out his phone and pressed a button.

"Hey, where are you?" He looked up at her as he listened. "We're right behind the club with Ravyn. He's down for the count. Care to come out here and lend me a hand getting him inside?" He held the phone away from his ear and she heard the commotion from the other end before he pressed it back to his head. "I know, but where else can we take him?" He paused. "Yeah, I'll see you in a sec."

Susan leaned over the seat. "Was that Kyl?"

"Yes, and for the record, he thinks you're insane, too."

"Oh, goodie. But I guess that's only fair since I think he's psychotic."

Otto's eyes sparked. "No thinking about it, he *is* psychotic. Which makes him great in a fight. C'mon, let's get this over with."

Susan looked around the darkened street before she got out. The back door of the club opened to show Kyl joining them. Susan held open the car door so that he and Otto could get Ravyn out. The two of them had to struggle under the weight of him and they weren't exactly gentle. In fact, they banged his head on the roof, trying to get him out.

She cringed in sympathy. "That'll leave a mark I have no intention of explaining."

Otto gave her a harsh glare as he grunted. Leo parked Ravyn's car near theirs, then went to hold the back door open.

Kyl staggered forward with Ravyn between him and Otto. "What happened to him?"

"We have no idea," Susan said as she shut the car door. "The Daimons hit him with some kind of trank."

Kyl paused for an instant until Otto dragged Ravyn forward. "I didn't know a Dark-Hunter could go down on a trank."

Otto gave him a dry stare. "Well, we learn something new every day."

Susan stood back as they reached the door to give them enough room to get inside.

They'd barely gotten in the back of the building before their route was blocked off by Ravyn's father.

"What the hell is this?" he growled angrily.

It was Otto who answered. "Ravyn's been hurt."

"Then dump him on the street with the rest of the garbage."

Otto let out a tired breath as he grimaced from the weight of Ravyn. "We can't do that, Gareth, and you know it."

Two more of the Were-Hunters appeared out of nowhere to stand behind Gareth. "He's forbidden access to the Serengeti. Permanently."

Those words struck something hard inside her. Damn them for being so cold. Her family had been taken from her and if she could have any of them back for even a minute, she'd take it in a heartbeat and not question it. How could Gareth turn his back on his own child, especially when he was hurt?

It made her burn as she thought about her own father. And that made her focus her suppresed rage on Gareth.

"Hang on a second," Susan said. "This is a sanctuary, right?"

Gareth slid her an angry glare. "Your point, human?"

She crossed her arms over her chest and returned that glare tit for tat. "Then you're not allowed to pick and choose who can stay here. I read in my manual that it was really hard for a place to become a . . . lemony—"

"Limani," Otto supplied for her.

"Yeah, that. And once you were granted that status, you had to welcome in anyone who needed your help. *Anyone*. Human, Apollite, Daimon, or Hunter."

She saw respect on Otto's face as he gave Gareth a shit-eating grin. "She's right."

Anger beat a fierce tic in Gareth's jaw. "He violated our laws."

"There was nothing in the book about exceptions. According to the rules, you have to take him in unless someone named Savitar bans him from it. Has this Savitar banned him?"

Gareth raked her with a nasty glare. "What are you? A fucking lawyer?"

"Worse. Reporter."

Gareth growled a sound that was animalistic and raw. "Phoenix!"

Ravyn's brother flashed in instantly. Susan frowned as a strange deep burgundy tattoo appeared on one half of his face before it faded out.

"Yes, Father?"

"Show these people to a room upstairs."

Otto curled his lip in disgust. "He can't be in daylight, Gareth, and you know it."

If looks could kill, they'd all be nothing but dust. "Fine. Dump him in the basement then. In the holding room."

Well, didn't that sound all warm and cozy? "I guess I was lucky not to have a father, after all, if this is how they act."

No one said anything as Phoenix obeyed his father and led them to a stairway that was off to the right, concealed by a door. But she still half-expected the animals to turn on them as they made their way down to the room.

And it was small. It could barely accommodate the full-sized mattress on the floor. The walls were painted a dull gray and the room held a nice, musty odor to it. Nice . . . like a moldy piece of bread.

"What do they hold in here?" Susan asked as soon as Otto and Kyl dumped Ravyn on the mattress.

"Problem clients," Otto said, stretching his arm as if he'd pulled it. "If someone or something steps out of line, they have to hold them until they can get a council order to terminate them."

That didn't sound pleasant. "Order from whom? The Squires' Council?"

Kyl shook his head. "No, the Omegrion. It's the ruling body for the Were-Hunters."

"By the way," Otto said, looking at Phoenix. "Thanks so much for helping us get him down here."

"Fuck you, human." And then he vanished into thin air.

Susan feigned happiness as she clapped her hands together like a kindergarten teacher before her class. "Wow, boys and girls, they're just so inviting, aren't they? Martha Stewart would be proud."

Otto laughed while Kyl shook his head at her. Even Leo snorted.

"The Were-Hunters may be fuzzy," Kyl said, "but they're seldom warm."

And that was definitely a shame.

Susan looked down at poor Ravyn, who was slumped in an awkward position on the mattress. "Could one of you at least get a pillow and blanket for him?"

Otto nodded. "I'll be back in a few."

The men stepped past her and left her alone with her charge. Although how he'd come to be her responsibility once more she wasn't sure. Then again, she was almost getting used to this.

Susan sat down beside Ravyn. As she was trying to make him more comfortable on the makeshift bed, she realized that he wasn't completely unconscious. "Ravyn?"

He gave a subtle blink but didn't really respond. He was as helpless as an infant, and that scared her. If he'd been hit with this while alone, he'd have been completely defenseless before his enemies.

It was one heck of an Achilles' heel to have. And now his enemies knew it. . . .

Her gut tight with that thought, she brushed his hair back from his handsome face. Even though they were half-hooded, those eyes were still breathtaking and disturbing and they melted a foreign part of her. She'd never been the kind of woman who lost her head over good looks. But something in her was definitely drawn to him.

It was hard to believe she hadn't even known him twenty-four hours yet.

Otto came back with a blanket and pillow. "How's he doing?"

"I have no idea."

He sighed. "I tried to get one of the doctors in here to examine him, but, big surprise, they refused."

She ground her teeth in fury at that as she very gently placed the pillow under Ravyn's head. "Why do they hate him so much?"

"I killed them all."

Susan frowned at Ravyn's whispered words. "What?"

"I killed my family," he repeated, his voice distant and slurred. "Isabeau lied. She told them and they came for us . . ."

"Who's Isabeau?"

But there was no answer as Ravyn's eyes closed and he went limp. Again.

Otto shrugged. "I have no idea what he's talking about. Any more than I know why they hate him. I'm sure it has something to do with his being a Dark-Hunter, but anything other than that would be a guess on my part."

Feeling for Ravyn, Susan spread the blanket over him.

"You want me to bring you something to eat while you tend him?" Otto asked. "That is, assuming you intend to stay here with him."

Where else would she go? Besides, she'd been ill enough times in her adult life to know just how lonely it was. There was nothing worse than to have to tend yourself when you felt like complete crap.

"Yeah, I'll stay with him. And as for food, I'll eat most anything that doesn't bite me back."

Otto nodded before he left.

No sooner were they alone than Ravyn rolled to his side as if he was trying to sit up.

Susan caught him and pulled him back toward the mattress. "You need to stay down."

He cringed. "Don't *yell* at me."

Oh jeez he was on ketamine. What else would they use on a shape-shifter? She should have known. She'd had a college roommate who'd loved experimenting with all kinds of recreational drugs, and Special K, an animal tranquilizer, in particular had been a favorite. If Susan remembered correctly, it often left her roommate highly sensitive to light, sound, and touch.

Wanting to test the theory, she reached out to stroke Ravyn's hair. Like a cat, he arched his back and actually purred. It was so out of character for him that she wondered what he would say if he weren't under the influence.

He raised his hand up to cup her cheek. "You're so soft," he breathed. He grimaced as if something pained him. "I don't feel good."

Susan looked around quickly until she spotted a small trash can near the door. Releasing him, she grabbed it and barely made it back to him before he unloaded the contents of his stomach into it.

She cringed. They must have seriously overdosed him. Her roomie had often been nauseated by the drug, but Susan couldn't ever remember her actually getting sick from it—just very stupid and extremely overaffectionate.

When he was finally finished, he fell back onto the mattress, where he panted and groaned.

Susan sighed wearily as she wondered what to do with the trash can. "What a perfect end to a perfect day."

Stryker *stood in* an alley outside of the Serengeti with three of his men and Satara. He glared at Trates, who'd allowed Ravyn to escape them yet again.

Stryker's second in command gave him a sheepish look that said he knew exactly how displeased Stryker was with him. "At least we know the tranquilizer works and it's every bit as fast acting as Theo promised."

Little consolation that.

Stryker licked his fangs meaningfully. "And where is the good doctor now?"

His face paling, Trates stepped back.

"Grow a ball, Stryker," Satara said irritably as she cast a glare toward the club. "March in there and take him down already."

"Grow a brain, little sister. You violate sanctuary and you open a whole can of worms that not even you can deal with."

"How so?"

Approaching her menacingly, Stryker backed her up against the wall. "I realize that as a handmaiden to Artemis you think you're immune to everythin. Lucky you. But the rest of us aren't that fortunate. You go in there after Ravyn and you'll bring the wrath of Savitar down on us all. Not to mention it would become open hunting season on Spathi. We use those places to run to as much as the Were-Hunters do."

Her nostrils flaring, she pushed him back. "Then what do you want to do? Give up on taking Seattle?"

"No," he snarled. "We've gained too much ground here, and so far the humans have proven themselves worthy. We will wait them out and kill them when they leave."

She let out a disgusted breath. "You know what your problem is, Stryker? You think like an eleven-thousand-year-old man."

"What's that supposed to mean?"

"You're too set in your ways. Give me a team of men to lead."

Yeah, right. Like he would trust her? She was too quick to act and too slow to think. "Are you insane?"

"No, but unlike you, I think outside the box." She gestured toward the buildings around them. "You want Seattle? I can give it to you."

Stryker hesitated as he considered her proposition. For centuries, Satara had kept to herself and only visited him whenever Artemis had no need of her. It was only in the last two years that she'd become a more frequent visitor to Kalosis. And with each visit, she seemed to get more and more agitated. Something had happened on Olympus to infuriate her, yet she never spoke of it.

But then maybe she had a point. He was old and tired. And set in his ways. Maybe she did have an idea that the Dark-Hunters and Acheron in particular wouldn't see coming.

"Fine." He looked back at his second in command. "Trates, go with her. If she makes a move to compromise any standing treaty, kill her."

Satara gave him a snide grimace. "I love you, too, Brother." She pulled the dagger out of her boot. "But don't worry . . . things are about to go deliciously our way."

CHAPTER EIGHT

Ash woke up in a cold sweat as fragmented, displaced images shifted through his mind like a broken kaleidoscope. Sitting up naked in bed, he could hear desperate voices calling out to him with unspoken pleas. . . .

And then he felt it. The cold, demanding hand on his bare shoulder that jerked his senses away from the nightmare.

"Come back to bed, Acheron."

Ash raked his hand through his long blond hair as he tried to center his attention on the loudest voice he'd heard. But it was lost now . . . drowned out by all the others until all the pleas were nothing but a dull roar that rang in his ears. "Something's happening."

Artemis made a sound of disgust deep in the back of her throat—a sound that was completely unbecoming for a goddess who had created an army supposedly to protect mankind from the Apollites and Daimons her twin brother had fashioned in his own image and then endowed with godlike powers. Then again, she'd immediately abandoned that army into Acheron's care and then used them to tie him to her forever.

"Something's always happening," she said in an aggravated tone. "When the cat's away, the rodents will scurry."

He let out an exasperated breath as he turned to look at her over his shoulder. She was lying back in bed, her body covered by the white, gossamer sheet that was softer than the most finely woven silk, and it left nothing of her body hidden from his gaze. Her red hair fanned out around her in perfection, but in spite of being a goddess, she was the furthest possible thing from perfection. "The mice will play, Artie."

She turned instantly huffy with him as she tried to pull him back into her arms. "Whatever."

Ignoring her, Ash got up and headed for the French doors that opened onto a golden veranda at his approach. He stepped through them to lean against the cold stone banister and stared out at the rainbow waterfall. It was truly beautiful here on Olympus and yet he cared nothing for it.

His thoughts were on the future that taunted him with scattered images that he couldn't bring into focus no matter how hard he tried.

Something was happening and it would affect those he was close to. He could feel it with every fiber of his being. Damn it.

"What are you up to, Stryker?" he asked in the faintest whisper, knowing there would be no answer from the other side.

Stryker had set something evil into motion. For thousands of years the Daimon lord had remained dormant. But something had happened four years ago to bring him back into the open. Now he was determined to hurt Ash any way he could.

Artemis moved to stand behind him. She placed one cold hand on his right shoulder while she nuzzled his left with her cheek before she nipped his skin with her teeth. "Come back to bed, love."

That was the last thing he wanted at the moment . . . well, honestly it was the last thing he wanted period. But long ago, he'd reconciled himself to the fact that he would never be free of the prison Artemis had damned him to.

Closing his eyes, he took a deep breath and counted to ten before he spoke a plea that stuck deep in his craw. He'd never been one to beg for anything and yet she managed to degrade him to this every single time they were together. "Let me go, Artie. My men need me."

Her nails bit deep into his shoulder blade as her temper flared and singed him. "You promised me a week of service if I let that woman's soul go, although why you wanted the soul of a Shade, I'll never understand."

That's because she had no concept of compassion and she never would.

"And you can release me from my word." He turned his head to look down at her uncaring expression.

She raked her nails painfully down his spine, no doubt laying his flesh open in vicious welts. Welts that would close instantly if not for her using her powers to make sure they stayed fresh and painful. His face stoic, Ash stiffened as his back burned. He knew what had always gone unspoken between them. She hated the fact that she loved him, and for the whole of their relationship she'd punished him because, in her mind, she couldn't live without him. Even though he would really, really like her to try.

She wrapped her hand in his long, blond hair and gave a vicious yank.

Bored with her childish games, he sighed. "Are you through?"

She gave another jerk before she released him. "I should have you whipped for your insolence."

Why not? His back was still sore from her last beating—part of the price she forced him to pay for Danger's soul. She'd always been sadistic that way. The fact that he could take a beating without flinching had always turned her on. But then he'd been weaned on brutality. Reacting to it had only served to worsen his punishments, so he'd learned early in life to suck it up and move on.

"Whatever makes you happy, Artemis."

"Then come back to bed with me." She brushed her hair back from her neck. Her long, graceful hand stroked the only part of her body that held any appeal to him. "I'll let you feed if you do. . . ."

He could feel his incisors growing at her invitation as his stomach rumbled with need. It'd been almost a month since he'd last eaten. That more than anything else was what had forced him to stay with her for a week. He had to eat from her soon or he'd turn into the very thing he hunted. "Don't tease me, Artemis. I'm too hungry for that."

She moved closer to him. So close that he could smell the blood that flowed through her icy veins. She nibbled the line of his jaw as she gently cupped him in her hand, and yet his body didn't stir in the least. "Give me what I want and I'll give you a small reprieve to check on them."

Ash clenched his teeth. He truly hated it whenever she bartered with him for sex. He'd rather be beaten. Again.

But then he was nothing if not her whore. For a semblance of affection, for the novelty of a gentle touch on his flesh, he'd sold himself to her eleven thousand years ago. No matter how much he hated it, no matter how much he hated her, he knew that he couldn't exist without her. Not if he wanted to maintain his compassion and live with his emotions under his control and not become an instrument for an even more selfish goddess.

He'd truly damned himself for something so trivial that he now wondered why it had seemed so important all those centuries ago. "I want your word that I can feed and then leave for twenty-four hours."

She licked her lips as she ran a hot gaze over his naked body. "Give me six orgasms within one hour and you can have ten. I swear it on the river Styx."

Ash laughed softly at that. Even after all these centuries, she still underestimated his abilities. Six orgasms and a feeding. Good. He'd be done with her in less than fifteen minutes. . . .

Susan *sat, bathing* Ravyn's hot brow as he whispered unintelligibly in his sleep. Otto had helped her clean up the earlier mess and now they were alone again while Ravyn drifted in and out of consciousness and she skimmed through more information in the handbook that Otto had also brought for her.

The Squires seemed to have an affinity for the monstrosity and were insistent that she learn every nuance of it, and she was anxious to learn absolutely everything. But she also didn't mind taking a break whenever Ravyn came to.

The hardest part though was whenever he was awake, he was either groping her or leading her hand to parts of his body that she really did want to explore—but not while he was this far gone. Something about it just wasn't right. Even so, she had to admit, he was scrumptious and while under the influence of the drug, he was also extremely affectionate. *Very* catlike.

He opened those deep, dark eyes to pin her with a lusting stare again. He pulled her hand from his brow so that he could nibble her fingertip, then the back of her knuckles. Each sweep of his tongue sent a razor-sharp spike of pleasure through her. This man knew his way around a woman's senses and how to elicit pleasure with the smallest move or stroke. It was what made pushing him away so difficult. That evil part in the back of her mind was dying to know what he'd be like naked in her arms.

"Sleep with me, black-eyed Susan."

How could a girl resist a line like that?

Oh wait, very easily. He was still out of it. *Yeah, and what would it hurt?*

No, she couldn't take advantage of him. She wasn't the kind of woman to take advantage of people while they were down. Not to mention the small fact that he'd never seemed that interested in her while at full capacity. If, when he awoke, he was still interested, there might be some grounds for negotiation. But at the moment, those talks were moot.

She pulled the cloth away from his brow with her left hand while she tried to get the right one away from that deliciously erotic tongue of his. "That's okay, Leopardman. I'll just keep bathing your brow."

"That's not what I want you to stroke." He pulled her head down toward his.

Tired of fighting him, she let him kiss her only to learn that that was a serious mistake. Her entire world spun at the decadent taste of him. He had a way with his tongue that should be illegal and it probably was in some states. She'd been kissed a lot of times in her life, but never like this. It was strong and powerful and left her completely breathless.

He led her hand back to the swollen bulge in his jeans. He held her hand there as he rubbed himself against her open palm.

Grinding her teeth, she could just imagine him doing that inside her. Feel him hard and deep, stroking her until she finally had ultimate satisfaction. . . .

But she'd gone a year without a guy. She could certainly go a little longer.

Reluctantly, she broke away from his kiss. "Easy, Puss in Boots."

He actually whimpered as she pulled her hand away. Pouting, he reached for her again, only instead of kissing her, he nuzzled her neck. Susan hissed at the warmth of his mouth on her flesh until something strange happened. . . .

Her eyes started watering and her nose immediately became stuffy. The more he nuzzled, the worse it got until she sneezed.

"Oh my God," she said, pulling back to wipe at her eyes. "I think I'm allergic to you."

He rose up and stalked her across the mattress. "I'm addicted to you."

"Ravyn!" she snapped, holding him back. "I'm serious." But now she was getting better. Maybe she was wrong.

"You're not allergic to me," he said, playfully grabbing her. He rolled her over onto the mattress and pinned her under him.

Susan was fine until he dipped his head back toward hers to kiss her again and his hair fell down over her face. She immediately became stuffy again.

Clearing her throat, she rolled him over until he was pinned under her. He gave her a grin so wicked that it alone could have made her horny. He lifted his hips, rubbing himself against her again.

"Stop that and listen to me. I *am* allergic to you," she said sternly.

At least to his hair, which made complete sense she supposed, since it was cat fur that set her off. But the worst part was that deep down inside her, a part of her was extremely disappointed. Which made no sense to her whatsoever.

It wasn't like she could ever have a relationship with a man who was an undead cat, Dark-Hunter thing.

"C'mon, Susan," he said in that deeply provocative voice as he lifted his hips to rub with a part of her that was way too interested in that swollen part of his body. "I need you."

Stifling the wicked imp that wanted her to strip him bare and sate both of their baser instincts, she shook her head. "What you need is a cold shower."

"Take one with me and I'll wash your back."

He was relentless!

Suddenly, a knock sounded on the door.

Grateful for the interruption, Susan immediately scooted off Ravyn, got to her feet, and straightened her rumpled clothes. "Come in."

The door opened to show Erika, who looked past her to see Ravyn stretched out on the mattress.

Ravyn snorted as he rolled to his side and curled into a very catlike pose. "Hey, kitten. Got any change?"

Erika wrinkled her nose as she stepped past Susan, into the room. "What is he? High?"

"Yes. Very," she answered, duplicating Erika's clipped tone.

That appeared to amuse her a great deal. "Man, any idea what it is?"

Susan folded her arms over her chest as she watched Erika slowly approach Ravyn, who was now singing something that sounded like it might be a lullaby in a foreign language, while lying on his side. "I'm not one hundred percent sure. Why?"

" 'Cause whatever it is, let's up the dosage. He hasn't called me kitten since I was ten." Erika gave her a wide, delighted smile, which might have amused Susan had they met on better terms. But given Erika's blasé attitude toward both her and Ravyn, Susan wasn't feeling overly charitable toward the younger woman.

"Is there a point to your visit?"

"I just wanted to make sure he was all right." There was an underlying tremor in her voice that made Susan feel like a heel for being so short with her. After all, Erika had known him all her life and with her father off in Hawaii, Ravyn was the only family she had here.

"He's fine," Susan said, softening her tone. "Are you okay?"

She nodded, but there was something in her eyes that was sad and hurt. "I just don't like people dying on me, you know?"

"Yeah, being alone sucks."

Erika tucked a piece of hair behind one ear. With that one, hesitant action, she went from being a snotty teenager to a little girl who needed someone to tell her everything would be okay. "You've no idea."

"Actually," Susan said, stepping closer to her, "I do. By the time I was your age, I was an orphan, and I've been alone ever since."

"Was it hard alone?"

Susan swallowed as old memories haunted her. "Yeah, most of the time. You stand there alone on graduation while all of your friends are surrounded by their families. You're alone the first day of college with no laughing mom and dad to tease you while you find your dorm room. Unless someone feels sorry for you, there's no place to go when the dorm's closed. But the worst are the holidays, especially Christmas. You sit in your house, looking at the one gift under the tree that you bought for yourself, and you wonder what it would be like to have a mom or dad, or just anyone to call."

Now she didn't even have Angie and Jimmy anymore. Angie had always been the one who'd invited her home. She'd always taken care to call her on Mother's Day and Easter to make sure she was okay. And she'd always lied and said she was fine, even though inside it still hurt to have absolutely no one.

She glanced over at Ravyn. How much harder were those moments when you knew your family was alive, but not to you?

It explained why he was so understanding of Erika. Annoying though she could be, she was better than being alone. Better than watching the rest of the world take for granted the very things you would sell your soul to have.

She saw a grudging respect in Erika's blue eyes as the girl nodded in mutual understanding. "I'm sorry about your parents. I lost my mom a few years ago. . . . It still hurts."

"I know. I'm sorry, too."

"Thanks." Erika looked over at Ravyn, then frowned. "*You* need anything? Like a cage or flea repellent?"

Smiling, Susan paused as she watched Ravyn move his hands as if he were singing "Itsy Bitsy Spider" in that lyrical language of his. "An antidote would be nice."

"I don't know," Erika said teasingly. "He's kind of amusing like this. It's like having a big kid around or something."

Ravyn rolled over onto his stomach and tried to push himself up. Susan rushed to his side to keep him down on the mattress.

"I need to go," Ravyn said, trying to push her back.

"No, no. You're right where you need to be."

"No," he said in a tone so whiny that it stunned her. She'd have never thought such a sound could have come out of a man with such a deep voice. "I have to *go*."

Why was he being so stubborn?

"No, Ravyn. You need to stay right here."

"But I can't go here and I really have to go."

Erika made an odd hissing noise. "Susan, I think what he's saying is he needs the litter box."

A feeling of dread consumed her. No . . . even her luck wasn't *that* bad. "Oh, surely not."

He pushed himself away from her grasp only to fall back down. He looked at the mattress as if baffled by it. "This isn't the bathroom. . . ."

Oh, shoot me, please!

But there was no reprieve. If he really had to go, she couldn't very well let him go in here. That would be gross *and* disgusting. "I can't believe I'm having to do this."

Erika indicated the door with her thumb. "You want me to get one of the guys to help?"

Susan let out a long, tired breath as she considered it for a second. "No. I somehow doubt they'll be any more enthused about this than I am." No doubt, they'd kill him if they had to help him with this. Dreading this down to the deepest part of her being, she assisted Ravyn to his feet and almost fell under his weight. The man was so solidly built that it was like lifting a car. "Could you help me get him to the bathroom?"

"Sure."

With Erika's help, Susan was able to get him across the hall to the small bathroom. The space inside was tight and cramped. She started to wait outside with Erika but then thought better of it. In his current condition, Ravyn might fall and damage himself. The last thing they needed was for him to whack his head on something.

She watched as he fumbled with his fly like a two-year-old. "My zipper's broken."

She rolled her eyes. "No, it isn't."

He dared to give her an exasperated look. "Yes, it is."

What did I do to deserve this? She figured it had to be divine retribution for something. There was no other reason for her day to have turned on her so viciously. Cursing her own fate, she moved forward to push his hands out of the way so that she could undo his pants. Which she learned were button fly. No wonder they wouldn't unzip. Unbuttoning them, her face flamed as she realized that he didn't have on any underwear. Not that she hadn't already seen him naked, but this was somehow different. More private. With a deep breath for courage, she helped him lower his pants, then turned her back while he took care of his needs.

This has to be the weirdest moment of my life. She'd never done something like this for a stranger before. But then again, if she ever somehow found herself in a situation like this, she only hoped that someone took the same mercy on her and helped her through it. What little she knew of Ravyn, she was sure he'd die of embarrassment about being this helpless. He seemed to pride himself on his independence.

And given the way his family treated him, it was obvious he'd been alone a lot longer than she had.

When he was through, she helped him dress and wash his hands. Susan paused while soaping them. His weren't pampered hands. They were large and callused, brutally scarred by untold fights against who only knew what. One in particular was wide and deep, and ran all the way up his forearm. Another one looked like something had taken a vicious bite out of him. Her stomach lurched at the sight of them. Yeah, her life and troubles seemed so mild by comparison.

"Your touch is so soft," he whispered. "Like a butterfly's wings."

It was stupid, but those words touched something inside her. No, it wasn't the words so much as it was the emotion she heard in his voice. The tone that told her he wasn't used to anything so gentle touching him.

"Thank you," she said, rinsing his hands off, then drying them with a small hand towel.

Placing his damp hand on her chin, he tilted her head back until their gazes were locked. "You are so incredibly beautiful."

Oh, yeah, the man was definitely high. Not that she was Quasimodo or anything, but Susan wasn't stupid, either. She wasn't the kind of woman that men thought of as beautiful. "Yeah, yeah. You just want me to sleep with you."

"No," he said in a deepened voice. "You are beautiful . . . like an angel." He pressed his forehead against hers before he gave her the gentlest kiss she'd ever known. Something inside her melted as he wrapped his arms around her and held her not like a horny man out to get laid, but like someone who actually had feelings for her. And it brought out an ache so deep inside her that her throat tightened.

All her life, all she'd ever wanted was to be loved. To have a family again, and this kiss only reminded her of what she didn't have.

Of what she'd most likely *never* have. And the pain from that thought washed over her like ice.

"Okay, Ravyn, we need to get you back in bed." She expected him to argue. Instead, he merely nodded before he withdrew from her, then opened the door.

"Kitten," he said as he saw Erika again. "When did you get so tall?"

She gave Susan a "duh" stare. "I grew while you were in the bathroom."

"Really?"

Erika snorted. "You know, this is a serious improvement over his regular temperament. I think I like it. We definitely need to find out what it is and spike his food."

As Susan tried to guide him back to their room, Ravyn caught the door frame with his hand and refused to enter. He gave her a harsh stare as she tried to push him forward. "I have to get back home."

"Yes," she said slowly, "it's right in this room."

"No!" he growled in a ferocious tone. "Zatira needs me. I have to go to her."

Who was Zatira? Susan exchanged a look with Erika, who

looked every bit as baffled by the name as she was. "No, you don't."

He pushed her away and he started down the hallway. "I have to save her." He took three steps before he froze. He stared at the floor as if it were a TV screen. Unbelievable pain twisted his brow as if he was reliving some kind of nightmare. She'd never seen a more tormented expression.

"No," he growled, punching at the wall. "Zatira! Mom! God, no! No more blood. They're not dead. They're not!"

He raked both hands through his hair before he threw himself against the wall and slid to the floor.

Susan went to him. Taking his hands into hers, she forced him to unclench them from his hair. "Ravyn, look at me."

He did, but she could tell he didn't see her. He was still being tormented by something in his past. "Zatira?"

"It's Susan."

He rolled away from her. "I have to save her. I can't let her die. I can't."

Susan tried to hold him back as he struggled without hurting her.

Suddenly, a shadow fell over them. Susan looked up, expecting it to be Erika.

It wasn't. It was either Dorian or Phoenix.

"Get up," he snarled at Ravyn. There wasn't a trace of compassion or sympathy on his face.

"Fuck you." Ravyn tried to crawl past him, only to have his brother grab him roughly by the arm and haul him to his feet.

"Not so rough," Susan snapped. "There's no need to hurt him."

Ravyn leaned back against the wall as he stared at his brother. His face was angry and feral, but his eyes spoke volumes of pain and hurt. "You going to kill me again?"

For once, his brother's expression softened. "It's Dorian, Rave. Not Phoenix."

"Dori . . ." The anger faded from Ravyn's face and was replaced by a profound agony. "I didn't mean to, Dori. I didn't. You have to believe me. I didn't want them hurt." He grabbed his brother by the shirt and held tight. "I didn't mean for anyone to die."

Dorian wrapped his hand around Ravyn's wrist before he removed his grip. "I know."

Ravyn snapped his head back so hard into the wall that it actually broke the Sheetrock. "We can save them," he said, taking a step toward the door that led upstairs. "We can go back and make it right."

"What is he talking about?" Erika asked.

Dorian didn't answer. Instead, he snapped at her. "Go upstairs, Erika."

It was obvious by her face that she wanted to argue, but for once she obeyed.

"We have to go," Ravyn insisted.

But there was no reprieve in his brother's stern expression. "Don't be stupid again." He shoved Ravyn away from him.

Susan glared at Dorian as Ravyn staggered and almost fell. "You asshole," she snarled, barely catching Ravyn against her.

Ravyn paused as their gazes met and held. For the first time since this episode had started, he saw her and not Zatira. His features relaxed. A small smile hovered on his lips. "You look like an angel. . . ." His eyes rolled back in his head before he collapsed.

Dorian let out an aggravated breath as Ravyn hit the floor. None too gently, Dorian picked him up and carried him back to the mattress. Susan wanted to protest his help, but there was no way she could move Ravyn by herself. Damn his brother for being so cold.

"How long has he been like this?" Dorian asked as he straightened up.

"About two hours."

Dorian shook his head as he looked back at Ravyn, who lay silent and still. "You need a breather?"

She crossed her arms over her chest as she gave him a suspicious once-over. "It depends. You gonna beat on him while I'm gone?"

The look on his face said he wasn't amused by her question, which was okay by her since she wasn't joking. "No."

That made her feel a little bit better . . . but only a little. She still didn't trust Dorian. From what she'd read in the handbook,

Dorian was an Arcadian Were-Hunter. Human in theory, he was able to shift into an animal. There were other kinds of Were-Hunters who held animal hearts. They were called Katagaria. Unlike Ravyn and his family, they were truly animals who could take human form. But from where she stood, she didn't see much difference since the so-called "human" branch seemed to be as cold as any animal she'd ever met in the wild.

Then again, as a reporter, she'd met plenty of humans whom she would definitely classify as animal. Some were even amoebas.

And the reporter in her had something else it was extremely curious about. "Who was Zatira?"

Pain darkened Dorian's eyes before he answered. "My sister."

"I assume she was Ravyn's, too?"

He cut her a look that said yes, but that Dorian didn't want to admit to it.

Which begged the next question. "What happened to her?"

The pain from his eyes seeped over his entire being. It was obvious that he felt her loss every bit as deeply as Ravyn did. "She was killed three hundred years ago."

Susan winced at that. "Killed how?"

"By humans." He snarled the word as if being human was the worst thing he could think of. He gave her the harshest, most hate-filled stare she'd ever seen in her life. "They brutally slaughtered her . . . our mother, Phoenix's wife and children, and our entire village."

Susan covered her mouth as the horror of that overwhelmed her. But then what had she expected? Dark-Hunters were created out of men and women who'd suffered unjust tragedy and who wanted revenge on those who'd wronged them. It was the screaming of their souls that summoned Artemis to them, and if they accepted the bargain, Artemis would bring them back to life and give them twenty-four hours to exact their revenge. After that, they became soldiers in her army that was dedicated to protecting mankind from the Daimons. The nature of their creation guaranteed that all of them had at least one major tragedy in their past.

"I take it their deaths are what made him a Dark-Hunter?"

He nodded. "He wanted revenge on the humans who'd killed them."

"And Isabeau? Was she part of your village, too?"

The look of hatred on his face was a resounding no. "She was Ravyn's mate . . . a heartless, human bitch. He told her about us and she in turn told her people. They're the ones who came for us. They thought we were evil minions of the devil and in their ignorance, they slaughtered our weaker members while we were out protecting them from the Katagaria who'd been raiding their village."

The Katagaria were the animal branch of their people who were at war with the "human" Arcadians. Susan winced as sympathetic pain swept through her. What awful irony to be betrayed by the very people you were attempting to help. But from what Dorian said, Ravyn sounded like a victim, too—all he'd done was trust the wrong person. Why would they hate him for a mistake that any one of them could have made? "How could you have banished him?"

He snorted at that. "We didn't *banish* him, woman. Phoenix killed him as soon as we found our families slaughtered . . . and the bastard should have stayed dead."

She was horrified by his words and the venom in his voice. "How could you people do such a thing . . . to your own brother?"

"How could we not?" he asked as if he was baffled by her question. He gestured toward Ravyn. "Every time we look at him, we're reminded that he caused their deaths. He is an abomination to us. And I hate that we're forced to run a sanctuary in the city where he's stationed. Damn the Fates for it."

Oh, that was stupid. "It wasn't his fault."

"It was *all* my fault. . . . I should have never trusted her."

Startled that he was awake, Susan looked at Ravyn, who had rolled over onto his back. At first she thought he was still delirious, but his gaze seemed clearer now.

His face grim, he pushed himself up and reached for his brother. "Dori—"

"Don't touch me, Ravyn." He curled his lip at Susan. "As soon as he's back to his senses, he needs to get out of here before the others turn on him again. Understood?"

"Yeah," she said, curling her own lip in response, "I completely understand. You're a heartless bastard and the rest of you aren't leopards. You're pigs."

His face hardened. "Be glad you're human and standing in a sanctuary right now. Otherwise, I'd rip your throat out." He cast one last hating glare at Ravyn before he vanished out of the room.

Unable to believe the gall of him, Susan turned back to Ravyn, who lay completely still. At first she thought he'd fallen unconscious again, but as she brushed his hair back from his face, she saw that his eyes were open.

The look he gave her singed her to the spot. There was so much anguish and self-loathing that it stole her breath. "I didn't want to be alone anymore. Was that so wrong?"

Her heart clenched at those heartfelt words. She knew exactly how he felt. "No, Ravyn, it wasn't wrong."

He started shaking uncontrollably as he reached for the blanket on the mattress. "I'm so cold."

Susan pulled the blanket over him, but his teeth continued chattering. She'd never seen anyone so cold. Figuring he was in enough pain from the raw emotions the drug was bringing out, she spooned up against him to try to warm him with her body heat. Poor man. And she'd stupidly thought she was all alone in the world. It was probably better to have no family than to have half of them dead while the other half hated you for causing the deaths.

She couldn't imagine anything worse. Well, maybe living with Erika, which he also did.

Ravyn continued to tremble in her arms. He covered her hands with his as she held him quietly in the dim light of the room. "Susan?"

She opened her eyes at his faint tone. "Yes?"

"I'm sorry about your friends. I wish it hadn't happened."

"Thank you."

He went suddenly limp in her arms as if he was unconscious again. Her first inclination to pull away from him, she laid her head on his muscular arm instead. How odd that two strangers would find themselves lying on a mattress in the basement of a popular singles club in the heart of Pioneer Square. They were both being hunted for a crime they hadn't committed and were trapped in a place where no one wanted them.

God, what a day.

Closing her eyes again, she let out a long, tired breath. What lay ahead was even more daunting than when she'd written the story about Senator Kelly and his questionable spending only to learn that her source was completely bogus. Even now she cringed at the memory of that day when her boss had tossed the paper with the story in it in her face and accused her of making it up.

Then she'd come under fire from all of her reporter brethren as they wrote story after story about her. There had been no kindness or forgiveness. Nothing but hostility and glee as they brought her down, and all because she, too, had trusted the wrong person to not lie to her.

And then there had been the lawsuits. Slander. Libel. Defamation. Not only had the senator sued her, but her own paper as well. It'd been the worst time of her life.

Up until now. Now she didn't even have Angie to hold her hand through it. No Jimmy threatening to kill the people who were hurting her.

Just say the word, Sue, and I'll arrest them for parking violations. . . .

She was completely alone.

Like Ravyn.

Susan blinked back her tears as she toyed with his silken hair that made her skin itch. But she didn't care. She needed to feel his presence. This wasn't the time for weakness. She needed her strength. Especially since she had no idea how all of this would turn out. How to even begin to get her life back.

What was she supposed to do?

You're a reporter, Sue. What would a good reporter do?

Find the truth. The only way to get back her life was to expose whoever was behind all of this. Granted, she couldn't expose the vampires without becoming a complete laughingstock, but Jimmy had spoken of a cover-up, and she did trust him. He wouldn't have lied to her. Ever. Someone in his department was definitely working with the Apollites and Daimons to hide the disappearances, which were probably all murders. Now that she knew what was going on, she could find evidence and expose him or her. . . . They could be brought out and exposed in a human court. Then the Apollites wouldn't have human help anymore.

Don't be stupid. The whole thing was ludicrous and she was living it. How could she sell this to people who couldn't see it for themselves?

Not to mention the small fact that going after a government official who was supposedly on the take was what had led to her disgrace.

"I'm too old to start over again."

More than that, she was too tired.

But even as she thought that, Angie's beautiful face hovered in her mind. She could see Angie and Jimmy on their wedding day, laughing as they waved good-bye to her from the limo before they headed off on their honeymoon. They were supposed to grow old together and make her a fabulous aunt to their whole brood of raucous children.

They had been her family.

This time there was no stopping the tears that flowed from her eyes. They—the only family she had—were gone and they would never have those kids to mooch off them. There would never be another call from Angie complaining about Jimmy watching football games on TV. No more Jimmy teasing Susan that he'd recently arrested a man who would be perfect for her.

No more late-night movies or laughter. No more Christmas dinners. . . .

They were gone and those bastards had killed them for no reason.

Fierce, unadulterated anger swelled deep from her soul to crawl all the way through her body. She couldn't let the people responsible for their deaths get away with it. Not to mention that every night they were still out there, ending other people's dreams. Other people's lives. Taking away the family someone else loved.

She had to stop them. Somehow. She couldn't just sit by and let someone else lose their loved one. Not if she could stop it.

Susan paused in her mental tirade as an idea struck her.

"Jimmy's journal. . . ." As far back as she could remember, Jimmy had kept anal notes in his journal. Both she and Angie had teased him about it endlessly. That incessant need to put everything in writing was what had made him such a great investigator.

Whatever evidence or leads he'd uncovered would be in that notebook. She knew it. There was no chance he didn't leave clues for her to follow.

But how could she get to his house while the police were looking for her? Not to mention they most likely had it staked out.

It didn't matter. She was going to find some way over there, and get those notes no matter what it took, and finish this investigation. *Even if it killed her.*

CHAPTER NINE

Ravyn woke up with his vision hazy and the scent of Susan heavy in the air. It was a delicate, warm smell. Unique and inviting. He felt like total shit and yet something about her scent soothed him.

It also set him on fire.

His right shoulder was so sore that he could barely move it. Not that he could anyway, since Susan was lying on it, facing away from him, sound asleep. At first he couldn't figure out where he was or why on earth she was on top of him. Then suddenly, the earlier events of the night came rushing back.

He'd been hit with a trank outside of the Happy Hunting Ground. Images of their flight and return to the Serengeti shuffled around him as he remembered bits and pieces of being sick . . . of Susan helping him.

She'd held him while the whole world had fallen apart.

Amazed by that, he rose up to look down at her and brushed a strand of blond hair off her silken cheek. She had the prettiest skin. Fair and unblemished, it was softer than silk. He laid his fingers over her cheekbone and marveled at the texture that was so different from his.

There was something lovely about her. Something that called out to the animal in him and lured it forward. He'd never felt such a pull toward anyone before. Not even Isabeau, and she had been his chosen mate.

He dipped his head down so that he could inhale the scent of her hair. The soft strands tickled his cheek even as the warmth of her body calmed him. He laid his other arm over her and held her close in the darkness. Like a lover. This moment awoke a long forgotten dream inside him. A dream of family. Of love. Of having someone he could love, who would love him, too.

God, it'd been way too long since he'd just held someone. . . .

"If you don't stop groping on me, Puss in Boots, I don't care if you are out of it, I'm going to hurt you."

He laughed in spite of himself.

Susan opened those striking blue eyes to stare up at him.

"I'm over it," he said softly to her.

Still she looked suspicious. "Uh-huh, that's what you said last time, right before you made a head dive for my boobs."

"No, I didn't . . . did I?" He frowned as he tried to remember, but the last few hours were all hazy and vague. And he certainly didn't recall that happening, but then given how much she appealed to him, he couldn't deny it, either. If he had a chance and a reason to get away with such a thing, he'd have probably taken it.

She narrowed her eyes on him. "You really are back, aren't you?"

He put the heel of his hand to his right eye in an effort to ease some of the pain that felt like it was cleaving his skull in two. "Yeah, and with a vicious headache."

Susan rolled over to look up into those midnight eyes. Okay, it was only one eye since he still had the other covered with his hand, but it was nice to see clarity there again. "Welcome back."

"Thanks." His gaze dropped to her lips that teased him with an invitation he was finding hard to ignore. "For everything."

"It's okay."

She licked her lips, moistening them with her tongue . . . it was his undoing. Unable to stand it, he lowered his head, half expecting her to pull back or push him away.

She didn't.

Instead, she moved forward in his arms to take his kiss. The instant their lips touched, Ravyn closed his eyes, letting the warmth of her wash over him. She wrapped her arms around him, causing him to tremble at the tenderness she offered. She was exceptional. His heart racing, he deepened the kiss, exploring her mouth.

Susan couldn't breathe . . . literally. Her allergies kicked in, but not even they were enough to make her let go as she tasted heaven. Every part of her fired at the touch of his lips. He cupped her face as his delicious weight pinned her to the mattress. She found herself actually resenting their clothing, even though she knew getting physical with him would be a mistake. Dark-Hunters couldn't have dates and girlfriends, and she had no interest in being someone's one-night stand.

They had nowhere to go except separate ways. Too bad her emotions weren't more rational because right now all they wanted was to keep him in her arms and to explore every inch of that wicked body with her tongue. But she couldn't.

Ravyn fisted his hand in her silken hair as images of her naked body writhing underneath him tormented him with desire. He nipped her lips as he felt her heart racing along with his. It took every piece of will he possessed not to lift her shirt and cup her breast in his hands. But she was a Squire, and they were off limits to Dark-Hunters. Even so, she appealed to him on a level he couldn't even begin to fathom.

If he could, he'd stay here with her for the rest of the night, but they had way too much to deal with at present. And the last thing he wanted was to be involved with another woman who could betray him. He pulled away, then groaned.

Susan put her hand on his sore arm as if she knew exactly what hurt. "You need to rest."

He shook his head. "We've got too much to do."

"Believe me, I know. But you're still hurt."

He snorted at that. "Trust me, this is nothing. I'll definitely live."

She shook her head at him as she sat up to face him. "Fine then. While you've been down and unconscious, I've been doing a lot of thinking. The Daimons are after all of you so that they can have a full run at Seattle, right?"

Ravyn remained lying back on the mattress. "That's what we think."

"Well, according to the handbook Leo gave me"—she picked up a huge leather-bound tome and held it against her chest— "whenever one Dark-Hunter goes down, another one is sent in to replace them, especially in an urban setting . . . such as say, oh, Seattle." She toyed with the edge of the book as she gave him a stern frown. "So what are the Daimons really hoping for? I mean if they kill you and more are sent in, why bother . . . right?"

She definitely had a point. "I don't know. It doesn't make sense, but you can't deny that they're doing it. Maybe they hope to pick us off one by one until the last Dark-Hunter falls." Even as he said it, he knew better than that. There were too many Dark-Hunters. It would take years, if not centuries, to get them all.

But then something weird had been happening these last couple of years. A lot of Dark-Hunters had gone free and an even larger number of them had died. Especially recently.

"Or maybe this is an experiment," Susan said. "Think about it for a minute. If they can get away with wiping out all of you here, then they could converge on other cities. Make a studied attack. Claim each city one by one. Right?"

"At this point, I would go with just about any theory. I've honestly never seen anything like this. I mean, there have always been a few stupid humans here and there who've been willing to help them. But never on this scale."

"Which brings up the question of why they're helping them? What are the Daimons promising them for their service?"

Ravyn shrugged. "It could be anything. My money says they've promised them eternal life."

"I don't think so. It's too easy. Think about it for a second. Someone fairly high up is helping them. Why? What could that person stand to gain by allowing Daimons to murder people in Seattle and take out the Dark-Hunters? The human would have to have a vested interest in this, and eternal life doesn't do it for me."

Ravyn grew silent. "You know, the Were-Hunters came into being for one simple reason."

"And that is?"

"Roughly nine thousand years ago, an ancient Greek king married an Apollite without knowing it. When she died on her twenty-seventh birthday by slowing decaying, the king realized that his sons were going to meet the same fate as their mother. Horrified at the prospect, he immediately set out to magically splice animal strength with his sorcery to Apollites. His goal was to make Apollites live longer."

"And?"

"It worked. He created the Arcadian race, my race, who have human hearts, and the Katagaria race, our enemies, who have animal hearts."

Susan nodded as she remembered that from her reading.

His dark eyes bored into her. "Do you see what I'm saying. Lycaon did everything he could to protect his family. He even defied the Fates when they told him to kill all of the hybrids he'd made. To kill his own sons. . . ."

Her jaw went slack as she finally caught his meaning. "One of the police has married an Apollite?"

"And what if that Apollite were to turn Daimon?"

Susan couldn't breathe as those words went through her like glass. It made complete sense.

An official who would have the ear of the media to help hunt them down. An official who could tamper with evidence and reassign investigators.

"It's either the police chief or the commissioner, isn't it?"

"That would be my bet."

She covered her mouth as her mind whirled. If they were wrong and she went after an innocent man, she'd never live this down. But if they were right . . .

"We need evidence. *Hard*, inarguable evidence."

Ravyn nodded. "And we need to cut off their human allies quickly."

Susan couldn't agree more.

"Yeah. It's going to be dangerous, but for now we have to get our hands on Jimmy's journal."

"What journal?"

She looked away as pain gripped her features. Clearing her throat, she met his gaze levelly, but he still saw the hurt she was trying so hard to hide. "My friend Jimmy, the investigator at the clinic, always kept a journal of his thoughts and what he did."

"Like a blog?"

"No, he was too private for that. This would probably be in his house somewhere. Either as a handwritten book or on his laptop. We need to search their house and find it."

Ravyn was skeptical. "Wouldn't the cops know about it?"

"I don't think so. Like I said, Jimmy was really private, especially around the guys he worked with. I don't think he'd have told them he kept a diary of all things."

She had a point. The gods knew he'd never admit to such a thing either. "But if they went to the trouble of killing him, wouldn't they have searched his place?"

"I'm willing to bet no. They think he's silenced and we're on the run. Searching his house might make someone suspicious."

Again, she had a good argument. But one thing, if the cops hadn't searched the house yet, they most likely would soon and whatever evidence or clues Jimmy might have left behind would be lost. So it was either get to it tonight or possibly lose it forever. "Okay, let's go. What time is it?"

She looked down at her watch. "Twelve thirty."

"Where does he live?"

"On Twenty-ninth Avenue West."

Good. Ravyn stretched before he sat up. "That gives us plenty of time to get there, search the place, and get back before dawn."

He noticed her hesitation as she sat on the mattress. "There's only one little problem with that."

He sighed as he caught her meaning. "I know. They don't want to let me back in here once I leave. But that's okay. I have a secret weapon."

She arched a brow. "And that is?"

"You," he said, smiling. "It was impressive how you got past my father earlier. You really should be a lawyer."

She blushed at his compliment before she set the book aside.

He stood up and held his hand out to her. Taking it, she let him pull her to her feet, but the tug was so forceful that she stumbled into him.

Ravyn's breath left him at the full frontal contact. Every inch of her was pressed up against his body, making him instantly hard and aching for a taste of her. There, for a moment, it made him almost want to be mortal again. There was just something about her that captivated him. "Sorry," he said, his voice faint. "I sometimes forget how strong I am."

"No problem."

But there was a problem, he wanted to pull her even closer to him and taste those lips again. *Get your head in the game, boy.*

Forcing himself to step back, he headed for the door and into the hallway. He led her upstairs toward the back of the club where his family should be away from human sight and hearing. From the sounds that echoed, it was obvious that at this time of night the club was hopping. The heavy, thumping beat radiated through his head, making it ache even more. But then he'd never been overly fond of this style of music anyway. He much preferred classic rock.

As they neared a partially opened door on their way out, he paused at the sound of his brothers' voices. And the more they spoke, the angrier he became.

"You know our laws, Dorian," Phoenix snarled. "He should be killed, now, while he's sleeping."

Dorian answered in a matter-of-fact tone. "The law of sanctuary—"

"Screw Savitar's laws. My mate and children are dead. The law of the jungle says—"

Ravyn pushed the door open. "The strongest survive. Always. And in my book, asshole, that's not you."

They jerked around to face him. He caught the look of shame on Dorian's face an instant before he hid it. But Phoenix was another matter. His eyes gleamed hatred. Ravyn braced himself as that look took him back to the night he'd died. To the look of tortured agony on Phoenix's face when he'd discovered his wife's body. She'd died beside their mother, trying to save her son and daughter.

Ravyn had stood in the doorway that night, too, paralyzed by the blood that soaked into the earthen floor of their cottage. Even though he'd been a warrior since the day he'd entered puberty and mastered his powers, he'd never seen such carnage. The humans hadn't been content to simply kill them. They had mutilated every member of their clan they had caught. Boy, girl, woman, child, infant . . . it hadn't mattered to them.

Phoenix had pulled his mate into his arms and roared with pain-filled horror. Until he'd turned on Ravyn.

"You did this!"

Overwrought with his own guilt and grief, he hadn't been able to move or to speak. His gaze had been morbidly caught by his mother's remains. By the look of terror that was permanently frozen on her beautiful face.

"Tell Isabeau the truth about us. About you. Ravyn, tell her what we are. Even if she is human, the Fates have chosen her to be your mate . . . surely, they know what they're doing. You must trust in the gods, my son. Always."

His mother's words had echoed in his ears that night as he stared at her through the tears that burned his cheeks.

And then Phoenix had lunged at him. At first, he'd thought nothing of it, until he felt the sharp, hot pain in his side. It was followed by another and another as Phoenix stabbed him repeatedly while Ravyn merely stood there, taking each blow without even raising his arms in defense.

"Die, you bloody bastard. I hope you spend eternity in Tartarus paying for what you've done!"

Dorian had grabbed Phoenix and pulled him back, but it was too late. The damage had been done.

Ravyn had staggered back as he coughed up his own blood. He'd looked down to see the lifeblood as it coated his hands and fled from his body to drip down his clothes, to the floor to blend in with the rest. He'd slipped on a pool of it and fallen to the floor.

The last sight that had carried him out of his human existence had been his own father coming forward to spit on him, then kick and curse him as his last breath had rattled painfully in his chest. It was a sight that haunted him still. A sight that came to him often in the light of day while he tried to sleep and tormented him anew.

But he was through being haunted by his guilt. Being hated for something he'd had no part in. His only mistake had been to trust a woman who'd told him that she loved him. He'd had no way of knowing she would betray him by calling down the wrath of her people before they formally mated.

And he was tired now. Tired of the hatred and the blame. It was time to put the past to rest.

Ravyn raked his brother with a sneer. "You want me dead, Phoenix, then let's go outside and end it once and for all. But I warn you now, I'm not feeling guilty anymore and I won't stand there and let you stab me again. You got your one shot in. That's it."

Phoenix moved to stand just before him. He narrowed his eyes. "You should have stayed dead."

Ravyn didn't flinch or blink. "No, I should never have let you kill me to begin with. I should have slapped your stupid ass down and gone for Isabeau and her people without losing my life over it. Or better yet, I should have killed you the night I took my vengeance for being such a selfish bastard. But I didn't. I forgave you for killing me, just as I forgave Dad for kicking me. But I'm tired of taking the high road while the rest of you spit at me. So stop crying, little boy, and suck it up like I've had to do."

He gave Phoenix a disgusted look. "You think you had it so bad? Trust me, you didn't. I lost everything that night, too, including *my* mate and my *entire* family. You and the rest at least had each other to console yourselves. What the fuck did I have? Not a damn thing. And now I'm sick of tiptoeing around you and I'm sick of being blamed for something I couldn't help. Had you been half the man you think you are, you'd have bonded yourself to Georgette and died with her."

Phoenix lunged at Ravyn only to have Dorian catch him and pull him back. "No, Nix, you know the law."

"Screw the law! Let me go, Dori!"

Dorian refused.

Ravyn shook his head at his brother while he struggled against Dorian. "Instead of bitching about what you lost, little boy, you should be damned grateful for what you had. You had almost a hundred years with Georgette. One. Hundred. Years. I didn't even get a day with Isabeau as my true mate and I've had nothing since then. So screw you, crybaby."

Phoenix lunged again, only to have Dorian catch him and pin him to the wall.

"Get out, Ravyn," Dorian said, his voice thick.

Ravyn stared at the twins. At one time in his life, he'd have died for them. Growing up, they had been more than just his brothers, they had been his best friends. The loss of that friendship still bothered him, but he'd learned to stop caring. Obviously he had never meant as much to them as they had to him.

"I'm going, Dorian, but I will be back."

Phoenix cursed as Dorian's face hardened. "You'll have to find someplace else to stay."

Ravyn shook his head. "There is nowhere else until I get this settled and you know it. By the Omegrion's law, you have to welcome me even if it sticks in your craw."

"I hate you!" Phoenix shouted. "You come back here and I'll kill you, you bastard."

"Take a number."

Dorian let out a tired breath as Ravyn took Susan's hand and led her to the door.

Susan didn't know what to say or do as they left the building and headed to the alley in the back. She could sense the pain inside Ravyn even though he was trying hard to hide it with an angry facade. Not that she blamed him. Given what she'd heard, she couldn't imagine how betrayed he must feel over his family's actions. How could they have turned on him like that?

Without breaking stride, Ravyn headed straight for a gray Porsche with tinted windows. Susan frowned as he opened his palm, waved it in a circle, and the door popped open.

"This may be an odd question, but whose car are we stealing?"

He didn't look up as he got into the car. "Phoenix's."

"How do you know it's his?"

"Look at the plate."

She did and sure enough, it had his name on it along with a bumper sticker for the club. Strangely amused, she got in. "Don't you think this is going to piss him off?"

"God, I hope so," Ravyn said in a sincere tone. "Otherwise it defeats the purpose of taking it."

"Won't he call the cops?"

"Nope. It would violate sanctuary. So let him simmer, we have a place to visit. Besides the cops won't recognize the car and the tinted windows will keep us hidden."

She shook her head at him as they buckled up. "I know it's a bit nosy—"

"A reporter being nosy? Damn, there's something you never see."

She ignored his sarcasm as he started the car without a key. That man had some eerie powers when they were working properly. "Yeah, back to my question. Why is your family in Seattle when it's obvious they don't want to be around you?"

Okay, that hadn't come out the way she meant for it to. Funny, it'd sounded much nicer in her head.

Ravyn cut an aggravated stare at her before he pulled out of the alley. "The Omegrion dictates where sanctuaries are to be set up, which means they didn't have a choice. If they wanted to be a sanctuary it was Seattle or nothing since this is where one was needed."

She considered that. "Why did they want to be a sanctuary?"

"I imagine it had to do with seeing most of our clan annihilated. A lot of my people tend to set them up whenever they're on the brink of extinction. It's a way of keeping our enemies at bay long enough for us to regain our numbers."

That made sense to her. "What about you? How did you end up here?"

"I was already here when they arrived. They just didn't know it. Acheron assigned me to this region almost two hundred years ago because it had enough open land to let me take on my cat form whenever I wanted, and Cael requested I get transferred with him. He didn't like the idea of coming out here solo."

"So the two of you have been friends a long time?"

He nodded. "He was the first Dark-Hunter I met after Acheron trained me. We were both stationed in London for a while and then later transferred to France, then Munich."

"Wow. You guys have been around."

"We had to move around a lot in the past because humans tended to get suspicious easier than they do now. Now most people are so absorbed by their own lives that they don't even bother to learn who's living next door to them, especially in a city."

She started to argue that until she realized just how right he was. She still didn't know the names of the couple who lived to the right of her, and they'd moved in almost two years ago.

The man had a vicious point.

"So where are we headed?" Ravyn asked.

"Hell in a handbasket."

He laughed. The sound of it was rich and deep. Gah, the man was so incredibly sexy. Especially with the moonlight shadowing the planes of his face. "Seriously."

"I was serious. It's exactly where we're headed," she said under her breath, but then louder, she added, "Forty-three thirty-five Twenty-ninth Avenue West."

"Nice area."

"Yeah, I know. Angie always had great taste in everything."

Wanting to distract herself, she focused on what Ravyn and his brothers had been talking about earlier. "So explain something to me. What is this mating thing you guys keep talking about?"

A dark shadow fell over his face, and she wasn't talking about the one from the moonlight. It was a strange light, as if her question bothered him on a deep, personal level. "Were-Hunters are different from humans."

No shit, Sherlock . . . But she kept that exact sarcasm to herself. "You mean other than the fact that you live for several hundred years, can turn into animals, time travel, and wave your hand to make freaky stuff happen?"

The corners of his lips turned up as if he was holding back a laugh. "Yeah, that, too. But unlike humans, we don't get the leisure of picking out our mates. The Moirae—"

"The who?"

"Greek Fates. They choose who we're mated to."

"Uh-huh . . ." she said, stretching the sound out. "Why am I suddenly channeling a cheesy Leo headline for this? Oh wait, I think I know. Maybe 'cause they're myths and not real?"

He gave her a peeved stare. "And neither are vampires, right?"

"Good point. Okay, they're real, too, and?"

"And they choose our mates."

If not for the ludicrousness of this day, she would recommend him for treatment. But there had to be truth in this even though it didn't make sense to her. "So what do they do? Jump here on earth, tap you on the shoulder, and say, 'Hey, bub, marry her.'"

"No. A matching symbol appears on the palms of the two people to let them know they're supposed to be mated."

"Intrusive and rude, but I'll go with it. So that's all there is?"

"Not exactly. Once the mark appears, we have three weeks to decide if we want to abide by it. If we do, then we sleep together and are mated. If not, then the symbol vanishes and we can never be mated to anyone else so long as we both live, and we can't have children."

She really didn't like the sound of that. "That sucks."

"You have no idea. The female can continue to have sex, but the male of the species is impotent until the day one of them dies."

"What if you're mated and one of you dies? Are you still bound to each other, or can the survivor go on to mate again?"

"Technically yes, but that rarely happens. One shot for a mate is pretty much all the Fates allow. They're bitchy that way. But at least death does free the survivor of the binding, which is why I can still have sex, even though I never finished the ritual with Isabeau."

"But you have no chance of being mated again?"

"Let's just say, I have a better chance of dying from grapefruit poisoning."

She laughed at that. "Oh, yeah, the Fates are definitely women. I love it."

"I'm glad you do, but I have to say it doesn't appeal to me. The idea of being impotent rather blows."

She could understand that. "So what makes the mark appear? You reach a certain age? You cross the street?"

"We have sex." He gave her a wicked grin.

"Yeah, right."

"No, seriously. The mark only appears after you've had sex with your predestined mate. Within a few hours it'll show up."

"And if you never have sex with your mate?"

"Then you never find your mate. You go the whole of your life without the chance of having children."

And she thought being human was hard. At least she had a choice about marriage and procreation. "You really have no control over the mating?"

"None whatsoever. Believe me, if we did, I would have never chosen a human for mine."

She didn't know why, but those words stung her. "You know, we're not all so bad."

He made a rude noise. "Pardon me if I reserve judgment on that."

Well, honestly, she couldn't blame him for his feelings. He'd been damaged rather badly by the actions of a single human. And it made her wonder what kind of woman would toss away a chance to have a man like Ravyn in her life. "So did you and Isabeau do the deed to finish off the mating?"

"No, I stupidly chose to be noble and to tell her what I was before I finished the ritual with her. Since she was human and it was the Renaissance period, she got a little . . . wiggy on me."

To say the least. "And the rest is history."

He nodded.

Man, she felt for him. How awful to lay himself bare before someone and have her betray him so badly. It made Alex leaving her because he didn't want to be tainted by her soiled reputation seem mild by comparison. His actions had been insensitive, but Isabeau's had been downright cruel.

"So what was the bonding thing you mentioned to Phoenix?" she asked.

"It's a special bond that we can make with our mates if both parties choose it. It combines our life forces together so that if one of us dies, the other dies, too. Instantly."

"Romantic and scary."

"Yes, it is. On the night our village was attacked, it was how we knew what was happening. Several members of our clan who were with us just keeled over. One minute they were with us and the next, they were dead at our feet for no known reason. Since so many of them fell, we knew someone was killing our families."

She let out a long breath as she tried to imagine the horror of that. "I'm really sorry, Ravyn."

"Thanks." But still she noted the way his grip tightened on the steering wheel and it made him ache for him.

They fell silent while they made their way over to Angie and Jimmy's. This time of night, the neighborhood was absolutely silent, with only an occasional house showing a light or TV on. Susan had always liked staying up late at night. There was something peaceful and pristine about the world. The silence was almost tangible.

As they neared the house, Susan spotted a patrol car parked on a curb. "Looks like they're watching the place."

Ravyn nodded. "After the day we've had, I'd expect no less."

Well, there was that.

He drove them past the patrol car, down the street, turned the corner, then parked. "We can go in the back way on foot."

"You know, it's a pity that with all the magic you guys have you can't just pop us into the house."

"Actually a typical Were-Hunter could."

"But you can't?"

He shook his head. "Not anymore. When I became a Dark-Hunter, I lost that power. It seems Artemis wants us to live chronologically, so I can no longer teleport. But I do have stronger powers in other ways and in cat form, unlike other Dark-Hunters, I can survive sunlight. It's not comfortable, but it doesn't kill me."

"Hence the burning cat-hair smell in my car earlier?"

"Exactly."

Susan watched the streetlight cut across the handsome planes of his face. Even though their time was limited, she had to admit he was stunning. And she would give anything to be able to kiss those lips again . . . to drape herself over that body of his until they were both sweaty and spent. But given his feelings about humans, she figured she was only one step up from an Apollite mauling him.

Sighing, she put that thought away. The last thing she needed after this day was rejection. "I guess life is nothing but trade-offs, huh?"

"What's your trade-off?" he asked as he opened his car door.

She thought about that as she got out and shut her door without slamming it. "I guess I got to keep my sanity and life, in exchange for working a really shitty job."

That seemed to amuse him. "Leo isn't that bad, is he?"

Susan wrapped her arms around herself as they doubled back toward Angie's house. "Actually, Leo is an unpolished gem most days. I just hate working for that paper so much that daydreams of torching it are a constant fixation for me."

Ravyn grabbed her and pulled her down behind a shrub as a car came down the street. The two of them huddled there while they listened to it passing by at an excruciatingly slow pace.

Afraid of being caught this close to their destination, Susan held her breath until the car vanished out of sight. Her gaze fell down to Ravyn's taut hand that held her in place. He had long, slender fingers that warmed her even if his grip was a little too intense.

As if he heard her thoughts, he loosened his hold and rubbed her wrist soothingly. That little gesture meant a lot to her as he peeped up to look.

Without another word, he motioned her forward and led her to Angie's house. They cut across the neighbor's backyard to avoid the patrol car that might see them if they approached from the front. Ravyn picked her up effortlessly and helped her over the fence before he jumped over easily.

She knew he was a cat, but whenever he did things like that it was almost spooky. Crouching low, he kept them in the shadows as they headed up Angie's deck. Again he did the strange hand gesture that allowed him to push open the sliding glass door without breaking into it.

Susan entered the house first. As she reached for a light switch, she caught herself. "This is useless. I can't see anything and if I turn on a light, the police will see it."

"It's okay." She was startled to find Ravyn so close to her that his breath fell against her cheek as he spoke. The warmth of his body reached out to her and actually calmed her nerves. "I have perfect vision in the dark. Tell me what I'm looking for."

Closing her eyes, she summoned a mental diagram of what the house looked like. "Upstairs, the second bedroom on the right is set up as an office. Jimmy's laptop should be there. Grab it and look around for a leather-bound journal that should be within easy reach."

"Anything else?"

"I don't know. If you see something else that he might have used to jot down notes, grab it."

He reached out and gently pushed her toward a bar stool. "Okay. Wait here and I'll be back."

Grateful that he'd helped to ground her in the darkness, Susan nodded as she leaned against the breakfast counter. She listened to Ravyn moving stealthily up the stairs . . . like a cat.

Yeah. This was an odd life she was having.

And as she glanced around the darkened house where all too familiar furniture faded into the shadows, grief settled deep in her chest. The last time she was here had been Angie's birthday a few weeks back. Jimmy had been teasing Angie about how she was becoming Merlin and aging backwards.

"You get more beautiful every year."

This had been the third time Angie had turned thirty-five. Angie had taken their jokes in stride as she reminded Susan that she wasn't that far behind her.

What she wouldn't give to be able to go back and live that night one more time. . . .

"Oh, Angie," she breathed, aching with the loss of them. How could they be gone? It was such a waste. Such a senseless tragedy.

"Don't think about it." And yet it was impossible not to. She wasn't supposed to grow old without her friends. They were her family. Without them, she felt completely lost and alone.

Adrift.

In spite of her resolve, she felt the tears starting to fall. Wiping them away, she hated herself for the weakness. They had something to do and here she was crying like a little girl.

"Susan?"

She jumped at the deep voice in her ear. "Ravyn! Don't startle me like that." She felt a muscular arm wrap around her and pull her close to his hard body. The scent of him soothed her even while it tickled her nose.

"It's okay."

But she knew it wasn't. It would never be okay that they were gone. Yet it was kind of him to try to offer comfort.

Then again, if anyone knew pain, it was the man holding her. He, too, had lost everything. Grateful for his presence, she leaned back against his hard chest and hugged his steely arm against her breasts. She was silent as she fought down the tears and drew a shaky breath.

Clearing her throat, she gave his arm a gentle squeeze, then stepped away. "Did you get it?"

"Yeah. It was just where you said. Now let's get out of here before someone sees us."

He adjusted the small box under one arm, then took her hand and led her back outside, to the deck. They crossed the yard silently, and headed back down the street to where they'd left the car. Every single step of the way, she kept expecting someone to catch them. She held her breath, waiting for the police or the Daimons to somehow discover where they were.

By the time they reached the Porsche, she was afraid her nerves were completely shot.

She got in first and buckled up before Ravyn placed the box on her lap. She frowned as he shut the door and walked over to the other side. At least until she saw what was on top. . . .

Grief and joy mixed inside her and closed her throat into a tight knot. It was a framed picture of her, Angie, and Jimmy from last summer when they'd been deep-sea fishing. She and Angie were pointing to the giant swordfish Jimmy had caught and he was standing there like a he-man with his arms up.

Clutching the picture to her, she looked over at Ravyn and was overwhelmed by his thoughtfulness. "Thank you."

He simply inclined his head to her as he started the car and headed them toward the Serengeti.

Susan put the picture back in the box and just tried to keep it together as her anger built over the injustice of their deaths. She wanted revenge. *You've got to keep yourself calm, Sue.* But it was hard. She'd always hated emotional basket cases, and yet that was what she felt like tonight. "I'm sorry, Ravyn."

"For what?"

"That you're stuck with the neurotic Susan. I'm usually much more together than this."

To her surprise, he reached over and took her hand into his. "Babe, don't you dare apologize to me. I have nothing but respect for the grace and strength you've had today. I don't know many men who could have held up as well as you have."

Those words made her heart pound. "Thank you."

He squeezed her hand before he let go to shift gears. Susan wiped at her eyes as she watched the streetlights cut across his face, bringing out his features. He was exceptional. But it made her wonder what he'd be like if he was just an average guy on the street.

No, she couldn't imagine that. He was so much larger than life. A guy like this could never be average. And it was why she knew a woman like her could never dare to have more than a moment with a guy like him.

Ravyn didn't speak as he drove them through the quiet Seattle streets. But he could feel Susan with every inch of his being. The Dark-Hunter inside him could hear her heart beating. Could feel her blood flowing through her veins. The predator sensed her unease and sadness. The man just wanted to kiss those lips she had parted and hold her until she smiled at him again.

It was hard to think straight with her so close to him. He'd never seen any woman more beautiful.

He dropped his gaze to the hand she had on the box. A hand he wanted to nibble and then guide down to cup him until she stroked the part of him that ached for a taste of her lush body. But an animal like him could never dare to touch something as precious as she. Susan was one of the very few decent humans he'd ever met. And she deserved much better than something like him. Shifting in the seat, he clenched his teeth. This wasn't the time to let his hormones lead him.

Sure it is. . . .

He wanted to growl at himself. Instead, he pushed the accelerator, needing to put some distance between them before he gave in to the feral need he had to have sex with her.

Not soon enough for comfort's sake, he parked the car right

where Phoenix had left it. He helped Susan out of the car and headed back inside the club. The hallway wasn't as loud as it'd been earlier. No doubt the club was winding down a bit, but it still had a good-sized crowd. He could hear the thumping beat of the dance music. The air was thick with the smells of alcohol, cheap perfume, and greasy food. Ravyn kept waiting for one of his "family" members to appear and try to drive him out.

As they rounded a corner, they were almost run over by Erika.

"Sorry," she said as she started past them.

"Where are you going?" Ravyn asked. Her father would have Ravyn's head if something happened to her while he was in Hawaii.

"Out."

"Out where?"

She sighed heavily. "To the dance floor, if you must know. I want to boogie till I puke."

He gave her a suspicious glare. "Don't you have school tomorrow?"

"Relax, Dad. Leo said that I should stay here until the threat is over. They're afraid I might get nabbed by one of the Doulosi."

"The what?" Susan asked.

Ravyn turned toward her. "It's a term for the humans who help the Apollites or Daimons."

"Oh."

Erika took a step toward the door that led to the club, then paused. "Oh hey, if you guys get hungry, tell the woman in the kitchen, Terra, and she'll make you something. I have to say the burgers here are delish."

"Thanks," Susan said, but Erika was already gone.

Ravyn took the box from Susan's hands. "Why don't you get us something to eat and I'll get this laid out in our room below so we can examine it."

"Okay."

Susan watched as Ravyn headed down the stairs, then followed the sounds of pans and glasses clanking until she located the kitchen. She wasn't sure if the people working in here were human or not. It was really weird to never know anymore.

"Can I help you?"

She turned to see a tall brunette woman. She reminded Susan of a chic model with extremely intense eyes. Crystal blue, they seemed to glow as they watched her like a predator in the wild.

Susan refused to be intimidated even though the woman was doing her best. "Erika said we could get something to eat."

The woman looked a bit reluctant as she glanced around the room in a very catlike manner. After a minute, she slid her gaze back to Susan. "All right, but don't let Dori know I fed you. The last thing I want is to hear about it from him."

This must be Terra and she was grateful that Terra had a heart. "Thanks."

"No problem."

Susan stood back as the woman made two plates of burgers and fries for them. "Are you part of the Kontis family?"

She held her palm up to show Susan a really cool geometric sign on her palm. "Dorian's my mate. I'm Terra."

So that's what the sign looked like. It was lovely. "Nice to meet you."

Terra snorted. "Yeah, right. You don't like being here any more than we like your being here—I can smell your emotions bleeding out of your pores. But that's okay. At least we all know where we stand." Terra handed her the plates. "You want a couple of beers?"

"That would be heaven."

Terra brushed her hands off on her apron, then pulled out two bottles from an ice tub behind her. She put them on the tray and indicated for Susan to place the plates there, too.

As soon as Susan did, Terra handed the tray to her. "You got it?"

"Yes, thanks."

Terra nodded before she went back to instructing one of the waiters to take an order of pretzels out to a table.

Susan took the tray and headed back downstairs to their room. Ravyn was already booting up the laptop. When he saw the beers, his face actually lit up like a child seeing Santa for the first time.

"You must have read my mind."

Susan smiled at him as she handed him a beer. "Terra did."

"Terra?"

"It appears your brother Dorian has a mate."

His jaw actually dropped. "Really?"

"Yep. She's an interesting woman. Kind of rough around the edges, but at least she fed us."

"I won't argue that, especially as good as it smells."

Susan set the tray on the floor before she pulled Jimmy's laptop toward her. "So what all did you find in his office?"

"Not too much. Some letters, a few file folders, a couple of leather journals, and the laptop."

And one picture that he didn't mention. Disregarding that thought, she started looking through his laptop file folders, but as she did so a wave of unbelievable pain engulfed her. These were Jimmy's private files. His whole life was on this computer. His tax records, family photos, e-mails to friends, jokes . . .

Everything.

She felt Ravyn's hand on her shoulder. "You want me to do it?"

"No," she said past the stinging lump in her throat as her anger returned. "I owe this to him."

Ravyn was amazed by her strength and resolve. He'd never seen anything like it. "Okay, while you search, I'm going to call the other Dark-Hunters and check in with them."

She nodded.

Not sure if she'd really heard him or not, he pulled his phone out and called Acheron. As before, there was no answer. Damn. He could really use some advice from the head honcho about how to handle this situation. If there was one thing in life Acheron seemed to understand, it was the Daimon mind-set.

Then one by one, Ravyn called the rest of the Seattle-based Dark-Hunters to find out that they were all on patrol, being vigilant.

The only one who didn't answer was Aloysius. A Scottish Dark-Hunter who'd been in Seattle since 1875.

Ravyn cursed.

"You okay?"

He looked at Susan and nodded even though he felt ill about it. "I think I know who they killed . . . he was a good man." Shaking his head in disgust, he moved closer to her. "Have you found anything?"

"Not yet. Just a few notes about things that disappeared out of his files at work. Some missing evidence. But no theory about who's behind it or why."

Ravyn leaned forward to read, but before he could, he heard something slam shut above.

More than that, he felt a wave of mass rage and fear in the air. The scent of it was overwhelming.

There was serious trouble above. . . .

CHAPTER TEN

Ravyn rushed upstairs, then froze with Susan one step behind him. He held her back with one arm while he stared through the crack in the door. He could see three uniformed officers and a tall, beautiful blond woman who was dressed all in black with the demeanor of a fighter. She appeared to be their leader. If not for the fact that she didn't have fangs and didn't set off his Dark-Hunter senses, he would think her a Daimon or Apollite.

"What is this?" Dorian asked as he looked at a piece of paper. Phoenix and their father stood just behind him.

The woman narrowed her gaze on Dorian. "It's a search warrant for this club. We have reason to believe that you're harboring a wanted fugitive."

Ravyn felt as ill as Dorian looked. They'd been so concerned about the Daimons coming after them that they hadn't even thought about what the humans could do. A search warrant was the one thing they couldn't hide from. One of the rules of a sanctuary was that they had to abide by human law.

Dorian would be arrested as well as him and Susan. . . .

"There's nothing here," his father said angrily. "This is total bullshit."

Ignoring his outburst, the woman turned to the officer on her right. "Get the others and tell them to be careful while they search. Remember both of them are wanted for murder and they could very easily be armed. If anyone gets in the way, arrest them."

Dorian lifted his hand in the gesture that said he was trying to manipulate the woman's thoughts. "There's no need to search our club. There's nothing here for you."

The woman gave him a peeved stare. "We'll see about that, won't we?"

Damn, she was too strong for them to tamper with her will. This seriously sucked.

His father turned and glared at the crack where Ravyn watched as if he knew exactly where Ravyn was while Phoenix told his father they should hand them over in Arcadian.

The cop turned, walked over to the door that led outside, and opened it. As he did so, Ravyn did a double take. Instead of a human standing there, he saw the one person he hadn't seen in centuries . . . and he meant *centuries.*

Susan pushed past Ravyn so that she could peer through the crack to see what was going on. She frowned as she saw the woman in front of Dorian and her heart stopped beating. "She was at the Happy Hunting Ground."

Ravyn scowled at Susan. "What?"

She lowered her tone so that only Ravyn could hear. "She was with the group of Daimons who tranked you."

"Are you sure?"

"Absolutely." And she was, too. She'd never forget the woman who actually put Cael's wife to shame in terms of beauty and grace.

But Susan's gaze was snagged away from the woman to the man who came into the back room with an aura so powerful that it instantly commanded everyone's rapt attention. Not to mention he had the determined stride of hell wrath and damnation. It was obvious he was here for blood and making no attempt to hide it. Wearing a black and blue scuba suit that showed off a lean, ripped body, and dripping wet, that man had a face that was both beautifully chiseled and rugged. He had at least a week's growth of whiskers and shoulder-length dark brown hair.

"You," he said to the cop on his left as he stopped beside the woman, "go outside and have a donut with your buddies."

The woman scowled her displeasure at him.

She raked him with a sneer that said she held him in the same estimation as something stuck to the bottom of her shoe. "Who do you think you are?"

His lips twisted into a mocking grin. "Oh, baby, don't ask *me* that question. I know exactly who and what I am . . . and more to the point, what I'm capable of." He wiped at a bead of water on his cheek before he spoke again. This time, his low, feral tone was sinister and cold and filled with his anger. "How dare you bring your prissy little ass into one of my clubs and pull this shit. You're lucky you're still breathing."

She was aghast at him. "I will have you arrested."

"And I will have your ass for breakfast, little girl," he sneered. "I'm not Stryker. There's no fraternal love in my heart for you. In fact, there's no love in my heart for anyone . . . much." He brushed his wet bangs back from his dark brown eyes. "Now, I just sent your boys in the alley off to Bainbridge Island. They're not sure how they got there and lucky for you, they have no memory of ever seeing you. For your sake, and that of your half-ass brother, let's keep it that way. You pull this shit again, and I don't care who you serve or who you think you know, you're dead. Got me?"

The woman appeared a bit subdued. "How do you know about Stryker?"

He gave her a dry stare. "I know everything about everything and before I dry off completely, which is something I truly hate, you better go outside, collect Trates, and have both your asses out of here or I'm going to lose what little patience I have." The air around him seemed to snap with powerful energy that appeared to be emanating from within him. "You will play by the rules I've set up for sanctuary, or I'll use your entrails for armbands. Understand me? Don't you *ever* chance exposing the Weres to the humans again."

The anger returned to her as she stiffened her spine. "If you know everything as you claim, then you know you can't stop me."

He laughed at her. "Yeah, and the next time you're fetching for

Auntie, tell her Savitar said hi and watch her bitch slap you for even bringing her to my attention."

"How do you—"

He cut her words off by moving to stand so close to her that she had to take a step back and crane her neck to look up at him. "I told you, little Satara, I know everything about everything. I even know about the goddess who really does scare the shit out of you. And you should be afraid of her. Trust me. The Destroyer earned her name for a reason, and it wasn't by posing. You might win this little battle you're trying to fight, but ask yourself if it's going to be worth the cost of it."

"I don't know what you're talking about."

An evil laugh emanated from deep within his throat. "Yes, you do. And when you find yourself back in Kalosis in a few seconds with a wide-eyed Trates and a pissed-off Stryker, remember that I'm watching you and that the Weres are off-limits in this game. You want to fuck with Artemis, fuck with Artemis. You want to fuck with me . . . make out your will."

The woman instantly vanished.

Savitar looked past Dorian, Phoenix, and their father, to the door where Susan and Ravyn were. "You two can come out now. They're gone."

Susan walked out first, but as she approached Savitar, the hair on the back of her neck rose. There was something so powerful and scary about him that it actually made her want to run for the door. The very air around him crackled with some kind of unholy energy. It was like standing next to a thrumming nuclear generator . . . that could explode and destroy you and the entire city at any second.

"Savitar," Ravyn said in a surprisingly friendly tone, extending his hand out to him. "It's been a while."

"Yes, it has." He shook Ravyn's hand, then turned to look at Dorian and his family. "No offense, Dorian. Oh, what the hell, take all the offense you want, it's not like I give a shit." He looked back at Ravyn. "I miss the days before you crossed over to the dark side. Back when you sat on the Omegrion, Rave. You were actually highly entertaining. Dorian, on the other hand, has a major stick up his ass."

"Glad to know I had some purpose."

A strange light darkened Savitar's eyes. "You have more than you've ever dreamed of."

Ravyn stiffened. "What do you mean?"

Savitar tilted his head. "Dorian and others, take a break." Before they could speak or move, they vanished.

Susan widened her eyes at the way Savitar seemed to be able to do whatever he wanted with people regardless of their will.

"Don't worry," Savitar said to her as if he knew her thoughts. "I won't send you off without warning. Just stand there and be awed by my beauty. It's the safest mode around me."

Yeah. . . . "Can I ask—"

"You're not ready for that answer," he said, cutting her off. "The only person who needs to know what I am already knows. That would be me. I like to keep the rest of the world guessing."

All things considered, she strangely liked this enigmatic man, even if he did have a titanic ego and frightening powers.

"But back to Ravyn." He placed a heavily tattooed arm over Ravyn's shoulders and hugged him like an affectionate brother. "You're going to do me a favor."

"I am?"

"Yes." Savitar stepped away to clap him on the back. "I have a small matter that I need you to help me with."

"You need *my* help?"

"Astonishing, isn't it?"

"You could say that." Ravyn exchanged a puzzled look with her as she wondered what a man like this could possibly want with Ravyn. "So what is this favor?"

"I have a friend who has a friend who needs to be trained."

"Trained for what?"

"To be a Dark-Hunter."

Ravyn was stunned by his words. For the first time in centuries, he was beginning to wonder about Savitar's mental capacity. "I can't train another Dark-Hunter. We weaken each other's powers."

"Normally, this would be true, but this particular Dark-Hunter is a little different from the others."

Now that made him nervous. Different wasn't necessarily a good thing, especially in this work. "Different how?"

"In many ways. He was entrusted to me, but I've found that training someone to fight just isn't my forte." Savitar screwed up his face. "It actually dawned on me that I don't fight. I just kill whatever annoys me, and it's over. Not to mention the kid is seriously cramping my style . . . which seriously annoys the hell out of me, and if I kill him, it'll just open a whole can of worms I don't want to deal with. Oh, and he's taken to complaining daily about how he wants to start training, wah, wah, wah." He sighed. "I just can't be bothered with it. Too many waves to surf . . . know what I mean?"

Not really. "Uh-huh, and who is this kid?"

Savitar snapped his fingers.

Susan gaped as a good-looking man in his mid- to late twenties appeared next to her. Standing a good six foot four, he had dark brown hair and black eyes, but what held her attention most was the double bow and arrow Dark-Hunter mark that covered his neck and part of his extremely unhappy face.

"What the hell is this, Savitar?" the man demanded.

"You wanted to be trained, Nick. Meet your new trainer. Ravyn Kontis, this is Nick Gautier."

Ravyn gaped at the name that was meaningless to Susan.

"Nick Gautier? The New Orleans Squire who went missing?"

Savitar gave him a droll look. "He's obviously not missing. Open your eyes, man. He's standing right in front of you."

Ravyn scowled. "No offense, Savitar, but this is a really bad time. I'm kind of in the middle of a situation here."

"Yeah, I know. You're basically screwed. But Nick can actually help you with this matter. Not to mention the fact that you're missing a Dark-Hunter. He can be the replacement."

"Can I ask one question?"

Savitar gave a heavy sigh. "I know you, Ravyn. I've known you for centuries, and Nick is a special member of this world. There's no one else I would trust to train him."

Ravyn wanted to protest, but one thing he knew about Savitar was that he didn't like to be questioned. As he said, he tended to kill things that annoyed him, and questions definitely annoyed him.

Savitar moved to stand beside Nick. "You've been entertaining, Gautier. At least most of the time. And you play a mean-ass game of pool. Before I leave you, I have two quick things I want you to keep in mind. One, stay away from the Charonte demons. They're really bad for you."

Nick didn't appear amused by his words of advice. "And the second?"

A wave of energy peaked in the room as Savitar's face lost all humor. "Is the life you seek to take worth the one you could one day create?"

Nick scowled. "What's that supposed to mean?"

"You'll learn." There was something in Savitar's eyes that looked like regret as he clapped Nick on the back. "Remember, Nick, there are only two people in the universe I care for . . . and you're not one of them."

"Damn," Ravyn said, with a hint of humor. "Savitar, that's cold."

Savitar took that in stride. "No one has ever accused me of being anything else. For good reason, I might add."

Ravyn nodded. That was certainly true. He glanced to Susan, who seemed to be completely subdued by Savitar's presence. "Before you go, can I ask one last question?"

"You can ask."

"Do you know where Acheron is?"

Savitar answered without hesitation. "Yes."

He waited for Savitar to continue. When he didn't, Ravyn prompted him, "And where would that be?"

"He's tied up at the moment."

"Tied up how?"

"Double-knotted to a bedpost, not that it's any of your business. That boy was always too trusting for his own good. You'd think by now he'd know better. But no. He's got to be stupid. Personally, I'd tie the bitch up, muzzle her, and ride her around the room with spurs on, but no one ever asks my opinion, do they? No. What do I know? I'm only omniscient."

Was any of that supposed to make sense? Before Ravyn could ask anything more, Savitar vanished.

He stood there with Nick standing between him and Susan. The air around Nick was rife with anger and agitation. It was obvious the man wanted to be anywhere but here.

Ravyn released a perturbed breath. "This is awkward."

"Yeah," Nick agreed. "I'm really getting sick of being dumped on strangers."

He could just imagine. "So why isn't Acheron training you?"

Hatred flared deep in the Cajun's eyes as he curled his lip. "You'll have to ask the bastard that for yourself. Seems he's not man enough to face me after he screwed me over."

Ravyn sucked his breath in between his teeth. He only knew Nick vicariously through the Dark-Hunter bulletin boards that Nick had run as a Squire. In those days, Nick had been friendly enough, if not a bit acidic at times. Then one night, about two years ago, Nick had gone missing. No one had known what had happened to him.

Until now.

Susan gave him a sympathetic smile. "I take it you and Acheron aren't on the best of terms."

"You think?" Nick looked around the room as if trying to place it. "Where am I?"

Ravyn exchanged an awkward glance with Susan before he answered. "Seattle."

Nick frowned in her direction. "And who's she?"

Something about that look and his tone greatly perturbed her. "You know, I am right here in the room, not outside looking in, and to answer your question, I'm a Squire."

"Bully for you," he said coldly. Nick curled his lip. "What's the date?"

Ravyn felt a stab of reluctance go through him. From his past when he was a member of the Omegrion, he knew that Savitar's home, which was a floating island, existed outside of traditional time. Nick most likely had no idea how long he'd been gone or, more to the point, what had been happening in New Orleans over the last few months. "June 3, 2006."

Nick's mouth dropped. "I'm missing almost two years of my life."

"No, Nick," Ravyn said quietly. "You're missing two years of your death."

He grew quiet at the reminder.

"Let me get Dorian," Susan said, her blue eyes filled with sympathy for a man she didn't even know. "I'm sure he has some place to put you." But before she could move, the back door opened to show Otto coming in with a large box in his arms.

He took one look at Nick and froze in place.

Time hung still as the two men faced each other with a shared look of stunned shock. It was obvious that they never thought they'd see each other again.

Nick was the first to recover himself. "Otto? What are you doing here?"

"Me? I thought you were dead. . . ." He set the box down as he approached Nick like a man seeing a ghost for the first time. He offered Nick his hand and when he took it, Otto pulled him against his chest for a man hug.

When they pulled apart, Otto's gaze narrowed on the bow and arrow tattoo on Nick's face. "Jesus, it's true. You are a Dark-Hunter."

Nick's features hardened as if he hated that fact. "Why are you in Seattle?"

"I—uh . . . I got transferred up here."

"Why?"

A veil fell over Otto's face. Ravyn had to give him credit, he had the best poker face he'd ever seen. Otto, along with a whole crew of New Orleans Squires, had been evacuated out of the city just before Katrina hit. Since then, they'd been slowly moving back to Louisiana, with Otto, Tad, and Kyl being the last to go. They'd been kept here a little longer while the New Orleans Council recouped. Not to mention that the Daimons hadn't been very active there since the hurricane.

"Council's orders," Otto said in a bland tone.

Nick nodded as if in understanding.

Otto's brow furrowed as he continued to stare at Nick like he was a bad science experiment. "What are you doing here?"

"I'm supposed to train him," Ravyn said.

The poker face slipped as Otto's jaw went slack. "You?"

"Apparently."

"What about Ash?"

Nick cursed. "He's recused himself." There was so much tension in the air that it was tangible.

"We need to find Nick some place to sleep," Susan said, trying to alleviate the unspoken hostility.

Otto shifted the box in his hands. "He can bunk in my room. I won't be sleeping for a while anyway." He stepped past Nick, toward the stairs.

They disappeared for a second before Otto came back alone.

He neared the two of them, then spoke in a low whisper. "Whatever you do, don't mention Katrina to Nick. I don't think he needs to know what's happened to New Orleans until he gets some bearing on being back here again. Not to mention, he was originally from the Ninth Ward."

"Don't worry," Ravyn said. "I'm not about to tell him."

Nodding, Otto left them again.

"Are you okay?" Susan asked.

Ravyn shrugged. "Honestly, I have no idea. Any more than I understand why Savitar would release Nick to me. How can I train him with all the crap that's going on?"

"Like he said, Savitar trusts you."

Yeah, but he couldn't imagine why. This day made no sense whatsoever to him. Tired and baffled, he held his hand out to her so that they could return downstairs. "C'mon. We still have a lot of stuff to cover."

Ash *growled low* in his throat as he twisted at the rope that held his arm to Artemis's bedpost. At the moment, he hated her.

No, wait, he basically hated her every moment of every day, but at this particular time, he really wanted to rip her head off and play a few games of baseball with it. He stared at the gold hourglass that was set on the shelf across from the bed and watched as the last few grains of black sand fell through it.

He should have known that nothing with Artemis would ever be simple. When he'd made the bargain with her, he forgot to stipulate that *she* had to stay in the room for a full hour. Instead, she'd finished her fifth orgasm, then vanished out from under him before he could uphold his part.

But not before she'd tied him to her bed to keep him from going after her. Leaning his head back, he ground his teeth in frustration. Yes, he could use his powers to free his arm, but whenever he did that, Artemis went wild on him because the other gods on Olympus could feel it. They weren't "supposed" to know that he was here.

Yeah, right. They'd known for centuries that he stayed with her in her temple, but all of them pretended ignorance so that they didn't have to deal with Artemis's temper tantrums. *If only I were that lucky. . . .*

Dressed in a long, flowing white gown, Artemis appeared beside the bed. She feigned shock as she saw her hourglass that was now empty. "Oh no, did the hour end?"

"You know it did."

She tsked. "Then I guess we have to start over, don't we?"

"Artie . . ."

"Don't take that tone with me, Acheron," she said sullenly. "You accepted the terms of your release." She freed his arm, then rubbed at the bruise on his wrist that had been caused by the rope. "Now, now, love, don't be petulant."

Ash recovered his features to the typical stoicism he wore around her. Fine. Now that he knew the rules, he could turn them on her. Rising from the bed, he went to the hourglass and turned it over.

Artemis watched him with a curious frown.

Ash returned to her side and reached for the brooch that held her dress over her body. He opened the brooch and let her dress fall in a puddle at her feet. "Now where were we?"

Susan *caught herself* as her head dropped down. Blinking, she stifled a yawn. Ravyn reached around her and took her hand from the keyboard.

"Let's call it a night."

"But—"

"Susan, you've been a trooper, but it's already dawn and you look like you're ready to keel over from exhaustion. You can't keep going like this. You're as likely to overlook something as you are to find it."

As much as she hated to admit it, he was right. She'd read the last paragraph at least a dozen times and she still wasn't sure what it said. Her head hurt and it was all she could do to keep her eyes open. "I guess you're right."

This time she didn't bother to hide her yawn as Ravyn shut down the computer for her.

"Did you find anything?" he asked her.

"Not yet. There are a couple of entries about some of the missing students whose parents called trying to locate them. Jimmy wrote that he took the inquiries to his chief only to be told not to worry about runaways. The chief told him he needed to focus his attention on other cases. That's odd, right? I mean, if he's covering up for Daimons, it makes sense. Otherwise why wouldn't he let Jimmy keep investigating their whereabouts?"

"I have no idea. Dealing with the police force isn't something I have much experience with. I tend to avoid them as much as possible."

Susan rubbed her eyes before she helped Ravyn pick up the files he'd been reading through. "What about you?"

"Not much to say. Just case notes. There are a few that mention a couple of witnesses who changed their testimony about an investigation he had that involved some woman he'd been trailing. But no real names or information. It's so vague that I'm not even sure what he was referring to."

"C'mon, Jimmy," she breathed as she put away the file folders. "Tell me something we need to solve this."

Ravyn pulled her up against his hard chest. It was the most soothing thing she'd ever known. And if she closed her eyes, she could almost pretend they were something more than strangers. But that was stupid. She knew better. "Enough, Susan. You need sleep."

"I know." She looked down at the uninviting mattress.

Ravyn got up and started for the door.

She frowned at him. "Where are you going?"

"To tell Dorian to set you up in a bedroom upstairs where you can get a decent day's rest."

"Why?"

He gave her a "duh" stare. "You're not allergic to daylight. There's no need for you to stay down here in this disgusting hole with me. At least one of us should get a good sleep."

His thoughtfulness warmed her. Susan caught his hand and pulled him back into the room. "It's okay. I'd rather be here with you."

"Susan—"

"Sh," she said, placing a finger over his lips. "Don't argue. Besides, I'm too tired to climb those stairs one more time and I'm sure you are, too." She pulled him back into the room and closed the door. "We can be grown-ups about this."

Ravyn wasn't so sure about that. All he could focus on was those lips that begged him for a kiss. He glanced down at her body and felt his own stirring in response. Not to mention the scent of her hung heavy around his animal's senses.

Yeah, he could be grown-up about this. . . .

Switching off the light, he allowed her to pull him down on the mattress. He grabbed the blanket and covered them. Then he turned his back to her, hoping that might ease some of the temptation.

She sneezed. "Ravyn?"

"Yes?"

"Could you roll over?"

His heart skipped a beat at her question. "Why?"

"I'm allergic to your hair and I have to sleep on my left side. I don't know why, but it's the only way I can rest."

That really wasn't the answer he'd been looking for. He was actually hoping she'd wanted him to flip over for her to molest him.

Unfortunately, he wasn't that lucky. "Are you serious?"

She sneezed again. "Yeah. I'm rather positive."

Great. Just great. She was allergic to him. Well, that was a new one. Sighing heavily, he rolled over only to realize that facing her was a big mistake. It brought the soft, delicate scent of her skin right up to him. Not to mention that his hand was dangerously close to the breast he wanted to explore.

She opened her eyes to look up at him with an expression that said she wasn't any more immune to him than he was to her. Normally that invitation would kick him into action.

But she was a Squire, completely forbidden fruit, and the last thing he needed was to be physical with a human he had feelings for. Not that he was completely sure what those feelings were, but she wouldn't be a one-night stand for him. He couldn't just sleep with her and leave. It was wrong, and it was the last thing either of them need.

Which meant he had to keep his hands to himself. Frustrated, he moved to the other side and lay back-to-back with her. "Is this okay?"

"Perfect," she said in a voice that was so laden with sleep he wasn't even sure if she was awake.

He smiled at the grogginess of her voice. "Night, Susan."

"Night, gorgeous." The words were barely out of her mouth before he heard her fall into a deep sleep.

How he wished it were that easy for him, but his erection was throbbing so badly that it was all he could do to lie still and not attend to it in some way.

Closing his eyes, he imagined Susan in his arms, her naked body pressed up against his as he sank himself deep inside her. Or better yet, her on top of him, riding him slow and easy as they both sought their own piece of paradise. . . .

It was an image that both tormented and soothed him as he felt sleep slowly overtake him.

W*ho exactly is* Savitar?" Satara asked as she faced an angry Stryker in the main hall at Kalosis. The dark hall was empty except for her and her brother, who sat on his throne, thrumming his fingers against the carved arm as he eyed her with malice.

"That would be the question *d'éternité*, little sister. Basically he is what makes everything evil and otherwise quake in its boots. I've never met a god yet who didn't flinch at his approach, and that includes the bastard who donated his sperm to create us. Savitar scares the gods so much that they won't even speak his name for fear of drawing his attention to them. Ironically, the only person who doesn't fear him is Acheron. No idea why."

That didn't bode well for her plans. As a handmaiden to Artemis, Satara had never even heard of this man, but then given what her brother said, that made sense. Artemis liked to keep her head down low. "How do we fight him?"

"*We* don't. I already told you, we don't screw with him."

She wanted to choke him for his obstinacy and fear. If there was anything she loathed it was weakness. "Then how do we get inside the Serengeti to drive out Ravyn?"

"Again, we don't." Stryker rose to his feet and stepped down from his dais. He strode forward with an eerie, silent gait until he was beside her. "My plan, such as it was, for Seattle has fallen apart. Now that the Dark-Hunters know what we're up to, there's no point in pursuing it. The game is over."

"Not so fast," she said as her mind played through everything that had gone wrong. "What was your original plan?"

"What do you mean?"

"Before Seattle opened its doors to you, what did you have planned?"

He didn't answer. But even so, Satara knew. "You're after Acheron. You want to see him suffer." She stepped closer to him so that she could whisper faintly in a voice that the goddess who ruled this realm wouldn't hear. "More than that, you're after Apollymi herself for all the pain the two of them have caused you."

He didn't react, but still she knew the agony Stryker harbored. To prove his devotion to Apollymi, he'd cut his son's throat and made Urian a bitter enemy.

Urian had been the only thing Stryker had ever loved. And that included her. He kept her around only because he didn't like to be totally alone, but at the end of the day, she didn't have any delusions about where she fell in his affections. If she died this instant, he would shrug it off and move on.

Urian, on the other hand, was a constantly festering wound that ate at him.

"Do you have a point?" Stryker asked from between clenched teeth.

She nodded as a new idea formed. "There are still ways to damage Acheron here and now."

"Such as?"

"Oh, Stryker," she said in a pitying voice. "Of all men, you should know exactly how to cripple someone. What hurts more than having someone you trust beyond measure turn on you?"

His face hardened and she knew he was thinking of the day he'd learned Urian had been lying to him while protecting the family Stryker was sworn to kill.

"Yes," she whispered in his ear. "Now imagine turning one of Acheron's men to our side without his knowing it? We can do to him exactly what he did to you. . . ."

Suspicion darkened his eyes. "How?"

She laughed low and evil. "What has always been the downfall of man, my brother?"

He didn't hesitate with his answer. "Pride."

"Hardly." She held her hand up to her face and blew a deep breath across her nails before she pinned him with an evil stare. "Love, my brother. It is the one thing that men will kill to possess. The one thing that will make them do things that they would never normally do. Things they can't even conceive of. And it will be the one thing that will ultimately bring Acheron to his knees. His Dark-Hunters are the one weakness that we can reach and exploit. We haven't lost Seattle yet. There are still ways to claim the city and drive a spike straight through Acheron's heart."

"And if you're wrong?"

"What have we got to lose? Honestly?" Satara stood on her tiptoes so that their gazes were locked and level. She offered him a tiny hint of a hopeful smile even though his face was still hard and unforgiving. "But if I'm right?"

He blinked and looked away as if considering her words. When his gaze came back to hers, it was filled with all the raw, aching need he had to win this war against Acheron and Apollymi. "If you're right, Satara, I'll deliver the Atlantean up to you on a silver platter and hand you the dagger you need to cleave his heart out of his chest."

"That's not what *I* want, Stryker. That's your dream."

His eyes flashed in greedy expectation. "Fine then. You get this for me and I'll give you the secret to kill Artemis and free you from her service forever."

Satara closed her eyes as she tried to imagine it. If she never saw that bitch another day in her life, it would be too soon.

Freedom . . .

It was too good to be true. Her heart racing at the prospect, she held her hand up to Stryker. "Have we a deal then, Brother?"

He took her hand in his and held it over his heart. "Yes, we do."

CHAPTER ELEVEN

Susan woke up suddenly. At first she couldn't tell what had disturbed her. But as she remembered where she was, she realized that Ravyn was twitching while he slept. She started to shrug it off and go back to sleep, but something in the way he moved reminded her of someone caught in a nightmare they couldn't wake up from.

"Ravyn?" She gently shook him.

Before she could blink, he seized her in a fierce grip and whipped her over him, onto her back. His breathing was ragged as he growled a sound so feral that she half-expected him to rip out her throat.

"Ravyn!" she shouted, afraid he might hurt her before he came to his full senses.

He froze for a full ten seconds before his touch gentled. He dipped his head down to inhale deeply by her hair as if savoring her scent. "Susan?"

"Yes."

He pulled back and ran his hands over her as if assuring himself that he hadn't broken anything. "I didn't hurt you, did I?"

"No," she whispered, trying to ignore just how good his hands felt roaming her body. "Are *you* okay?"

"Yeah." He got up from the mattress and moved toward the door. She couldn't really see him until he opened it and the light from outside illuminated his tough stance. He'd removed his shirt and wore nothing but the black jeans as he stepped across the hall to the bathroom.

Susan didn't move while she waited for his return. When he came back to bed, his hair was damp as if he'd washed his face and then raked his hands through it. He wiped the back of his hand over his face before he shut the door and rejoined her on the bed.

He turned his back to her as if nothing had happened. But even so she could sense his unrest. There was an aura of deep sadness and something else she couldn't quite place. His actions reminded her of a tough kid who glared at the world through angry eyes. One who wanted nothing more than kindness and yet any time someone tried to offer it, he rebuffed them rather than take a chance on being hurt again.

There in the darkness, Ravyn's pain reached out to her and it made her want to soothe him.

"You want to talk about it?"

Ravyn lay there with visions of his nightmare still tormenting him. He really hated to sleep. It was the only time he was truly vulnerable. Awake, he could control his thoughts and emotions. Then as soon as he slept, all the things he wanted to forget came back with a vicious clarity. If he could, he'd purge those memories from him entirely.

But they were his memories and his feelings. Two things he didn't like to share with anyone else.

"Not really."

He could sense Susan's disappointment. But what confused him was her gentle kindness that was all but unknown to him. He didn't understand why it was important to her that she try to soothe his unrest.

She rolled over on the mattress so that she was facing his back. When she spoke, her tone was low and comforting. "You know,

when I was a little girl, I used to have these awful dreams about . . ."
She hesitated as if considering whether she should continue. With a
soft laugh, she admitted her nightmare. "Well, okay, my mother's
dolls coming alive while I slept. It was kind of stupid, but it used to
scare me to death."

Ravyn let out a tired breath even though he appreciated what
she was trying to do. "I assure you, I'm not dreaming about dolls,
Susan."

"I know. But whenever I woke up from my nightmare, my
mother would always make me tell her what I'd been dreaming—
no matter how stupid it seemed. She said that when you talk about
it, you get it out of your mind so that you can dream about good
things instead."

"I don't want to talk about it."

But then he felt her hand in his hair, gently stroking his scalp.
"Okay."

Ravyn closed his eyes as a foreign emotion went through him.
He couldn't remember the last time someone had offered him comfort. The last time a woman had touched him like this. She moved
her hand lower, over his shoulder to his arm, where she gently
rubbed his biceps. Her touch . . . no, her kindness singed him with
heat.

Susan didn't say a word as she rubbed his back. She merely lay
there, comforting him, gliding her hand along his flesh. Reminding
him that he wasn't alone in the darkness. Reminding him that it
was okay to be human. He didn't sense her judging him. She didn't
think him weak or ineffectual.

And before he realized what he was doing, he was speaking to
her about his nightmare. "It's always the same memory . . ." he
whispered. "I'm meeting Isabeau by the lake where I first saw her.
She was a merchant's daughter in the town that wasn't far from
our village. She and a small group of her friends had been picnick-
ing when my brothers and I were passing through. They'd waved
to us, and Dorian had headed for them."

Ravyn could still see that day so clearly in his mind. It'd been
an absolutely perfect warm spring day. The three of them had ridden to town for supplies and were on their way home. He and Dorian were on horseback while Phoenix drove the cart.

The women had been laughing and drinking wine . . . a *lot* of wine. Before Ravyn and his brothers had ridden by, the women had been bathing in the lake. Then they'd climbed out to sun themselves on the banks. Half-dressed in soggy chemises that kept falling off their bare shoulders to expose their better assets and giddy from their play, the women had actually catcalled to him and his brothers.

But he left those details out of his story as he told it to Susan. "Since Phoenix was mated, he'd gone on ahead while Dorian and I joined the women. They offered us food and wine." And other things best left unsaid. "I don't know why, but I was instantly attracted to Isabeau. There was something about her that seemed more vivacious than the rest of her companions."

Susan felt an inexplicable stab of jealousy at his words. She didn't like the idea of him cavorting with another woman. But she didn't say anything while he continued to talk.

"After it started getting late, the women packed up to return home. So Isabeau and I made plans to meet again in a few days. Alone."

"You were on the make."

"Yeah, and she wasn't a virgin." He gave a short, bitter laugh. "She was a woman with a hefty appetite and I didn't mind being her main course."

Susan had to force herself not to yank a hank of his hair at that. *Bastard.*

But then he'd paid dearly for his dalliance with the little tart. It was something Susan wouldn't wish on her worst enemy.

Ravyn took a deep breath before he continued. "One thing led to another and the next thing I knew, we'd set up our meetings fairly regularly."

She frowned at his words. "Weren't you afraid of making her pregnant?"

"No. Weres can't have children with anyone but their mates. Since we weren't mated, there was no chance of that."

Susan would give him that, but pregnancy wasn't the only thing to be concerned about. "Not to be rude, but what about STDs? Given how quickly she threw herself at you, weren't you afraid she'd give you a gift that kept on giving?"

He snorted. "No. Again, my people can't get those diseases. Our magick keeps us immune from the rest. The only human diseases we share are cancer and common colds."

Lucky you. Susan had to bite back the sarcasm. She didn't want him to pull away while he was telling her his story. "So how long did the two of you keep meeting?"

"About four months. And after a while, I was really infatuated with her. She kept asking me to marry her and I kept putting her off."

"Because she wasn't your mate?"

"Exactly. There was no point in bringing her into my world when she couldn't really be a part of it. And I didn't want to tie myself to someone who wasn't my mate. I used to have this stupid idea that one day I'd have a mate and kids and live happily ever after."

Susan's heart jerked at the hurt that underlined those words. "It's not such a stupid idea, Ravyn. You know a lot of people have the same exact thought."

"Yeah," he said in a tone that told her he thought those people were fools. "Anyway, when the mark finally appeared on our hands, I thought it was too good to be true. She'd been telling me for months that she loved me. I wasn't sure if I loved her or not, but I enjoyed her company so I proposed as soon as I saw the marking. Isabeau was scared, of course. She thought it was the mark of the devil and I tried to tell her not to worry, but she ran off before I could explain it."

"You went after her?"

"No," he said to her surprise. "Something in my gut told me to leave her alone . . . she'd been really hysterical before she took off. So I went home and that night my mother saw the mark on my palm and asked me about it. I told her the truth and tried to make her understand just how distraught Isabeau had been. She assured me that Isabeau was just taken by surprise. And that I owed it to both her and myself to tell her the truth about who and what we were. She was sure that a woman who loved me would accept the truth of it and join us."

He rolled over onto his back to stare up at the ceiling. She could feel the guilt and anger inside him, reaching out to touch her heart. "You have no idea how much I wish I could go back in time and change that night. It's probably why Artemis stripped the ability to time travel from me. God knows, it eats at me constantly and I'm sure if I could, I'd go back and do something stupid."

Susan rubbed his arm soothingly. "Is that what you dream of?"

He turned his head to meet her gaze. "In part. I always see my mother as she urged me to go to Isabeau and bring her back to our village, and then it shifts to the night I became a Dark-Hunter. I keep seeing Isabeau's terrified face in my mind as I killed her father while she screamed and cowered in a corner."

She hesitated to ask the next question, but she wanted to know the answer. "Did you kill Isabeau, too?"

"Yes."

Susan pulled back at that as her heart hammered. She'd seen Ravyn in action, but even so she hadn't thought that he could be *that* cold.

He winced as if he could still see the past. "While her father died, Isabeau found some courage. She grabbed a short sword from the wall and ran at me with it. I wasn't armed so I tried to dodge her swing, but she caught me across the arm with the blade. Acting on instinct, I knocked her away from me and cupped my arm. She stumbled back into the hearth and dropped the sword as the tail of her dress went into the fire. I reached for her to help her, but she bit me and went running for the open door as the fire spread up the back of her gown. As I ran after her, more of the men came between us and attacked me. By the time I'd killed them, it was too late for Isabeau. I found her lying in a heap not far from her cottage. As I rolled her over, I realized she was still alive. Her eyes flared as she saw me, then she spat in my face and died in my arms. I can't get the sight of her burned face out of my dreams. The hatred in her eyes as she spat on me. I keep thinking that I should have somehow known how it would all play out. That I could have done something to save all of them."

"It wasn't your fault Isabeau was stupid."

"No," he said, his dark eyes burning into hers. "She was just a woman of her time who was convinced I was the devil out to steal her soul. I should have never touched her."

"But then you wouldn't have found your mate."

"Yeah, and what good did it do me to find her?"

He did have a point. Sighing, Susan squeezed his hand in hers. "I'm sorry, Ravyn. Everyone deserves to have someone who loves them."

By his face she could tell that he didn't agree with that. Instead of hating Isabeau for her ignorance and stupidity, it was obvious that he hated himself for setting it all into motion. How she wished she could ease that guilt from him. But there was nothing she could do. He would have to learn to forgive himself someday.

"What about you?" he asked quietly as he played with her fingers.

"What about me?"

"Did you ever love anyone?"

Susan bit her lip as her own regret and sadness gnawed at her. "No. Not really." And it wasn't from lack of trying on her part. She just couldn't seem to find anyone who was in sync with her. Someone who could make her laugh. . . . Someone she wanted to grow old with. "At least not like you read about in books or see in movies. I've always wondered what it would be like to be swept off my feet by some sexy stranger. To have that one person who I can't imagine living without come into my life and make me his." She sighed wistfully as an image of it happening played through her mind. Oh, what she wouldn't give to have that feeling just once in her life.

"Yeah. It's such bullshit."

"No," she said seriously. "It does exist. I saw it with Jimmy and Angie. They were so in love that there were times when I would have to leave the room to get away from the jealousy I felt. It wasn't that I begrudged them their happiness, it was just hard to see them so happy while I had no one in my own life."

Susan felt a sad smile play at the edges of her lips. "When I was a little girl, I remember going to see *Urban Cowboy* with my mom. Remember the scene at the end when John Travolta punches out the bad guy for hurting Debra Winger and then carries her outside? I always wondered what that would feel like."

His callused fingers continued to play with hers. "Well, considering the fact that he doesn't carry her out at the end, that would be hard."

Susan started at his words. "What?"

"She gets carried outside at the end of *An Officer and a Gen-*

tleman. Not *Urban Cowboy.* Bud and Sissy walk out arm in arm at the end of that one."

"Oh." Susan frowned as she thought about that. He was actually right and she was amazed that he knew that. She turned to give him a chiding stare. "By the way, I find it fascinating that you know this."

His grin was wicked as he moved her hand to his chest while his thumb stroked her palm and sent little waves of pleasure through her. "Don't. Remember that I live with a girl who's recently gone through puberty. Erika watches those movies over and over again and then cries and carries on for hours about how men like that don't exist and how we're all insensitive pigs who should be neutered."

Susan laughed. She could just see Erika tirading against poor Ravyn, who would most likely look completely baffled by the attack. "You know, she's amazingly astute at times."

"Thanks."

She rolled her weight playfully into his side. "I was just teasing."

"Sure you were. Admit it, you agree with her."

"Some days," she joked. "After all, you guys are a little self-absorbed at times."

"Yeah, like we're the only ones."

Susan paused as she realized just how comfortable she was with him. She hadn't teased like this in a long time. And it felt really good. Licking her lips, she stared at their joined hands and wondered if Ravyn even realized what he was doing.

Ravyn's breath caught in his throat as he saw the tender look on Susan's face. As dark as the room was, he knew she couldn't see him all that well, but he had a perfect view of her face. And she was beautiful. Her blue eyes were tinged with dark circles, but they in no way took away from her angelic features. Her long blond hair was a complete mess and yet he'd never seen anything sexier in his life.

In that instant, he knew that he should get up and sleep somewhere else, but he didn't want to leave her. She'd been right, talking about his nightmare had made him feel better. A *lot* better. The haunting images were gone now, replaced by her hesitant smile and her gently teasing voice.

And deep in the back of his mind was the question of what his life would have been like if Isabeau had been more like Susan. . . .

Without thinking, he cupped her face in his hand and watched as she closed her eyes to savor his touch. Her skin fascinated him with its softness. Before he could stop himself he leaned down and captured her lips with his. The taste of her invaded every part of his body. Her kiss was tender and precious, and there in the darkness it chased away the shadows of his past and eased the pain that had lived way too long inside him.

Susan sighed as she tasted Ravyn. His whiskers chafed her skin and prickled her lips making them both itchy, but still she didn't want to give up that mouth. There was something about him that she wanted to possess. Something that addicted her in a way she wouldn't have thought possible.

Her heart pounded as he left her lips to nibble his way down to her neck. Chills spread through her. His fangs gently nipped her skin that had been made sensitive from his whiskers. She wrapped her arms around him, delighting in the way his muscles rippled and bunched under her hands as he moved. It felt so good not to be alone in the darkness. So good to just hold someone, but especially this man who'd protected and comforted her.

Desire pooled itself to the center of her body as she reached out for him. But as he shifted, his hair fell into her face.

Her nose started burning immediately as her eyes watered and she sniffed. Then she sneezed.

Ravyn let out an irritated breath as he pulled back. "You really are allergic to me, aren't you?"

She gave an extremely undignified sniff. "Only to your hair."

"Fine then. I'll shave it off."

"Don't you dare. . . ." She caught herself and the heated intensity of her voice. "I mean . . ."

His eyes gleamed at her with humor. "I know what you mean."

Susan cocked her head as his hair was immediately gathered back from his face into a ponytail without either one of them touching it.

"How did you do that?" she asked in awe.

He winked playfully at her. "Magick."

And before she could speak again, he returned to her lips to kiss her blind. Her body burned as he lifted up her shirt and exposed her stomach. He dipped his head down to tease her skin with his fangs. She shivered and groaned at the sensation of his hot lips on her cool skin. Nothing had ever felt better.

Ravyn growled at the taste of Susan. He wanted to bathe in her scent. To roll himself all over her until she coated every part of him. And when she reached down between them to cup him in her hands, he actually saw stars from it.

He moved farther up her body to recapture her lips as she slowly unbuttoned his fly to free him. Unable to stand it, he closed his eyes and melted their clothes from their bodies.

A light, gentle laugh filled his ears. "You know, that little talent could get you arrested in most states."

"If you'd like to break out some handcuffs . . . I wouldn't be inclined to resist that arrest."

She laughed again as she wrapped her body around his and then rolled him over onto his back. Her eyes dark and hooded, she straddled his stomach, then slid her body down his. Ravyn hissed as pleasure tore through him. The hairs at the center of her body tickled his stomach as her wetness teased him with promise.

His heart racing, he cupped her breasts in his hands as she leaned forward to trace the outline of his jaw with her tongue.

Susan delighted at the sensation of his whiskers prickling her lips. A part of her was appalled that she was making out with a guy she barely knew, and yet she felt as if she'd known him an eternity. There was something about him that called out to her. Something inside her that wanted only to be with him . . . at least for this moment in time. No, that was wrong. She felt a connection with him. This wasn't just scratching an itch. It was something more.

She didn't know why having sex with him seemed so important, but this was something she had to do.

He ran his warm hands down her back before he lifted her up ever so slightly to stroke her gently between her legs. Susan moaned as she slowly rode his fingers. It'd been so long since any man had touched her like this. She'd almost forgotten just how good it felt.

Wanting to taste more of him, she trailed her lips from his jaw to his chest so that she could lave his nipple. She laughed deep in her throat as she felt chills spread over his body.

Ravyn couldn't think straight as Susan made her way down his body. Her sweet mouth was working the most amazing magick on him as it caused his own magick to swell and increase. Sex always invigorated his kind. He watched as she moved to kneel between his thighs. He reached to brush her hair back from her face only to have her capture his hand in hers and lead it to her mouth.

His entire body burned as she gently suckled his fingers. And when she pulled away, he actually wanted to whimper until she took the tip of him into her mouth.

Arching his back, he buried his hand in her hair as she ran her tongue around him, taking his cock even deeper into her mouth. Something inside him shattered at the sight of her tasting him. It'd never been in his nature to let anyone close to him. And yet he found himself softening for her. She was the kind of woman a man fought for. The kind he kept near him no matter what.

That thought scared him. He was a Dark-Hunter. Women were a passing curiosity for them. A scratch for a biological itch. But as he watched Susan, he realized that he didn't want to walk out of her life. He wanted to spend more days with her like this. . . . well preferably without people trying to kill them. Most of all, he wanted to get to know everything about her.

Susan paused as she caught Ravyn's hooded gaze. There was something so tender in his expression that it actually made her breath catch. He looked so good lying on the bed, his prone body just waiting for her.

Pulling back, she ignored her stuffy, itchy nose and gave one long, wicked lick from the base of his cock all the way to the tip, delighting in the salty taste of his body. She was on fire for him. He pulled her up his body so that he could kiss her.

She ran her hands over his steely arms, seeking out every dip and curve of muscle. Unable to stand it anymore, she shifted her weight so that the center of her body was pressed against the tip of him. Pulling back from his kiss, she slowly inched herself down his shaft until he completely impaled her.

She ground her teeth at the incredible sensation of his hard length inside her. She lifted her gaze to lock with his as she lifted herself up and then slid back down to take him in all the way to the hilt.

Ravyn growled as pleasure tore through him. He lifted his hips, driving himself even deeper into her as she rode him at a furious pace. His entire body was on fire as he cupped her breasts in his hands.

Susan covered his hands with hers as her pleasure mounted. Never in her life had any man felt so good inside her. She quickened her strokes, wanting to feel him even deeper. And then she felt it . . . that magical moment when her entire world exploded into white-hot ribbons of ecstasy.

Ravyn growled as he felt her orgasm. His Were-Hunter powers were fired by it, and as they gained strength, his own pleasure built until he joined her release.

Throwing his head back, he groaned aloud. Susan collapsed on top of him, covering his body with hers as they both struggled to breathe.

His entire body covered in a fine sheet of sweat, he held her close, his heart racing, his magick snapping. Her breath fell in gentle puffs against his skin while he held her and marveled at the tenderness she awoke inside him. "That was amazing," he said quietly.

"You've no idea," she said as her fingers toyed with his right nipple.

"Oh, I think I do," he teased, nuzzling her until he had her lips again. The warmth he felt for her both delighted and scared him. He wasn't supposed to feel this way, and especially not toward a Squire. They weren't supposed to touch, and yet he couldn't seem to stop himself.

Susan's eyes widened as she realized that he was already growing hard again. Pulling back, she looked down to see that she wasn't imagining it.

Shocked, she met his evil grin.

"Welcome to the world of the Were-Hunters, baby. We're not like human men."

"No kidding. . . ." Before she could move, he sat up with her in his arms.

"Now let me show you how a cat makes love to a woman."

She stiffened instantly. "I don't do bestiality."

"Good, neither do I."

He faced her to the wall and placed her hands there to brace her weight as he nudged her thighs wide apart. Susan turned to see him over her shoulder before he brushed her hair from her neck and nibbled the skin there. Chills exploded over her. What was it about him that made her crave him so?

As he pressed himself closer to her, she could feel his earlier release start to trickle out from her. Until he moved his hand down around her stomach to trail to the center of her. He gently separated the folds of her until he could stroke her.

Susan cried out as her muscles jerked in response to his hot touch. He took a nip of her skin in his fangs an instant before he drove himself deep inside her again.

She clenched her hands into fists against the wall as unimaginable pleasure filled her. He drove himself so deep inside her that she swore he actually touched her womb. His fingers teased her in time to his thrusts while his hot breath singed her neck.

Ravyn closed his eyes as he moved even faster against her. This was a position that most of his kind reserved only for the mating ritual, and he'd never used it with any woman before. He wasn't even sure why he did so now except that he wanted to know just once what it was like to make love to a woman like this.

And he couldn't think of anyone better than Susan to experience it with.

Susan pushed herself away from the wall and leaned back against him as he continued to thrust himself into her. He felt so incredibly good there. She fell back in his arms so that she could reach over her head and sink her hand into his silken hair even though it made her skin itch. He moved his lips so that he could tease her lobe while she massaged his scalp, and chills consumed her. No man had ever felt better. And her body was growing hotter and hotter.

She tightened her grip in his hair an instant before she cried out in ecstasy. Still he kept his hand buried between her legs, wringing out every tremor of pleasure from her body until she fell forward and begged him for mercy.

He moved his hands and then braced them against her hips as he quickened his strokes until he, too, found his release. He kept himself deep inside her as he nuzzled and licked the flesh of her back.

Susan trembled as Ravyn held her while he was still inside her. Their bodies still joined, he pulled her with him down to the mattress.

"You know," she said as she slowly floated back into her body. "Aside from the allergies, I think I could get used to you being a cat."

He laughed gently in her ear before he wiggled his hips against hers. She moaned at the sensation of him stroking her deep inside.

Then suddenly the blanket was over them again.

"Ravyn?"

"Yes?"

"Do you think we'll ever get our lives back to normal?"

Ravyn was silent as he considered that. The concept of normal to him was actually laughable. But he knew that wasn't what she was asking him.

She wanted him to tell her that everything would be all right.

"I'm sure you'll get your life back, Susan." The only problem was that he knew he, too, would go back to being a Dark-Hunter, but after spending this day with her he didn't think that his life would ever be the same again. How could it?

He'd shared things with her that he'd never shared with another living being. More than that, she'd touched a part of him that he didn't even know he still had.

But he also knew that in the end, he was going to have to walk away from her. It was all he could do. He was a Dark-Hunter and she was human.

And that reality broke the heart he thought had died more than three hundred years ago.

Cael jerked awake as a sense of foreboding terrorized him. Amaranda rolled over in bed to stare up at him with her brow furrowed by concern.

"Are you okay, baby?"

He couldn't speak as he tried to pull his dream into his conscious mind. One of his gifts as a Dark-Hunter was the power of precognition.

Yet this vision escaped him completely. Except for one thing that he remembered clearly.

Amaranda's death.

He pulled her into his arms and held her as pain racked him. He couldn't lose her. He couldn't.

"Cael? You're starting to scare me."

Still, he couldn't speak, not while he saw her dead at his feet. And as in the past, the thought of her death weakened his Dark-Hunter powers. He could feel them slipping, even as he drew personal strength from her.

"Cael?"

"It's okay, Randa," he said, finally. But inside it wasn't. He'd already lost everyone who'd ever meant anything to him. He didn't want to ever feel that grief again.

And yet what choice did he have?

She was going to die. Their time together was so finite that he couldn't even let himself think about it.

Tightening his arms around her, he laid a gentle kiss on her cheek. "Go back to sleep, love."

He reluctantly pulled away from her.

She frowned at him. "Where are you going?"

"Bathroom." Cael pulled up his plaid and wrapped it around his hips before he opened the door and stepped through it toward the bathroom in the hallway.

He'd only taken a few steps when he felt a preternatural frisson go up his spine. He turned just as a door opened on his right to show him a man almost even in height to him. And even though the man had black hair, he oozed the scent and aura of a Daimon.

But unlike a Daimon, this man had swirling silver eyes that Cael had only seen on one other being.

Acheron Parthenopaeus.

"Who are you?"

The man smiled to show him a set of fangs. "Stryker."

"You don't belong here."

He arched a brow at that. "I would think, as a Daimon, that I have more right here than a Dark-Hunter does. Tell me, why is the enemy living in peace in a commune of Apollites?"

"That's none of your business."

"Isn't it?"

Cael started for the Daimon only to have him vanish. Two heartbeats later, he appeared at Cael's back.

"I'm not your enemy, Cael."

"How do you know my name?"

"I know lots of things about you, including your marriage to Amaranda. More than that, I know what you fear most."

He curled his lip at the Daimon. "You don't know shit about me."

"Oh no, that's not true. But tell me something? If I told you there was a way to save her, would you take it?"

Cael's heart literally stopped beating. "I won't let her go Daimon."

"What if there was another way to save her?"

Dare he even hope for that? "What other way?"

Stryker moved to stand just before him. So close that Cael could feel the heat from his body. "Join my army, Cael, and I will give you the secret you need to keep Amaranda alive as an Apollite past her birthday."

He cut a suspicious glare at Stryker. "What army?"

"The Illuminati. We serve the goddess Apollymi, mortal enemy of Artemis and Acheron."

Cael stiffened at those words that asked him to betray two people he owed his loyalty to. "I made my oath to Artemis. I won't go back on it. Ever."

Stryker tsked at him. "Pity you then. I hope your oath keeps you company after your beautiful wife disintegrates in your arms."

Cael sucked his breath in sharply as his dream came back to him in crystal clarity and again he felt his powers drain.

Stryker handed him a small medallion. "Think about my offer, Dark-Hunter, and if you change your mind—"

"I won't."

Stryker gave him an evil smile. "As I said, if you change your mind, use the medallion to call me."

Cael didn't move as the Daimon summoned a bolt-hole and stepped into it. He looked down at the golden medallion that held a dragon flying in the center of a sunburst. It was the universal sign of the ancient Spathis.

Was the Daimon serious? Could there be a way to save Amaranda's life?

He's lying to you, Cael. Don't be a fool.

But what if he wasn't?

Clenching his fist over the medallion, Cael went to the bathroom, then returned to his bedroom. He stood over the bed, staring at Amaranda, who'd returned to sleep. Her long blond hair was fanned out around her as she lay on her side completely naked.

He reached out and touched her supple arm. She meant the world to him. Before he'd met her, he'd been nothing but an empty shell who'd been incapable of feeling anything at all. She'd taught him to laugh again. To breathe. He owed her everything and the thought of living for even one minute without her crippled him with pain.

He put the medallion on the dresser, then dropped his plaid and joined her in the bed. If she were awake, she'd be angry at him for even thinking about betraying his oath.

"We'll enjoy what we have and be grateful for it, Cael. Don't wish for more than what the Fates have decreed for us."

Her compassion and strength was only part of why he loved her so much.

And it was why he didn't want to lose her.

Swallowing against the lump in his throat, he pulled her warm body flush to his.

And as he closed his eyes, he could have sworn he heard Stryker's voice in his head.

"One single word, Cael, and you'll never have to lose her. Just one."

Cael whispered a prayer for strength and courage. But in the end, his gift of second sight laid out a future that scared him. Because in his heart, he knew the truth.

He would do *anything* to keep this woman by his side. The only question was what exactly Stryker would ask him to do in order to save his wife's life.

CHAPTER TWELVE

Susan came awake just after dusk—at least that's what she thought. Since there were no windows or a clock in the room, she didn't really know what time it was, except for the fact that the music from the club upstairs was already hopping. That meant it had to be after sundown, but it was quiet enough that she figured it couldn't be too late.

Ravyn shifted behind her as if he knew she was awake and laid a gentle kiss on her bare back. She shivered as chills shot down her spine in the wake of his hot lips on her flesh. "Good morning," he said as he stretched languidly. Rolling over, she could swear that she felt that stretch herself. The faint light showed his naked body off to perfection. His lean muscles were taut and bulging . . .

Along with another part of him she couldn't help noticing.

"Evening, you mean."

He yawned without responding. She was mesmerized by the definition of his abs as he arched his back. Oh, yeah, a woman could do laundry on that. And it made her want to rub herself against him.

"Did you sleep well?" he asked, reaching over to brush her hair back from her face.

"Like a baby. You?"

He rolled to his side to give her a devilish grin. "Yeah, I actually did for once."

Before she could ask him another question, Grieg's "In the Hall of the Mountain King" started playing. It took her a full second to realize it was Ravyn's phone.

Making an aggravated noise, he rolled over to pull it out of his pants before he answered it.

"Yeah?" He reached over and idly toyed with her hand as he listened.

Susan savored the roughness of his fingers on her skin, even though a part of her wished it was something else he was fondling.

"Okay, I'll be there." He hung up the phone.

"What's up?"

He raised her hand up to his lips so that he could nibble the back of her knuckles before he answered. "They're calling a meeting here tonight with all the Dark-Hunters."

That surprised her. "I didn't think you guys could be together without weakening each other."

"We can't, which tells you how important the Squires think this meeting is. Acheron is usually the only one to call together something like this." He leaned over to give her a kiss, and as their lips touched, she felt warmth seep through her body. She couldn't believe the things this man made her feel for him when they shouldn't even be together.

Susan melted under his assault until he pulled back sharply.

"We have half an hour," he said quietly. "Chop-chop."

She groaned. "I wish that were half an hour for sex, but I think you mean half an hour for dressing."

He gave her an arch stare. "I could never have sex with you in only half an hour, my lady. Truly not possible."

Biting her lip, she reached down to cup his warm sac in her

hand. "You keep talking like that, Leopardman, and we won't be leaving this room any time soon."

He nibbled and laved her neck. "Yeah, but then they'd come after us and I'd have to kill one of them, which would really be a bad thing. Ash tends to get testy when we kill off Squires."

He laid himself down on top of her to savor her skin against his, then he stood up with a deep groan.

Susan allowed him to pull her to her feet before they quickly dressed and headed upstairs. Part of her wanted to stay downstairs and keep reviewing files . . . among other things such as testing how long his stamina would last, but her curiosity got the better of her.

What could be so important that they would call a meeting when it was obvious that the Dark-Hunters needed their strength to fight the Daimons who were trying to kill them?

Susan hesitated at the top of the stairs. "You don't think this is a trap, do you?"

"How do you mean?"

"Well, if I were a Daimon and I knew that to get you guys together would weaken you, wouldn't I do that if I could?"

"Yeah, but they don't have our phone numbers."

Good point.

He opened the door. Terra met them in the upstairs hallway before they could reach the kitchen. "They're in the back office," she said, handing each of them a sack and a soda.

"What's this?" Susan asked.

"Breakfast. I figured the two of you would be hungry during the meeting."

"Thank you," Ravyn said.

"No problem." Terra led them down another hallway that shot off the kitchen, to a large office that had a desk along one wall and a huge conference table in the center. Leo and Kyl were already there, along with Erika and Jack. Susan looked around for Jessica, but there was no sign of her.

"What's up?" she asked Leo as Terra left them alone.

"A lot of shit."

"Good," Susan said as she put her sack lunch on the table. "I'll make sure and get my waders out."

Kyl snorted as he reviewed something on his laptop.

As Susan and Ravyn sat down, the door opened to show Otto and Nick. Otto's face was stoic, but Nick's was angry, as if he really resented this meeting. He took a seat opposite her and folded his arms over his chest like a sullen child.

Kyl cocked a brow as he looked up from his computer. "What? Being a Dark-Hunter doesn't agree with you?"

Nick curled his lip. "Shut up, schmuck."

"Schmuck?" Kyl was completely indignant. "What the hell happened to you, boy? I thought we were friends. *Best* friends."

"Kyl," Otto snapped as he sat down beside Nick. "Lay off."

Kyl held his hands up in surrender. "Whatever."

Susan looked up as the door opened again and froze with her turkey sandwich halfway to her lips. Eyes wide, she stared at a man she hadn't seen in almost twenty years . . . and he hadn't changed a bit. Seriously. Not a bit. Not a wrinkle, not a gray hair. Nothing.

Still stunningly gorgeous, he was six feet even in height with short jet-black hair that set off his Asian features to perfection.

She set her sandwich back on the table. "Sensei?"

His own mouth dropped as he met her gaze and she finally saw a set of fangs that she'd somehow failed to notice during the two years she'd trained in his studio. "Susan?"

Ravyn darted a curious gaze between them. If she didn't know better, she'd swear she saw a hint of jealousy in those dark eyes. "You know Dragon?"

Susan nodded.

Ravyn looked less than pleased. "How well do you know him?"

"She was one of my students at the dojo," Dragon said as he smiled at her. "One of my best students, I might add."

Susan continued to stare at him in disbelief. "Wow, I can't believe you're here. Then again, this explains so much."

Finally relaxing, Ravyn laughed at that. "Let me guess, never a day class available, and a lot of family emergencies that had him running out at odd times?"

It was true. Dragon had been a great teacher, but he'd also had two assistants and they'd often joked that he dashed off like Superman after a criminal. Who knew how close they'd been to the truth?

Susan shook her head. "Jeez . . . you guys really are everywhere, aren't you?"

"Yes," Dragon said. "Which explains why I'm here, but not how it is that you're in our company."

"She's a new Squire," Leo said as he sat down at the head of the table.

Coming forward, Dragon held his hand out to her. "Welcome to our world. It's good to see you again."

She shook his hand and smiled. "You, too."

As Dragon started to take the chair beside her, Ravyn cleared his throat.

Dragon arched a single brow as he hesitated with his hand on the back of the chair. She could see his inner debate of whether to sit there and irritate Ravyn or not. Winking at her, he moved to sit on the other side of Ravyn.

"Have you known Ravyn long, Susan?" Dragon asked.

"Just met."

"Uh-huh—"

"Drop the subject, Dragon," Ravyn said as he picked the tomatoes off his sandwich.

Dragon put his hands in the pocket of his black windbreaker and cast a knowing look at them.

Susan felt the heat sting her cheeks before Dragon started chatting with Leo over the latest story in the *Inquisitor* about an alien baby being found in Greenland.

While they talked, Susan noticed Nick's hand. Like Leo and the others, he had the same spiderweb tattoo. How very interesting. . . .

The next Dark-Hunter to join them was a former Nubian priest named Menkaura. Tall and lean, his skin was a perfect shade of mocha. He wore his long black hair in braids that were tied back at the nape of his neck. But what fascinated her most was that he was dressed in black jeans and a black sleeveless vest that showed off a tattoo of the eye of Horus on his right biceps. There was also a line of tiny hieroglyphics beneath it.

"I have to know what that says," she said, indicating the tattoo.

He glanced at it before he answered, " 'Death is a doorway. Think before you knock on it.' "

"That's profound."

He inclined his head to her as Jack made an aggravated noise.

"Dang, and I always thought it said something like 'Die, Scum, Die.' How disappointing."

By his pained expression, Susan could tell Menkaura didn't appreciate Jack's humor. Unlike Dragon and Ravyn, Menkaura was completely reserved and said very little. Something about him reminded her of a cobra lying in wait for its next victim.

Susan took a second to glance around at the men. . . . "You know, I suddenly feel like I'm on that *Cover Model* show. Is it just me or is there some unwritten rule that says all the Dark-Hunters have to be really hot?"

Erika snorted. "C'mon, Susan, think about it. If you're an immortal goddess and you're putting together an army of warriors to fight the undead, are you going to fill it with slugs or with the hottest pieces of cheese you can find? Maybe I'm shallow . . . okay, I'm highly shallow, but in this I give Artemis two thumbs-up."

"You have a point," Susan said as she let her gaze wander over the four Dark-Hunters who were present. Then she looked at Leo. "You know, this would have made a good headline, huh? 'Greek Goddess Commands Army of Hot Cheese.' "

Leo flipped her off before he returned to sorting through his folder.

"Ooo," Susan said, feigning hurt. "I think I've been dissed by the Master of Sleaze."

Menkaura had just taken his seat when the door was suddenly thrown back.

"Dammit, Belle!" Leo snapped as he jumped completely out of his seat. "Don't do that."

Susan had to force herself not to laugh.

"Aw, sit your ass down, Leo," Belle said in a voice that was thick with a Texas drawl before she slammed the door shut with the heel of her foot. Tall and blond and also dressed in black jeans and a black blouse, she reminded Susan of an angel . . . one that was chewing her gum like a cow going to town with cud. She moved forward to set two bottles of unopened tequila on the table. "Now boys and girls, let the party start."

"All right, Annie Oakley," Ravyn said in a teasing tone. "Last time you threw a party, half of Chicago burned down."

Belle narrowed her eyes playfully on him. "That was *not* my fault."

Ravyn leaned back in his chair and gave her a doubting stare. "Uh-huh. The least you could have done was take the blame yourself and not put it off on Mrs. O'Leary's cow."

"Hey now, they couldn't hang old Bessie for starting the fire." Belle moved to stand by Susan. She folded her arms over her chest as she stood there with her feet slightly apart. The stance reminded Susan of a gunfighter about to draw his gun. "You're new. Who the hell are you?"

She glanced about nervously, but the men didn't seem concerned at Belle's antagonistic nature. "Susan."

"Uh-huh," Belle said in a tone that was less than impressed.

"She's a Squire," Leo said.

"Uh-huh." Belle sized her up again. "Can you shoot a gun?"

Susan frowned at the odd question. "Yeah."

"Can you hit anything after you pull the trigger?"

"Most of the time."

"Cool." She held her hand out to her. "Welcome to our little group here."

Susan shook her hand as Belle's entire demeanor changed over to friendly. "Thanks."

Menkaura shifted in his chair. "Belle used to travel with a Wild West show."

Belle opened the bottle nearest her with her teeth. "Yeah," she said as she pulled a small shot glass from her pocket and filled it, "and I kicked Annie Oakley's ass in my last show, but do they ever mention that? No. I got the shaft and she got the fame. Life's just not fair, I tell you."

Kyl opened the other bottle before he poured the tequila into the plastic cup he had before him. He held the cup up in toast to Belle before he met Susan's gaze. "Belle shot the reporter who failed to mention her as the winner." He knocked back the drink in a single gulp.

"Yeah, but he took a shot at me first." Belle tilted her head back to empty her cup, then refilled the glass. "Not my fault he missed. I just showed him up close and personal who the better shot was . . ." She frowned as she set the bottle aside. "But then I probably shouldn't have killed him 'cause then he could have fixed that article."

Leo gave her a dry look. "*And* you wouldn't have become an outlaw."

"Shut up, Leo."

Belle grabbed the chair next to Susan, spun it around, and straddled it. At the same time an unbelievably attractive woman walked in.

Susan had to keep her mouth from dropping. She'd truly never seen a more beautiful woman in her life. And she was incredibly tall . . . at least six foot five, with long auburn hair that was scraped back from her face to fall in a braid all the way to her thighs. Like the others, she was dressed in what must be their uniform of black clothes. Only this Dark-Hunter had on leather pants and a black brocade corset. She was also clutching a venti-sized cup of Starbucks coffee and wearing a pair of five-inch steel-spiked boots, which accounted for some of her unbelievable height.

She stopped beside Nick's chair and took a minute to size him up. "Gautier?"

He didn't even bother to look at her while he poured his own shot of tequila. "Hi, Zoe."

Narrowing her eyes, she reached out and tilted his head to the side so that she could see the Dark-Hunter mark that was on Nick's face and neck. "Damn, boy, what happened? Artemis bitch slap you?"

He grabbed her wrist and glared up at her.

Zoe broke his hold as she shook her head. "Kyrian said he thought you'd gone over to the *dark* side, but I didn't believe him."

Nick gulped down his tequila. "Yeah, well, I guess he isn't as dumb as he looks."

Zoe looked surprised by the venom in Nick's voice. She took a drink of coffee before she frowned at Susan. Zoe inclined her chin toward her. "Who's the new chick?"

"Who's the old bitch?" Susan asked, looking over at Leo.

"Ooo," Zoe said with an evil laugh, "snotty." Still there was respect in the woman's eyes. "You got anything to back that up?"

Dragon gave a low laugh of his own. "Yes, she does. *I* trained her."

"Okay. A smart- and tough-ass. Can't ask for better than that. I know she's not one of us, so I take it she's a Squire then."

"Yeah," Leo said.

Susan put her sandwich wrapper back in the sack as she looked over at Ravyn, who was watching her with a seductive gleam in his eyes. "Should I have a shirt on that says 'New Squire'?"

"Nah," Kyl said, "it should have 'Squirehood: what an indenture.' "

All the Squires plus Ravyn laughed. The rest didn't seem to have much of a sense of humor about it.

After taking another swig of coffee, Zoe gave Susan a once-over that was extremely sexual. "Who does she serve?"

Erika answered. "No one. She's Dorean."

There was no mistaking the interest in Zoe's eyes as they lingered on Susan. "Really?"

Ravyn cleared his throat meaningfully. "You've already got a Squire, Zoe."

"Yeah, but I can't stand him—he's more woman than I am. Be nice to have an actual female Squire for a change."

Dragon snorted. "It doesn't work like that, Zo, and you know it. You can't have a Squire you're sexually attracted to."

She let out an aggravated breath. "I really hate that rule," she muttered as she took a seat next to Belle and Cael joined them.

He greeted them all before he took a seat beside Leo. Unlike the others, Cael wasn't dressed in black. He had on a pair of baggy blue jeans and a loose V-neck sweater that seemed at odds with his spiked hair. Poor Cael looked like he'd just crawled out of bed and tossed on the nearest clothes he could find.

Susan frowned as she watched him. He seemed extremely subdued, as if something had him completely preoccupied. The reporter in her was instantly intrigued.

Dragon checked his watch. "I don't mean to be rude, but my powers are starting to wane. How much longer before we start this meeting?"

"We're just waiting on—" Leo's voice broke off as the door opened and a short, stout man walked in. In his mid-thirties, he was dressed in a flannel shirt and jeans. He didn't strike her as a Dark-Hunter but rather another Squire.

His face was completely grim as he swept them with a soulful stare.

"What are you doing here, Dave?" Leo asked. "Where's Troy?"

A tic worked in Dave's jaw. He swallowed before he answered in a voice that was thick with grief. "Dead."

With that one word, it felt as if all the air had been sucked out of the room. For a full minute it was so quiet that all Susan could hear was a faint buzzing in her ears. No one moved.

Even though she didn't know who this Dark-Hunter was, she felt the sadness of his loss. And she knew it deeply affected everyone there, especially Dave.

Ravyn was the one who finally broke the silence. "How?"

Tears gathered in Dave's eyes as he visibly struggled for composure. "Last night, he'd run into a group of Daimons at the Last Supper Club and got seriously injured fighting them. He called me from the alley and said that he was bleeding badly. That he couldn't drive back or go inside without exposing himself to the humans. I told him to wait behind the club and I'd be there as fast as I could. Before I could get him into my car, the police showed up and arrested us. He was too weak to fight—not that Troy would have anyway. There's no way he'd have ever done something to hurt a human."

Ravyn looked as ill as Susan felt. "You're kidding."

He shook his head. "We weren't allowed a phone call or anything. They took us to a cell on the east side of the building . . . no shades or anything else over the windows. I kept shouting at them to move us to another cell, but they'd just laugh and make jokes about crispy critters and toast. There was nothing we could do but wait."

He shook his head and turned so green that Susan halfexpected him to be ill on the floor. When he spoke again, his voice was barely more than a whisper. "Troy kept moving out of the way of the sunlight, and I kept trying to cover the window, but by nine o'clock, it was over." He winced at the pain of his memory. He looked around the table at the Dark-Hunters. "Pray to whatever

God you worship that none of you ever die like that. Forget what Apollo did to the Daimons . . . this is a whole hell of a lot worse. You don't die right away. It's slow and painful. You just smolder while your skin and bone melt until there's nothing left. Not even ashes." He covered his eyes with his hands as if trying to banish the images that were haunting him. "He was totally aware of everything right up to the end. He kept praying over and over, between crying and screaming from the pain." Dave let out a sob. "Why wouldn't they at least give me an ax to put him out of his misery?"

Susan covered her mouth as bile rose in her throat. She glanced around at the Dark-Hunters who were there. All of them felt the pain of what he described. All of them. It was plain on every face. But it was Ravyn her gaze settled on. In the back of her mind was an image of him in the same situation.

It was more than she could stand.

"How did you get out of jail?" Otto asked.

Dave clenched and unclenched his fist as a myriad of emotions played across his face. Rage. Hurt. Even bitter humor was there. But it was the hatred that flared so bright, it was blinding. "They were watching it. After Troy died, they came to the cell and opened the door. . . . 'Guess we were wrong about you. But you should be more careful about who you befriend.' Then they stepped back and walked me out of there."

"We can get them for murder!" Erika said angrily.

Leo shook his head. "How? I'm sure by now they've erased whatever surveillance data they had. Even if they hadn't, who would have believed it? Human beings don't disintegrate in real life—only in Hollywood movies."

"And there's no body," Otto added. "No evidence. As far as we can prove, all they did was arrest one man who they let go a few hours later. No harm. No foul. They're untouchable."

Dave's gaze went to Leo. "And that's why I quit. I'm completely out of this."

Kyl got up and reached for him.

"Don't touch me," Dave snapped as he stepped away.

Kyl's features turned harsh. "You've got to pull yourself together."

"No, hell, I don't." His face was ashen. "I'm a sixth-generation

Squire on my father's side, Kyl. Eighth- on my mother's. I grew up in the house with Troy and I never doubted what I would do with my life." He gestured meaningfully with his hands to emphasize his words. "We are here to protect the Dark-Hunters' identities. We're their lifeline when they're hurt and we're the only ones they're ever allowed to rely on. Dammit, I failed him. And now I know the man who was like a brother to me is stuck as a Shade suffering for eternity because he tried to protect us. Where's the justice in that?" He turned toward Leo. "I don't care if you guys kill me. I'm done. I can't go through this again."

"He's right," Nick said in a deep voice. He gripped the cup of tequila so tightly that his knuckles were white. "This is just like New Orleans. The Daimons are screwing with us and laughing while they do it. There's no telling what they've done that we don't even know about . . . yet." He cut a look around the table that was so cold it could freeze fire, and it chilled Susan all the way to her bones. "For all we know right now, one of you could be a Daimon who's already killed a Dark-Hunter and who is now using his body to spy on us." His gaze stopped on Cael. "You even live with them."

Cael's face turned to stone. "What's that supposed to mean?"

"When a cow lives with the butcher, sooner or later he gets eaten unless he helps the other cows off to their slaughter."

"Bullocks!" Cael shouted as he came to his feet.

Still Nick didn't back down. He merely sat there, staring at Cael as if he were trying to figure out if it was Cael or something else. "How *do* we know Stryker or one of his chief minions hasn't possessed you?"

Otto scowled at him. "Nick, what are you talking about?"

He pinned that deadly glare on Otto. "You don't remember anything about the night my mother died, do you?"

"We were attacked."

"To say the least." His voice dripped sarcasm. "We weren't just attacked, Otto. We were fucked over royally. Don't you remember the phones and how the Daimons played us? I'd get a call from you, only it wasn't you. . . . It was them screwing with our heads."

Susan and Ravyn exchanged an eerie look. The hair on the back of her neck rose at Nick's words.

"No one screwed with the phones, Nick." Otto snarled.

"I don't remember that either," Kyl added.

"How could they get our numbers?" Ravyn asked.

Nick scoffed. "Do I look like a Daimon? How the hell do I know? But they did it. Night after night they led us on a merry chase through the streets as they killed us and any innocent by-stander who caught their attention." He looked over at Otto. "Don't you remember the night they almost killed Ash?"

By Otto's face it was obvious he had no idea what Nick was talking about. "No."

Nick growled deep in the back of his throat. "Let me guess, when all was said and done, Acheron took all of you aside one by one and erased your memory, didn't he?"

Kyl shook his head. "Ash wouldn't do something like that."

"You idiot. Of course he would. None of you know Jack Shit about him. But *I* do." He raked his hand through his hair as his eyes burned with anger. "When you think back, is everything fuzzy? You can remember some things clear as a bell, and others are vague?"

"That's true of any memory," Otto scoffed.

"Yeah, and do you remember when we were trying to get ahold of Ash and no one knew where he was?"

"Yes."

Kyl frowned. "Ash said his phone wasn't working."

"Trust me, it was working just fine. He knew what was hap-pening, but he stayed out of it and left us alone to deal with the Daimons, knowing we weren't capable of fighting them without him. And then the Daimons came out and went to town all over us. While we were distracted with trying to fight them off, their leader, Desiderius, possessed Ulrich so that he could kill Amanda's sister and my mother. As a possessed Dark-Hunter he was able to enter Kyrian's house without an invitation. He took off Kassim's head and then he killed Amanda and Kyrian."

Kyl rolled his eyes. "You're the idiot, Nick. They didn't die."

"Oh, yes, they did. Trust me. Artemis had already dumped me into Hades when Kyrian showed up. Even though he was dead, he was beside himself because Amanda wasn't there with him. Since she was a Christian and he was an ancient Greek, she'd gone off to her heaven while he was on his way to his. Still bloody from our deaths, we stood there on the banks of the river Acheron, waiting for Charon to ferry us to the other side. While we waited, Kyrian spilled his guts to me about everything that had happened to cause his death."

"Kyrian isn't dead," Kyl insisted.

Hatred flared deep in Nick's eyes. "Not now he isn't. Acheron brought him back."

Still Kyl argued. "Ash doesn't have that power."

"And you're stupid if you believe that." Nick sat forward and punctuated his words by pounding his hand on the desk. "News flash, folks. Ash is a god."

Leo and Otto laughed at him.

"Nick, are you high?" Zoe asked.

He turned on Zoe like a demon looking for a victim. "No. Deny it if you want, but I know the truth. I might be the youngest Dark-Hunter created, but I've been in this world a long time and I know *exactly* what I'm talking about. The rest of you are just fools in a game that's being played behind your backs. The Spathi Daimons that you're up against now aren't stupid. Until Desiderius went after Kyrian the first time, no one even knew that Daimons could live a hundred years, never mind a thousand . . . or more to the point, *eleven* thousand. But Ash knew and even when I asked him about them, he didn't say a word. Why is that?"

Dragon narrowed his eyes on Nick. "Ash didn't know or he would have."

"Ash is the king of secrets. You all know that. I don't know how the Daimons are related to him, but I know there's a link."

Now it was Belle's turn to laugh. "What are you saying? Ash is a Daimon?"

"No. He's a god and somehow he's linked to them." Nick looked at each one of them. "These aren't what you're used to dealing with, folks. These are so much more and now they have human help, too."

Menkaura frowned. "What do they want with us?"

"They want to bathe in your blood and trust me, they will."

Erika made a rude noise. "Well, aren't you just Mr. Sunshine?"

Nick turned his head slowly toward her like something out of a bad horror movie. Not to mention the fact that his face reminded Susan of a king addressing a peasant who'd dared to breathe his air. "Who are you, little girl, and why are you even in this meeting?"

She pointed to Ravyn. "His substitute Squire and I have no idea, but at least I'm not bringing everyone down with this doom and gloom bullshit."

Now he looked to Susan like the king after the peasant had wet his shoes . . . and she didn't mean with water. "Substitute Squire? What the hell is that?"

Erika gave him a "duh" stare that had to be one she reserved for those who were a bit slow. "It's a person who doesn't want to be a Squire, but who got drafted into this because Mr. Kontis won't let anyone else around him for more than twenty-four hours. I think my father has lasted longer with him than anyone else in the past because he's half-deaf and can't listen to Ravyn's razor-sharp sarcasm. Something I can only tolerate because, well, he taught it to me from the crib."

Nick didn't look impressed by her speech. "Then as a Squire you should know to sit there and keep your mouth shut."

Erika's jaw dropped in indignation. "What do you know about being a Squire?"

"He used to run the Dark-Hunter Web site," Leo said under his breath.

She turned on him in a pique. "And that makes him an expert?"

Kyl shrugged. "He's the one who put the Squire's handbook online."

"So he can write HTML, so what? My grandma could do it, if she were still alive."

"Erika . . ." Leo said in a warning tone.

"Shut up, Leo," she snapped.

Nick hissed at her, "You don't talk to a Theti like that."

"Why not?"

The look on Nick's face would have made anyone with half a brain shudder. Erika, on the other hand, appeared to be missing the part of her brain where her self-preservation should be located.

"You need to learn to respect your elders," he growled dangerously.

"Oh, yeah?" she challenged him. "Like you would have?"

"As a Squire, I always followed orders."

Cocking her head, she folded her arms over her chest and glared at him. "Yeah, right. If you followed orders, then how did you get to be a Dark-Hunter, huh? Last time I checked, we weren't supposed to be doing that, now were we?"

"Erika!"

"What?" she snapped at Leo.

He gave her a harsh stare. "We have more important things to discuss and we're running out of time."

She held her hands up. "Fine. Talk. I'm going to get a sandwich." As she crossed the room, she mumbled to herself. "Like he's going to save us with his sage bullshit—the man don't know shite about shit. He couldn't even save New Orleans and he lived there."

Those words went through the room like a pall as everyone sucked their breath in sharply.

Erika tried to open the door only to find it locked.

His face contorted by rage, Nick shot to his feet. "What did you say?"

Erika ignored him while she tried to get the door to open. "Why won't this door open?"

"What. Did. You. Say?"

"Leave her alone, Nick," Otto said, rising.

Nick threw his hand out and Otto went crashing into the far wall. "What happened in New Orleans?" Nick demanded of Erika.

Finally her survival sense kicked in. Erika turned around, eyes wide as Nick approached her. Gulping, she pressed herself against the door and made a tiny squeak noise.

Nick was only two feet away from her when he went flying across the room to land not far from Otto.

"Two can play that game, boy," Ravyn said in a feral growl as he stood up. "And I've had a lot more practice with my powers than you have. Don't you *ever* threaten her."

The door opened a crack.

"Erika." Ravyn's tone was eerily calm and pleasant. "Go get your sandwich."

She hurried from the room as Nick pushed himself up from the floor.

Nick glared at Kyl and Otto. "I want the truth about New Orleans."

It was Otto who answered as he straightened his clothes with a tug. "New Orleans was hit dead-on with a category three hurricane about nine months ago."

Susan's breath caught at the horror she saw on Nick's face.

"What happened?" he asked, his voice thin and breathy.

Otto sighed before he answered. "The levee broke and flooded the city. It completely wiped out the Ninth Ward."

Nick leaned against the wall as horror played across his face.

"Your house is still standing," Kyl said gently. "It had some damage from the winds, but it's repaired now. Kyrian made sure of it."

"Screw my house. What about the people?"

Otto and Kyl exchanged a sick look. "It was bad. But we're—"

"Why are you here?" Nick demanded. "Why aren't you down there helping people?"

Anger flared in Otto's eyes. "We were sent here before the hurricane hit."

"You just walked out and left the city?"

"We did what we were told to do, Nick. We're Squires, remember?"

Nick curled his lip. "You bastards." He pinned a hate-filled glare on Kyl. "I don't expect better from Otto, but you were born there, same as me, Kyl. How could you turn your back on the city and our people?"

"You don't know what you're talking about, Nick," he said between clenched teeth. "Damn you, how dare you take that tone with me? I lost family down there, boy. We weren't the ones sitting on an island with Savitar, learning to surf. We were in the thick of it. I stayed there through the storm, with Kyrian, Valerius, Talon, and the rest. I was part of search and rescue teams until I couldn't take it anymore. And then I got up and started it over. Every single day. I wasn't transferred up here until three months ago. So don't you dare stand there and judge me."

Leo whistled. "Enough! Squires, out of the room. Now."

Susan felt like she'd been caught by shrapnel. She started to argue that she hadn't been the one causing problems, but Leo didn't look like he could take any more arguments from anyone.

Ravyn squeezed her hand reassuringly before she got up. Ironically, Nick took two steps for the door before he must have remembered that he was no longer a Squire. He was a Dark-Hunter.

There was so much agony in his gaze that it stole her breath as he returned to his chair. Feeling for him and for Dave she followed the men out of the room.

She paused to look back at Ravyn, who gave her a small smile. That smile warmed her and gave her strength as she closed the door and headed back downstairs to start her research again.

All right," Leo said as soon as the Dark-Hunters were alone in the room with him. "We have a unique problem here. We not only have to avoid the Daimons, but the police, too. Anyone have a suggestion?"

"Bend over and kiss your ass good-bye," Nick said.

They ignored that oh so not helpful comment.

"Don't we have some cops on the Squires' payroll?" Zoe asked.

Leo shook his head. "Not in Seattle. We have some in Internal Affairs and with the DA's office, but none on the force itself."

Belle made a sound of disgust. "Why not?"

"The last one retired," Leo said irritably. "The other one died a year ago of a heart attack. We haven't had a chance to replace them."

"Well, that blows." Belle reached for the tequila bottle and didn't bother with her glass. She took a giant swig. "No offense, but I don't want to be barbecue."

Zoe gave her a pointed stare. "None of us do."

"Has anyone been able to get a hold of Ash?" Dragon asked.

One by one, they shook they heads.

Except for Nick. "You won't hear from him until it's too late.

Any time he vanishes, the Daimons go wild. I told you, they're linked somehow."

Leo cleared his throat. "That doesn't help us, Nick."

"And neither does staying together like this," Ravyn added. "We've been together too long. We need to break."

"Yeah," Menkaura agreed.

Belle set the half-empty bottle back on the table. "I just wish we knew what they were up to!"

"That's a no-brainer," Nick said snidely. He looked around the table as if they were all morons, and honestly, Ravyn was getting a little tired of his attitude. Train him, hell, the man would be lucky if Ravyn didn't kill him.

"Care to enlighten us blind sheep?" Zoe asked.

"Most of you are ancient warriors. Can't you figure it out? Think about it. All through history, what has brought down every great civilization or people?"

"War," Cael answered.

"No," Zoe whispered. She looked around the table at them. "It's what has brought all of us over to Artemis."

Ravyn nodded as he understood what they meant. "Betrayal. Sabotage. None of us were brought down by the enemy who attacked us in the open. We were brought down by the enemy within. By the traitor we didn't see coming at our backs."

"That's right." Nick's gaze went back to Cael. "It's always the one you least expect who does it, too. We won't be destroyed by the Daimons. We're going to be destroyed by one of our own."

Ravyn stiffened at words he knew were all too true. It was why, as Erika had pointed out, he didn't let anyone near him. He'd had enough of trusting people. God, he'd been killed by his own brother. A brother whose life he'd saved only a year before Phoenix had taken his.

Zoe stood up. "And on that sobering thought, I'm going to patrol."

Menkaura fell in behind her.

"Watch your backs," Leo called.

Zoe paused at the door. "Don't worry. It's what I'm best at."

"And beware of the phones," Nick said. "I don't know how the Daimons do it, but not even the caller ID works right."

She scoffed at him. "Yeah, thanks."

Dragon and Belle went next, leaving Cael, Ravyn, Nick, and Leo alone in the room.

Cael met Ravyn's gaze. "August 14, 2007."

"What's that?"

When he spoke, his tone was barely a whisper. "That's the day I need you to help me do the right thing."

Ravyn's heart clenched as he realized it must be Amaranda's birthday. That more than anything else told him that Nick was wrong to accuse Cael. He was the one person Ravyn had faith in. "I'll be there."

Cael nodded and then passed a hostile glare toward Nick before he headed to the door.

As soon as it closed, Ravyn sighed as he looked at the Cajun. "Well, you certainly know how to win friends and influence people. No wonder Savitar wanted you off his hands."

"Don't start with me, Katagari. Out of all of them, you know I'm telling the truth."

How he wanted to deny it, but yeah, he could feel it. His animal senses picked up on it with an eerie accuracy. There was something highly out of the ordinary here. "For the record, I'm Arcadian, not Katagaria. Jeez, you've been hanging around Talon too long."

Nick sneered. "For the record, I don't give a shit."

Turning away from the angry man, Ravyn looked at Leo. "So what's our next move?"

"You have to stay hidden," Leo said as he handed him the folder he'd been thumbing through.

"What's this?"

"A file I was collecting. About a year ago, I got a call from a hysterical woman who said she'd seen her neighbor come home one night with blood on her clothes. A neighbor with fangs. I investigated it and found out the woman was on all kinds of medication, so I wrote it off."

"Okay, so why give it to me?"

"Open the folder."

Ravyn did. His gaze went straight to the third paragraph where Leo had underlined four words that leaped out at him. *Chief of police's wife.*

"That's who she lived next door to."

Ravyn narrowed his eyes as those words went through him.

"Give it to Susan. Believe me, if anyone can find the truth, even while the cops are hunting her down, it's her." Leo patted him on the arm and left.

Alone now with Nick, Ravyn closed the folder. "Just so you know, Cael would never betray us."

"Yeah, and two years ago I thought Ash was a friend of mine. You know what that got me? A bullet to my brain."

"I don't know how you died, but I know Ash didn't kill you."

Nick gave a bitter laugh. "I wish I still had your blind faith. Unfortunately, mine was stripped from me the night I died."

Ravyn felt sorry for the man. What he had inside him was actually very typical for a new Dark-Hunter. That sense of outrage and of being wronged. The need to strike out at everyone around you. Hell, he'd even attacked Acheron when the Atlantean had shown up to train him. But then, he hadn't really needed training. Unlike a human warrior, he was used to his powers and used to fighting preternatural beings.

"When do you want to start your training?"

"I don't need training," Nick said. "I was a Theti and I know how to stake a Daimon."

As a former Squire, Nick also knew the basics for Dark-Hunter survival.

"Fine. I guess for the first time in history, Savitar was wrong."

"He wasn't wrong. He just wanted an excuse to get me off the island. Now, if you'll excuse me, I have things to do."

Ravyn didn't even want to go there. He didn't say anything as Nick left the room. That was one troubled man. But until he was willing to let go of the bitterness, there was nothing Ravyn or anyone else could do for him.

As Ravyn started for the door, he froze. There was something strange in the air . . . a whispering.

Closing his eyes, he summoned his powers of cognition and tried to hone in on it. But for his life, he couldn't. Instead, it settled as an uneasy feeling deep in his gut. Something bad was about to happen. He just couldn't tell what it was.

CHAPTER THIRTEEN

Ash laughed deep in his throat as Artemis clutched him to her in the throes of her latest orgasm. Sighing in complete contentedness, she held him close as the last tremor shook her body.

"Ah," she breathed in his ear as she draped one arm around his neck while her long, shapely legs slid from around his waist to the floor so that she could support her own weight.

Ash wiped the sweat from his face with his hand. Every muscle in his body was twitching from the marathon she'd put him through over the last six hours. His long blond hair was damp while his entire body was covered in a fine sheen of sweat. He gladly welcomed the cool breeze that whispered in from the veranda.

Leaning back against the wall, Artemis laughed seductively. "Surely you're not giving up so quickly, Acheron. Only two more to go now. I wonder what position we should try next?"

He pulled away and gave her a crooked smile as he summoned a towel and used it to wipe at his chest. "Actually, that was your sixth and now you owe me a feeding before I leave." Completely uninhibited by his nudity, he draped the towel over his shoulders and held it in place with both hands.

Her face fell immediately. "What?" She looked past his shoulder to her hourglass on the shelf above her bed. It was still half-full of sand. "You're wrong, Acheron. That was only four since I started timing this."

Leaning on one arm against the wall where she stood, he savored the sensation of having bested her again. One day she'd learn not to play these games with him. But what the hell? At least it kept him on his toes. "From when you started logging your time, yes. But not from when I started logging mine."

He snapped his fingers and five hourglasses appeared beside hers. Each one had started right before her orgasms began. One hourglass to mark the hour from when one started until he had given her six within the allotted time.

All had expired except for the last two, but it was the fourth hourglass that was important. Held between the hands of two black gargoyles as the last few sands were quickly making their way from the top to the bottom, it was his key to freedom. He held his hand out and it shot from the shelf to his waiting grip so that he could show it to her.

"This one started earlier, right before you had your last two orgasms and vanished out of the room to delay our bargain. You came back after *your* hourglass had expired to begin again, but mine was still going . . . marking the time from when the last two left off to these four. Now I've fulfilled our pact, Artie. You've had your six orgasms in one hour."

She shrieked in outrage. "No! That wasn't what we agreed. You—"

"Yes, it was," he said calmly, cutting her off before he returned the hourglass to its shelf. "That was the exact wording of our contract. You set up the terms and I abided by them. Now you have to free me for ten hours."

She balled her hands into fists as her face turned as red as her mussed hair. He knew she was having to mind her tongue to keep from calling him a liar. But then she knew what he did—he couldn't lie. Once his word was given, it was unbreakable.

"I hate you!"

He snorted. "Don't keep saying that, Artie. It's cruel to get my hopes up."

In her anger, she threw her hair over her shoulder as she continued to fume at him. His gaze narrowed on her exposed neck, which caused his stomach to rumble.

She paused instantly. Her green eyes darkened as her heartbeat picked up.

Unable to stand the temptation, Ash jerked her to him with one arm, dipped his head down, and pressed his lips to the throbbing vein that enticed him like a Siren's lure. The sweet fragrance of her blood made his own heart pick up speed as he opened his lips to taste her. He felt his incisors growing until he knew they were long enough to give him what he needed.

Growling deep in his throat, he sank his fangs into her neck and tasted the life that flowed inside her. Feeding was the only time he really wanted to be in her presence. The only time she didn't infuriate him beyond his best tolerance.

Here, for a moment, he found her soothing. Her blood calmed him as it nourished his hunger. Without breaking from her, he separated her thighs again and drove himself back into her body.

Lifting her legs from the floor, she cried out in happiness as her hands roamed his back while he continued to take what he needed.

He would be free of her soon. . . .

Susan *looked up* from the floor as Ravyn entered the room with an air of distraction hovering around him. There was something strange about his demeanor. It wasn't like him to be so preoccupied. Normally when he was in a room, he was *in* the room.

"Are you all right?"

His face grim, he rubbed at the back of his neck. "I don't know. Nick's words keep chasing themselves around in my head. Kind of like ferrets or something else vile and evil. Not that ferrets are particularly vile, they're actually kind of tasty when I'm in leopard form."

Susan screwed her face up. "That's disgusting."

He winked at her. "I know and I'm only kidding. I don't like anything raw in either form . . . except for female flesh."

"Ew! That's worse, you cannibalistic necromaniac."

"You mean necrophiliac?"

"No. *Necromaniac* as in 'lunatic with the dead.' "

He appeared to consider that. "Actually, wouldn't it be *un-necromaniac,* as in 'the undead'?"

Susan held her hands up in surrender. She knew when she'd been bested verbally. "Switching topics back to Nick. What's bothering you exactly?"

"After you left, he kept saying that he thought one of our own, a Dark-Hunter, would betray the rest of us."

That bothered her, too. It was really a scary thought, but she had a hard time believing the men and women she'd met upstairs would turn on one another. There seemed to be an unspoken respect and brotherhood that existed between them.

"Boy, as Erika said, he's just a ray of sunshine, isn't he?"

Ravyn didn't seem to find the humor in her sarcasm. "Yeah, but I think he's right. Can you imagine how much damage a Daimon could do if they possessed a Dark-Hunter?"

More than she really wanted to think about. The Daimons had done enough damage in Daimon form. Imagine one masquerading as a good guy . . . that could get ugly really fast. "How easy could that be to do? I mean you guys kick serious Daimon ass, right?"

"I don't know—they've taken out two of us already and came too damned close to killing me. It's enough to make me wonder how much of Nick's crap is true and what isn't." He cocked his head as if realizing that his words were really getting to her.

She didn't like the thought of being Daimon bait. But then neither did he.

"Don't worry about it, Susan. I'm just thinking out loud." He moved forward to hand her the manilla folder in his hands.

"What's this?"

"A present from Leo."

Susan set it aside as she watched Ravyn withdraw back toward the wall. Something really wasn't right about him. It was like he sensed something that she couldn't, and it reminded her of a pet that was staring at the wall. And just like that pet stare, it unnerved her. "Hey?"

He looked over at her.

"I wanted to ask you about something Erika said earlier where you're concerned."

He scowled at her. "I don't wear purple panties to bed and I don't chase cat toys when they're thrown down in front of me."

Susan was stunned by his unexpected response. Uh-huh. It was obvious the man had some hidden issues.

"What was that action? What are you talking about?" she asked with a laugh.

He looked baffled by her question. "Isn't that what she said about me? It normally is . . . and it's most definitely not true."

Susan couldn't speak as she fought down her laughter. Most likely, he wouldn't think it funny to be laughed at, but it was hard to bury. Her mouth merely opened and closed like a guppy as she sought a suitable answer.

Finally she got enough control to speak again. "Well, I can certainly vouch for the lack of panties myself. I've been down there enough to know. As for the other . . . that could be interesting. Maybe we should try an experiment?"

Ravyn shook his head at her. "So what was your question then?"

Susan hesitated as she considered what he might answer. Not to mention, she was a bit captivated by the rugged appearance he made standing in the room as if ready to battle someone. "Erika said that, as a rule, you don't allow people around you for more than twenty-four hours."

He nodded. "It's true."

She couldn't imagine how he tolerated that kind of isolation. She liked to be alone, but not always. There were definite times when she liked having friends over. Or honestly, times when she *needed* someone around her. "Why is that?"

His face droll, he made an interesting noise. "Ever notice most people are major pains in the ass? I'd rather save myself the trouble of dealing with them and just avoid being around them to begin with."

In spite of the sincerity of his tone, she didn't buy that answer. It came too automatically, as if he'd rehearsed it repeatedly. More to the point, she was learning a lot about this man. There was a weird blankness that came into his eyes whenever he wasn't being honest, or whenever he was hiding something.

He had that look now.

Getting up, she walked over to him. They stood so close that she could feel the heat of his skin. Smell the sharp, tingling fragrance of his aftershave. His expression turned guarded.

"Talk to me, Ravyn."

He looked away as a veil descended over his features. Susan placed her hand against the muscle that was working in his jaw. The dark whiskers of his cheek gently scraped the palm of her hand as she felt an inner connection to him. It reminded her of taming a wild beast.

His eyes flared at that as if her action irritated him. "I don't need you to soothe me, Susan. I'm not a child."

"Good," she said seriously. "I'm not a nanny. I personally like to avoid most children, since they're rude, ill-mannered, and usually smell like freaky kinds of juice and mixed fruit." She frowned as those words struck her with a bit of humor. "Wait a second, given all that, you *do* remind of a child."

He gave her a peeved glare.

She smiled at him as she patted his cheek playfully. Something that reminded her she was actually petting a wild leopard who could tear her arm off if he wanted to. That thought sent an odd sensation through her. She really was taunting the devil.

"Sorry," she said, not out of fear, but out of guilt that he didn't find her comment funny. "I couldn't resist." She lowered her hand from his face before taking his large, scarred hand into hers. "Now you know I'm a reporter, so you might as well answer my question truthfully, or I'll just keep asking it until you lose your mind."

Ravyn growled low in the back of his throat. It wasn't in his nature to confide in people. Even when he'd been mortal, he'd always preferred to keep his personal business just that—personal.

But he'd learned enough about Susan to realize she wasn't joking. She would stay on his tail like a hound running a fox to ground. In a way, he actually respected her persistence and some alien part of him actually liked being honest with her. He liked having someone who knew him.

So to save both of them a lot of time and pain, he answered her. "Honestly? I don't want people around me for two reasons—they ultimately betray you or they die on you. Either way, you're screwed and you spend all your time obsessing on why you didn't see it coming. Or that you did something or didn't do something to cause it. No offense, but I don't like to be hurt and I'd rather just avoid it."

He saw the compassion in her blue eyes as she stroked his hand with her thumb. "Tell me about it. My father ran out on us when I was too young to even remember what he looked like. He donated his sperm, then fled his responsibilities. My mother never mentioned him, but I knew she was never the same after he left. To the day she died, she refused to date anyone. And when I got into trouble with my career, all those people who'd been my so-called friends ran like frightened rats from a sinking ship. People I'd known and trusted for years, even the one person I thought I loved. The only ones who stayed were Jimmy and Angie, and strangely enough, Leo . . . and don't get me started on the dying part. I'm trying hard enough not to have a breakdown."

Even though it was against his nature, Ravyn pulled her into his arms and held her quietly against him to give her whatever comfort he could. Looking down he saw the faint scar on her wrist.

"Tell me something, Susan."

"What?"

"When did you try to kill yourself?"

Susan swallowed as she remembered that awful, cold November night. It'd been about a week after Alex had left her, and she'd been forced out of her house into a roach-infested dive.

They'd even repo'd her car that afternoon.

On a holiday.

"It was Thanksgiving," she whispered as she felt the tears pricking her eyes. "Jimmy and Angie hadn't been able to spend it with me because his parents had come in from out of town. They'd invited me over, but the last thing I wanted was to put on a happy face when everything in my life was going wrong. Not to mention I didn't want to answer any questions from his parents about the news reports they'd been watching, where I was served up raw.

"So there I was, in my crappy, rundown apartment. Alone. Thinking about my mother, and how much I missed her, and I realized at that moment, that all the things I'd wanted as a little girl—my dreams of having a family and career—were all gone. All the things I'd worked so damned hard for had been stripped away, one by one. There wasn't someone to stand by me through the scandal. Someone to hold my hand and tell me it was going to be okay and that they would be there for me. I only had me, and I was just too tired to take another step alone. I hurt so badly and there was no one else who understood what I was going through. No one who'd seen their entire life crumble to nothing. So I decided the world would be better off without me in it."

He cradled her head against his chest. "But you didn't die."

"No," she said, sniffing back her tears. "After I'd cut my wrists, I realized how stupid I was being. More than that, I realized that if I killed myself, then those bastards who set me up would win. They wouldn't care that I was gone. They'd probably gloat, and that gave me the strength I needed to survive. After all they had taken from me, I wasn't about to let them have that, too. So I called an ambulance and promised myself that I would never be that weak again. My enemies can take what they want, but my life is mine and so long as I breathe, it has value. I won't ever give up. Not again."

Ravyn felt something warm go through him at her words. She was amazing. And she was stronger than anyone had a right to be.

It was weird, but of all the people he'd known in his long life, with the exception of Cael, she was the only one he really believed understood his feelings. She knew firsthand exactly what he was talking about when it came to loss.

"Damn, we're a pair, aren't we?" he said quietly.

"Could be worse."

Her words surprised him. "How so?"

"We could be Nick."

He laughed gently at her never-ending humor. Sometimes it was gallows and dark, but it never failed her. She wore it like armor. "Good point."

Clearing her throat, she pulled away. He didn't miss the very subtle gesture of her wiping away a tear with her pinkie before she looked up at him. "What's his deal anyway? Why does he have the bow and arrow mark on his face while the rest of you have them in more private areas?"

"I have no idea. I've never seen a Dark-Hunter have one in such an obvious spot before. I think Zoe might have had something when she asked if Artemis had slapped him."

Susan smiled at the thought. "Well, if he was as kind to her as he's been to the rest of us, I might understand her motivation."

"Yeah, but in a way I feel sorry for him. He's not the same man who used to run the Web site. He was always sarcastic, but I can respect that. Now he's bitter and angry."

Ravyn shook his head as he remembered the way Nick used to be. There was nothing he could do to change that. Only time would allow Nick to regain some semblance of what he'd been before. "Enough about Nick. You need to check that folder out. Leo thinks it's a lead to who's helping the Daimons."

That caught her interest immediately. She headed back for the folder and sat cross-legged on the mattress to read it.

Ravyn's groin jerked at that and he wasn't sure why . . . well, okay, he was. There was something very inviting about that position as inappropriate thoughts went through him. He'd give her credit, she was hot in bed and on the floor, and he wondered how she'd be in other places such as the kitchen counter, the shower, and out in the woods, under the stars.

His body was really burning at those thoughts.

But she was completely engrossed by her work right now. She didn't even appear to know he was in the room as she started fanning pages around the mattress to read them. Her brow furrowed, she grabbed the laptop and pulled up Google.

"You want something to drink?"

"Coffee," she said in a distracted tone as she grabbed a pencil and started making notes.

"Black?"

"Cream and sugar, or a caramel Macchiato is always welcomed."

"Ooo, a Starbucks woman after my own heart."

That finally made her look up. "That's the best part about living in Seattle. Twenty-four stores in a ten-block radius. It's the only thing I don't miss about living in D.C."

He laughed. "All right, I'll see you in a few."

She went back to her research while he made a coffee run.

Ravyn paused in the doorway for a second just to watch her. She looked beautiful but tired. Most of all, she looked determined. He remembered a time when he'd had that kind of fire. A time when he'd lived for the thrill of the hunt. He wasn't sure when those feelings had faded. When he'd learned the complacency of just going through the motions of life. Of finding a temporary partner for sex one night and then leaving to find a new one the next.

Now he wondered what it would be like to have a woman who knew his likes and dislikes. To have a woman who knew what he was and who didn't seem to mind that he was both a leopard and a man. . . .

Repressing those thoughts before they got him into trouble, he left the room and headed upstairs. No matter how much Susan appealed to him, she was off the menu. There was no hope for them. He'd been given his one shot at a mate, and he'd sworn himself to Artemis. No matter how much he might wish otherwise, there was no kind of future for them. He went to the kitchen to find Terra bustling around the kitchen as she helped prepare appetizers for their clients in the club.

She paused as she saw him. "You need something?"

"Yeah, he needs to leave."

Sighing in disgust, he turned to see Phoenix behind him. "Lay off me, Nix. I'm really not in the mood for your bullshit."

"Yeah, that's because you're a pussy."

Anger whipped through him so fast that Ravyn was actually stunned he didn't go for his brother's throat. Ravyn turned slowly to glare at him. "Me? *I'm* the pussy?"

"That's what I said."

"Uh-huh. If I'm the coward here, then why am I dead while you're alive? You were mated for what, two hundred years, and you never bonded to Georgette? What were you waiting for, Phoenix? There were several blue moons during that period."

Growling in rage, Phoenix started for him only to have Terra knock him away. "Sanctuary, Nix."

His breathing ragged, he had bloodlust all over him as he glared at Ravyn.

Terra let out a deep breath. "Leave the kitchen, Phoenix. You can either go on two legs or I'll carry you out."

His gaze slid to hers. "You wouldn't dare."

"Oh, trust me." she said in deadly earnest. "I would and I'm man enough to do it, too."

He curled his lip at her before he headed out the swinging door that led to the club.

Terra wiped her hands on her apron before she looked back at Ravyn. "Now where were we?"

"Coffee."

"Coffee coming right up."

Impressed by Dorian's mate, Ravyn watched as she made her way over to the counter where the coffeepots were set. His brother's mate was an interesting beast. She didn't look like Dorian's type at all. And for some reason, Ravyn's curiosity got the better of him. "Are you bonded to Dorian?"

She paused in filling the mug to look up at him. "Yes. Unlike Phoenix, he isn't a pussy."

Ravyn laughed in spite of himself as she returned to filling the mug then she pulled a thermos out and filled it, too. "How long have the two of you been mated?"

"Seventy-five years." She placed the mug and thermos with a small container of sugars and cream on a tray for him.

"How long have you been bonded?"

"Nosy much?" Her gaze burned into his, and to his surprise, she answered. "Seventy-five years. Dorian never wanted to come home and find his mate dead after what all of you had been through. He said that the Fates joined us for a reason and that his place was to be by my side, even in death."

A newfound respect for his brother welled up inside Ravyn. But more than that, he remembered the horror of the night his village had been destroyed. When the men had started falling around them, the assumption had been that those who were standing had mates who'd survived.

They'd rushed back home only to find out just how many of their clan hadn't bonded to their mates.

The hardest blow for Ravyn had been his mother. Given how much his parents supposedly loved and respected each other, he'd just assumed they were bonded. But apparently his father hadn't loved her enough.

"Thanks, Terra," he said, taking the tray.

"Ravyn?"

He paused to look at her.

"Dorian thinks about you all the time and he holds himself responsible for not stepping up to defend you against Phoenix." She looked around as if embarrassed that she'd confided that to him. "I just thought you should know."

Ravyn's throat grew tight. So he did have a brother who still loved him. Not that it changed anything. Dorian was still too much of a coward to stand up to the others or to let Ravyn know that he didn't agree with the pack about his banishment.

So be it. He'd lived these past three hundred years without them, he could certainly live longer.

He inclined his head to Terra before he left her to return to Susan, who was gnawing her pencil to a nub.

"You're going to break your teeth on that." He set the tray down beside her.

She appeared baffled by his words. "What?"

He pointed to the pencil. "Are you hungry?"

She looked at it and laughed. "No, it's a bad habit I started in grade school. My old boss used to say he could tell whenever I was on to something good by the number of teeth prints in the pencil on my desk." She set the pencil aside and reached for the coffee.

"I assume by the state of the pencil that you've found something."

She poured the cream in and added sugar. "Yes and no. Apparently the chief of police's wife died a couple of months ago while visiting Europe with her son."

"Really?"

She nodded. "I've pulled up a few photos of her at various social events, but nothing that leaps out at me." Cradling the mug in one hand, she held up a piece of paper from the folder where Leo had written a small note: *Makes the Mad Hatter Look Sane.* "I think Leo was right."

"Well, so much for that."

His phone rang. Ravyn pulled it out of his pants and answered it. "Ravyn here."

It was Otto's voice. "Hey, Ravyn, we have a bit of a situation we need you for. Can you meet us at Post Alley?"

"When?"

"Fifteen minutes?"

"I'll be there." He hung up the phone to see Susan's quizzical stare. "Otto wants me at Post Alley."

"Why? I thought you were supposed to be lying low."

Ravyn shook his head. "Otto didn't say why, but it must be important though for him to call."

Susan nodded in agreement. "Can I hitch a ride over?"

"Why?"

"Curiosity. C'mon. You're a cat. Surely you, of all people, can appreciate that."

"I don't know. . . ." Ravyn hesitated.

"Oh, don't take that tone with me. Either I go with you or I find my own way."

"And if I don't want you to?"

She gave him a miffed stare. "You know, you'd look really weird in a dress and high heels."

"What's that supposed to mean?"

"It means you're not my mother. Now stop arguing and help me find my shoes."

By the expression on his face she could tell he wasn't happy, but he did help her search out her shoes, which were buried under a pile of Jimmy's papers.

It didn't take them long to reach the alley, which wasn't far from Pike's Market.

They'd just gotten out of Phoenix's Porsche and walked over to it when they heard Zoe's aggravated voice in the darkness.

"Don't make me run up that hill, Daimon, and spill my coffee. If I do, I can assure you that you'll suffer unmercifully before I kill you."

"I strangely like that woman," Susan said to Ravyn as she followed him toward Zoe's voice.

They'd only taken a few more steps before they ran into Dragon.

"What are you doing here?" he asked them.

"Call from Otto," Ravyn said.

Dragon paused. "Me, too. How weird that he'd want us both here. Out in the open."

That *was* odd. Susan looked back and forth between the men. "Did he say what he needed?"

"He didn't," they said in unison.

Dragon and Ravyn exchanged a wary stare. "Is it just me," Ravyn asked, "or do you suddenly have a bad feeling about this?"

They heard Zoe let out a war cry.

The men took off at a dead run up the hill. Without thinking, Susan ran up after them, but as they crested the hill and she saw Menkaura, Cael, and Belle also there, she realized this was a trap.

And they'd all fallen right into it.

CHAPTER FOURTEEN

Ravyn cursed as he realized what was going on. Susan had been right. The Daimons had put them together while their powers were weakened knowing that this would drain them even more—which would make them easy pickings for the Spathis. Dammit, they should have listened to Nick. He'd even warned them about the phones. Who knew the crusty bastard had been telling the truth?

And of course, Nick was the only one of them not here. . . .

"We need to separate." The words had barely left Cael's lips before bolt-holes began opening all around them, trapping them in the narrow, grungy alleyway.

Spathis were emerging from the top and bottom of the hill.

"Oh, we're screwed," Belle said as she pulled the whip off her belt and snapped it in the air before her. "Anyone got a bright idea?"

"Yeah," Zoe said as she pulled a knife from the top of her boot, "we learn to teleport."

They all looked at Ravyn. "Wish I could help folks. But that power was stripped from me when I died."

Belle made a face at him. "Well then, what good are you, leopard?"

He didn't know at present. This was a bad situation and they all knew it.

His adrenaline rushing at the prospect of a fight that would most likely be to his death, he turned to Susan. "We need to get you out of here."

She scoffed at him as she gestured toward the top and bottom of the hill where the Spathis were gathering force. "No offense, Catman, unless you know something I don't, I don't think the Daimons are going to let me out."

As much as he hated to admit it, she was right. Angry that he'd allowed himself to be caught like this, he manifested a stake in his hand. "You know the legend. Stab them in the heart and they'll die." He handed her the stake.

Susan's eyes held a degree of fear as she wrapped her hand around the stake and offered him a brave smile. "Call me Buffy. I'm even blond, but don't ask me to wear a halter top." She glanced over to Zoe. "Or corset."

Ravyn lifted her hand with the stake in it and kissed the back of her knuckles. Standing there with his death imminent, he felt a wave of respect for her the likes of which he'd never known. More than that, something sublimely tender touched his heart.

Whatever happened tonight, he only hoped that she got out of it in one piece.

Susan offered him an encouraging smile before she stepped back. Reluctantly, he let go and turned around to fight.

As the Daimons came toward them slowly, the Dark-Hunters formed a circle with their backs to one another.

Ravyn tried to put Susan behind him, but she wouldn't go. "Susan, get in the middle."

She met his gaze without flinching. "Get your head in the fight, Ravyn, and don't worry about me. I'm the only one here who isn't having my strength depleted right now."

Zoe scoffed at her bravado. "You're also the only one of us who has a soul they can steal and blood they can drink."

Susan opened her mouth to respond, then snapped it shut. "Very valid points." Then she literally hopped behind him.

Ravyn reached around his back to assure himself that she was as far from harm's way as she could be for the moment.

Dragon whipped out his nunchakus while Menkaura wrapped a strange golden chain around one fist.

The Daimons didn't attack right away. Rather, they crept toward them as if savoring the picture of them crowded together.

"What are they waiting for?" Belle asked.

Ravyn ground his teeth as he realized the answer. "For us to grow even weaker."

"Screw that," Cael snarled before he let out a war cry. He ran at the Daimon closest to him.

Without thinking, Ravyn broke formation to help Cael as two Daimons ran at Cael's back. Suddenly all hell broke loose as the Daimons swarmed over them.

Susan couldn't breathe as she watched the Daimons go after the Dark-Hunters. There were so many of them, she wasn't even sure if the Dark-Hunters were still standing.

She staggered back as a Daimon came at her, then paused a few feet from her. He sniffed the air in a way that reminded her of a dog who'd caught wind of something it found appealing. "You're not one of them," he said with a gleeful smile. "You're human."

"And you're not."

He came at her.

Susan grabbed his shirt and fell to the ground with him in tow. Rolling onto her back, she raised her legs up and kicked him over her head, away from her, then continued the roll until she was back on her feet. He landed in a heap by the Dumpster as the next Daimon came at her. She elbowed the woman in the face, then twisted around, trying to stake her.

The woman sank her fangs into Susan's arm.

Susan hissed as the pain spread through her. "I hate to girl fight, but . . ." She grabbed her by the hair and yanked as hard as she could.

The Daimon cried out before Susan head-butted her.

Ravyn turned to see Susan fighting off her attackers. Stunned by her skill, he missed the Daimon coming for his back. Something hot ripped into his shoulder. He turned with a curse to punch the Daimon in the face. He staggered back but left the knife embedded deep in Ravyn's shoulder. Pulling it out with a curse and a fierce grimace, he tossed it straight into the Daimon's chest. He exploded into a golden shower that rained down on Ravyn.

Ravyn caught the knife before it fell to the ground and headed for Susan. She executed a *mawashi-geri* or roundhouse kick so perfectly that even Bruce Lee would have been impressed. Gods love her, she did know how to handle herself. Dragon really had taught her well.

And before Ravyn could reach her, she turned on the Daimon nearest her and stabbed him with the stake.

Ravyn skidded to a stop as she killed the Daimon like a pro. She started for Ravyn, then caught herself as she realized he had black hair.

He gave her a crooked grin. "Remind me to never piss you off again."

"You got it."

He started for the Daimon who was coming at her back, but before Ravyn could take more than one step, she'd elbowed the Daimon in the face and flipped him to the ground, where she pinned him with his arm twisted behind his back and with her right foot on the small of his spine.

Realizing she was fine to fight on her own, Ravyn turned to see Belle surrounded by a group of Daimons. She was wounded and bleeding profusely as an extremely large Daimon swung an ax around.

Belle caught the Daimon against his cheek with her whip. The Daimon recoiled, then snarled before he swung the ax. He narrowly missed her as she lunged to the right.

Ravyn rushed at the Daimon's back to kick him away from Belle.

The Daimon spun on him as two more joined them. He could hear Belle cracking her whip and Dragon fighting with his nunchakus while he kept his eyes trained on the Daimon's ax so that he could dodge the deadly swings. Ravyn dropped to the ground and rolled, then kicked the Daimon's feet out from under him. Grabbing the ax as it fell toward the street, Ravyn arced it toward the Daimon's chest and killed him.

And still the Daimons kept coming.

One dove at Ravyn's back, knocking him forward. The ax flew out of his hand as he hit the ground and landed at the feet of another Daimon. Laughing, the Daimon picked up the ax and came after him.

Ravyn tried to back up, only to stagger against another Daimon who shoved him back toward the ax. Ravyn changed into a leopard at the same time the Daimon swung. He missed Ravyn and decapitated the other Daimon. But before Ravyn could think, another Daimon caught him with another ax against his back leg.

Yelping, his powers snapped from the pain and turned him back into a man against his will. He barely had time to summon clothes onto his body and roll away before they were on him.

To his surprise, Susan was there with an ax she must have taken from another Daimon. "Back off," she snarled, driving them away from Ravyn.

Ravyn tried to stand only to have his savaged leg buckle under his weight. His strength was starting to fail him and he knew the other Dark-Hunters weren't in any better shape. No matter what he might like, his pain would keep him in human form.

They were going to die.

The Daimons seemed to be growing stronger while the Dark-Hunters were weakening by the heartbeat. But even so, Ravyn wasn't going to die on the ground like a scared rodent. He forced himself to his feet. A Daimon caught him a punch to the jaw that felt like a sledgehammer striking his bones. He tasted blood as his lip split. Spitting it out onto the asphalt, Ravyn head-butted the Daimon, then kicked him away as a flash caught his attention to the right.

It was two Daimons with axes trapping Belle between them. Frozen by the horror, he watched helplessly, knowing he couldn't reach her in time.

A frisson of grief spun through all of them as they saw her fall to her knees an instant before the Daimons coldly executed her. Susan stared in horror at the woman's body as she lay in a pool of blood on the dark asphalt while the Daimons high-fived each other.

Zoe cried out and started for them, only to have her legs swept out from under her by another Daimon. She hit the ground face-first, then rolled to her back to kick out at the Daimon who was trying to stab her.

Ravyn was kicked so hard, he swore he heard three ribs crack.

Before he could regain his senses, Menkaura was flung down on top of him. The weight from him was enough to finish breaking Ravyn's ribs. His breathing labored from the pain, he caught the man's look of panic as Menkaura realized the same thing he had.

They had no way to escape.

Ravyn pushed the larger man off his chest and tried to breathe past the awful pain that seemed to seep into every part of him.

"Summon Stryker," one of the Daimons called out to the others. "He'll want to be here to see them die."

"Yeah," a deep, angry voice said, echoing off the brick walls around them, "summon the bastard. I'd really love to get my hands on him right now."

Ravyn held his breath as he heard the last voice he'd expected.

Susan hesitated as the Daimons froze in the middle of their attacks. They were all staring at the bottom of the hill.

She turned to see what had them transfixed and felt her own jaw drop.

Yeah, that'd do it.

Highlighted by the bright moonlight, the man there was incredibly tall, with long black hair that had a red stripe in the front. A strange ethereal fog swirled around him as if it were caressing his entire body like a lover. Dressed in black leather pants and a long leather coat that had its sleeves pushed back to expose his forearms and fingerless black leather gloves, he looked like the typical Goth who hung out around Capitol Hill. But as he walked slowly up the hill with a long, predatorial lope there was an aura of power so dangerous that it made every hair on her body stand up on end.

The Daimons summoned their bolt-holes.

"I don't think so," the newcomer said as each hole fizzled shut before they could use it.

A powerful boom rent the air. It emanated out from the man like a sonic wave. She felt it go through her and chill her very soul.

And as it touched each of the Daimons, they screamed out in pain, then burst into a colorful dust.

Damn, they could have used some of that themselves.

Not completely sure this man was a friend, Susan ran over to Ravyn, who was clutching his ribs and bleeding profusely from his leg, shoulder, brow, and mouth. Menkaura lay beside him, also badly hurt. Menkaura's brow was laid open and by the way his arm was twisted it was obviously broken. She knelt beside Ravyn and helped him to sit up.

"It's about time you showed up, asshole," Zoe snarled as she wiped the blood from her own chin. "Where the hell have you been?"

The man ignored her as he went silently to where Belle had been killed as if he knew exactly what had happened before his arrival. His features tormented, he knelt down on one knee and picked up a small silver necklace that had been around Belle's neck. He clenched it tight in his fist before he bent his head as if in prayer and held it to his forehead.

Susan was held transfixed by the agony he betrayed. It was obvious he mourned the loss of Belle.

He moved the necklace to his lips to kiss it before he rose slowly to his feet and faced them. He slid the necklace into his pocket.

Susan was going to take a wild guess that this was the mysterious Acheron who led the Dark-Hunters. But dang, who knew the big bad was going to be a child, and not some ancient wise man? Even though he was completely ripped, he couldn't be any older than his early twenties.

Still, there was something powerful about him. Something compelling and terrifying. Like Savitar, it was obvious he wasn't human and that he commanded primal powers no one should possess.

And it was then as he looked around that she saw his eyes. Susan actually fell back onto her butt on the street at the sight of them. They were unlike anything she'd ever seen before and they held so much power, so much wisdom and pain, that it sent a jolt through her.

Those weren't the eyes of a human. They swirled like silver

mercury as he took in the scene around him. And as those eyes went to each Dark-Hunter, the Dark-Hunter's injuries instantly healed.

"Thanks, Acheron," Dragon said irritably as he wiped his bloodied hands off on his coat. "But couldn't you have gotten here a little sooner?"

Anger bled from every pore of Ash's body as he held his hand out to help Dragon regain his feet. "Trust me, I got here just as fast as I could."

Ravyn pushed himself up from the street, then turned to help Susan up. "I heard you were *tied* up. Double-knotted to a bedpost as I recall."

"Excuse me?" Ash asked as if offended. "Who told you that?"

"A big, angry birdie on a surfboard."

Ash gave a painful grimace. "He knows? Great. That's all I need."

Zoe curled her lip at that. "We've been dying because you were making time with your girlfriend?"

Ash cut a nasty glare at Zoe. "Mind your own business, Amazon. I'm really not in the mood for your sniping." He looked around at the others. "How are the rest of you?"

"Other than pissed off, with severely damaged egos, we're fine," Cael said. "Why haven't you been answering our calls?"

"I wasn't able to."

"Uh-huh." Cael looked less than impressed by that answer. "Well, welcome to Seattle. We have a major situation with the Daimons. They're in league with the police force and are kicking our asses all over the streets. We've lost Troy and Aloysius and now Belle."

"Thank you for the recap, Cael. But I already got the picture."

"Good, 'cause I'm heading home. You can get your ass kicked for a while."

Menkaura walked over to Ash. "I'm glad you made it, but I really wish you'd been here sooner."

As Menkaura left, Susan heard Ash whisper, "Not half as much as I do."

He looked around at the others. "Anyone else have a complaint?"

Zoe opened her mouth.

"Don't start," Ash snapped. "I'm already hearing the entire tirade in your head, Zoe. I did the best I could, okay?"

"Yeah, well, your best sucks." And with that, she turned on her heel and left, muttering about her spilled coffee and worthless men.

Ravyn patted Susan on the arm, before he walked over to Ash. "You okay?"

"No. I have people who are dead and an extremely limited amount of time before I have to leave again. As Zoe says, it sucks."

"You know how Zoe is." As Ravyn clapped Ash on the back, he hissed and stiffened as if he were in an incredible amount of pain.

"Are you all right?" Susan asked.

Ash recovered himself almost instantly. "Fine. We've got bigger problems right now."

She looked over her shoulder to see what he was staring at. . . . It was a police car.

She held her breath until after it'd rolled past and vanished. She looked up at Ravyn. "That was close."

"We need to get the two of you back to the Serengeti."

Susan was baffled by Acheron's words. "How do you know where we're staying?"

"I'm omniscient, Susan."

A chill went down her spine because he knew her name. "Uh-huh. There seems to be an abundance of that going around." She glanced to Ravyn. "You ever feel left out?"

"All the time."

Well, that answered that.

As the men headed back up the hill, Susan couldn't help looking around the alley. There was no sign of a battle having been fought here. Not one. Not even dust from the Daimons, not a trace that Belle had ever lived. . . .

A gentle breeze stirred down the narrow alley and everything looked oddly peaceful and quiet. This was a tragic life the Dark-Hunters lived. They gave their lives for mankind and no one even knew they were here. And when they died, they vanished into nothing.

It brought everything home to Susan with painful clarity. How many battles like this had Ravyn fought over the centuries? How many injuries had he tended without Acheron there to fix them? He really was alone with no one there for him.

Good God, Ravyn would have died had she not gone to the shelter and taken him out. That thought made her ache for him.

"Susan?"

She looked up at Ravyn.

"You okay, babe?"

Nodding, she headed for them and took his hand, needing to feel a physical connection to him while her emotions were so raw.

Acheron gave her a look that said he knew exactly what she was thinking.

"Can you help us stop the humans from attacking the Dark-Hunters?" she asked Ash as they headed for Phoenix's car.

Ash opened the car door for her. "That's a loaded question, Susan. And not as easy to answer as you'd like."

Ravyn paused by the driver's side. "Will you be at the club later?"

"Yeah. I'll catch you guys then."

Susan got into the car. Ash closed her door at the same time Ravyn closed his.

She watched Acheron step back from the car and turn back toward the hill. As Ravyn started to pull away, she could swear Acheron evaporated into the mist.

"That is a strange man."

"Yes, he is."

"Can't he just kill off all the Daimons like he did tonight?"

"Probably."

"Then why doesn't he?"

Ravyn glanced at her as he shifted gears. "I have no idea. I guess it comes down to what Ash would say. Just because you can do something doesn't mean you should. There's a lot of stuff in this world that doesn't make sense. I would imagine the Daimons and Apollites are in some kind of balance with the rest of us and if he killed them all off, it would destroy it."

"But you don't know that's true."

"No. I'm only guessing."

Susan considered that as they headed down the dark streets. Balance . . .

It seemed like hogwash to her, but then what did she know? She was only a reporter who up until two days ago knew nothing of their existence.

"What do you think the Daimons will do now that Acheron is here?" she asked Ravyn.

"I don't know for sure, but if I were them, I'd run for cover."

A*cheron let out* a long, tired breath as he flashed himself to the alley behind the Serengeti. He could feel a presence inside the club that saddened him to the deepest part of his consciousness.

Nick Gautier.

Acheron hadn't seen him since the night Nick had killed himself and Ash had removed him from Hades and Artemis's clutches. Nick hated him and he had every right to.

In one fit of anger, Acheron had been the one to curse him to his death. The guilt of that festered inside Acheron like an open wound he knew would never heal.

And because of Nick's hatred, Ash had been unable to train Nick and so he'd sent him to live with Savitar. He didn't know why Savitar had freed him to this time and place. No doubt Savitar knew, but he would never share that information.

He was even better at keeping secrets than Ash was. How he wished he could see Nick's future. But Ash was forbidden to see his own future, or the future of anyone he cared about.

"No need to postpone the inevitable," he said under his breath. He wasn't a coward.

Steeling himself for what he knew was coming, Ash entered the club through the back door.

He met Dorian first as the Were-Hunter was taking a box of bottles from the storeroom.

"Ash," he said, his eyes wide. "You're in town."

"Hi, Dori. How's the mate?"

"She's fine. How's Simi?"

He could feel his Charonte demon in tattoo form crawling up his biceps to lay herself over his shoulder where she liked to sleep. "Same."

"Is she with you?"

Simi was almost always with him. "She might pop in later."

"Give us a little warning and I'll have Terra stock up on barbe-cue sauce."

"You got it." Ash moved past him, into the kitchen. He called a greeting to Terra and the cooks before he pushed his way through the door, into the club. The hip-hop music here was loud. It was "Grillz" by Nelly.

Ash was surprised Nick could hang out with that playing. Per-sonally, Ash liked all kinds of music, but Nick didn't really care for hip-hop or rap. He only listened to metal and Cajun Zydeco.

And Ash knew the instant Nick saw him. The hatred went up his spine like an electric shock.

Dreading the encounter, Ash turned to find Nick standing just behind him. Gone was the good friend who used to tease and laugh with him and in his place was an enemy Ash knew was plotting his death even while he faced him.

Nick's face was completely stoic. "Well, look who the leopards dragged in. I'm surprised you bothered."

"Hi, Nick."

"Fuck you." Nick knocked back his glass of whiskey, then glared at it. "You know what I hate most about being a Dark-Hunter?"

"The fact you can't get drunk?"

Nick put the glass on the tray of a waitress who was passing by. "It's having to deal with you."

Ash shook his head. It was still too soon for this. Nick needed more time. "I'll catch you later."

Nick grabbed Ash's arm as he started away and spun him around to face him. "You'll catch me now, you bastard."

Before Ash could move, Nick punched him in the jaw. He stag-gered back from the force of it. And if Nick had been paying at-tention, he would have realized something significant. Ash didn't feel the blow he'd just been given. Dark-Hunters couldn't strike each other. But then Ash wasn't like the others.

His first instinct was to strike Nick back, but Ash caught him-self before he did more damage to the Cajun. The crowd around them cut them a wide berth as people moved to get away, while the Weres looked around in nervous debate about whether or not they should come between two Dark-Hunters, or more importantly, if they should interfere with Ash.

Nick's face was contorted by rage. "How could you destroy New Orleans?"

Ash frowned at him. "What?"

"You heard me. Wasn't it enough that you killed me? Did you have to punish all my friends and family, too?"

"Nick, get a grip."

He shoved Ash back, into a table. "I've just spent the last few hours looking at the pictures . . . at the people. You could have stopped it and you didn't."

Ash felt his anger snapping. They were drawing way too much attention here in the bar. "You don't know what you're talking about."

Nick was relentless as he stalked Ash. "Yes, I do. I know what you are. You brought Kyrian and Amanda back from the dead. You saved their baby from the Daimons and you did *nothing* to help my mother. You claim you loved New Orleans and yet you did nothing to help the city when she needed you most."

"That's not true, Nick. I was there and I did what I could. But even I have limits and rules about what I can and can't do. My God, you were like a brother to me. How can you think that I'd ever do anything to hurt you?"

"You killed me, remember?"

"No. I've loved you and your mother like I've never loved another human being in my entire life. I never wanted to see the two of you hurt."

"Bullshit! One snap of your fingers and you could have deflected the storm. Talon could have deflected it. You refused to let him, didn't you?"

Ash shook his head. Fate wasn't that easy to control. "It's not that simple."

"It *is* that simple." He shoved Ash again.

The people in the bar were getting restless now, especially the Weres. Nick was drawing way too much attention to them and he was speaking of things that no one was supposed to talk about.

"Lay off me, Nick. I mean it."

Nick grabbed Ash by the front of his coat and pulled him close enough that he could whisper in his ear. "Or what? You'll kill me again?" He laughed at that as if it amused him greatly.

Letting go, Nick stepped back and smoothed Ash's lapels. "You know, I'm sorry. I'm forgetting all the manners my mother tried so hard to teach me." He narrowed his eyes meaningfully. "How's Simi doing? Has she picked up any new guys lately?"

That succeeded in breaking the hold Ash had on his temper. He bellowed in rage as he felt himself slipping. Throwing his head back, he froze everyone in the bar. Everyone. They stood silently in place as the music continued to play while he and Nick faced each other. Not as friends. As enemies.

Nick's face actually paled as he saw Ash's true form.

"You never knew when to shut your mouth, Cajun." His voice was a guttural demonic growl.

"What are you?"

Ash looked down at his blue hands that were marbled by silver. His gaze was hazy now from the fire that swirled in his irises and pupils.

Closing his eyes, he shoved his emotions aside and returned to his human form. How he wished he could erase Nick's memory, but Nick was one of those one in a trillion people who were immune to Ash's mind manipulation. It was what had made them friends.

Unfortunately, Nick wasn't immune to Ash's god powers, and that was what had made them enemies.

"For your own sake, Nick. Stay away from me and never say Simi's name in my presence again."

Nick gave an evil laugh. "One day, Ash, I'm going to find a way to kill you for what you've done to the people I love."

"Don't threaten me, boy. You don't have those powers."

"It's not a threat," he said, his eyes burning. "It's a promise."

Ash growled low in his throat as he pushed his way through the frozen people.

"Keep walking, Ash. But remember when you feel my hand delivering the death blow to you that you're the reason I'm here."

Ash paused and turned toward him. "No, Nick. You're just another mistake Artemis has made that will cause me nothing but misery."

Nick grabbed a bottle from the table beside him and flung it at Ash.

Ash splintered the glass bottle before it reached him. The pieces hung silently in the air for a full ten seconds before they fell to the floor as harmless dust.

Turning on his heel, he headed for the door intent on putting as much physical distance between them as possible.

He was so intent, in fact, that he failed to notice the one person in the corner who wasn't frozen. The one person who had witnessed the entire encounter.

As the room returned to normal and Nick went back toward the bar, the woman in a dark wig smiled evilly.

Now this was something they could definitely use. . . .

CHAPTER FIFTEEN

Satara flashed herself straight into Kalosis. For once, Stryker wasn't in the hall or "war room," as it had once been aptly called. In fact, the vast room was oddly empty, with his throne sitting alone on the dais.

The unexpected silence was eerie.

All of the Daimons who normally gathered here must be in their own homes, which lined the dark streets outside in this realm where sunshine was eternally banished.

Atlantean legend once claimed that this was the palace of Misos, the Atlantean god of death and violence. Archon, the peaceful king of the gods, created this realm to control Misos and keep him prisoner, along with all of his minions who preyed on both the Atlantean people and mankind.

Styker's black throne of carved dragons, skulls, and crossbones had been fashioned by Thasos (the Atlantean personification of death) for Misos himself while he ruled over all the damned who were sent to Kalosis to be punished. Ultimately, Archon had even sent his queen, Apollymi, to this realm to be held so long as her natural son lived.

After her beloved son had died, Apollymi had left her prison in this realm and destroyed all of the Atlantean pantheon—just as the Fates had prophesied. And as she made her way across Greece, bent on destroying the entire world, somehow the Greek gods had found a way to return her to her prison in Kalosis.

No one knew how they'd done it and not once, in all this time, had any of them breathed a word of it.

But it wasn't long after her new incarceration began that Apollymi had mentally reached out of this prison and summoned Stryker to her so that she could teach him how to take human souls and save his people.

That had been a hell of a day . . .

And Satara was grateful her brother had lived, because through him, she had a shot of ending her enslavement as a handmaiden to Artemis once and for all. That was if she could find the missing bastard to tell him her news.

Knowing her time was extremely finite, she rushed through the rooms of the palace, looking for him.

Oddly enough, she found him where she least expected . . . his bedroom.

And he wasn't alone. There were half a dozen Daimons, male and female, sprawled all over him and his bed. That wasn't counting the two who were making out on the floor in front of her.

She didn't know what stunned her most, the fact that it was an orgy or the fact that Stryker was actually having sex with someone. Given his coldness, she honestly hadn't thought he'd bother.

Then again, he didn't seem to be particularly involved with the two women and one man who were trying to please him. Rather, he looked bored and preoccupied.

"Excuse me," Satara called. All of them froze at the sound of her voice. "I really hate to interrupt this, but I have a situation I think Stryker will be very interested in and I don't have time to wait until you're through."

Stryker pushed the woman on top of him off and sat up. "Leave us."

Without a single word, they quickly gathered their clothes and walked past Satara, out the door.

Stryker was a bit more leisurely as he pulled on a robe but let it hang open as he moved from the bed.

Fine. If his nudity didn't bother him, it certainly didn't bother her.

Facing her, he wiped away the bit of blood at the corner of his mouth with his finger before he licked the digit clean. "Since you interrupted my dinner and I'm still hungry, could you make this quick?"

Satara was amazed by his words. "*That* was dinner?"

He gave her a bored stare as he closed the distance between them. "Yes. I like to play with my food before I eat it."

That sounded more like the vicious Daimon she knew. But that wasn't what had her here.

"Acheron is free of Olympus and I've been recalled to Artemis's temple. I thought you'd want to know that he's in Seattle with his Dark-Hunters now."

Stryker let out a long, aggravated breath. "I guess it was too much to hope that she'd actually keep him this time." He paused before he looked back at her. "Is that all?"

"No. I was at the Serengeti a few minutes ago and learned something *very* intriguing."

Susan *winced as* Ravyn held an ice pack to her eye.

"For a woman who can handle herself so well in a fight, I can't believe you got taken out by a defenseless doorjamb."

She narrowed her eyes on him. "Given the size of my goose egg, I would argue the defenseless part. That doorjamb has a mean left hook. Besides, it's not my fault. I was distracted."

"By what?"

His butt, if the truth were told, but she wasn't about to give him the satisfaction of knowing she'd been so preoccupied by his body that she wasn't paying attention to where she was going. "I don't remember."

"Uh-huh."

"I don't."

He brushed her hair back from her forehead with a gentle touch while he kept the ice over her brow. "You were amazing tonight by the way."

"Thanks, but not half as much as you guys were." Her heart clenched as she inadvertently thought about Belle and right behind that thought was another, even more disturbing one. It was an image of Ravyn down on the ground . . . being executed in the same way.

Looking up at him now, she couldn't get that out of her mind. Belle's death had been way too easy to accomplish. To be so powerful, the Dark-Hunters had an awful Achilles' heel.

Then again, most beings, supernatural or otherwise, usually died once their head was removed. There really was no way back from that unless you were a character on a soap opera or in a horror movie.

Suddenly, someone screamed from upstairs, causing Susan to jump and scrape her brow against the ice bag. It was followed by running feet and something very heavy hitting the floor.

"What now?" she breathed, tired of the constant fighting for their lives. Honestly, she just wanted a few minutes of quiet.

"I don't know." Ravyn handed her the ice bag before he went to check it out.

Susan left the bag on the mattress before she followed after him. They rushed up the stairs to the hallway.

All of Ravyn's family was there, along with a couple of other Weres and the doctor she'd seen on their arrival.

But it was Jack who held her attention. He sat on the floor, crying with his arms wrapped around his legs, rocking.

"What happened?" Ravyn asked Terra, who stood off to the side, looking perplexed by Jack.

Terra's eyes were deeply sad. "Patricia died a few minutes ago from her injuries."

Susan felt ill from the news.

"It's not right," Jack wailed as he pulled at his hair. "She never hurt anyone. Why is she dead? Why!"

The doctor patted him on the back as she looked up at Dorian. "I think you guys should go back to work. I'll take care of Jack."

They nodded before they complied.

Ravyn's father took a moment to narrow his eyes on his son and curl his lip in disgust. "Why are you still here?"

Ravyn didn't give him the satisfaction of showing any emotion whatsoever. "Love you, too, Dad."

His face was so contorted by rage that Susan expected him to lash out at Ravyn. And he probably would have had Dorian not pulled him away.

Ravyn's face didn't betray anything, but his eyes spoke a tome about how much his father's rejection hurt him. And in that moment, she hated his father for the pain he caused Ravyn.

Her heart breaking for both Jack and Ravyn, Susan started to return downstairs until she realized that Ravyn wasn't behind her. Instead, he went to Jack and knelt on the floor beside him. The doctor looked a bit surprised but didn't say anything while Jack sobbed.

"Why couldn't she have at least woken up for a few minutes?" Jack whispered. "I just wanted to talk to her one last time. I wanted her to know how much I loved her. How much she meant to me."

Ravyn reached out and touched his forearm to comfort him. "She knew, Jack."

He shook his head. "No, she didn't. I was always complaining whenever she asked me to do something. Why did I complain all the time? I should have done something, just once, without lipping off. Oh God, I just want her back. I'm so sorry, Mom."

Susan's eyes teared as she listened to him and remembered her own pain when she'd learned about her mother's death. It'd been the worst moment of her life.

It still was. And like Jack, all she could think about was how many things she wanted to change. How many things she wanted to say, that she couldn't.

She watched silently while Ravyn sat on the floor beside him. The two of them sat shoulder to shoulder with their backs to the wall as the doctor pulled back to give them space.

Ravyn let out a tired sigh. "You know what I miss most about my mother? She used to sing to herself every night while she knitted by the firelight."

Jack looked up with a frown. "Your mother didn't knit. She was a Were."

"Yeah, I know. It was such a strange hobby for her to have, but she loved it. She'd make all kinds of things, but her gloves were my favorite. I could always feel her when I wore them. Smell her scent. For some reason, I could never keep up with them. So she'd make a new one to match the one I still had, kiss it, put it on my hand, and then say to me, 'My poor little kitten had better keep up with his mittens or I'll skin 'im.' I'd laugh, go off with them, and lose one again every time."

"My mom liked to read," Jack whispered. "When I was a kid, I subscribed her to one of those book clubs where you get a bunch for free, not realizing that you had to pay postage for them. She acted so excited, but I felt like a complete asshole when my sister Brynna told me Mom had to pay for the books. So I hired myself out to Erika to carry her books home from school for two months to pay Mom back."

Ravyn looked aghast at that. "And you survived?"

Jack actually managed a tentative smile. "Well, let's just say I earned every cent and then some." Sniffing, he looked up at Ravyn. "Does the pain ever stop?"

There was nothing but raw agony in that dark gaze as Ravyn stared at the floor in front of them. "Not really. There will always be a part of you that misses her. You'll see something that reminds you of her and want to tell her about it, only to realize she's not there anymore. Then you'll feel her loss all over again."

Another tear fell down Jack's cheek. "You're not helping me, Ravyn."

"I know, buddy." He turned to lock sincere gazes with Jack. "But you will eventually make peace with yourself, and that's the most important thing. Eventually, you'll even be able to smile again when you think about her."

Jack wiped the tears from his cheeks and drew a ragged breath. "Thanks for talking to me."

"No problem. There's nothing worse than being left alone to grieve. You want to talk, you know where I am."

"The basement."

Ravyn nodded. "You going to be okay?"

"Yeah. Tad and Jessica are handling everything. I just have to pick up Brynna when she gets here in a few hours."

Ravyn patted him on the arm before he got up and realized

that she was still there, watching them. He actually blushed before he walked past her, back down the stairs.

Susan stood there for a moment, completely overwhelmed by the tenderness she felt for him, and as it surged, she realized how easy it would be to fall in love with Ravyn. In fact, a tiny part of her was already there. Most men who'd been so callously thrown aside wouldn't have any compassion at all for someone else.

And then she realized something else. That was why he tolerated Erika. She might make him crazy, but in his mind she was the closest thing he had to a family.

It was probably why he even tolerated her, a stranger, being with him. He knew how much she was hurting from the loss of Angie and Jimmy.

Feeling strangely weepy, she followed him down to the basement, where he was going over Jimmy's notes. He had his back to her while he stood with the light falling down on his hair. Susan closed her eyes and inhaled the warm scent of him. Needing to be near him, she crossed the room and pressed herself against his back, then wrapped her arms around his waist.

Ravyn actually trembled at the unbounded wave of tenderness that swept through him over her actions. His emotions were roiling through him. Anger and hate over Belle's death. Pain and compassion for Jack. And something he couldn't even begin to fathom for Susan.

He turned in her arms to capture her lips with his. He cupped her face in his hands as he explored every inch of her decadent mouth. She tasted like honey and heaven.

Susan's head swam as she literally ripped the shirt from Ravyn's back. She didn't know why, but she had to have him. Right now. Right here.

He looked down with the cutest stunned expression as she pulled his shirt down his arms. He gave her a wicked grin. "If you're in that big of a hurry . . ."

Their clothes vanished.

Susan laughed even as the cold air chilled her. At least until he pulled her to him and pinned her up against the wall. Giddy with the sensation of his hard body against hers, she wrapped her legs around his waist and buried her lips against his neck to suckle his prickly skin even while her sinuses clogged.

Ravyn pressed his cheek against hers while he savored how soft and warm her body was. He loved the feeling of her legs around him, of her tiny hairs teasing his stomach while her breasts were pressed flat against his chest. It was the sweetest sensation he'd ever known.

Unable to stand it, he thrust himself deep into her body. She cried out as she dug her nails into his shoulders. He leaned his head against the wall until she started sneezing. Her body tightened around his, enhancing just how good she felt.

Until she sneezed again.

He groaned as he realized his hair was in her face. "This really sucks." He pulled back to see her twitching her nose. "Are you okay?"

She answered with another sneeze.

Aggravated and really wanting to shave his entire body, he pulled out of her and stepped back to give her room so that she could recover.

Susan felt awful as she sniffed. Not to mention, he reminded her of a little kid who'd had all of his candy stolen. It wrung her heart. Poor Puss in Boots.

But she wasn't going to let something so petty rob them of this moment.

Looking up at him, she pressed the back of her hand to her nose to help open the passageway so that she could breathe better.

Ravyn was just about to summon their clothes back when Susan knelt down in front of him. Before he could move, she cupped him gently in her hand.

A chill went straight up his spine at the sensation of her fingers massaging his sac. "What are doing, Susan? You're allergic."

She looked up at him, licked her lips, and gave him the hottest seductive stare he'd ever seen on a woman's face. "Some things are worth suffering for."

And the next thing he knew, she dipped her head to gently lave the tip of him. His cock jerked in response to her warm, sweet tongue. He growled deep in his throat as she took more of him into her mouth.

His heart pounding, he buried his hand gently in her hair and leaned forward with one arm against the wall so that he could watch her. Every so often, she'd pull back to sneeze, but then she'd return to him.

In all his life, he'd never had anything touch him more. God, how he admired her, even though he knew he had no right being with her. He destroyed everything he touched, and yet he desperately wanted to stay with her. If only he could . . .

Susan licked her lips before she returned to him again. She loved the way he tasted. But most of all, she loved the gentle expression on his face while he watched. The feel of his hand tenderly caressing her while she pleasured him.

And when he came, she didn't pull away. Instead, she continued until there was nothing left. She pulled back to lean against the wall so that she could look up at him. A slow, loving smile spread across his face as he stared down at her.

"You're the best," he breathed, fingering her lips.

She suckled his thumb. "Not really, but I'm glad you think so."

He helped her to her feet, then turned her so that her back was to his front. He wrapped his arms around her and held her to him. She could feel him nuzzling against the back of her head.

"What's going to happen to us, Ravyn?" she asked quietly.

"I don't know. But right now I'm glad that you're here with me."

Susan ached with the knowledge that they couldn't stay like this. And the worst of it was the fact that she couldn't go back to her old life. She knew things about the world now that would haunt her forever.

But none of them more than the fact that she would have to deal with Ravyn in the future without being a part of his life. Why did she feel this way for a man she knew she couldn't have? It wasn't right for her to crave the one thing she could never claim.

Then she felt it, the soft tickle of his fangs against her neck. She groaned at how good that felt as she arched her back in expectation of what was to come.

Ravyn cupped her breasts in his hands and teased her sensitive nipples with his palm as his breath scalded her skin. Then he lowered one hand to tease her before he slowly slid himself into her one sweet inch at a time until he was buried deep inside her.

She ached with how good he felt thrusting into her. He took her hand into his and led it to his mouth so that he could nibble on her palm.

Susan couldn't explain it, but she felt like she was a part of this man. Like they were connected. It didn't make any sense to her. There was no explanation. She'd never felt like this in all of her life.

She didn't feel alone. Even though tomorrow should scare her, she wasn't afraid. Nothing seemed to matter to her while she was with Ravyn.

Ravyn inhaled the sweet fragrance of her skin. There was nothing on this earth that smelled better than his Susan. Nothing that felt better than her skin gliding against his. Her hand touching his face. Closing his eyes, he savored that precious touch.

He didn't know how they were going to get out of this, but one thing was certain. He wasn't going to let anything happen to her. Ever. He would give her her life back. She deserved at least that.

And then he felt her tighten around him an instant before she cried out in orgasm. He clenched his teeth and held her tight in his arms while he quickened his thrusts until he could join her there.

They were both breathing raggedly as they stood by the door. Ravyn didn't want to move, but unfortunately his body slid from hers and left him feeling strangely vacant. He didn't want to leave her. Not even for a second.

She turned around to smile up at him before she nibbled his bottom lip.

"You still stuffy?" he asked.

"Yes, but you're worth it."

He laughed at that before he kissed her. He'd barely tasted her before he felt an awful stinging pain in his palm.

His heart stopped beating at the sensation he hadn't felt in hundreds of years.

It couldn't be. . . .

Susan hissed, shaking her hand as if to cool it. "What on . . ." Her voice broke off as she saw on her palm what he knew was on his.

The mark.

"Ravyn?" she breathed.

His vision darkened as conflicting emotions tore through him. "I can't mate." Not as a Dark-Hunter. It wasn't possible . . . was it?

What the hell was this?

Confusion furrowed her brow. "But that is what this is, right?"

He nodded, unable to believe his cursed luck. He was dead. How could he mate? It defied logic. He couldn't have children, he couldn't commit.

And after this, he wouldn't even be able to have sex again. . . .

"Damn you, Fates," he hissed. *What were they thinking?*

Susan clenched her hand to conceal the ornate scrollwork. She didn't know what she'd expected from him, but this anger sure wasn't it. "I didn't know I was so repugnant to you."

The anger melted from his face. "How could you think that? But damn, Susan, do you understand what this means?"

"Yeah. You're screwed."

Ravyn leaned his head back. "I can't believe this."

"Well, look on the bright side, in this day and age if I told people you guys existed, they'd lock me up and laugh about it *with* you."

"You're not funny."

She reached up to cup his face in her hand. "I know. Look, I'll make this easy on you. You mate with me and then I can just leave and you'll be free to, pardon the pun, cat around all you want."

"It doesn't work like that."

Susan frowned. "What do you mean?"

"So long as you live, I can't have sex with anyone *but* you. Ever."

"And if we don't mate, you're a eunuch."

"Basically, yes."

A tremor of fear went through her as she considered what he'd just said. So long as she lived . . .

"You're not going to kill me, are you?"

He looked both offended and baffled by her question. "What? Are you insane? Why would I do that?"

"Let's see, ten seconds after I met you, you ripped out a guy's throat, and now you're telling me that so long as I'm alive you're screwed. Murder seems like the best course of action for you even though *I* strongly vote against it."

"Don't worry. I can't kill you. I took an oath to protect human life."

She didn't know what offended her most about that. The fact that he considered killing her or the fact that the only thing that kept him from it was an oath. "Well, gee, thanks, hon. I'm so glad I mean so much to you."

His face lightened up. "I wasn't serious."

"Uh-huh."

He leaned his forehead against hers and let out a frustrated breath. "I can't believe I'm mated to someone who's allergic to me."

"You? I'm the one who should be having a hissy. How do I introduce you to people? Hi, this is my . . . what? Significant other? Mate? Pet?"

He closed his eyes and clenched his teeth. "Why must every relationship I have be so damned impossible?"

Susan pulled back and tilted his head so that he met her eyes. "Hey now, defeatist talk from a catman like you? I'm the one who should be freaking out here. I mean, damn, you could give me fleas or something."

He laughed. "I'll give you something all right." He popped her playfully on the rump.

"You better stop that. I could lure you out in daylight and then take you to be neutered."

"You don't need daylight for that. All you have to do is walk out that door and stay gone for three weeks."

Her humor died at his dire words. "I won't do that to you, Ravyn."

"Why not? What does it matter anyway? We can't live together. Acheron will never allow it."

"He's not stopping Cael."

Ravyn paused as he considered that. She was right. "Have you any idea what living with me would entail?"

She wrinkled her nose as if she smelled something foul. "If you're like most men, it probably means dirty underwear and socks on the floor. Toilet seat left up at night. You eating all my peanut butter and not telling me. But," she said in all seriousness, "you better not expect me to clean out that cat box. Erika needs chores, too."

He was stunned by her. She could always find humor in everything.

"Your life will be in constant danger."

"Excuse me? Do you have amnesia? Did you miss the last four dozen attacks on us? And that's not counting the doorjamb that almost decapitated me."

"Susan, I'm serious."

"So am I. I mean, yes, I would rather have had time to fall in love with you and I'd really like for you to be human. But no one's perfect. Granted most men are dogs and not cats . . . and I am allergic to you—"

He cut her words off with a kiss. "Look, we don't have to settle this right now. I'm asking you for the rest of your life. Literally. There's no such thing as divorce in our world. We have three weeks to act on this. So I want you to really understand what you're signing on for, okay?"

"Okay, but let's not forget that in three weeks, we could be dead or in jail, which for you would probably mean death anyway."

"True."

Susan let him pull her into his arms. She honestly wasn't sure about this, and she was glad he was giving her time to think it over. But she couldn't let him be alone and not have any shot for making a human connection again. That was just wrong and cruel. Especially given how kind he'd been to her through all this.

Still, they had a long way to go and it was getting scarier by the minute. She didn't know what tomorrow would hold. She only hoped that for them, there was a tomorrow, period.

What do you mean, they got away?"

Trates sighed as he faced the human bastard he'd rather suck dry than deal with. But Stryker wanted this human alliance even if he thought it was completely stupid and beneath them. So here he was, playing nice with the chief of police when what he really wanted to do with Paul Heilig was rip his throat out and drink in his putrid soul.

"We had them trapped in an alley when Acheron showed up

and killed every Daimon there. Now we're going to lie low until he leaves."

"Bullshit! You promised me my—"

"Listen to me, human," Trates sneered through his clenched fangs. "You don't want to mess with this Dark-Hunter. He's not like the others."

"They're still bound to the night and when something lives perpetually on the dark side of the moon, all you have to do is drag it into daylight to kill it."

Trates held his hands up. "I'm just here to tell you what Lord Stryker said. You do what you want. It's your funeral." He turned to summon the portal to return to Kalosis.

But as soon as he had his back to Paul, the chief of police ran at him.

Trates hissed as he felt a deep, biting pain in his heart. Gasping, he looked down to see a small sword blade piercing his chest . . . right through his Daimon's mark.

Paul jerked his sword out an instant before the Daimon exploded into gold powder. "You're wrong about that, Trates. It's *your* funeral."

And soon there would be a lot more of them. If Stryker was too big a coward to do what was necessary to protect his children, then that was his loss. But Paul wasn't the same.

He'd already lost his wife to one Dark-Hunter, he wasn't about to lose his sons. No matter what it took, he was going to keep them safe.

Ravyn Kontis still lived and as long as he did, Paul could hear his wife's voice calling out to him to avenge her. And as long as a single Dark-Hunter roamed the streets of his city, his sons were at risk.

That he couldn't allow.

Pulling his cell phone off his belt, he called his deputy chief. "Hey, I need a search warrant."

"For?"

"The Happy Hunting Ground." If Trates wouldn't tell him where Ravyn was hiding, he knew one person who would.

CHAPTER SIXTEEN

"Cael?"

Cael paused as he heard Acheron's voice behind him. He turned around on the sidewalk to see him walking through the night's mist. There was something really spooky about Acheron. There always had been.

He'd first met Acheron on September 15, 904, on a cool night much like this one in Cornwall. Cael had been covered in the blood of an entire raiding party of Vikings that night. The fires he'd started had singed his hair and blistered his skin.

But he hadn't cared. All that had mattered had been avenging his wife, brother, mother, and sister who had been slain by the Vikings.

Even after all these centuries, he could still see Morag's beautiful freckled face, hear the gentle lilt of her voice as she called out his name. With hair redder than the sun and a smile every bit as radiant, she had been his entire world.

Her and his baby sister who'd been on the brink of adulthood.

Corynna had held eyes so blue they rivaled the sky and a laugh so musical that it should have belonged to a songbird.

And his father had sold them all into slavery to save his own life. But the Vikings hadn't wanted slaves. They'd wanted victims to practice on. Bound in chains, Cael had watched helplessly as every one of them had been tortured and killed for fun while their cries of pain and pleas for death had echoed in his ears.

Not even his own death had been able to silence their agonized voices. It hadn't erased the sight of them being beaten and dismembered. There were times even now when he came awake, shaking from the memory of it.

Acheron had appeared to him after he'd taken his vengeance on those who'd preyed on his family, and had shown him, a simple peasant bastard, how to fight the Daimons and how to live again when he had nothing in this world worth living for.

He owed everything to the Atlantean leader of the Dark-Hunters. Had Acheron not shown him how to put the past behind him and go forward with his life, he'd have never made it to this time and place.

Never made it to Amaranda.

Through her, he'd found the one thing he'd thought was lost to him forever.

Love.

Most of all, she gave him solace, peace, and acceptance. She was his haven in a harsh life that had been nothing but violence and fighting until the day she'd entered it. And he would do anything to hold on to that and to her.

Except hurt Acheron. Cael was nothing if not loyal, and he hated being torn between the two people he loved most in this world.

He offered Acheron a lopsided grin and used a greeting from one of Acheron's favorite cartoons. "Greetings, O Great Gazoo. How nice of you to join us here on planet Earth again."

Ash rolled his eyes. "Thanks, Barney. How's Betty and Bam Bam doing?"

"Great, if I could only get them away from Wilma and Pebbles. Those women are nothing but trouble."

"Nah, they're good women. It's the ones in red who are always the downfall of good men."

Laughing, Cael extended his hand to Acheron. "Ain't it the truth, my braither?"

Ash reached out and took his hand. Cael went to clap him on the back, only to have him move out of reach.

Cael didn't miss the grimace Acheron quickly hid. "You okay?"

Acheron shrugged his shoulders as if trying to alleviate something uncomfortable. "I hurt my back earlier. It'll be all right though."

Cael nodded. "It's good to be immortal, huh?"

"Some days, anyway."

They grew silent as they stood out on the open street, in front of a small coffee shop where a group of college students were lolling about, studying and talking while music filtered out of the store. Cael wasn't far from home, but he had no intention of taking Ash there. He'd always kept as much distance as possible between his boss and his wife.

Acheron knew things that no one had a right to know and it always chilled him.

"Did you need something?" Cael asked.

Ash didn't speak as a thousand thoughts went through his mind. He wanted to warn this man and knew that if he did so, he'd change so many more fates than just Cael's. The endless chain of change was playing out in his mind.

A thousand lives rewritten because of one spoken word . . .

Don't speak.

That was so much easier said than done. How he hated knowing what was to come and being constricted by a human conscience from preventing it. Then again, if not for that conscience, it wouldn't matter what happened to Cael one way or another. He wouldn't care about anything except himself.

He'd become Savitar. . . .

Ash winced at the thought. Recovering himself before Cael realized what he was doing, Ash rubbed his cheek. "No, I just wanted to wish you a good night."

By Cael's face he could tell the Celt didn't believe him. "Yeah, okay. I'll catch you later." He turned and started heading for his home.

Ash stood on the street, watching him walk away. Every part of him wanted to call Cael back and warn him.

And every part of him knew why he couldn't. He didn't know if he should curse or thank Artemis for this gift.

But then the only thing worse than knowing the future was not knowing it, which happened whenever the future involved him or someone whose future directly influenced his.

"Hi there, cutie."

He turned his head to find an extremely attractive college student by his side. With black curly hair, she was dressed in jeans and a tight green top that displayed her curves to perfection. "Hi."

"You want to go inside for a drink? It's on me."

Ash paused as he saw her past, present, and future simultaneously in his mind. Her name was Tracy Phillips. A political science major, she was going to end up at Harvard Med School and then be one of the leading researchers to help isolate a mutated genome that the human race didn't even know existed yet.

The discovery of that genome would save the life of her youngest daughter and cause her daughter to go on to medical school herself. That daughter, with the help and guidance of her mother, would one day lobby for medical reforms that would change the way the medical world and governments treated health care. The two of them would shape generations of doctors and save thousands of lives by allowing people to have groundbreaking medical treatments that they wouldn't have otherwise been able to afford.

And right now, all Tracy could think about was how cute his ass was in leather pants, and how much she'd like to peel them off him.

In a few seconds, she'd head into the coffee shop and meet a waitress named Gina Torres. Gina's dream was to go to college herself to be a doctor and save the lives of the working poor who couldn't afford health care, but because of family problems she wasn't able to take classes this year. Still Gina would tell Tracy how she planned to go next year on a scholarship.

Late tonight, after most of the college students were headed off, the two of them would be chatting about Gina's plans and dreams.

And a month from now, Gina would be dead from a freak car accident that Tracy would see on the news. That one tragic event combined with the happenstance meeting tonight would lead Tracy to her destiny. In one instant, she'd realize how shallow her life had been, and she'd seek to change that and be more aware of the people around her and of their needs. Her youngest daughter would be named Gina Tory in honor of the Gina who was currently busy wiping down tables while she imagined a better life for everyone.

So in effect, Gina would achieve her dream. By dying she'd save thousands of lives and she'd bring health care to those who couldn't afford it. . . .

The human race was an amazing thing. So few people ever realized just how many lives they inadvertently touched. How the right or wrong word spoken casually could empower or destroy another's life.

If Ash were to accept Tracy's invitation for coffee, her destiny would be changed and she would end up working as a well-paid bank officer. She'd decide that marriage wasn't for her and go on to live her life with a partner and never have children.

Everything would change. All the lives that would have been saved would be lost.

And knowing the nuance of every word spoken and every gesture made was the heaviest of all the burdens Ash carried.

Smiling gently, he shook his head. "Thanks for asking, but I have to head off. You have a good night."

She gave him a hot once-over. "Okay, but if you change your mind, I'll be in here studying for the next few hours."

Ash watched as she left him and entered the shop. She set her backpack down at a table and started unpacking her books. Sighing from exhaustion, Gina grabbed a glass of water and made her way over to her . . .

And as he observed them through the painted glass, the two women struck up a conversation and set their destined futures into motion.

His heart heavy, he glanced back in the direction Cael had vanished and hated the future that awaited his friend. But it was Cael's destiny.

His fate. . . .

"Imora thea mi savur," Ash whispered under his breath in Atlantean.

God save me from love.

Susan leaned back against the wall as she sorted through files on Jimmy's computer. "Dammit, Jim. I'm just a reporter, not a mind reader," she said, feigning a Bones McCoy quote from *Star Trek*. "Couldn't you have at least left me an obvious crumb to follow? Is one loaf of bread too much to ask?"

Sick to her stomach, she decided to take a break and clicked on the photos folder.

A bittersweet pain lacerated her chest as she flipped through pictures of him and Angie at a party last year. God, what she wouldn't give to hear Angie tell her she was five by five again. To hear Jimmy's raspy voice teasing her about being too uptight all the time.

"You okay?"

Startled, she jumped at Ravyn's deep voice as he entered the room with that silent cat walk of his. "You scared me. . . ." She paused to watch him come closer. Honestly, he was the best-looking thing she'd ever seen in her life. He had his hair pulled back in a ponytail and even though his shirt was untucked, it didn't disguise the fact that he was ripped with sinewy muscles. Distracting herself from that thought, she indicated the laptop with her chin. "I was just spying on Jimmy's pictures."

He handed her the coffee he'd gone upstairs to get for her. "Maybe you should close the file." He sat down beside her so that he could look at the screen, too.

"No, it's okay. I just found this one set of pictures from Jimmy's Halloween party at his precinct last year. He went as Frankenstein and Angie was—"

"Bride of Frankenstein?"

"No . . . she went as a Holy Cow." Susan smiled at the memory. "She was always a bit offbeat that way."

Ravyn laughed as she showed him the picture of Angie in a cow suit with a halo suspended above her head and a giant wooden cross around her neck. He'd only seen her a couple of times in the shelter while they'd held him, but the woman had seemed decent enough.

But his smile died when Susan flipped to the next picture and he saw the people in it.

It couldn't be. Surely he was mistaken. . . .

Susan flipped to another.

"Wait! Go back."

Susan frowned. "Why?"

He set his own coffee aside and frowned as he examined the picture of a tall blond woman who was dressed as a classic campy Hollywood vampire, complete with all-too-real-looking fangs, standing with her arm around Angie. "I know her."

Susan gave him a less than pleased glare. "For the record, Puss in Boots, I hope you're not speaking biblically. Because if you are—"

"No," he said, interrupting her tirade, even though a part of him was flattered that she felt that way. "She's a Daimon . . . or was. I killed her."

Susan scoffed at him. "Not *her* you didn't."

Ravyn looked again and studied the woman's sharp patrician features. In the back of his mind, he could still see her dressed in a black pair of slacks and a red blouse as he found her standing over her victims. The sight had sickened him as she had wiped the blood from her mouth and laughed about it.

"It was her, I'm sure of it."

Still Susan had doubt in those blue eyes. "How would you know? Do you memorize the face of every Daimon you snuff out?"

He gave her a droll stare. "No, but I remember her."

" 'Cause she's a bimbo?"

He shook his head. "Because she didn't run from me. She actually dared me to kill her. She said that she had a get out of jail free card and that unless I wanted every Dark-Hunter in Seattle to die, I'd leave her alone."

Susan was unamused by that. "So naturally you just had to kill her."

If a dry stare could mutilate, she'd be in several pieces on the floor.

"She'd just taken the life of a pregnant woman and her small child outside of a Laundromat. I had to kill her to release those two souls or both of their souls would have died."

"While fascinating and gross, that can't be *this* woman."

"How do you know?"

"Because she's the wife of Paul Heilig, the chief of police. And she died in a car wreck in Europe. I saw the photos of it."

Ravyn went cold at her words as they confirmed his suspicions. "What?"

"You heard me." She flipped through the pictures until she got to one of the Daimon with two very tall blond men, who were also dressed as Bela Lugosi vampires, and a short, pudgy man with dark hair, highlighted with gray, and glasses, dressed as an explorer. The man appeared to be around the age of fifty, with thinning hair and sharp gray eyes. "That's her, her sons, and her husband."

Ravyn narrowed his gaze on them before he looked up at Susan. "Don't you think it odd that the chief of police is married to a woman who looks to be the same age as her children?"

"Plastic surgery, baby. Some of the best surgeons in the country live right here."

"Yeah, and so do some of the best Daimons."

Susan went cold as she stared at the woman, and her emotions sobered. It all made sense now. "It's just what you said, isn't it? He married an Apollite who turned Daimon, and now he's using his position to keep them safe."

"Except for the wife I killed. No wonder they wanted to torture me in the . . ." His voice trailed off as he remembered something the half-Apollite vet had said.

"Paul wants to see this one suffer. . . ."

Since he didn't know who Paul was, he'd completely forgotten that. But now he understood. Paul was Paul Heilig. Chief of Police and father of two Daimon sons.

They were screwed.

"When did you kill her?" Susan asked.

"I don't know. About two months ago, maybe."

That was around the same time the chief's wife had died. Susan remembered the articles about it clearly. No body had been returned to the States for a funeral, but they had held a memorial service for her.

Of course if she was a Daimon, there wouldn't have been a body to bury. Oddly enough, it made a perfect cover.

Oh jeez, now you're thinking like Leo. But then Leo wasn't the crackpot she'd taken him for. . . .

"Do you remember anything about her?"

"Yeah," he said breathlessly. "She was a nasty bitch with a mean left hook."

"Not that," Susan snapped. "Something that could help us identify her as the chief of police's wife."

"The words *get out of jail free card*—"

"Maybe she played a lot of Monopoly. Who knows what weirdness Daimons partake in to pass the time." At his withering stare she held her hands up in surrender. "Okay, bad stab on my part. Please continue."

"Couple that with Jimmy's paranoia that someone high up in his department was covering up murders and disappearances. C'mon, Susan, this is too much to be coincidence."

"I know I'm playing devil's advocate here. We have to have concrete proof before we accuse this man of framing us and hiding murders."

"Susan . . . ," he said in a chiding tone.

"Look, Ravyn, I already ruined my life because something that looked like a duck and quacked like a duck turned out to be a tiger with an entire battery of attorneys bent on taking everything I might ever own again. All the evidence was there, clearcut and perfect, and I leaped at it and, in the morning, everything that said he was guilty was just a bad coincidence for me. I don't want to make that mistake again." She held up her wrist to show him the scars she still bore. "I *really* don't want to relive my past."

Ravyn's gut clenched at the sight of the scars where she'd cut her wrist. "Susan . . ."

"Don't patronize me, okay? I know it was stupid. But I was completely alone. Everything I'd ever believed in caved in on my head and I had to sit through lawsuit after lawsuit until the rubble settled and left me homeless, friendless, and hopeless. I clawed myself up every morning from bed so that I could be kicked again. And then I decided that though I was ruined, I wasn't dead, and that my life, such as it was, was mine and I refused to let them take that from me, too. I've come a long way, but it's been hard and brutal, and the last thing I want is to accuse an upstanding, highly decorrated official and relive that nightmare all over again. Understand?"

Ravyn's throat tightened at the pain he heard in her voice, the agony she held in her eyes. He kissed her wrist, and held it in his hand as he locked gazes with her. "You won't ever relive that, Susan. I promise you."

"Don't make promises you can't keep."

"I *can* keep this one. And if I'm wrong, I'll go down alone with my error. But if we're right . . ."

"Jimmy's avenged."

Cael had just reached the back door of the Happy Hunting Ground when his cell phone started ringing. He pulled it off his belt to see it listing Amaranda's number. Flipping it open, he held it to his ear. "Yeah, babe?"

"Don't come home."

"What?" he said, not sure he'd heard her right with the loud music that was drowning out her voice. He reached for the doorknob.

"Don't. Come. Home," she repeated only slightly louder than the last time.

"Is this a joke?" he asked angrily. Amaranda would never tell him not to come home. "If this is you, Stryker, go fuck yourself." He slammed the phone shut, then opened the door.

As usual, the club was thumping and loud with college kids gyrating on the dance floor and guzzling alcohol at the tables that surrounded it. He inclined his head at Amaranda's cousin who was waiting tables as he passed by.

Nothing seemed out of the ordinary.

Cael closed his eyes and searched the building mentally for any telltale sensation of a Daimon. Nothing set off his radar. Wanting to double-check in case he was still unnerved by the earlier fight, he pulled out his phone and ran the Daimon trace program that was in it.

It, too, came back negative.

Cool, there was nothing here that needed his attention . . . except his wife.

Cael pulled his thin jacket off and slung it over his shoulder as he descended the stairs to the basement. Looking forward to spending some quality time with Amaranda, he began whistling while he headed for his room.

Until he opened the door.

His whistling stopped mid-tune. Kerri was in his room, bound and gagged. Her eyes were large and terror-filled as she begged him with her gaze to set her free.

And in that instant, he came face-to-face with his past. The pain of it was almost crippling. And most of all, he could feel his Dark-Hunter powers wane.

Was it some kind of joke? If it was, he damn sure didn't find it funny.

"What the hell's going on, Kerri?" He'd only taken one step toward her when the door slammed shut behind him.

He jerked around to find a human male there, glaring at him. In his mid-fifties, the pudgy little man had shifty gray eyes that reflected his insanity. "What the hell's the meaning of this?" Cael demanded.

"Where's Ravyn Kontis?"

Cael forced himself to betray nothing. "Who?"

"Don't play stupid with me," the man snarled, spewing spittle in his rage. "Answer the question."

"I can't. I don't know anyone named Ravyn."

Disbelief twisted his features. "No?"

"No."

The man tsked as he moved forward toward Kerri's chair. "Too bad. I guess I'll have to kill you and your whore then." He headed for Kerri, whose eyes widened even more as she started squealing through her gag.

"She's innocent."

The man gave him a vicious glare. "No one's innocent. And even if she was, I don't give a damn." He pulled a hunting knife out from his jacket and angled it at Kerri's throat. "Tell me where that bastard is or watch her die."

"But I don't—" He broke off as the man pressed his knife so close that it pricked Kerri's neck.

She screamed, trying to angle her neck away from the blade.

"Okay, okay," Cael said, trying to stall for time as his powers weakened even more. But what concerned him most was where had Amaranda gone? Obviously, she was the one who'd called him and this idiot had mixed the two of them up. Even so, if anything happened to Kerri, Amaranda would never forgive him.

Nor would he forgive himself.

And then he felt it . . . that prickling sensation of a Daimon's presence.

Only there were two of them.

The door opened and Cael's entire world shattered. Amaranda was between the two Daimons with her hands tied behind her back. She was pale and shaking as she bled from a wound at her neck.

They'd been feeding from her and by her appearance, they'd almost drained her dry.

"Look who we found trying to warn him, Dad."

"Damn you!" Cael snarled. Without thinking, he rushed at them.

Even though his powers were all but gone, he caught the first one about the waist and they went sprawling into the hallway. The Daimon didn't let go of Amaranda, who landed on top of Cael.

He took a second to make sure she was okay before he cut the rope on her hands then kicked the second Daimon away from them. Growling, Cael reached for the one he'd tackled only to hear a gun firing.

He recoiled as the bullets ripped through his body in rapid succession. The pain of it stole his breath as he bled all over the floor.

The Daimon picked him up and slugged him hard in the jaw. The impact knocked him back into the wall so that the other Daimon could kick him in the stomach.

As the Daimon moved to kick Cael again, he grabbed his leg and shoved him back. The Daimon slipped on Cael's blood and hit the floor with a thud. He kicked the Daimon in the ribs and turned to grab the other one.

"Freeze, asshole, or I give your little playmate here a bullet in her brain. And since she's an Apollite, it'll cut her short life even shorter."

Cael froze instantly.

"Turn around."

He did and saw that the older man had Amaranda in front of him with his gun angled at her head. Cael's heart pounded at the sight of her fear as anger clouded his vision. Damn this bastard for scaring her.

"It'll be okay, baby."

"Not if you don't answer my question." He cocked the snub-nosed .38 against her temple.

Cael heard Amaranda praying in Atlantean under her breath.

If he gave up Ravyn's location, they would kill him. If he didn't, they'd kill Amaranda.

His best friend or his wife. How could he make that call?

"Fine," the man snarled. "Have it your way." He started to squeeze the trigger.

"No!" Cael shouted, taking a step forward. "He's . . ." He couldn't say it. He just couldn't. Having been betrayed, how could he betray someone else?

"Don't play with me, boy."

Cael took a deep breath and leveled a sincere look of hatred on the bastard. "He's at the Last Supper Club in Pioneer Square."

The man narrowed a doubting gaze on him.

One of the Daimons grabbed Cael by the hair and pulled his head back. "Are you lying to us, Dark-Hunter?"

"No," he lied with conviction. "I wouldn't dare."

"What do you think, Dad?" the Daimon holding him asked the man with the gun.

"He's either telling the truth or he's a damn good liar. Since I don't know which, I think we should keep them alive, just in case."

Images of his family dying while he'd been powerless to stop their torture ripped through his mind. He looked at Amaranda and her sister and saw the terror in their eyes.

There was no way in hell he would relive that moment. He wasn't about to let them be tortured in front of him while he was powerless to stop it. And with that thought, the last of his Dark-Hunter powers seeped out of him.

The man tossed a pair of handcuffs at the Daimon, who caught them and snapped one over Cael's wrist. He swung about and elbowed the Daimon straight in the face.

"Derrick!" the man shouted before he opened fire on Cael again.

Cael refused to stop. He pulled his dagger out and turned to kill the Daimon.

Another gunshot rang out, an instant before Cael felt something sharp and hot pierce his back. It was the knife the man had used to threaten Kerri. Cael knew it the instant the blade didn't protrude out of the front of his chest. The man twisted the blade sideways and then snapped it off at the hilt to leave the blade buried deep in Cael's heart.

Cael's ears buzzed as he tasted his own blood. He heard Amaranda's screams through the haze as his vision dimmed.

He was dying. . . .

Unable to breathe for the pain, he fell to his knees.

Amaranda screamed out loud at the sight of Cael falling. Agony and grief assailed her and it awoke the fighter inside her. Her rage taking root, she ran at the man who'd stabbed him. Before she could reach him, his Daimon son turned to fight her. He grabbed her and slapped her hard. She spun around to face him again and then acted on pure Apollite instinct.

She launched herself at his throat and sank her fangs into his flesh. His father cursed as he tore her away from his son, but by doing so he caused her to sever the Daimon's jugular. Instead of dying quickly, he fell to the floor and lay there as his blood ran over him and he shook uncontrollably.

His father let out an anguished cry before he shot Amaranda and her sister.

Her vision dimming in pain, Amaranda fell to the floor and couldn't move. It was as if she were completely paralyzed.

"So help me," the man shouted, "I will see all of you dead. Dead!" He stomped her hard on the small of her back before the other Daimon pulled him away from her.

"C'mon, Dad, we'll mourn Derrick later. We have to get out of here before the Apollites realize we're here and what we've done."

"I have a search warrant."

"And you just killed two members of their family. Search warrants are for your people, not mine. They'll kill us both."

He stomped her one last time before they left.

Amaranda could barely see for the tears in her eyes. She'd never known physical or mental pain like she felt right now.

"Cael," she whimpered, needing to touch him. Even though all she wanted was to close her eyes and let death carry her away from the agony of her body, she refused to go without holding his hand.

It was what he'd promised her on the night they'd married.

"I won't leave you alone to die. I'll be there with you, hand in hand, until the end."

She wouldn't let him die without knowing she was there for him. Hand in hand.

Her limbs shaking, she pulled herself across the slick floor until she reached him. To her shock, he was still alive, but only barely. There were tears in his eyes as he breathed in shallow gasps. No longer the black of a Dark-Hunter, his eyes were a beautiful amber.

"Cael?"

She saw the fire in his eyes as he stared at her. "Sunshine," he breathed.

She choked on a sob as he called her the nickname he'd given her during their wedding vows . . . vows he'd written just for her. *"Even though I walk only at night, I will never know darkness as long as you, my sunshine, are by my side."*

He swallowed as he reached out to touch her cheek. "I'm sorry I didn't listen to you."

Amaranda licked her lips, retasting the Daimon's blood. "It's okay, baby." She laid her head down on his chest and held him while he played with her hair.

She fully expected to die like that. Closing her eyes, she waited for death to take her.

Or so she thought. But as the seconds ticked by and Cael's breathing grew more shallow, hers only grew stronger.

And stronger.

The pain of her body receded as something started to burn in the center of her chest. It wasn't overly painful, but it wasn't comfortable.

It was . . .

She felt her vision turning more sensitive, her hearing sharper. Gasping, she lifted herself up as she realized what was happening.

She was turning Daimon.

But how? She hadn't . . .

Her gaze went to the Daimon she'd killed. "Oh God," she breathed as full knowledge assailed her. She'd drunk the blood of a Daimon and in that blood was the human souls he'd taken. Now it was converting her body.

And it was saving *her* life. . . .

She looked down at her chest to see the small black stain over her heart—the place where the human souls gathered so that they could nourish her Daimon's blood and keep her Apollite body from decaying. And as she watched, her body expelled the bullets out of her flesh and then healed itself.

Her heart raced. She looked to the Daimon whose blood was still pouring out of him. There were only three ways to kill a Daimon. Sunlight, piercing their Daimon mark over their heart, and tearing out their jugular.

The Daimon wasn't quite dead. Once his blood was completely expelled from his body, he would crumble into dust.

But she could save Cael. . . .

He'll never forgive you.

Maybe, but if he died, he'd become a Shade and spend eternity suffering in perpetual hell. There would be no goddess to offer him clemency. No more bargains with Artemis to get his life back. His body would crumble to dust and he would be trapped without his soul. Forever. No way to rest. No way to regenerate or reincarnate.

Just an eternity of pain.

Most of all, he'd be alone.

"Forgive me, Cael," she whispered, laying her lips over his to kiss him gently.

Without another thought, she grabbed the Daimon's arm and pulled him to her. Grabbing a knife from the Daimon's belt, she sliced open his wrist. She hesitated. Dark-Hunter blood was poisonous to Daimons, was Daimon blood also poisonous to Dark-Hunters? By trying to save Cael would she destroy him? But what choice did she have? If she did nothing, he would certainly die. Deciding she would have to take the risk, she held the Daimon's wrist over Cael's lips.

Too weak to turn away, he had no choice but to let the blood flow into his body.

His eyes flew open as he cried out in pain. He writhed on the floor as if in utter agony.

Amaranda pulled back, dropping the Daimon's arm.

He rolled to his side, cursing and jerking as if something were trying to tear him to pieces.

"No," she breathed, terrified that she'd only hurt him more. She pulled his head into her lap and held him close as he gripped her shirt so tightly that the bones of his knuckles protruded.

And then she saw it. . . .

The knife was working its way out of his back. Slowly, painfully, inch by inch, it crept out until it landed on the floor with a sharp clatter.

Amaranda stared at it as she felt Cael's breathing steady itself. He loosened his grip on her.

She looked down and saw something that according to Dark-Hunter laws was not supposed to happen. Cael's eyes were now an unnatural shade of amber with black streaks running through them.

"What have you done to me, Amaranda?" he asked in a ragged, demonic tone.

"I saved you, Cael." But even as those words left her lips, she knew the truth. She hadn't saved him.

She'd damned them both straight to hell.

CHAPTER SEVENTEEN

Ravyn leaned back against the wall with his eyes closed. His head was throbbing from exhaustion and tension. How could someone trap a public official in the police department without getting burned?

Even if they did catch him, could they clear Susan's name? He wasn't particularly worried about himself. He could be transferred to a remote part of the world for a few decades and then moved back here. But her . . .

He smelled her the instant she returned to the room. He kept his eyes closed as he savored the scent. There was nothing more soothing to him. Nothing more gentle. Her feet made only the slightest of sounds as she crossed the room and then knelt by his side.

She brushed the hair back from his forehead, firing his body with her careful touch. And then she pressed her lips against his. Ravyn hissed at the taste of her as he returned her kiss.

But when she reached for his fly, he caught her hand in his and moved it away.

He opened his eyes to find her frowning at him. "Did I do something wrong?"

"No, love. But we can't have sex until you're sure you want to mate with me. That's how we seal the deal. One tiny penetration, whether intended or not, and you're mine. Forever."

She nipped his mouth with her teeth. "Would that be so bad?"

He teased her lips with his tongue. "No. Not at all. But I already told you that I want you to take a few days to really consider this. Once we're mated there's no way back." Not to mention the fact that as a Dark-Hunter he wasn't supposed to mate at all.

"Okay." She pulled back. "So what's our game plan?"

"That's what I've been trying to think of. I mean, if we're right, and I'm sure we are, we have a motive and a name. It explains why the police are so gung ho to hang us and how they're getting away with all this."

"And if you're right and his sons are both Daimons, he doesn't want them to die like his wife, which explains why he wants to wipe out the Dark-Hunters in Seattle."

He nodded, then had a bad thought go through him. He pushed himself away from the wall. "We have to get Erika out of here."

"What?"

"We need Erika gone. First thing. I don't want them to use her as a hostage."

"Wouldn't all Squires be in danger?"

He shook his head. "Think about it, Susan. *I* killed his wife."

"He wants your blood more than the others."

"Yeah, and *that* is how we're going to get him."

Stryker *walked into* his study on Kalosis to find the clock that marked human hours on his mantel. It would soon be dawn and Trates hadn't returned. . . .

What could be keeping him?

It wasn't like his second in command to stay gone so long. Feeling stupid for even caring, Stryker picked up the *sfora* from his desk and cradled the small clear crystal orb in his hand. The Atlantean word for "eye," the *sfora* was a way for those in Kalosis to keep tabs on the humans or anyone else on earth or here.

"Where are you, Trates?" he mumbled under his breath as he searched for him.

He found nothing.

Stryker frowned. "Show me Trates," he commanded the magical orb.

There was nothing but the red and gold swirling mist.

He gripped the ball tight in his hand as he conjured an image of the Daimon he sought in his mind. "Show me what has happened to him."

He relaxed his grip enough so that he could see the mist that was clearing into images of Trates and Paul. At first they seemed to be talking . . . until Paul staked him in the back.

For a full minute, Stryker couldn't breathe as disbelief soaked him. Finally the numbness that incapacitated him dissolved into rage. Growling deep in his throat, he threw the orb against the wall and it splintered into a thousand shards.

Trates was dead.

Unimagined pain tore through him and he didn't even know why. Sure Trates had been with him for thousands of years and had served him well, but he was a servant to Stryker. Nothing more.

Yet the grief he felt told him the truth. He had cared for the man. Through it all, Trates had been a good friend to him, and now he was gone.

Slain by a human hand.

If there was anything Stryker hated more than a Dark-Hunter, it was a human being. He could at least respect Dark-Hunters as worthy adversaries.

But humans . . .

They were cattle to be slain and eaten. And now one of the cows had dared to attack them. Fine, if that was the way Paul wanted to play it, then the rules were changed. The truce was over.

His anger raw, he left his study and headed for the hall, where he summoned his soldiers to him. Within seconds the entire room was filled with Spathis.

He glanced to where his elite Illuminati warriors stood on the left of his throne as he ascended the dais to stand before his regal seat. Because of their skills and ruthlessness, the members of his Illuminati had risen through the ranks of the others to be bodyguards to the Destroyer. Or, more to the point, to be the personal entourage and Valkyries of Stryker.

"Davyn," he said to the male who stood in their center. Davyn had once been a close friend to his son, Urian, before Urian had betrayed him and sided with Acheron and his bastard Hunters.

Like Urian, the Daimon had long white-blond hair that he kept tied at his neck with a black cord. Stepping forward, Davyn placed his right fist to his left shoulder and bowed slightly. "My lord?"

"You are my new second in command."

Straightening his spine, Davyn looked about nervously. "My lord?"

"You heard correctly. All of you have heard it. Davyn is to be my new right hand and you will all treat him accordingly."

Davyn bowed his head with a jerk. "Thank you, my lord. But may I inquire as to what has happened to Trates?"

Stryker clenched his teeth as his virulent emotions threatened to overtake him. But he wouldn't show weakness to his people. They relied on him to be strong and he would be rock solid for them. "Our brother has fallen to a human hand."

Curses and whispers of shock filled the room as the news went over everyone like a pall.

"The experiment with humans is off. If we're going to die, then we'll die as soldiers fighting Artemis's army, face-to-face with our worthy enemies. We will *not* die by being stabbed in the back by cattle. As soon as Acheron is gone from Seattle, it's feeding time for the zoo, and we're starting with Paul Heilig and his sons."

"But, my lord," Arista said from her place with the Illuminati, "his sons are one of us."

"Not anymore they're not. I'm calling for vengeance on the human and his spawn. I want his head and the lives of his sons."

He beat his right hand against his breast before holding it up in salute to Trates, who'd died carrying out his orders.

His army followed suit.

"Sleep well," he told them. "And be prepared to attack."

Susan *was tired* and more than ready for bed as she left their small room to head across the hall to the bathroom. All she wanted was a cold cloth for her face to help her wake up so that they could formulate a plan of attack against Chief Heilig.

So used to it just being the two of them in the basement, she didn't even think to knock before she pushed open the door.

She froze instantly. Acheron was standing with his back to the mirror as he tried to rub ointment down his spine. But it was the sight of his tawny, muscled back that held her enthralled. Never in her life had she seen anything like it. It was raw and bleeding, with vicious welts covering every inch of it. They disappeared below his belt and even curved around his biceps, except they'd somehow missed hitting his small dragon tattoo.

"I'm sorry," she said quickly. She knew she should leave him to his privacy and yet she couldn't make her feet obey her. All she could do was stare at his ravaged skin and try to imagine how badly it must hurt him.

Before she could lose her courage, she stepped forward and held her hand out for the tube.

He moved so quickly that she barely saw him before he had grabbed his shirt from the towel rack.

"Ash," she said, reaching for the tube again. "I can help you smear that."

His face blank, he shrugged his shirt on. "It's okay. I don't like for people to touch me."

She was dying to know what'd happened to him, but due to his demeanor and the aura of "don't mess with me or I'll kill you" that he wore wrapped around him like a tight glove, she refrained from asking.

There was something extremely powerful and at the same time

highly vulnerable about him. More than that, he oozed an unnatural wave of primal sex. He was completely compelling, captivating. And a part of her actually wanted to touch him.

He sidestepped her as if he knew her thoughts and was made extremely uncomfortable by them.

As he started for the door, she stopped him. "Ash?"

"What?"

"How do you punish a Dark-Hunter who breaks the rules?"

He scowled at her. "Depends on the rule and the circumstances. You have something in mind?"

She clenched her hand into a fist, afraid that he might see her palm and the telltale marking there. "No. I was just wondering."

"I see." Once again, he started to leave, then paused in the doorway. His eerie silver eyes burned into her. "But you know something, Susan . . . I personally don't believe anyone should be punished because they want to share their life with someone." His gaze turned empty as if he were thinking of something from his past. "No one should have to pay for love in flesh or in blood."

And with that, he left her alone to think about what he'd said.

Ravyn was right. Acheron was one spooky man. And it made her wonder what price he must have paid to hold that view.

As she reached for a washcloth, she heard Ash knocking on the door across the hall.

"Hey," he said to Ravyn in that strange lilting accent of his. "I just wanted to let you know that I have to leave now."

"You just got here."

"I know. I told you that my time here was extremely limited. But don't worry. I'll be back in a few days."

"Don't worry?" Ravyn asked, his voice dripping with sarcasm. "Why would I worry? We only have humans and Daimons dropping out of the sky to murder us. Nothing to fret about at all."

"Yeah, well, it could be worse."

"How so?"

"You could be mated to a human."

Susan's stomach hit the floor at those words. Her eyes wide, she moved to the door and cracked it open to see Acheron heading down the hall while Ravyn watched after him with his face stern.

She quickly closed the distance between them and waited until Ash had vanished out of sight. "Do you think he knows?" she whispered.

"I have no idea."

Her heart hammering, she looked back down the hallway to make sure Ash was really gone. He was, but those words lingered and left them both unsettled.

So much so in fact that when Ravyn's phone rang two seconds later, it actually made her jump.

Ravyn scowled as he saw Cael's number. Given their earlier words, he was rather amazed to have his friend calling him so soon again.

He flipped the phone open. "Yeah?"

"Hey, Rave. We have a serious problem."

"I'm aware of that."

"No, leopard, you're not. I was just paid a visit by the chief of police, who dropped by with two Daimons."

Ravyn went cold with dread as he looked at Susan, who was watching him with a curious frown. "What?"

"You heard me. They busted up the place pretty badly and killed Amaranda's sister."

Ravyn winced at the news. Granted protecting Apollites had never been a mandate of his, he still hated to see anyone killed so needlessly. "What about you? You okay?"

"I'm hurt, but I'll live."

"And your wife?"

Cael paused. When he spoke, his voice actually broke. "Thanks, Rave."

"For what?"

"For the kindness of asking about her without having venom in your voice."

Ravyn glanced over to Susan. He was actually beginning to understand Cael's stupidity. "Yeah, well, I might not like it. But we've been friends for a long time."

"I know, which is why I'm calling. While they were here I learned some interesting things."

"Like I killed the chief's wife who was also a Daimon?"

"Yeah," Cael said, his voice full of disbelief. "How did you know that?"

"Lucky guess."

"Well, it gets better. He wants you like there's no tomorrow."

Ravyn had pretty much figured that one out, too. "Did you tell him where I was?"

"You know me better than that. I told him you were at the Last Supper Club. I assume he's there now, looking for you. The man won't stop until you're dead."

Ravyn scoffed at his dire tone. "I don't think he's going to stop until we're *all* dead, Celt."

"Probably."

Ravyn pulled the phone away and checked the ID again as Nick's words and their earlier encounter with the Daimons went through his mind. "Just out of curiosity. How do I know this is you?"

Cael paused before he answered. "Because I know you have three knitted gloves. It was the last pair your mother made for you, and on the night you took your vengeance, you found the third glove that she'd made to match the other two because she knew you were going to lose the left one soon. For some reason, the left one was always the one that got misplaced."

It was Cael. He was the only person who knew Ravyn still had them. "Hey, Celt?"

"Yeah?"

"Thanks for not ratting me out to the chief. I owe you."

"Don't worry. Just make sure you kill the bastard before he kills anyone else." And with that he hung up.

Amaranda *stared at* her husband as fear held her close. "Are you sure that was the right thing to do?"

"Yeah. Ravyn needs to know who's gunning for him. And we need the chief dead before he realizes we're alive and tells someone that he killed us both."

Amaranda walked herself into his arms, where he felt her trembling against him. "I'm so sorry I did this to you, baby. I just didn't want you to suffer."

"I know." He leaned his head down so that he could rest his cheek against her hair and let her touch soothe the fear he felt, too, about a future that was even more uncertain than the one they'd had before.

All these centuries, he'd been the hunter. Now he was going to be the hunted.

Ravyn *returned his* phone to his pocket.

"What's up?"

"That was Cael confirming our suspicion. It's the chief and he busted Cael and his wife up, trying to find me."

"What do we do?" she asked, her voice thick with worry.

Ravyn rubbed her arm comfortingly. "We give him what he wants."

She looked aghast as she shrugged his touch off in a huff. "I don't think I'm following this whole line of suicide that you're planning. What are you talking about?"

"I'm going to face him once and for all and end this."

"Whoa," she said, matching his tone with an equal amount of determination. "Wait a minute, Clint Eastwood. This isn't some spaghetti western with bad music playing in the background while you face off at high noon. We're talking about the chief of police. A man who can arrest you."

"Yeah."

Susan ground her teeth. By his tone of voice she could tell he wasn't listening to her.

So she whistled.

He cringed as if that caused him excruciating pain. "Don't do that. Being both a leopard and a Dark-Hunter, I have doubly sensitive ears."

"Good. I now know how to get your attention. And back to what I was saying. What are you planning to do?"

"Go to his house."

"Oh, yeah. That's a good plan. Want to fight him with a marshmallow gun while we're at it?"

He gave her a pointed glare. "Lay off the sarcasm long enough to think about it. If I don't go to him, he's not going to rest until he finds me. I don't want any more innocent people getting killed while I hide from him. I'm a trained fighter, Susan, with centuries of battle experience backing me. I somehow doubt I have much to worry about."

Uh-huh. Men and their egos . . . "And who was sitting in the cat cage when I found him?"

His features tightened in anger. "They caught me by surprise. This time the surprise will be on him."

She let out an irritated breath. He was so stubborn. She wanted to choke him, but she could tell that she was fighting a losing battle. He was going to do this no matter what she argued. "Fine then. I'm going with you."

"No, you're not."

"Why not?" she asked, feigning innocence. "Because maybe it's a *stupid* idea?"

"Susan—"

"Don't Susan me, you're not my father."

"No. I'm your mate."

She cocked her head with attitude. "Not till we do the deed, bud. And we haven't done the deed and if you keep this up, we're not going to do the deed, either, Mr. Limp. So if you go, I go. After all, between the two of us, I'm the one with the biggest ax to grind . . . upside that man's head. He took from me all I had, and I'll be damned if I don't pay him back."

Ravyn wanted to argue, but he knew the determined gleam in those blue eyes. Besides, she was a damn good fighter. It would be nice to have her by his side even if the thought of losing her was crippling to him. "All right, but I want you to promise me that if something goes wrong, you'll get out of there immediately and come back here for protection."

"You got it. 'Super Susan Becomes Terrified Rabbit. Runs to Ground.'"

"What is that?"

"A cheesy headline. I'm finally getting good at them, too. Leo's going to be impressed."

Ravyn shook his head at her. They didn't need a cheesy head-line. What they needed now was one hell of a miracle.

And a cavalry.

Unfortunately, said cavalry had walked up the stairs and most likely out of the city.

But at any rate, one way or another, this was about to be over. At least for him.

As they made their way upstairs, Ravyn paused as he came face-to-face with his father and Phoenix.

"Leaving?" his father sneered. "Dare I hope this is permanent?"

He didn't respond as he pushed his way past them.

Susan paused as she watched Ravyn leave the room. Unable to stand it, she turned on his father. "You are such a rank bastard."

"How dare you!"

"Oh go ahead," she goaded. "Hit me, kill me. I really don't care. But how can you stand there so sanctimonious and judge him when he didn't do anything except try to find someone to love? How could you hate your own son for that?"

She turned her gaze to Phoenix. "Your own brother? My God, you killed him. And instead of hating you people for what you've done to him, he's forgiven you. Why can't you do the same? Don't you think he hurt too? That every morning when he goes to sleep, he sees that night just as the rest of you do? I've listened to him talk about his mother and his sister, I've held him when the night-mares racked him, and I know how much he misses them. I've lost everyone who's ever meant anything to me, and I don't know how Ravyn has stood it all this time alone. He's going out right now probably to die. I'm sure that means nothing to you, but it means something to me. You should be proud of the son you fathered. He's more of a man than anyone I've ever known."

"What do you know, human?"

Susan shook her head as tears filled her eyes. She couldn't stand the thought of Ravyn getting hurt. Of what might very well befall him in the next few hours. She'd already lost too much in this bat-tle. "I don't know anything, really. I just know that if I had a son . . . a brother, I would fight heaven and hell to keep him safe, and I would be damned grateful that, having lost so many in my family, I still had one more. Be damned if I'd lose him, too." Curling her lip at them, she followed after Ravyn.

Gareth narrowed his eyes as he watched the human leave. "Stupid, human."

"No, Dad," Dorian said behind him as he stepped out of the shadows. "I think she's smarter than all of us put together."

CHAPTER EIGHTEEN

Susan took a deep breath as they headed for the chief's house on 18th Avenue South, not far from South Lucille Street. This time of night, it was totally peaceful as the moonlight dusted each house with becoming shadows.

"It's hard to believe how tragic the world can be when it's like this, isn't it?"

"Yeah," Ravyn agreed. "It's why I don't mind being a Dark-Hunter. There's something about the serenity of night that soothes the soul."

Susan gave him an amused smile. "I thought you didn't have a soul."

He cut his eyes toward her as he drove. "I was speaking meta-phorically."

"Ooo, there's a big word for you."

By his face she could tell he enjoyed her teasing. "Be nice to me, or I might leave you here alone."

"Considering how close we are to dawn, I don't think you should be antagonizing me, do you?"

He gave her a feigned sullen look that was positively gorgeous. She really liked the fact that he could take a joke and see her humor for what it was. Too many people mistook her sarcasm for scorn. But it was her defense mechanism. Ravyn not only understood that, he seemed to actually enjoy it.

Before she could say anything more, he stopped the car a block over from the house and turned the engine off. "I don't think we should give them any warning."

Susan couldn't agree more. Personally, she still didn't even think they should be there. She glanced around the silent, dark upper-middle-class neighborhood. There wasn't a single light on in any house. No movement. Nothing to say that she and Ravyn weren't the last two people alive on earth.

It was a bit eerie.

"You think they're home yet?" she asked.

"I don't know. It'll be dawn shortly. I'm sure the chief has to work, so if they're not, I'm sure they're not far away."

She nodded, then frowned as a thought crossed her mind. "This may be a stupid question, but could you humor me?"

"Sure."

"What exactly are we going to do here?"

He looked at her with an arched brow. "The plan is to fight it out with the bad guys and win the day."

She nodded at his dry tone. "Good concept, any idea on how to execute it?"

"Not a one." He got out of the car and slammed the door shut.

Gaping, Susan jumped out and caught up to him on the side of the road. "Wait a minute. You're joking with me, right?"

"No," he said in all sincerity. "I'm going to break into his house and then confront him."

She let out several scoffing staccato laughs. "Can I tell you just how stupid I think this plan of yours is?"

"You just did." He placed the keys in her palm that held the mating mark and folded her fingers over them. "Feel free to head back at any time. In fact, I really wish you would." He started away from her.

She pulled him to a stop as fear tore through her. "You're going to get yourself killed, Ravyn. Do you understand that?"

A tic worked in his jaw. "Fighting Daimons is what I do, Susan. It's why I was created." He glanced up at the sky that was growing lighter by the minute. "Besides, it's a moot point. I don't have time to make it back to the Serengeti before dawn. This ends today. On my terms. Not his."

"At dawn. How cliché."

He shook his head at her as he turned and walked toward the chief's house.

Susan stood there in indecision. Every part of her screamed at her to get into Phoenix's car and just leave. To keep driving until all of this was behind her.

But as she glanced to Ravyn, who was making his way steadily toward the chief's house, she knew she couldn't do that. He'd been alone for all of these centuries. If he really was heading for his doom, then she would go with him.

You're an idiot.

Yes, she was. And maybe she would die this morning, too. But at least she would have confronted the man who was responsible for Angie's and Jimmy's deaths. She owed them that much. And she wanted to look the man responsible for their fate in the eye and personally tell him what a scabbing bastard he was.

Tucking the keys in her pocket, she ran to catch up to Ravyn.

Ravyn wasn't expecting Susan to join him, but when he felt her tugging at his hand he couldn't keep from smiling inside. He laced his fingers with hers before he took her around back and crept along the chief's house.

"You think he has an alarm system?" Susan whispered as Ravyn located a window low enough to crawl through.

"Probably."

"Then how do we get inside?"

He covered the windowpane with his hand and closed his eyes to sense if there was anything electrical around the window. There was. He put both hands on the glass and used his powers to interfere with the electrical connector. Then he unlocked the window and pushed it open.

There was silence as the alarm continued to think nothing had been breached.

Susan shook her head at him. "How do you do that?"

"He's a magic man, Mama," he said, quoting the song from Heart, with a grin before he lifted her up to crawl inside.

As soon as she was safe, he joined her, then slid the window closed and locked it. He took a minute to rearrange the curtains over it.

The house was completely dark and silent. There were heavy brown and gold jacquard drapes pulled closed over every window so that not a single ray of sunshine could enter. Definitely the residence of nocturnal beasts who had one serious allergy to daylight.

The house was decorated with a hodgepodge of contemporary and antique furniture. But even so, it looked like a typical home. There were photographs on the wall of Paul, his sons, and his wife.

Susan stared at the pictures, especially the ones of the boys. They appeared so normal. Until you realized their clothing was identical to what she'd worn as a child. His sons weren't in their twenties as they appeared. They had to be in their mid- to late thirties.

Suddenly, she and Ravyn heard the growling sound of a garage door opening. Someone was coming home.

"What do we do?" she breathed nervously, looking around for a place to hide.

"We wait," Ravyn said aloud.

Nonchalant to the danger they were facing, he went to lean against the arm of the brown leather sofa with his arms crossed over his chest. He crossed his ankles and for all intents and purposes looked like someone waiting on an errant child to come home after being out all night.

She couldn't fathom his cool exterior. And she really didn't like his strategy. It was a good thing the man didn't work for the Pentagon. The "I'll figure it out as I go" just didn't jibe with her.

"Don't worry, Ben," a man said, closing a door that she was sure led to the garage. "We'll get him."

"I can't believe that bastard lied." The voices were getting closer and closer.

Susan stepped back into the shadows and whispered a small prayer that this would go the right way.

"Like I said, don't worry about it. He paid for his lie. We'll get Kontis and the others. Mark my words."

"They're marked and noted," Ravyn said in a snide tone as the two men joined them in the room.

Paul and Ben pulled up short.

"What are you doing here?" Paul demanded, his face alternating from pale to red.

Ravyn didn't move or even blink. "Heard you were looking for me. I figured I'd save you the trouble of having to search."

Paul seemed to get control of himself as he adopted Ravyn's calm tone and stance. "Hmm . . . interesting. So what do we do now? Slug it out?"

Ravyn shrugged. "Sure. Why not?"

"I don't like that plan," Paul said, exchanging a smug look with his son.

Well, at least she and Paul saw eye to eye on something. She didn't like the idea, either.

"No?" Ravyn asked as he put his hand to his chin introspectively. "Then what do *you* propose?"

"That we kill you."

That plan she liked even less.

Luckily, Ravyn agreed. "I have to say that I don't like your plan. Too much . . ."—he hesitated as if searching for the right word while he waved his hand around his face in a circular motion—"dying on my part, I think." His face turned deadly earnest as he crossed his arms again. "I'd much rather kill *you*."

The threat didn't appear to concern Paul at all. "You can't do that."

"Why not?"

He took a step toward them. "If I die, the two of you will never be absolved of the murders. You'll be hunted by the police forever."

Ravyn laughed. "Forever. There's a concept you can't even begin to fathom." He sobered. "Trust me, human. That takes on a whole new meaning in my world. But that's beside the point. I think you seriously overestimate your people and their attention spans. More than that, you definitely overestimate my giving a shit about them. I'm a Were-Hunter, moron. I've spent six hundred years being hunted by things a lot scarier and smarter than you."

"I think you're wrong. I think you seriously *under*estimate my kind."

Ravyn paused as he felt something odd run down his spine. It was like there were multiple Daimons in the house, but he knew better than that. He hadn't felt any when they'd first entered and Ben was in front of him. . . .

"Really?"

"Ravyn!"

He turned to see Susan in the arms of another Daimon. Dammit! How had he gotten behind him?

But then he knew. He could sense a Daimon's presence, but he couldn't really pinpoint it. They must have opened a bolt-hole somewhere in the house.

Now there was no telling how many of them might be here.

Paul laughed smugly. "Meet my brother-in-law. He sometimes travels with my sons to keep them out of harm's way."

Ravyn glared at the Daimon but knew if he moved to take Susan away from him, the Daimon could rip her throat out. "Let her go."

Smirking, the Daimon shook his head.

"Why should we?" Paul asked, drawing Ravyn's attention back to the chief. "We're holding all the cards now."

Ravyn locked gazes with Susan, whose face was stricken by her panic, and he hated that she was endangered.

She tried to flip the Daimon over her body or break his hold, but she couldn't. He held her so tightly that the only way to get her free would be to kill him and since she was covering the Daimon's heart . . .

They were screwed.

Smiling, Paul made his way over to the curtains and pulled one panel back ever so slightly. "Oh look. Daybreak. What great timing." He turned to level a sinister smirk at Ravyn. "Why don't you come see this for yourself, Dark-Hunter?"

"You know I can't."

"True. But I really think you're going to."

"Like hell."

"Fine then." He looked past Ravyn to the Daimon. "Terrence? Kill the bitch and take her soul."

"No!" Ravyn shouted. "Don't you dare touch her."

"If you don't like this scenario, how about this one? You die painfully so that I can enjoy your suffering. I let Susan go in exchange for her writing a piece about how you killed all the students that my wife and sons have fed on. You're dead, my wife is avenged, my sons are protected, and Susan lives, as long as she swears to forget all about me and everything she's seen."

Ravyn snorted at the very idea. "That would require me to trust you. I have no guarantee that if I die, she lives."

"You have no choice but to trust me, Dark-Hunter."

Ravyn cursed, hating the fact that Paul was right. "And how exactly would this work?"

"Simple. Both of you go to the window. She opens it up, you fry, and then she can crawl through it and leave. Obviously neither Terrance nor Ben can follow after her."

Ravyn turned it over in his mind, then shook his head. "Empty your gun so I know you won't shoot her in the back as she runs across the lawn. You're the chief of police. It's not like anyone would question it."

By his face it was obvious Paul didn't like the idea, but agreed.

"You can't do this," Susan said, her tone a mix of anger and fear. "I won't help you to die."

"Yes, you will, Susan," Ravyn said calmly. "Law of the jungle. You do what you have to to survive. And your survival hinges on my death."

"You're not trying to survive. Shouldn't you be fighting this?"

"No. I'm allowing my mate to survive. It's our way."

Susan clenched her teeth as pain and sorrow tore her apart. It wasn't her way. She didn't want to have to kill him in order to live. That wasn't right.

Ravyn looked at the chief. "Give her your bullets."

No! her mind cried as she tried to fight Terrence. Damn the bastard and his Bondo grip. She had to get free of him. She had to. She couldn't let Ravyn die.

Not like this.

Paul pulled the gun out of the holster at the small of his back and unloaded it into his hand. Then he handed the bullets to Susan.

Ravyn narrowed his gaze on Paul. "Fire the gun at the wall so that I know it's empty."

His features disgusted, Paul did as he said. The gun merely clicked, proving that he was abiding by the agreement. "You satisfied?"

"That your gun is empty, yes. With this solution, not hardly." He turned to look at Susan.

She stopped struggling. Her heart froze at the sad resolve she saw mirrored in his black eyes. The grim determination that marked his handsome features. "Don't do this, Ravyn. We can find another way out."

Ravyn offered her a comforting smile, but what he really wanted to do was touch her one last time. To feel the softness of her skin. "It's okay. I've had a really long life."

Susan felt the tears prick the back of her eyes. She couldn't believe he'd be willing to do this for her. That he'd damn himself to being a Shade simply to save her life.

And in that moment, she realized that she really did love him.

More than that, she didn't want to live if he died.

The Daimon led her to the window.

"Open the latch, Susan," Paul said snidely. "Then Ravyn can join you at the window to help you out."

She parted the curtains only enough to let her hand reach the latch. But as she did that, a thought struck her. She knew how to get out of this.

How to save Ravyn.

"It's unlocked," she said.

Nodding, Terrence stepped away from the window to a safe corner of the room near Ben.

"Good," Paul said with a laugh. "Now go check out the daylight, Dark-Hunter."

Her heart pounding, Susan felt Ravyn at her back as he approached her. She closed her eyes and savored the strength of him. The heat of his body warmed hers.

And her conviction grew.

"I know I just met you, Susan," Ravyn whispered against her ear. "But I think I love you."

She froze her hand on the latch as a wave of anger went through her. Instead of warming her, those words went over her like ice. Looking at him over her shoulder, she glared at him. "You *think*? You *think* you love me? You don't *know*?"

His face baffled, he scowled at her. "Why are you so angry? I'm trying to die here . . . for *you*. Nobly."

"Then you should have just dropped dead and not opened your mouth to piss me off. You *think*? Think? What is that? Obviously it's only wishful thinking on your part, because if you had thought for a single second, you'd have known it would upset me. Ugh!" Wanting to really kill him, she grabbed the heavy drape and before anyone realized what she was doing, she jerked with all her strength.

The curtain rod was torn free from the wall. Still angry at the beast behind her, she stepped back so that the curtain would fall over Ravyn to protect him as the room was flooded with daylight.

The two Daimons screamed out in pain as the light struck them and set them both on fire. Susan shielded her face from the horror of their deaths. If only she could protect her nose. The stench of burning flesh was revolting.

And in less than a minute, both of them were dead. Black, smoldering piles of ash on the green Persian rug.

"Ben!" Paul shouted in an agonized cry. "No!" He turned on her with his fury blazing. "You fucking bitch! I'll kill you for this."

He rushed at her, only to have Ravyn, now in leopard form, launch himself at him. The two of them hit the floor hard. Ravyn caught him a vicious swipe on the shoulder.

Rolling over, Paul pushed himself to his feet and held his injured arm to his side, then ran pell-mell to the interior of the house, toward the staircase, with Ravyn bounding up the stairs after him.

Susan followed them, then pulled up short as a hugely tall man stepped out of the shadows at the top of the landing. He was dressed in a pair of jeans with a black turtleneck and motorcycle jacket. Ravyn stopped halfway up the stairs as Paul continued on to the man's side.

"Stryker," he breathed, turning to point down at them. "Kill them!"

Susan's jaw went slack at the mention of the Daimon's name. So this was their infamous leader Nick had mentioned. Tall and lean, with short jet-black hair and wearing a pair of black wraparound sunglasses, he didn't look like the other Daimons, who were all blond.

But even so he did make an awe-inspiring sight. An aura of brutal, cold power bled from him. He had a demeanor that said he relished cruelty and that he was here for blood.

Their blood.

Ravyn flashed to human form and summoned clothes as he faced the Daimon with grim features.

"Why would I kill *them*?" Stryker asked Paul in a bored tone.

Paul's anger melted into a look of confusion. "He's a Dark-Hunter. Death to all Dark-Hunters . . . right?" There was no mistaking the fear in his voice now.

Stryker nodded. "That *is* my motto. But today it seems my agenda is a little different." He grabbed Paul by the throat and slung him against the wall, where he held him so high that the shorter man's feet didn't reach the floor.

Paul grabbed Stryker's hand in both of his as his face turned bright red while he struggled to get free.

Stryker's entire face was one of hell wrath. "You lying bastard. You betrayed my trust and you stabbed me in the back."

"I did no such thing," Paul choked out in sharp sobs. "I-I-I didn't touch you."

"Yes, you did." Stryker pulled him away from the wall, then slammed him back into it again. "When you stabbed Trates, my right hand, my second in command, you in essence stabbed me. *Me.* And no one stabs at me. Do you understand, you pathetic fool? If I were to let you live after what you've done, I would become weak, ineffectual in the eyes of my men, and that I cannot allow."

Ravyn took a step up the stairs.

"Halt!" Stryker snapped at him. "This doesn't concern you, Dark-Hunter. You and your woman are free to go."

Ravyn shook his head. "I can't and you know it. Even if he's a lying sack of shit, he's still human, and I took an oath to save the humans from Daimons."

Stryker let out a tired sigh before his face hardened. "Spathis!"

Before they could move, twenty Daimons flashed into the room. Three were by Susan while the rest were on the stairs between Stryker and Ravyn.

Ravyn ran at them only to have them drag him down the stairs to stand by her side.

She didn't even try to fight, since it was obvious the Spathis were more than able to kick their butts and take their names.

Stryker turned to Paul and opened his mouth to expose his fangs. "Before I kill you, I want you to know that the minute the sun sets tonight, I'm turning my warriors loose on every human who has helped you. Every single one, as punishment for your betrayal. No pathetic human slaughters one of my Daimons. Ever."

Paul's eyes were bulging. "No. How can you do this? We were going to combine our men and rule Seattle. We were allies!"

"Are you serious? After you killed Trates? But now I have an even better ally than you."

Without another word, Stryker removed his glasses and then sank his fangs into Paul's throat.

Revolted by the sight, Susan turned her face away and clenched her eyes shut an instant before she heard Paul's painful scream. It rang out through the house and chilled her all the way to her soul. In spite of everything he'd done, she still felt sorry for him. No one deserved to die like this. . . .

She could even hear his feet kicking the wall as he continued to beg for mercy while Ravyn tried to fight his way past the Daimons to help Paul. But it was useless.

Suddenly there was utter silence.

It echoed through the house and set her nerves on edge. Were they next?

There was a sharp thud on the landing above.

Feeling sick, she looked back to see Paul lying on the floor at Stryker's feet as he wiped his forearm across his face to remove Paul's blood from his lips and chin.

Putting his glasses back on, he stepped nonchalantly over the body and walked leisurely down the stairs until he was in front of Ravyn. Stryker smacked his lips with his face twisted as if the taste didn't agree with him. "What a wuss. His pathetic soul barely qualifies as an hors d'oeuvre."

"You bastard!" Ravyn tried to reach him, but the Daimons wouldn't let him.

Stryker merely laughed. "Yes, and I revel in that title."

"Do we kill him, my lord?" one of the Daimons asked.

Stryker cocked his head as if considering it. "Not today, Davyn. Today, we show a bit of mercy to our worthy opponent. After all, he taught me that you don't trust the human cattle. Only other immortals understand the rules of war."

He broke through the ranks of Daimons to stand before Ravyn. "I have to say you've impressed me, Kontis. You've survived everything I've thrown at you. And the way you handled yourself here . . . really, I was wondering how you'd get out of this."

He looked at Susan then and his harsh features actually softened. "You remind me of my own wife. She was one hell of a lady, and like you she'd fight with me even while we were battling others."

For some reason she couldn't even begin to understand, she actually felt a pang of compassion for him. It was obvious he'd loved his wife a great deal.

"There's only one thing I have ever respected. Strength." He returned his attention to Ravyn. "We'll fight this battle another night, Cousin. For now . . . peace."

And with that, the portal opened and Stryker stepped through it. The Daimons released her and Ravyn and quickly followed after him.

Susan stood there, completely stunned by what she'd seen and heard. "This par for the course?"

"No." Ravyn looked every bit as baffled as she felt. "I think we may have witnessed an all-time first for the Daimons."

Susan expelled a long breath. "Damn. It's been one hell of a day and it's not even six thirty yet."

"Tell me about it."

Just grateful that they were both alive, she smiled at him and walked herself into his arms. Closing her eyes, she held him tight . . . until his earlier words repeated themselves in her head.

"You *think* you love me?"

"We're not going to go into this again, are we?"

"Yeah, we are. How heartless is that? Here I was thinking I

meant something to you because you were willing to die for me and the next thing I know, you tell me that you don't even know whether or not you love me. That you'd rather kill yourself than stay alive and what? Be mated to me? Thanks a lot. You weren't making some declaration of loyalty. You're willing to die for any bimbo you meet."

He scowled at her. "That's not true. If you were just some bimbo I wouldn't have tried to make it meaningful."

"But you would have died for her anyway?"

"I didn't say that."

"You implied it!" As she opened her mouth to continue her argument, he captured her lips with his and kissed the daylights out of her.

Susan melted as his tongue teased hers. Her head spun as all her conflicting emotions settled down into just one. . . .

The one that loved this man.

Ravyn licked her lips playfully before he pulled back to press his forehead to hers. "You feeling better yet?"

"I don't know. I think I need another kiss to be sure."

Laughing, he picked her up in his arms and kissed her again.

Yeah, that was doing it. She was definitely feeling better. At least until she realized something.

"How are we getting home?"

"Looks like you'll be driving." He glanced up the stairs to where Paul was. "We need to head out and call the police."

"Yeah, I don't want to be here anymore. I've seen enough death for a while."

He kissed her one last time before he stepped back and turned into a leopard.

Susan paused as she looked down and laughed. So this was her life now. . . .

It was too bizarre even for her. "You know," she said quietly, "I've always wanted to pet a wild cat."

"Babe, you can pet me anytime you want."

It was so strange to have his voice in her head. "You're not like Ash, where you can read my thoughts or anything, are you?"

"No."

Oh thank God. She didn't know why, but the idea of that really screwed with her head. Relieved, she bent down and sank her hand in his soft pelt. And then she sneezed, and sneezed again.

"Remind me. Benadryl. I think we may need to buy some stock in the company." Sniffing, she straightened up and headed for the door only to realize that the sun was still painful to Ravyn even in leopard form.

He actually stepped back with a hiss instead of going through the door.

Susan's heart ached as he pulled her coat off to wrap it around him.

"It won't help."

She gasped at the sound of Dorian or Phoenix's voice. Looking up, she found the twins in the living room, along with their father. Afraid of what they were going to do to Ravyn since he didn't have the protection of sanctuary here, she put herself between them. "What are you doing here?"

Gareth moved forward with that lethal predatorial lope that reminded her so much of Ravyn. Narrowing his gaze, he sniffed the air around her as if he caught a whiff of something he found puzzling.

Ravyn immediately flashed to human form. "Let her go. Your fight is with me, not her."

Before Ravyn or she could move, Gareth grabbed her hand and turned it over to see the mating mark. His grip bit into her wrist. "Do you love him?"

"That's none of your business."

"Let her go," Ravyn growled.

Gareth didn't. Instead, he turned that cold gaze to Ravyn. "It would be so easy to kill you here and now." And then something odd flashed into his eyes. "In spite of what you think, I loved your mother more than my life. I wanted to bond with her, but she refused. Her worst fear was that we would die and leave all of you orphaned. I think about that at night. How angry she'd be to know what we did to you."

Susan looked to see the anguish in Ravyn's eyes.

Gareth turned his gaze to her. "You were right and I'm glad he has you." He let go of her wrist. "I don't expect you to forgive us. But now you need us to get you home in the daylight."

Gareth held his hand out to Ravyn.

Ravyn hesitated as all the pain of his past washed over him. And in the end, he was still that little boy who loved his father. That little boy who just wanted to go home again. But the home he'd known had been shattered three hundred years ago. There was no way to go back to the family he'd known then.

He looked at Susan, whose gentle eyes waited expectantly for him to respond to his father. She was his family now, and he knew he would do anything for this woman.

But in order to protect her . . . to love her, he would have to live.

He wasn't ready to forgive everything, not by a long shot. Still, his father was making an effort, and he wasn't the kind of man to shun an honest offer.

Unsure of his future, Ravyn took his father's hand.

"Phoenix? Bring Susan home."

Susan watched as Ravyn and Gareth vanished. "What's he doing?"

"Relax," Dorian said. "No one's going to hurt him."

"Well, I might," Phoenix said in a surly tone. "Where the hell is my car?"

Susan laughed as she pulled the keys out of her pocket and held them up. "A block over."

"Is it damaged?"

"No."

Phoenix let out a relieved breath as Dorian laughed.

Dorian took the keys. "I'll drive it home." And then he flashed out of the room.

Phoenix reached for Susan. "Trust me?"

"Not a bit, but I trust that Ravyn will eat your head if you let anything happen to me."

He dipped his gaze down to her marked palm. "You didn't answer my father's question. Do you love him?"

"Why does it matter?"

"Because if you do, bond with him. Take my word for it. The worst hell imaginable is knowing you lost what you held dearest because you were a coward. Don't make my mistake."

And in that moment, she had a newfound respect for Phoenix. Standing on her tiptoes, she kissed his cheek. "Thank you."

He inclined his head before she put her hand in his. In an instant, they were back inside the Serengeti.

The next two weeks went by in a blur as they returned to their lives. With Leo's help, along with the help of the Squires who worked for Internal Affairs in Seattle, they were able to put the blame for all the deaths Susan and Ravyn were accused of where it belonged.

On Paul's shoulders.

She was even allowed to write it up and have her story picked up by the Associated Press. And as soon as her piece on surviving forty-eight hours with an insane serial killer chief hit wide syndication, papers all over the country contacted her about working for them.

And to be honest, she was actually considering it. Having a legitimate job again was all she'd dreamed of.

But in order to do that, she'd have to leave Ravyn. . . .

It was a cool, breezy afternoon when they buried Angie and Jimmy together. Because it was daylight, Ravyn wasn't able to be with her in human form. But he'd insisted that she carry him as a cat so that he could be by her side.

It was the kindest thing anyone had ever done for her. She kept the cat carrier covered with a dark cloth, and during the service she stroked him through the bars.

When it was over and they were back at his house, he'd held her for hours while she cried and remembered all the years she'd had with the two of them.

And with every hour she and Ravyn spent together, she realized that she loved him even more.

"Susan?"

She jerked away from her thoughts as she heard Ravyn's voice. Getting up from her chair in front of the computer, she headed toward the hallway, then down toward the balcony so that she could look to the great room below where Ravyn was standing.

"Yes?"

"The Post is on the phone. They have to have an answer."

She saw the fear in his eyes. They still hadn't mated officially. Ravyn wanted her to have all the time she needed, but his deadline was looming, and if they didn't mate soon, he would be neutered. "Okay. I'll tell them."

Ravyn *swallowed as* he watched Susan turn around and head back to his office. He had a sneaking suspicion she was about to take the D.C. job. After all, it was her dream.

But her dream was killing him. He didn't want her to leave. He wanted her to stay.

Be strong. As an animal, he knew that you couldn't put someone in a cage and expect them to live. She had to be free to make her own life . . . with or without him.

His heart heavy, he went back to his bedroom and picked up the receiver. Part of him wanted to listen to her conversation, but he wouldn't do that to her.

It was up to her to tell him the news.

Sitting down, he picked up the book he'd been reading and tried to focus on it. He couldn't. All he kept doing was thinking of what his life would be like without her in it.

And he knew the answer. He'd been living that way for centuries.

The door opened to his room. He glanced up to see Susan coming in with a glum look on her face.

This was it. She was going to tell him and then pack. Bracing himself, he watched as she moved to the side of the bed and handed him her latest article. No doubt this one would solidify her as a legitimate reporter again.

He forced himself not to betray his hurt as he picked it up to read and his heart slid to his stomach.

I MARRIED THE CATMAN OF SEATTLE

So my husband has a litter box. At least he doesn't stray at night. . . .

"What the hell is this?"
"My article."
"I don't understand."

She laughed. "I have to turn it in to Leo. I just called and he told me that I can have my old job back."

"I thought you hated that job."

"Not anymore. I just realized that I can have a lot more fun working for him than I ever could writing for the *Post* or *Wall Street Journal*. Not to mention, I get to cuddle up with the best-looking catman in town."

Ravyn still couldn't believe it. "You're staying?"

"Are you deaf, kitty? Yes. Now are you going to make an honest woman of me, or what?"

Ravyn laughed as he pulled her to him and dissolved their clothes. "Yeah, baby. I intend to make sure that you never stray, either."

Susan shivered as the cool air caressed her skin, followed immediately by the warmth of Ravyn's hand as he glided it down her spine. His hair pulled itself back from his face into a ponytail so that he wouldn't cause her to sneeze too much.

She laughed at his consideration. Pressing herself against him, she pulled his head down so that she could taste his lips. It was still hard for her to believe that after this she would never be alone again.

Ravyn would be here for her.

He was her family. So was Leo, and even Otto and Kyl. They were more like her homicidal cousins, but they were family. It was more than she'd ever hoped for.

No, Ravyn was more than she'd ever hoped for. How could Mr. Wrong, be so right? It didn't make sense and yet he was. She couldn't imagine ever being this comfortable with another man. He fit her perfectly.

The more she learned about him, the more she loved him.

Ravyn's senses whirled as he tasted the sweetness of her mouth. In all these centuries, he'd never thought to have another mate and yet here she was.

Susan. Soft, irritating, beautiful. She was more than he'd ever dreamed of. Pulling back, he lay his cheek against hers and inhaled the floral scent of her hair. . . .

At least until she sneezed.

He smiled before he turned her in his arms.

"What are we doing?" she asked.

"The ritual," he breathed in her ear. He held his marked hand out before her. "Put your marked palm against mine."

Susan did, then he laced his fingers with hers and nuzzled her neck with his whiskered cheek. She loved the sensation of his skin scraping hers. It sent chills all over her.

"Now I need you to guide me into your body."

Susan snorted as she realized that with his arm across her chest while he was behind her, that was easier said than done. "For the record, I'm not Stretch Armstrong. How am I supposed to do that?"

He laughed before he kissed her cheek and made her entire body burn as he cupped her breast with his free hand and teased her nipple with the calluses on his palm.

"I can do it then, but you have to tell me that you accept me as your mate."

"That's why we're naked, right?"

"Susan," he said, his tone gravely serious. "This is a big step to my people. By our laws, I'm not allowed to take a woman as my mate unless she is one hundred percent accepting of me and our ways. I'm not a Katagari, forcing my will on you. I'm an Arcadian and we would never breach the sacredness of this."

She leaned back so that she could meet his midnight gaze. "I've never been more serious about anything in my life, Ravyn. I want you as my mate."

"For eternity?"

"For eternity."

His features softened as he dipped his head down to nip her on the back of her neck. Susan shivered in pleasure an instant before he slid himself deep inside her. Her hand burned as she rose up on her tiptoes, then lowered herself down onto him, taking him in all the way to his hilt.

He kept one hand on her hip while his arm crossed her body, holding her against him. It was the most incredible moment of her life. So this was mating. . . .

She liked it.

Ravyn growled deep in his throat as he thrust against her hips, and she met him stroke for stroke. She was so warm and wet that it almost drove him over the edge, but he wanted to time this carefully. This was the first time they would make love as mates and he wanted them to come together.

She was his. A wave of possessiveness consumed him. So long as they lived, he would never again be able to take another woman. Susan alone would sustain him, and it wasn't just because the Fates decreed it. It was because he loved her. Deeply. With every part of himself.

There had been a time when that kind of commitment would have sent him running for the door, but after all these centuries, he was looking forward to having her in his life.

She wasn't just another lover to come and go. She was a companion. A friend. She alone knew how much he liked to have his ears rubbed. And even though it made her hand itch, she always made sure to rub them at night while they lay in bed. Just as she was doing now.

Her touch sent chills over him, and when they came together, it was the most blissful moment in his entire life.

He quickly released her hand before their union went further. He wasn't ready to bond with her just yet.

Not until she was as committed to him as he was to her. She still had her own life to live and he didn't want to trespass there. Having had his life taken from him by one person's selfishness, he wasn't about to do that to her.

"I love you, Susan," he said, kissing her gently on the cheek.

Susan purred as she continued to rub his ear with her hand. "I love you, too, Ravyn."

CHAPTER NINETEEN

Stryker sighed as he sat at his desk, looking for his cell phone, which was no place to be found. "Trates!"

He winced as he accidentally called for his old second in command. Damn, he was never going to get used to Davyn being here and Trates being gone.

It was almost as bad as having lost Urian.

Before he could call for Davyn, Satara appeared in the room beside him. "Hello, Brother."

Her presence amused him and he wondered if either Artemis or Acheron knew that he had a direct link to whenever Ash visited Stryker's auntie. "I take it Acheron is back on Olympus."

She nodded as she leaned against his desk. "Have you thought about what I said earlier?"

She'd had one hell of a plan to give them an informant that no one would ever suspect. Of course it hinged on her being correct, and he wasn't so sure that she was. "I have."

"And?"

"If he's really alive and you can convince him to go through with it, I'll convert him."

She laughed deep in her throat as she tapped him on the chin. "Oh, Brother, you constantly underestimate me." Leaning back, she snapped her fingers, and an instant later a Dark-Hunter was standing between them.

Stryker actually gaped at the sight. Satara had been right after all.

It was Acheron's friend from New Orleans. The one Desiderius had caused to kill himself. "Gautier . . ."

Nick looked around as if confused. "Where am I?"

Satara licked her lips as she leaned against him and rested her arm on his shoulder. "I told you, sugar. This is where you can get what you need to kill Acheron. And this is the man who can do it."

He narrowed his eyes on Stryker, but lucky for Stryker, Gautier didn't know him by sight and it was obvious Satara hadn't given his name to the man.

Good for her. She was a clever girl.

"He's a Daimon," Nick sneered.

Duh . . . Stryker masked his Daimon's aura. "Not entirely, Dark-Hunter. Not entirely. I'm also the son of a god."

He saw the confusion on Nick's face now that he could no longer sense him as a Daimon. "How can you mask your essence?"

"I told you. I'm the son of a god, and I can share those powers with you. *If* you're willing."

Suspicion darkened his eyes. "At what price?"

"Submission to me. You have to agree to abide by my rules. Same as Artemis required of you . . . only with a twist."

"Yes," Satara said. "You'll actually get your Act of Vengeance with us. Unlike Artemis, we won't deny you."

Nick's eyes gleamed at the prospect. "Is that all I have to do?"

"Not quite," Stryker said honestly. "Once I convert you over so that you can share my powers, you'll be required to drink from me in order to live. If you go too long without feeding, you will die."

Nick was silent as he considered that. The idea of drinking blood disgusted him. The idea of drinking it from a man . . .

He shivered in revulsion.

But you could kill Acheron.

That idea thrilled him. Ash had taken everything from him. Or if not taken, he'd allowed it to be taken by others. And Nick wanted revenge. A vengeance Artemis had refused him when she'd taken his soul. But for Ash, he would still be alive. More than that, his beloved mother would be alive. New Orleans would still be intact. Rage darkened his vision.

"Is it a deal?" the Daimon asked.

"Yes," Nick said before he could chicken out. "Give me what I need to kill him."

Stryker stood up slowly as he savored this victory. Now here was something Acheron wouldn't see coming. Because he loved Nick, Nick's future was shielded from him. He'd never know this man was going to betray him.

Not until it was too late and the death blow was upon him.

Thrilled, Stryker unbuttoned his shirt so that his neck was exposed. He sat down on the corner of the desk so that Nick would have an easier time reaching him. Though Dark-Hunter blood had been made poisonous to Daimons, Daimon blood wasn't poisonous to Dark-Hunters. The fact that Dark-Hunters could drain emotions and powers from others was why they were banned from drinking blood. Nick was about to learn one of many secrets Acheron kept from his Hunters.

"Whenever you're ready, Dark-Hunter."

Nick stared at the Daimon's neck and the vein that throbbed there. If he did this, there was no way back for him. None.

And then he saw his mother's gentle face. Saw her sitting in her favorite chair, dead in their house on Bourbon Street.

Ash needed to pay for the people he'd allowed to die. The people he hadn't brought back to life.

His breathing ragged, he took a step closer and sank his fangs into the Daimon's neck.

Stryker laughed as heat poured through his body. He cupped Nick's head in his hands and tilted his head so that Nick could drink his powers into him. Stryker knew what was happening to Nick's body. The lust and craving the man was feeling as Stryker's life force invaded him. There was nothing else like it.

And when Nick became more feral from his newfound strength, Stryker pushed him away, into Satara's arms.

Nick whirled on her then and pinned her to the wall before he feverishly kissed her. He needed to release the fire in his body or it would consume him.

Wiping at the blood on his neck, Stryker licked it from his fingers. "Call me when he's through with you."

He wasn't sure Satara could hear him as Nick furiously pulled at her clothes. Stryker left them alone to screw while he savored this moment.

He now had two of Ash's Hunters. One Ash knew about. But the other . . .

He would be the death of the Atlantean.

Susan *was still* smiling from the mating ceremony with Ravyn as she entered the offices at the *Daily Inquisitor*.

"Hi, Joanie," she said, heading for Leo's office.

"Hi, Susan." Joanie leaned over her desk to whisper loudly. "Did you hear that there are vampires who live here in Seattle?"

"Oh, yeah. A lot of them hang out at the Happy Hunting Ground, too."

She watched as Joanie made a note. Shaking her head at the woman, she opened Leo's door. "Hey, boss man, what'cha up to?"

He was sitting with Otto across his desk. "You look awful chipper, Sue. What's up?"

Walking in and shutting the door, Susan handed him her article and watched his face as he read it, then laughed nervously.

"What is this?"

She smiled at him. "I have learned Ibsen. I now know how to embrace the absurd."

Otto arched a brow at her. "I think she's learned to embrace the bong."

Susan slapped at his shoulder playfully. As she pulled her hand back, Otto grabbed her wrist. "What's this?" he asked, turning it over to see her mark.

A pall went over the room.

Susan balled her hand up, but it was too late for that.

"You can't mate with him," Otto growled. "It's against the rules. You're a Squire."

Susan's heart pounded as she tried to think up a lie.

"Actually," Leo said, leaning back in his chair. "That's not true."

Otto released her. "What do you mean?"

Leo squirmed a bit before he answered. "I kind of forgot to swear her in. She's still technically a civilian."

Otto was aghast. "Leo . . ."

"Hey, we had a tough week, you know? I was going to get around to it, but things came up."

To her amazement, Otto visibly relaxed. "Damn. Another good Dark-Hunter lost. And I really liked the leopard, too."

Susan went cold at his words. Were they going to kill Ravyn for mating with her? "What do you mean, you're going to lose him?"

Leo gave her an agitated glare. "You haven't read all the manual yet, have you?"

"Well, no. The thing's something like five thousand pages long."

Leo tsked at her. "You should read chapter fifty-six."

"Why?"

It was Otto who answered. "That's the chapter that tells you how you can free your Dark-Hunter and marry him."

Susan gaped at that. Ravyn hadn't said anything about that to her. "Are you serious?"

"Always. I don't have a sense of humor . . . well, Roman general and Tabitha not withstanding."

She had no idea what he was talking about and honestly she didn't care.

"You know," Leo said, distracting her. "I like this article, Sue. What say we make it front-page?"

Her head still spinning from her latest discovery, she nodded at him. "That'd be great. I'll . . . um . . . I'll see you guys later."

She left them alone and headed back to her car as quickly as she could. Could she really be able to get Ravyn out of his service to Artemis?

The thought thrilled her.

At least until she got home and brought it up to Ravyn, who didn't seemed pleased by the prospect at all.

"No," he said firmly.

She couldn't believe his automatic answer. "What do you mean, no?"

He crossed his arms over his chest as he faced her in the hallway.

"What I said. No. I'm not getting my soul back from Artemis."

"Why not?"

"I don't want to be mortal."

That didn't make any sense. Why wouldn't he want to be free? For someone who hated cages, he seemed awfully happy to live in bondage to a Greek goddess.

"But you can leave—"

"No, Susan. I can *die*." He shook his head. "I don't want to die and I damned sure don't want you to die on me, either. I want us to bond when you're ready and I want us to be together forever." He gestured at the window that looked out onto the city. "I have a job to do here in Seattle. A really important one. I go back to being a Were-Hunter and then I go from this to being a Sentinel again and that's the last thing I want to do."

She frowned at the unfamiliar word. "What's a Sentinel?"

"Essentially, it's the Arcadian equivalent to a Dark-Hunter. Only instead of chasing Daimons, I chase down other Were-Hunters. And I lose all immortality. But wait, it gets better. The minute I return to being mortal again, the Katagaria have a clear shot at you because you're my mate."

"Oh. . . ." Suddenly the idea of him getting his soul back wasn't so appealing to her, either. "They'd really do that?"

"Yes. We are at war and they'll stop at nothing to hurt us." He cupped her cheek in his hand as his black eyes and the sincere adoration there warmed her. "But if you really want that for us, then I'll call Ash and we can ask for the test to restore my soul. I leave it up to you."

"Really?"

"Yes."

Susan bit her lip as she considered that. "What if Ash won't let us be together if you continue being a Dark-Hunter?"

"He let Cael have Amaranda. Do you really think he'll stop us?"

He had a point. "I don't know. I mean, after all, you only *think* you love me. . . ."

Ravyn laughed at that and rolled his eyes. "There's no thinking to this, Susan. I *do* love you. Why else would I volunteer to spend eternity with you? Have you any idea how long that is?"

"No," she said, giving him a devilish grin before she kissed him. "But I'm going to find out."

EPILOGUE

Spent from sex, Nick lay naked on the floor, panting beside Satara who was laughing as she stroked his chest. His entire body burned and he now heard voices in his head that echoed and screamed.

What have I done?

When Satara had come to him and told him about her connections to the Daimons and gods, he should have turned her away, but her offer to strike back at Ash had been too good to pass up. He knew that as a Dark-Hunter he'd never have the ability on his own to kill Ash. But with his life force tied to a god's . . .

He could do it.

And he felt that power now seeping through him. It hummed and sang with an unimagined beauty. He wasn't human. He wasn't Dark-Hunter.

He was . . .

Nick frowned as he saw his reflection in a silver globe that was on the bottom shelf of the Daimon's bookcase. Rolling toward it, he pulled it closer to him until he could see his eyes.

His breath caught sharply in his throat as he stared at his distorted face.

It couldn't be.

The door to the room opened to show him the demigod Daimon who'd allowed him to share his powers. No longer wearing sunglasses, he looked at Nick with the same swirling silver eyes that Ash had.

The same eyes that Nick now had, too.

"Who *are* you?" Nick breathed.

"I would be the one man on your list, after Acheron, who you want to kill, and you're now my minion, Nick. Welcome to my hell."